Tackling the Team
The Vassi Collection
Volume VI

Tackling the Team

Marco Vassi

OPEN ROAD

INTEGRATED MEDIA

NEW YORK

ISBN 978-1-4976-4086-3

This edition published in 2014 by Open Road Integrated Media, Inc.
345 Hudson Street
New York, NY 10014
www.openroadmedia.com

Introduction

Were the Sixties put on earth so that Marco Vassi could happen? Or was Marco Vassi put on earth so that the Sixties could happen? To read his classic works of erotic fiction and his masterpiece of autobiographical fiction, THE STONED APOCALYPSE, is to realize that the man and the era were created out of the same fire and primordial elements. It is not, however, enough to say that Marco Vassi was a child of his age. It could just as accurately be said, that the age was Marco Vassi's fantasy, a fantasy so intense and compelling that it is impossible to read any of his books in one sitting: one must either jump into a cold shower, relieve oneself sexually, or go for a long contemplative walk to reflect on the profundity of his insights into human behavior.

Vassi had done many things before he became a writer, but writing was not one of them except for some translations from Chinese and critiques of manuscripts submitted to a literary agency where he was employed for a few years. He had also tried numerous identities on for size as he acted out and lived out the experiences that were to pour from his mind like water raging over the spillway of a dam. When in the late 1960's "Fred" Vassi announced that he was embarking on a journey, his friends knew that it was not to a place but to a state of mind.

The state of mind was what came to be known as The Sixties, and anyone seeking to live in that state must enter it through the vision of the author of these works. In cartographic terms it was a journey from the East Coast to California, a trip that resonates with meaning for every student of The American Experience. Speaking metaphorically, however, it was a trip into the heart of life, love, laughter, horror, and sweet pain. Fred Vassi came back Marco Vassi, having recreated himself in the name of the intrepid voyager to the ends of the known world hundreds of years ago.

Heart fecund with all that had happened to him, he started writing the work that was eventually to become THE STONED APOCALYPSE, a book that captured in coruscating words what others of his generation were capturing so brilliantly in music.

With no source of regular income he tried his hand at what were then popularly known as sex novels, a genre of tame pornography that pandered to the fantasies of repressed males still mired in postwar inhibition. With the wide-eyed innocence and self-deprecating humor that characterized every venture he undertook, he showed them to me, his friend and a fledgling literary agent. He merely hoped to raise a few dollars with them. I told him that they were the most incredibly arousing works of erotic literature since Henry Miller, and arranged for them to be brought out by Olympia Press, Miller's publisher. Critics and reviewers confirmed my assessment. What distinguished his books from the rest of the pack was the application of Vassi's intelligence. He knew that the mind is the most erotic organ of all. He termed this fusion of mind and sex organs "Metasex."

For Marco Vassi, the liberation of sexual emotions, paralleling the liberation of so many others in the late 1960's and early 1970's, promised a new age of beauty, love, and honesty, and he lived his vision to the hilt—quite literally. For a long while it seemed to him impossible that this vision did not rest on the bedrock of reality.

But, in the words of Robert Frost, nothing gold can stay. The bloody hand of Vietnam and the corrupt fist of the Nixon presidency crushed the fragile beauty of the flower generation. The unbridled commercialism that became the 1980's captured and exploited the butterflies of Woodstock, enriching half of them and killing the other half with sex, drugs, and rock and roll. Finally, the horror of a new scourge, AIDS, visited death upon the bodies of those who had dreamed of eternal love, irresponsible fun, and self-realization. It was then that Marco Vassi awoke from his dream of The Sixties. When he did, the virus had entered his blood. The first malady of any consequence to come along, in this case pneumonia, conquered his defense less immune system and made short work of him.

Marco Vassi's body died, but not the body cf his work, which lives again in these new editions. Like a rainbow over a bleak landscape, his dream of The Sixties shimmers above the depressing, sordid, and tragic decades that succeeded his. And ultimately, it triumphs over them.

Richard Curtis

ONE

By the time I reached the end of my sophomore year in college, I knew that the whole higher education scene was pretty much a crock of shit. Not for those few who had specific goals, like wanting to be engineers or Sanskrit scholars, but for the rest of us who had been told by our parents that a college education was necessary, something like having your teeth fixed when you're a kid. We went through the motions of going to class, and every now and then might meet a teacher who wasn't completely bored with his work, and might even learn something from him. But other than that, all but the most naive kids soon figured out that the entire thing was a game: it kept a lot of people employed and met all the mythic standards of respectable society.

I suppose I would have stuck it through until graduation if I hadn't met Jeff. The only alternative was getting a job, and without a degree there weren't too many interesting possibilities in that area. Also, on the basic level of material comfort, I didn't have anything to complain about. The campus was extremely pretty, almost luxurious. The southern California climate in which it was located was one of the finest in the world. And aside from the periodic stupidity of having to sit through meaningless lectures and performing the rituals of examination time, there was more than ample opportunity for swimming, tennis, exploring the night-life of Los Angeles, and, of course, sex.

It was because I was suffering a dry period in the last category that the event which was to affect the direction of my life took place. My first experience had been at the age of seventeen with a suave business acquaintance of my father's. I often suspected that my father even encouraged it, so that I would be "broken in right." My old man had a mania for efficiency that bordered on obsession, and it wouldn't surprise me to learn that it extended as far as making sure that his daughter lost her virginity in as commodious a fashion as possible. Manfred had proved himself to be an understanding person as well as a superb technician, so I began my erotic existence with a very high set of standards.

That was to prove to be something of a handicap at school, for the freshmen who were my classmates were, as might be expected, as raw and awkward as they were enthusiastic. I fucked my way through half a dozen of them before I came to the conclusion that getting laid provided a challenge far more complex and difficult than anything being presented to me by my formal studies. Of course, I harbored many of the conventional romantic notions about meeting "Mister Right" but I was level-headed enough to understand that that might not be for some time, and until then I had to discover an intelligent means to take care of the constantly increasing demands of the mouth between my thighs, an organ that was developing a hunger as vital as that felt by my stomach.

On the night I first saw Jeff I had been without sex for almost three months, and it was making me more than a little jittery. So when I was invited to a fraternity party by a tall, handsome imbecile whose whole repertoire of facial expressions rarely went beyond a vacant leer, I found myself accepting. The sub-adolescent ambience at those bashes was revolting, but that very fact fed my feeling of desperation. Hank, the lunk who presented himself for stud service, was stupid enough for me to manage him with little more than vocal inflection, and his intentions were so palpably obvious that I foresaw no complications. It may sound unladylike to put it this way, but when he asked me to the party all I could think was, "Wow, do I need a good stiff cock right now."

My plan, albeit a little coldblooded, was to spend an hour or two at the party, drink enough vodka to make me really woozy, and then have Hank drive me somewhere and fuck me in the back seat of his car. I didn't want to spend a night in the same bed with him. I sensed, rather than articulated to myself, that part of the process involved my assuming a feeling of degradation, of getting into a whorish state of mind. It was to be a night during which I would make no pretence at being a woman, but would just become a cunt. There was some risk in the matter, for if any of the seven or eight people who formed my circle of peers saw me they would ride me about it for a long time. And although I had no concern for any abstract reputation I might have on campus, still I didn't want to be pestered by the kind of attention I would receive when Hank told the boys in the locker rooom what a fine piece of ass I was.

The night went pretty much as I had planned, and the party was exactly as I had expected: it fell to the level of the infantile within a half hour, and by the end of the hour the place was like a kindergarten with all the children run amok. Bad music, loud raucous laughter, an incredible amount of booze, thick clouds of smoke from grass and tobacco. I dealt with it with an efficiency that would have made my father proud, proceeding with my strategy. And within a short time I was irrevocably drunk, enough so that I could even be amused and slightly turned on by the bird-dogging that went on in relation to me, friends of Hank's asking me to dance and, when he wasn't looking, running their hands over my ass, pressing their erections against my crotch, cupping my tits.

At one point I needed to use the bathroom and, swimming in a sea of wooziness, I barged into one of the johns without bothering to knock. And what I saw brought me up short, even in the context of the vulgarity of the total evening. A young man in a wrinkled tuxedo was standing in the middle of the floor and pissing in the sink. The sight was so odd that I forgot my instinctive reaction of distaste and drifted into the room, absentmindedly closing the door behind me. As I lurched forward he turned his head to the side and watched me approach, a slow smile forming on his lips. The sense of unreality engendered by all the alcohol I had consumed was noticeably heightened by this strange vision.

"Why are you doing that?" I asked.

"Water conservation," he said in an even, well-modulated voice.

"Huh?" I replied, my mind too fuzzy to make connections swiftly.

"It's a criminal waste of water to use five gallons to flush down a half pint of waste fluid," he went on in a dry tone. "This way, after I'm finished, I turn on the hot water and it only requires about a glasssful to rinse the sink."

"Something in me tells me I'm supposed to find what you're doing disgusting," I said. "But somehow it all seems very logical. I wonder why I never thought of it."

He put his cock back in his pants, zippered his fly, and dutifully washed the bowl with hot water. He regarded me quizzically, by far the most intelligent expression I had observed all evening.

"Well," he began, his manner suddenly diffident, "it's rather inconvenient for a woman, isn't it?"

For a moment I didn't catch his meaning, and then I saw it, and burst into laughter.

"Want to try?" he asked.

Already reckless, I answered, "Why not?"

"Well, prepare yourself, and I'll give you a lift," he said.

Without thinking, I hoisted my skirt and dropped my panties. He looked at my legs and cunt appreciatively for a moment, and then slipped his hands under my armpits and swung me up onto the sink. I yelped at making contact with the cold porcelain, and then relaxed as I felt the heat from where he had run the hot water.

I waited, but nothing happened. "I don't think I can," I said, "with you standing there."

"Be my ghost," he quipped, and walked gingerly out of the room.

As soon as he had closed the door behind him, I began giggling again. It was clearly the most absurd situation I had ever been in, and the laughter shook my entire body. I relaxed, threw my head back, and still chuckling, began to let loose, following the example of the strange man who had been there before me.

And it was like that, sitting bare-assed on a sink in a frat house bathroom, drunk and giggling, and gaily pissing in the sink, that I met Jeff. The door opened and he stepped inside. It wasn't until I heard his sharp intake of breath that I turned my head, and at that instant the blood froze in my veins.

He was the most strikingly beautiful man I had ever seen. He stood six and a half feet tall, his shoulders were as wide as the door frame, his face seemed carved out of granite, and although he couldn't have been more than twenty-one, he had the air of a successful man of forty. But more than all that were his hands—I will never forget his hands!—more than three times the size of mine and emitting a sense of fierce power that almost frightened me.

We locked gazes and for a few seconds all time ceased. I forgot myself, the surroundings, the whole universe. There was only this terrible and magnificent vibration, this rush of overwhelming male energy. It was as though he had some irresistible magnet inside him, and I felt that my very soul was being drawn out of my body.

Then he shook his head, snorted once, and began to back out of the room. "That's got to be the weirdest goddamn thing I've ever seen in my life," he said out loud, and then turned and disappeared.

I wanted to shout for him to wait, but I only fell back against the mirror behind me, feeling weak and empty. My stomach turned sour, and I verged on nausea. I jumped back to the floor, and got my clothes back in place, and then used the sink for its more common purpose, to wash my face and run cold water over my wrists. I took several deep breaths and staggered back out into the roar of the party, still stunned at the apparition which had shaken me so deeply.

And stepped right into the arms of the boy—I can't call him a man—who had taken me, and had, through great effort, reversed the process of evolution and become a gorilla. He was the last thing I wanted at the moment, but the heat was upon him and he was impossible for me, in my shaky condition, to fend off. Besides, fucking him was the commitment I had implied, and I really didn't want to be a bad sport. I've never thought of myself as a particularly moral person, but I like to keep my word and pay my debts. Besides, I had come there to get laid, and I was determined to accomplish my aim.

Hank wheeled me to the room where the bar had been set up and we began another round of drinks. Other couples had already begun to sink into couches and corners and the room was thick with the moans of heavy necking. I was still too stunned to feel very much, and wanted just to be alone to bring the incident of that astonishing meeting back into focus and dwell on it, but that was not to be permitted. So I did what I had come to do: I shut off my mind and flung myself into the theater of the body.

Within moments, Hank had me stretched out on the floor, his mouth pressing mine, his tongue blind and insistent between my lips, his hands flying like crazed moths over the flames of my erogenous zones, not knowing where they wanted to settle. He was crude, staying almost exclusively with the tried-and-true duo of tits and ass, pummeling my breasts with one hand and piercing into my ass crack through the cloth of my dress with the other, all the while he rubbed his very hard and hot cock against my cunt. But for all its lacking in nuance, his approach was effective enough, and within a short time I found myself responding, twisting my hips and grinding my ass on his hand and opening my mouth to moan and letting his tongue slide down as far as my throat. He was exactly what I had imagined he would be: pure, unrefined lust. And I let myself loll under him as he pushed his weight and desire into my body, getting my nipples hard and my ass itchy and my cunt wet.

He rolled off me part way and his right hand went from my tits to my crotch, his fingers stroking my pussy. That really got to me and I felt my legs opening as he rubbed my clit through the fabric. But when he began to pull my skirt up, I stopped him. I knew that it was one of the general status symbols among the fraternity boys to be able to fuck a date in full view of everyone. It was taken as a sign of irresistible virility for a man to be able to "get a bitch so hot" that she would let herself be plowed before the eyes of fifty or a hundred people. Such incidents usually ended up in gang bangs in one of the upstairs rooms, and while I must admit that the idea had its appeal, I was not willing for my initiation into that particular form be at the hands of juvenile delinquents. I was later to look back on those boys with fondness, because despite all their baseness they still had a kind of inocence, but that night I hadn't yet had experiences to judge them against.

"Come on," he cajoled, tugging at my dress.

"No," I said firmly, and in his eyes I saw the beginnings of anger, and I knew that the word "cockteaser" would be one of the first from his lips.

"In your car," I said.

For a second he was disbelieving, and then his face lit up with all the unselfconscious joy of a child's. *I* was asking *him* to take me to his car. He could barely contain himself.

I couldn't resist the impulse to goad him on a bit. "I want to put that thing in my mouth," I said running my fingers over his cock, "and I can't do that here."

On the way to his car, and during the ride to the deserted spot that he took us to, I wondered at the situation. From one point of view, I should have been disgusted with myself. I felt nothing but disdain for the boy I was with. I considered myself his complete superior, not only intellectually but in terms of sexual experience. And yet I would be giving him the use of my body, knowing that he was seeing me as a conquest, as a star on his report card. But it was that very condition which had prompted me to choose him, for the only thing about him that appealed to me was his cock. I didn't know the roots of the impulse; all I knew was that I had a hungry hole that needed to be filled periodically, in the same way that it bled periodically. And that filling it would involve a series of trial-and-error situations until I found the man with whom I could feel whole. As I said, I was not without visions of falling in love, but until that happened, or until I met someone with whom I could have a rational affair, I would go about stuffing my pussy in whatever way I could, much as I would eat a hotdog at a roadstand when I really wanted steak, but could not wait until I found a good restaurant. And on top of all this was the tingling awareness that I was indeed about to do something "dirty," because Hank was seeing the whole thing with such an obvious lascivious glee that I could not help but be infected by his vibrations.

The scene in the car was as gaudy as I had hoped. We drank brandy from a flask until I was practically paralyzed, which is what I suppose he wanted. And I just went along and drank until I fell back on the leather seatcovers, almost in a swoon. In a flash he was all over me, pawing my breasts, grabbing my ass, flinging his body on top of mine. Before I went completely under, I saw myself as I would appear through the window of the car, a pretty and sophisticated girl, her dress up over her thighs and pulled down over her breasts, lying almost spread-eagled in complete abandon, while a young man vented his lust upon her.

He climbed up on the seat and unzippered his fly. "This is what you said you wanted," he panted. "Now come on, open your mouth. Open those beautiful lips and suck my cock. Come on, put my fat cock in your mouth."

I rolled my head toward him and felt the swollen head of his cock brush against my lips. I felt a constriction in my chest. It wasn't something I had done that often, and my sophistication began to desert me. He pushed forward and the huge thick rod insinuated itself between my lips. And then before I could take a breath, it was inside my mouth. I gasped, and he took the chance to push further, and his throbbing cock lodged itself right into my throat. I gagged and tried to push him away, but he pinned my hands down.

Now I was under him, and he was fucking me in the mouth. "Oh, beautiful," he hissed. "You look beautiful with my cock splitting your mouth open." He pulled back and I gasped for air, and to my astonishment, found myself covering his cock again. This time I wrapped my tongue around the shaft and began to lick it. I could feel it swelling and throbbing. I became slightly delirious and went a little wild. I started to moan and he began pumping again, his hips beating rapidly as his cock slid in and out of my mouth. It was now slick and engorged and hot, and I could taste the first drops of pre-seminal fluid.

"Suck it, suck it, suck it," he chanted, and I responded by doubling my activity, drawing him in and letting him slide into my throat until I choked, and then expelling him, panting, and beginning again by slowly licking the rod from its base to the tip.

"Come on, Julie," he said, his voice cracking slightly. "Oh . . . you cocksucker," he crooned, and with that let his orgasm burst, his cock spurting wildly in my mouth, the sticky jism splashing on my tongue and into my throat. I retched and almost vomited at the sensation, but I held onto my control until his entire climax had spent itself and his cock hung between my lips. I didn't want to swallow his cum but I couldn't hold it any longer without gagging violently, and so I relaxed and let the load ooze down until I gulped and consumed the entire thing. His cock pulsed once more and he pulled it out slowly.

I sank slowly away from the experience and from consciousness, and wasn't roused until I felt his fingers between my legs. My panties had been removed and he was shoving two fingers violently in and out of my pussy. I could barely feel anything at all, and lay as though I were tied down. He may have thought me unconscious and that seemed to be adding to his frenzy. The thought that I had passed out from too much drink and he was now fucking me seemed to describe the epitome of any erotic fantasies he may have had.

He lifted my legs until they were over his shoulders, and my cunt and ass curved out at him, utterly open and vulnerable. "Gonna fuck you . . . fuck you . . . shove it up your hole . . . put it in your pussy . . . hot pussy . . . wet pussy . . ." he crooned to himself. And then fell upon me, his cock, hard and re-charged, plunging between my thighs. I groaned, and passed out again.

I don't know how long he fucked me, but I remember coming to a number of times, and each time the scene that greeted me was the same. Hank was crouched over me, his arms holding my legs, his pelvis pumping steadily, his cock churning deep into my cunt, sliding, sliding, sliding. I felt no specific sensation, but a gradual heat began to build, until near the end my box was like an oven, burning with friction. I had lost all distinction between cunt and asshole. There was only a huge hot pit between my thighs, and each stroke of his cock was like another shovel of coal thrown onto the flames.

I did nothing but open and open, and even when my legs would split no wider, my cunt continued to spread. It was ironic that I needed to get so drunk to allow this to happen, and that very drunkenness was taking the edge off the experience. But then I thought that if I were cold sober, I wouldn't be able to stand the heat that was boiling in my loins and belly.

Finally, I heard him begin to build. His breath changed rhythm and pitch. "Come on," he urged, "come on, you cunt. Come!"

His words triggered the connection between my mind and my pussy, for I had disassociated one from the other, my cunt building its enormous charge and my mind either spinning off or lapsing into darkness. Now I brought them together and began to direct myself toward orgasm. As he rode me faster and more vigorously, I let the deep throbbing in my twat settle into a single, discrete rhythm, and I focused my attention on it, nursing it along. I began to cooperate with his movements and started to thrust my pelvis up to meet his swoops into me, at the same time twisting my ass on the seat to feel his cock hit different parts of my cunt, also adding to his sensations.

The timing clicked, and before I could do anything else we were both swept up into a single climax, his entire body jerking spasmodically from his toes to his neck, while his cock pulsed violently deep inside my hole. At almost the same second, heat and rhythm coalesced in me into a single sensation of melting, and I yielded totally to it, crying out as my legs trembled and my ass shook and my cunt pounded and the juices ran out of me and over his cock and onto the leather.

I heard Hank whisper, "Christ, what a fantastic fuck," just before I passed out for the final time that night.

He must have taken me back to my room, undressed me and put me into bed, for the next thing I remembered was the doorbell ringing insistently. I opened one eye and looked at the clock. It was one in the afternoon, a Sunday. I wasn't expecting anyone and hoped it wouldn't be Hank back for more. My head ached, my tongue was thick, and my cunt felt like it had been filled with tabasco sauce. But the caller wouldn't stop, and I rolled off the bed and onto my feet, my legs almost collapsing under me, the muscles sore from the sustained stretching they had received. I looked around for something to wear, couldn't see my clothes, and finally tore the sheet off the bed and wrapped it around myself. Looking and feeling like the survivor of a car crash, I staggered to the door.

"All right," I yelled, "I'm coming."

I reached the door just as I remembered that those were the last words I had used before falling into unconsciousness, and the incongruous link struck a chord in my sense of humor. Ready to let my visitor have no nicety for waking me up, I started to laugh at the situation and opened the door. And almost fell on my face.

Standing there was Jeff, the incredibly beautiful giant who had come into the bathroom the night before. We stared at each other for a full fifteen seconds, and then he smiled.

"Still laughing?" he asked.

My mouth fell open and forgetting that I was holding the sheet, I let my hands drop. The cloth fell to the floor and suddenly I was standing in front of him without a stitch of clothing.

He took a long look at me and said, in a voice that held an edge of amused irony, "And *totally* naked this time." He gazed at my breasts, then looked back into my eyes, and added, "I liked the bottom half very much last night. The top makes you one of the most beautiful women I have ever seen."

A breeze blew in from the street behind him and I was suddenly aware that there were people passing by on the sidewalk, and even though his huge body largely hid me from view, I suddenly felt extremely embarrassed.

"I thought that after the party you might be needing a cup of coffee." He paused. "May I come in? I'll fix it while you're getting dressed."

I stepped back, dumbfounded, and he came into the living room closing the door behind him. Seeing the expression on my face, and handing me back the sheet which he had picked off the floor, he said, "There's nothing mysterious. You turned me on. And I wanted to see you again. That's all."

"But how did you know who I was?" I began.

But he cut me off. "Put something on," he said. "If you stay naked I'll probably wind up fucking you right here on the rug. And I think it would be more pleasant if we talked first. Don't you?"

"I'll take a shower," I mumbled, and turned to go to the bathroom, aware that his eyes were drinking in my ass. I couldn't think coherently enough to build a quick context for what was happening, but I decided not to try until I had showered, dressed, had some coffee, and talked to the man who I already instinctively felt was about to change the course of my life.

TWO

From the moment I stepped into the living room and found Jeff sitting on the couch, a pot of steaming coffee and two cups on the table in front of him, I knew that I was in a different league from any I had played in before. The sheer size of him continued to astonish me, and it was the most natural thing in the world for me to imagine what it would feel like to have that gorgeous body ramming violently between my legs. I later learned that he weighed two hundred and forty-six pounds, every bit of it hard, rippling muscle. I wondered if his cock was in proportion to the rest of him.

He stood up as I entered, and just seemed to keep rising as he towered over me. I'm five-nine and have considered myself a pretty big girl, but next to him I felt like a child.

"You look refreshed," he said as he came toward me. Before I could reply his arms were around my back. I grew weak and melted in his embrace. His chest was like cliff rock, his belly a flat sheet of iron, and his thighs like tree trunks against my own. He crushed me to him and I realized that he could easily crack my entire rib cage without even trying. His hands slid down and cupped my buttocks, although he could have held my ass in one of his huge hands. When his lips covered my own, I almost fainted; I was drawn into the magnetism of his animal strength. But his lips were gentle, soft, and his kiss was as soft as a falling autumn leaf touching the earth. When he released me, I was trembling from head to toe.

"Who are you?" I whispered.

"My name is Jeff Arnheiser," he said, and paused, as though waiting for a reaction.

"If that's supposed to ring a bell, I'm afraid it doesn't."

"Football?" he coaxed.

"Oh, *you*," I said, his name suddenly flashing in my memory. He had been one of the school's great all-time players, and his exploits filled the papers weekly during the season. I had read of his receiving a contract to play for Seattle, at a starting salary of $40,000 a year plus an undisclosed bonus.

He smiled. "But I know who you are without your having to tell me. Name: Julie Shepherd. Major: Psychology. Voted by a secret meeting of professional girl watchers as the woman who combines the most beautiful ass, the most luscious tits, and the most dangerous mind of any coed on campus."

I was taken completely aback, and wasn't sure whether he was joking. His grip tightened around my waist and I was pulled tightly into him, feeling his cock hard against my belly. I was in peril of being swept off my feet and while part of me was thrilled, another part told me that it was unsafe to let a man, even one as glorious as this one, take too commanding a position.

But he was relentless. "I didn't recognize you last night," he said. "That scene was just so strange, and it wasn't until a half hour later that I realized who it was that was sitting there. But by then Hank had whisked you off, probably, if I'm not mistaken, to fuck you in the back seat of his car."

"That was my idea," I told him, looking into his eyes and continuing to melt from the heat of his body. "Is he part of your team of women watchers?'"

"Hank's all right," Jeff said, "just a little dumb, that's all. Tell me," he intoned in a low lascivious voice, "was it good?"

"Why don't you ask him," I shot back, a little angry.

"I already did," he said. Then, without warning, he slipped one hand between us and cupped his fingers over my cunt. I had put on a pair of shorts and a blouse after the shower, and now his hand had slipped between my thighs and was massaging my pussy and ass crack. I squirmed in pleasure and discomfort. "And I figured that if a girl like you is fucking a boy like him, you must be more than a little horny."

"I don't know whether I like your attitude," I said.

I don't know how our little bit of badinage would have

continued if the doorbell hadn't rung. "Damn," I said, and went to answer it, and was stunned to see Hank standing there. He leered at me, and then his face fell when he saw Jeff in the living room. I saw fear and resolve in Hank's eyes, and he stepped inside.

"Cutting in on my girl is a dirty trick," he said in a voice that shook a little. I had to admire his courage, but had to agree with Jeff that he was a little dumb. Jeff walked up to him very slowly and then planted his weight right in front of Hank's body. Hank wasn't small, but Jeff made him look like an adolescent.

"She isn't *your* girl," Jeff said. "She's her own woman. And right now she is choosing to be with me, so maybe you'd better go peddle your papers somewhere else."

Hank started to protest but Jeff grabbed his shirt, gave one yank, and lifted him clear off his feet. Then he pushed him backwards and pinned him against the wall. His eyes were blazing. I got a sense of his enormous strength and felt my knees wobble at the thought that he would probably soon be fucking me. I knew he wanted me, and I knew there was no way in the world I could resist.

"You're a nice kid, Hank," Jeff said, "I'd hate to have to break your arms and legs."

He let Hank down and stared at him until the poor boy turned sheepishly and went back out the door. Jeff turned to me, and his eyes were smoldering. "Now," he said, "get out of those clothes. I've waited long enough."

All my resentment at being bossed around by men disappeared in the realization that up to that moment I hadn't met a man who was man enough to get away with it. And an ancient female sense of surrender filled me and made me subservient. I didn't know where this was taking me, but I didn't care. I turned around and walked toward the bedroom, feeling Jeff's piercing gaze penetrate the cloth and cover my ass.

He followed me into the bedroom, closed the door behind him, and crossed his arms over his chest. I knew what he was waiting for and I was more than a little ready to oblige. I reached down, grabbed the bottom of my blouse, and lifted it slowly over my head. As I pulled it up, first my belly and then my tits were bared to his gaze. I threw it to one side and stood there, my breasts thrusting out proudly, the nipples already wrinkled.

"The shorts," he said, "I want to see your cunt."

I unhooked the button and slid the zipper down. Then, in a gesture that is as old as burlesque, I raised first one leg and then the other, slipping each out of the brief pants. In a few moments my suntanned body was completely naked.

He grinned and followed suit, jerking off his shirt and then stepping out of his pants. He wore no underwear and I was quickly able to see what my bed-mate to be looked like. I almost gasped in astonishment. He was perfectly proportioned, his legs solid and tapered, with thickly muscled calves and immense thighs, his chest broad and covered with curly black hair. His arms were as thick as my legs, and my glance went finally to his cock, already stiff, and jutting out what seemed like a foot in length from his pubic hair. Looking at him, I felt utterly feminine, soft and curvy and receptive. My cunt twitched and I knew that the hunger I had tried to satisfy the night before was only the pale shadow of a ravenous need that I had been afraid to fully admit. And if there were a man anywhere who could satisfy that need, surely it was Jeff.

He came toward me and without thinking I fell on my knees, almost worshipfully. He put his hands on my shoulders and directed his cock toward my lips. I felt faint at the thought of that huge engine in my mouth, and I leaned forward to kiss the flaring purplish crown, and then licked the few drops of fluid from the tip.

"A beautiful and intelligent woman on her knees sucking cock is the most thrilling experience in the world," he said. And with that he pushed his cock toward me, parting my lips, and forcing the whole huge head of it into my mouth.

I was totally overwhelmed. Just the smell of him was exciting, a rich pungent aroma of male flesh. I took a deep breath and took the cock as far into my mouth as it would go, but I was only a third of the way down the shaft. I was stuffed with cock and it seemed not another bit could enter me. But he had other ideas. He pushed my head downward and changed the angle of penetration until he was hitting at the base of my throat. I began to gag and he pulled back, but soon renewed his efforts.

"Down your throat, Julie," he hissed, "I want to shove my cock down your throat."

I started to struggle, but something in me gave way, and I just relaxed and let him do it. I made my mouth as soft and pliable as my cunt, and let him fuck me the way he wanted. He began to stroke in and out easily, leaving me time to breathe, but his movements soon became more insistent and harder. With each thrust he penetrated more deeply. My legs started to vibrate and my tits were pressed against his thighs. My eyes started to water and my brain was darkened over. He reached down and started pinching my nipples, and when I went to cry out, his cock went deeper into me.

I closed my eyes and gave myself up to being fucked in the mouth by this strange and compelling man with a giant cock. I used my tongue to lick the underbelly of his prick each time it slid out, now glistening with wet. I began to want to drink his sperm. My jaw ached and my lips were stretched almost to being torn, but a raging desire had been sparked in my chest and I wanted his fluid to quench the flames.

I started to moan. "Come on, Julie," he said, "want it, want it bad! Beg for it. Lick for it. Suck for it."

I lost all sense of what I was doing. Suddenly I was a madwoman, sobbing, sucking, licking, groaning, feeling that huge cock pound in my throat. I put my hands on his buttocks and pulled him toward me. His ass cheeks were deep and round and firm from exercise, and as he pumped his cock into my mouth, they flexed and relaxed. I dug my nails into his flesh and he doubled his pace.

Abruptly, I heard him start to pant and let out short, harsh sounds. His movements built to a frenzy and I knew he was at the brink. Finally, he gave one deep thrust and his cock slid completely inside me, and my lips sank into his thick bush of hair. With that came the explosion, the eruption of semen spurting from his balls, down the length of the tube, out of the crown, and into my gullet. His cum spilled straight down inside me, cascading down my chest and into my stomach. He continued to cum, and as he did so he pulled out, the jism still spurtting, splashing the back of my throat, the back of my tongue, the inside of my mouth, and finally onto my lips and chin, until his cock stood over my head, splashing out its last drops on my face.

I was almost drowning in sperm, feeling it burning my insides where he had begun his orgasm, clogging my throat, coating my tongue, and beginning to coagulate on my lips. I felt sticky and sexy and dirty and good. I sat back on my haunches and licked my lips, feeling like a grand cocksucker. I swallowed and swallowed and swallowed until there was no spunk left in my mouth, and then I put his cock back in my mouth once more and sucked hard, draining him of his last dangling drop.

He looked down at me and the expression on his face was a mixture of gratitude and wonderment. "Wow," he said, "you're better than anything I had even hoped. You're so fucking hot when you get going."

"That weapon you have between your legs is a major incentive," I said.

I thought we might take a rest but I wasn't counting on his stamina. Jeff reached down and without a sign of strain lifted me off the floor. He kept lifting until he was holding me over his head. He shifted my weight until his hands were under the back of my thighs, right where my buttocks start to swell, so that I was sitting on his hands. And then he lowered me until my cunt was right above his mouth.

"What are you doing?" I squealed, sounding like a schoolgirl and loving it.

"Eating you like you've never been eaten before," he said.

He lowered me a little further until my cunt covered his lips, and then he began licking the length of my crack, from asshole to cunthole. His long broad tongue swept over the whole valley, sending delicious thrills up my spine. He glued his lips against my pussy and began to suck, drinking in my juices which had begun to flow copiously. My mouth was still tingling and now he had begun to get my ass and cunt excited. I felt like a leather wine bottle being hoisted in the air and squeezed of its contents.

My legs hanging down, my hands massaging my tits. I luxuriated in the splendor of the position.

He moved up to my clitoris and started to nibble the small exquisite button. I was hotter than I had thought for when he began to stimulate that trigger, I could feel myself beginning the first waves of orgasm. I cried out and started to rock back and forth on his hands, rotating my hips. But just then he began to dance across the room, spinning around like a dervish.

"Jeff!" I yelled, "be careful."

But he was beyond hearing. His lips and tongue punishing my clit, his thumbs sliding inside my cunt, he spun faster and faster until the whole room began to rock crazily. My mind went reeling as my cunt climbed toward climax. My head grew lighter and lighter as my pussy grew hotter and wetter. I tried to hold on but he was too insistent, spinning wildly through space as he sucked my clitoris and chewed my pussy lips until I couldn't find anything to grip, and I let myself go completely. With that, my climax swelled inside me, seizing my cunt and belly and brain. I cried out and prepared to ride it on to conclusion.

But at precisely that instant, Jeff stopped whirling and with a single motion hurled me across the room. And my orgasm ripped through me as I was flying through the air, my arms flailing, my legs kicking, my tits flopping, my ass clenching. I screamed at the top of my lungs and came crazily in space.

But his throw had been perfectly planned, and as I spent myself, I landed flat on my back in the center of the bed, spread-eagled, my eyes wild with terror and ecstasy. I crashed with a loud whomp and bounced three or four times before coming to rest.

Jeff did not give me a second to recover before he had rushed across the room, flung himself on top of me, and without allowing me a second to compose myself jammed his enormous cock its full length into the deepest recesses of my cunt. I screamed once more, jack-knifed in the middle, and was skewered totally on his steel-hard prong.

Maintaining his momentum, he grabbed my ankles and lifted my legs high in the air, spreading his arms so that my limbs formed a wide V, apart at the top and narrowing to a single

point, which was none other than my very hairy, very wet, and
slightly awestruck pussy. At that moment I knew I had crossed
a threshold. It was not only the size, although that in itself was
enough to send me into transports even if that cock had been
attached to a syphilitic donkey. It spread my pussy lips until
I thought my cunt would crack at the seams. It reamed me as
neatly as a blow torch burning barnacles out of a rusty pipe.

I suddenly realized that what I had thought was sexual
experience had up to that point been little more than hors
d'oeuvres, and that my real erotic education was just beginning.
Lying there with that mountain of a man driving me into the
mattress, his horse cock beating into my belly with the force
of a triphammer, and my being able to not only contain it but
envelop it and enjoy it, gave me some sense of the scope of my
capacity.

I wrapped my legs as much as I could around his broad
waist and pulled him toward me with my thighs. He was now
supporting himself on his palms, stiff-elbowed, while his pelvis
swung with delicious fury and abandon. Although it almost
felt as though I had no operative muscles in my vagina left to
work with, I began to contract my cunt and squeeze his cock.
The sensation triggered off a higher level of explosion in him,
and his movement became somewhat frenzied, although he still
maintained admirable control. I shuddered to think what it
might be like if he really let go and allowed himself to go wild!
It would be like having a maddened bucking bull driving into
my cave.

I opened my eyes and saw him staring down at me. He was
smiling, a warm, beatific smile. Without knowing why, I began
to smile too, and then we were beaming vibrations of love at one
another while our bodies continued their magnificent animal
dance.

"I really dig you," he said.

"I kind of like you too," I replied, lightly.

But his face became serious. "No," he said, "I *mean* that."

I let something flip slip out "Why, Mr. Arnheiser, are you
asking me to marry you?"

But he didn't answer. For a reply he buried his face into my bosom and began to savage my chest with his tongue and teeth. I cried out and grabbed his hair with my fingers, pulling his head back and side to side. But he only dug in deeper, now taking one breast into his mouth, sucking the nipple, licking it, and then biting it sharply. A shout escaped my lips, but my ass responded, bucking up off the bed and pushing my cunt harder against his slamming rod.

What I had feared was happening. He slipped his arms behind the backs of my knees again and forced my thighs to my chest, exposing my cunt and ass most fully. I was prone and flat and open and helpless under him, and he cut loose. He started to pant, hoarse jagged sounds, his long sandy hair tossed about on his forehead and face. His biceps knotted up into veined mounds of muscle. His feet pressed against the foot of the bed and using full leverage he hurled himself into me, again and again, a wild eruption of sheer driving lust.

I was beyond all differentiated feeling; everything was one vast and thunderous rush, a roaring breaking wave that caught me up and tossed me endlessly into the foaming surf of my own seething passion, all the more ferocious for being refused any gross expression of the body.

Only my mouth was left to tell what I felt, and the words spilled out heedlessly, astonishing me.

"CRAM ME!" I shouted. "Shove it . . . shove it . . . shove it . . . ooohhh . . . fuck . . . fuck . . . cock . . . god . . . cock . . . cock . . . aah . . . aah . . . aarngh . . . pussy baby . . . pussy baby . . . fuck my pussy baby . . . take it . . . fuck it . . . bust my pussy baby . . ." And on like that, a kind of rancid parody on Molly Bloom's soliliquy.

But the feeling that spawned those words was anything but facile. It shook me in my heart and bowels and brain. It took everything I thought and felt and imagined about myself and subjected it to a blinding light and searing heat. My ego screeched in horror as it felt itself being torn to shreds by the furnace demons of the unleashed id.

I heard him scream, a long ululating yell, like an apeman swinging on a long vine rope across a deep chasm from one tall tree to another. And all I could do was hold on and hope that he made it because whether I liked it or not, he was holding me in his arms. I surrendered entirely and let myself be nothing but the conscious shape of his primeval orgasm. And in that I felt a climax in me that went so far deeper and sang so far wider than anything I had ever known, that even my terror stopped its jabbering and was still to observe this paradigmatic orgasm.

I don't remember what happened next. It was all shimmering lights and surreal sounds and choirs and insights and para-sensational experiences, and when we had stopped thrashing and twitching and rolling and spewing, we were a tangle of arms and legs lying on the floor. We had literally flung ourselves off the bed!

As might be expected, we didn't speak for a long time. We lay and breathed and marvelled. And returned, level by level, to the basic aspect of perception which human beings have largely agreed, for better or worse, to accept as the common reality.

The first words he spoke startled me.

"The coach would have had a fit if he had seen that."

I shook my head, not sure where the syntax fit in with what had just happened. "The coach?" I repeated.

He rolled over, disentangling himself, and lay on his back, his head resting against the bed, one arm under my neck, his other hand curling the hairs in his chest. "We're not supposed to fuck," he said.

"I didn't know football was a religious activity," I said.

"It's energy," he replied. "The amount of energy that goes into a fuck like that is worth three hundred-yard runs returning a kickoff from the goal line. Or it's the equivalent of an hour of practice. I don't know, he's got the charts that explain it in terms of calories and metabolism. The thing he told us was that if we fucked we would be too debilitated to play as well as we can. But that if we did fuck, we should stay cool and not move too much. He said the best thing was to get a blowjob. He even gave us the address of a whorehouse."

"But that's bizarre," I said.

He frowned and looked thoughtful. "Not really," he explained, and I could see that he had become quite serious. When I recalled that within a few months he would be earning almost fifty thousand dollars a year just because of his prowess, I could understand why he was disturbed about the issue. "It's like you wouldn't let a surgeon get drunk very often," he went on. "A man has to be careful not to do things that jeopardize his work."

"You make me sound like an occupational hazard," I told him.

He suddenly turned and looked deeply into my eyes as though he were searching for something. "I've had my eye on you for months, and I knew it would be like this when we got together. That's why I didn't come on to you sooner. But after I saw you with Hank, I knew that you were ready to really cut loose. And I have only three more weeks before I have to report to training in Seattle. I had to have you, and I knew that if I did I wouldn't want to let you go."

I was speechless. The fucking itself had turned me inside out, and now that I was especially open and vulnerable, he was making what almost sounded like a declaration of love. I knew it wasn't love per se, although we had shared some really tender and deep feelings while we were balling, but his voice held such affection, such warmth, such *sincerity*, that I found myself being won over.

"Well," I said, still attempting to skate away from what I intuited was coming, "we can have a bang-up three weeks and maybe I can visit you when your team plays near here."

He raised himself on one elbow. "Julie," he said, "why don't you come with me?"

I shot him a lancing glance. "Oh, listen, Jeff," I said, "I know I mentioned marriage earlier, but that was just in joking."

"I'm not talking about marriage," he said. "But just to have you near me."

"But what would I do? And what about school?"

"Well, you don't really take school seriously any more, do you?"

I had to consider. "No," I said, "I guess not. It is a bit of a farce for someone who doesn't have a specific goal."

"Then what's the problem?"

"Well, what would I do in Seattle?"

"I don't know," he said. "I could set you up in an apartment and visit you when we got passes from camp."

"God," I sighed, "it sounds like the Army."

He didn't reply, but instead put one hand on my breasts. It was so huge he was able to cover both tits at the same time. He pressed down, squashing the sensitive globes into my chest. I felt the heat from his palm, and found myself thrusting my tits toward him. He pinched one nipple and I squirmed in response. He leaned over me again, and brought his mouth to mine. His full curved lips pressed into mine. My mouth opened spontaneously, and my tongue went up to find his. For a long stretch of time our tongues slithered over one another, licking, curving, dancing. By the time he broke away, I was breathing heavily.

He reached under my back and gently lifted, turning me over. I lay on my belly next to him, my shapely ass rising slightly from the floor. He ran his fingers up and down the crack, causing me to squirm, and finally slipped two fingers down between my legs and into my already open and sopping cunt. I arched my buttocks even higher and spread my legs. His other hand went down to my crotch, and from the front two more fingers entered my pussy. He grabbed my cunt from two directions, pulling it open, and then sliding his fingers even more deeply inside, and then pulling again. He was prying me apart.

"Oh, Jeff," I moaned.

He increased the force of his pressure and within a minute he was buried inside me, now three fingers from each hand plunged in up to the knuckles. I began to grind into him, pushing my cunt into one hand and then lifting my ass to impale my pussy on the other hand. And all the while his fingers kept moving, thrusting, twirling, pulling.

"Oh sweet God," I cried. "I never . . . never . . ."

He covered my neck with his lips and began biting the tendons lightly, sending shivers down my back. I was being impelled once more into the vortex, rising from the depths of my cunted being into a cyclone that would lift me bodily once more, toss me through the sky, and fling me into yet a different place. Each time Jeff touched me, it changed my reality. And while I was terrified of the violent changes, I could not help myself. Something profound in me was stirring, and would not be denied.

"Oh, Jeff, fuck me, oh, fuck me," I pleaded. His hands were driving me mad with desire for more. He was taking me up to the point where nothing but total penetration would do, and forcing me to acknowledge that.

"What do you want?" he teased.

"Your cock," I moaned, "please give me your cock. I want your big hard cock all the way up my snatch."

He ranged himself over me, letting his hands slide from my pussy to my thighs. He lifted me a foot, exposing my pussy and bringing it up to his cock. I could feel it throbbing between my thighs and I began to twitch and roll around trying to get the tip of it to the edge of my lips. He went up on his knees, drawing me back, so that I was now kneeling, my ass high in the air, my face on the floor, my tits hanging, nipples grazing the rug. And with deliberate slowness and sureness he brought his rod to my dripping cunt and plunged easily and lustily inside, my pussy parting like butter to a hot knife.

A deep shudder ran through me and I felt skewered, like a sizzling hunk of meat on a steel rod.

"Oh, baby, take me," I said, "it's all yours. Do what you want, baby. Fuck me any way you want."

And he did that. Once again I found myself becoming utterly passive, an open hole for him to use, and while all the conditioning of my liberal education shrieked in protest, that deep need to be had, to be taken, to be owned, to be possessed, overtook me.

"Possessed," I thought. "It's like being possessed by a demon, or a powerful spirit. It's too great for me to defend against." It was not Jeff that I was giving into, but the thing I became when I let myself be empty, a space to be filled.

And he filled me and filled me. His raging cock once more took to the heat and propelled Jeff into an insane ride. Only now it was as though he were a cowboy on a bucking horse. I caught some of his movement, and began to twist from side to side. He was so big and so strong that I was afraid to try to match movements with him before we had settled into a mutually understandable rhythm and routine. One misthrust and he could easily tear my vaginal opening. So I rotated my ass just enough to provide a small counterpoint to his major theme, his theme of wild frenzy.

He fucked me for almost half an hour, and I screamed until I was hoarse and it seemed there was nothing in me left for him to fuck, but again and again he renewed his attack, coming from a different angle, using a different intensity, and each time he uncovered yet another layer within me. Finally, when I was certain I would pass out, I could feel him beginning to cum. He bucked and rocked and slammed into my ass, his cock churning up my foaming pussy, until the climax was triggered, and once again he sprayed a shower of shimmering sperm into the aching recesses of my slit.

He collapsed on top of me and we both fell to the floor, breathing heavily, until our pulses returned to normal. He rolled off me again, again lying on his back, his head against the bed, his hand curling the hairs on his chest.

I looked up, saw him there in that same position, and all at once the ludicrousness of the thing hit us, and we both burst into gales of laughter, so happy that we had fucked, so happy that it had been splendid, so happy we liked each other, so happy we could laugh together.

We roared and tittered until we calmed down, and to my surprise Jeff stood up abruptly. He towered over me like a colossus, and I felt spent and drenched in my cuntiness lying at his feet. He looked down and seemed extremely stern.

"Julie, I don't know if this is right or wrong. And I don't even know just what it is I'm offering you. But I've never known anything like that with another woman, and I don't want to give it up. And if we keep seeing each other, it will get harder to leave you."

My heart sank. I thought he was going to get dressed and leave, and that I wouldn't see him again. I reached up toward him, but he stepped back.

"You have to decide now," he said. "I want you to come with me. And I'll think of something you can do so that you don't have to spend all your time in an apartment waiting for me to have a pass out of camp." His words were coming rapidly and I knew he was thinking hard as he went along. "Maybe I can find you a job with the team, in the office or maybe even on the field. And then we can see each other often."

"I don't know, Jeff," I said, "it's such a big step. Leaving school, going off with you up north."

"Well," he said, "where's your spirit of adventure?" His face got serious and he added. "Tell me now. Come with me and we'll stay together. But if you won't, then I'll leave now. Because I'm falling for you and I don't want it to get any deeper if we have to part in three weeks.'"

It was reckless, insane, all out of proportion, and the single most daring thing I had ever considered. I imagined how my father would sneer. And how my mother would weep. But in a flash I realized that it *was my* decision to make, and perhaps it was time to take myself firmly in my hands and throw myself into me current of life.

I looked up at the extraordinary man looming over me, and I smiled, and I said, "All right, Jeff. I'll come with you."

But before he smiled, and took me in his arms, and kissed me, and told me how glad he was, I could swear I had seen the faintest whisper of disappointment and—could it have been?—fear pass across the back of his eyes. But the die had been cast. And I turned my face toward a new direction.

THREE

The following three weeks were among the most vibrant of my entire life. Jeff spent his mornings in class, his afternoons at the gym and his nights in my bed. But by the end of the second week I forced him not to see me. It was hard for me to do because our fucking had, incredibly, become even more wild than it had been the first day.

One night he fucked me in the ass. It took almost half an hour for him to get the full length and width of his immense club into the tiny opening and all the way up the small, hot canal, having to ease into me and then pull out again, doing that over and over until the muscles relaxed and stretched. Three or four times I thought I would faint from breathlessness. But he moved so slowly there was never any pain, only an unbelievable filling up that had me wriggling and squirming and bleating like a new-born calf. By the time we were finished, I was amazed to find myself bent over the edge of the mattress, my feet on the floor, my full round buttocks curved high in the air, as he plowed my ass with long powerful strokes, driving deep into my bowels until he exploded and erupted, cumming with thick splashes of sperm in my belly. For a whole day afterwards I was giddy and lightheaded, and when I sat in class I could feel my whole ass throbbing, the cheeks still flushed. I was certain that anyone looking at me could tell what I had been doing, and a few of my friends commented that I looked almost manically cheerful.

But I began to feel guilty, thinking I was draining Jeff of the strength he should be conserving for his summer practice sessions in Seattle. The day he left, we hadn't seen each other for almost a week, and that night we treated ourselves to a marathon fuck, lasting until dawn, and when I saw him off at the airport I was too sleepy to feel the pangs of parting. It wasn't until I received his first letter three days later that I experienced the vacuum created by his departure, and my cunt throbbed to have him in me again. My own vacation had begun and I spent most of my time selling my books, sorting out my wardrobe, and arranging to get rid of my apartment. I ran into Hark one morning but he took one look at me and darted away as though I were a poisonous snake. I couldn't keep from laughing.

A week to the day after Jeff left, he sent me a letter outlining the arrangements he had made for me. "I spoke to a few of the older men on the team and they told me that some cf the wives take on jobs as cheerleaders," he wrote. "I nosed around a bit and found that there is a position open. I know this might sound weird to you at first, but it has a couple of advantages. The first is that you can travel with the team and get paid for it. The second is that we won't have to be separated at all. And"—and here I could hear him chuckle—"all the exercise you get will keep your thighs firm and your pretty ass hard and you'll be continually excited from having your tits bounce up and down as you cheer me to touchdowns. I know this isn't exactly what you might have had in mind, but it will always be something you can tell your children (our children?) about."

I found the letter disturbing. Not the idea of being a cheerleader; that was enough of a goof to interest me even if it didn't mean that I could be with Jeff. But that he was starting to talk in terms of years and children. And while he was certainly the most exciting man I had ever known, I wasn't at all sure I wanted anything permanent with him, certainly not marriage and children. I felt too young to be making decisions like that.

But I figured I would handle that part of the problem as I went along. All I knew was that my body craved Jeff's body, and I was already itchy for more of that dazzling fucking we shared. I wrote back that I would be glad to go into cheerleader practice, thinking how thrilling it would be to be dressed in a tight shirt, my tits bulging out, and a short skirt, with the panties outlining my pretty ass flashing every time I jumped into the air, and having the eyes of fifty thousand people on me, and the millions who would be looking in on television.

I settled my affairs, and within two days I was in Seattle, getting off the plane, seeing Jeff in the crowd, his height and bulk making him stand out among the rest of the people.

"He's a giant," I thought, and my heart beat faster.

I ran across the terminal floor, and then I was in his arms, and everything seemed to fall into place. Jeff was holding me, and pressing me to him, and kissing me, and telling me how much he had missed me. We picked up my luggage and went out to his car. It was a blue Pinto, and still shiny from the showroom.

"Like it?" he said, his voice tinged with boyish pride. "It's one of the first benefits I'm experiencing from all the money I'm making."

I had to restrain myself from telling the truth, that I thought it was a tacky little car, and as I fell silent, Jeff grew extremely chatty, telling me all about practice, about the new friends he had made. "I'm only off one day a week," he said, "but since cheerleaders practice at the same time as players, I'll really be seeing you every day." He reached over and put one hand on my breasts, kneading the firm flesh through the cloth of my dress. He took one nipple between his fingers and pinched it gently. My cunt twitched and I bit my lips.

"Jeff, look out," I yelled, as the car swerved dangerously toward the divider in the middle of the highway. He jerked the wheel around and righted our course. "Be careful," I said.

He laughed. "I can't help it," he said. "You know I've been dreaming about your tits all week. When I get the football in my hands, I feel your tits instead. I'm beginning to get a reputation as a guy who never fumbles. They don't know what I'm holding on to."

I smiled, but I thought the conceit a trifle coarse. To my astonishment, Jeff was beginning to get on my nerves.

"The training program is fantastic," he went on. "Pro football is something else again. I realize that college football is in many ways a kindergarten. The coach drives us in ways I didn't think possible. I've gained nine pounds and I'm tougher than before. And I'm as horny as a bull in springtime. I've been dying to feel your body under me, your cunt going soft and mushy as you spread your legs and let me plow into you." He put one hand on my thigh, this time keeping his eyes on the road. "I've been thinking of your ass rolling around on my cock, and your mouth splitting wide to take me in, and even when I eat all I can taste is your pussy juice."

His talk was having a double effect: turning my body on but turning my mind off. We went through the city to one of its outskirts and Jeff finally parked the car in the driveway of a one-story ranch house. It sat smugly in the middle of a bland suburban neighborhood. The car rolled to a halt and I looked around at the wide lawn, the trees, and listened to the quiet.

"Jack Karnovsky lives just four houses down with *his* family," Jeff said with a touch of pride.

"Oh God," I thought, "all his unconscious mamma-pappa patterns are coming to the surface."

There was no way for me to say what went through my mind at moments like this. The very boyishness and ingenuousness which made Jeff so dear also made him a bit of a bore at times. His taste was so *pedestrian*. I didn't come from a wealthy family, but my father had impeccable taste. Even when he bought things from Woolworth's, they were always precisely right. Jeff had a predilection for the banal, including his choice of cars and places to live. Going from a poor student to an affluent football player did something for his pocketbook but hadn't affected his imagination. I wondered where all this left me.

Jeff was oblivious of my mood, and he rushed us out of the car and into the house. I took one brief look around. It was as plastic inside as it was outside, done in a style I can only describe as motel kitsch. As soon as we were in the living room, he came up quickly behind me, threw the luggage down on the floor, and wrapped his arms around my breasts. His body pressed into mine and I could feel his cock, already hardening, pressed into the crack of my ass. As always, the physical sensations were overpoweringly strong, and despite the fact that I was distracted and slightly depressed, I found myself responding, coming up on my toes so he could get the full length of my buttocks along his rod. He slid his hands down and pressed his fingertips into my crotch, pushing my dress into my cunt slit. I squirmed and rubbed myself against him, my cunt riding his hands and my ass riding his cock.

"I don't know what to do first," I said. I spun around, dropped to my knees, and buried my face in his crotch. It was the only part of him that seemed worth relating to at the moment. The huge penis bulged inside his pants like a billy club. I licked it through the fabric, my tongue tingling on the cloth.

"I love you like that," he rasped, "on your knees in front of me, hungry to get me inside your mouth. Take it out. Open the zipper with your teeth and fish out my cock with your tongue."

I grabbed the top of the zipper with my teeth and tugged it down, letting his hair spring out through the opening, releasing the deep pungent aroma of his maleness. I pressed my mouth into the bush and worked my tongue around, licking and curling, reaching for his cock. It was pressed down against one thigh and I couldn't get at it. I strained and strained, pushing my face more and more fully into his bush.

Finally, I reached up and unfastened his belt and the top button of his pants. I snaked the pants down over his hips and when they had fallen almost to his knees, his cock sprang up, hot and hard, thick, juicy, and throbbing, pointing right out at me. I went to take it, to cover it with my mouth, but his fingers went into my hair and yanked my head back.

"Do you want it?" he hissed.

"Oh, yes," I moaned.

"Beg for it," he said.

I looked at his huge rod pulsing in the air and my legs shook with weakness. Whatever else was true at the moment, the thought of having that piece of meat stuffing my throat was making me giddy. My mouth started to tremble and my tongue started to lap the air.

"I want it Jeff, please, please give it to me," I pleaded.

He moved back, stepping out of his pants, and pulled off his shirt. When his hands released me I went after him, walking on my knees. But he pushed me back again. He kicked off his shoes and I tried once more to get at his cock. This time he reached down, grabbed the front of my dress, and with a single yank ripped it off the top part of my body. I knelt there, naked to the waist, startled by the suddenness of his movement.

He grabbed my hair again and this time he pushed me forward and down, until I was lying on my belly between his feet. He leaned far over and tore the rest of my dress until it was nothing but a ragged piece of cloth under me. Now my ass was naked to his eyes.

He raised his right foot and pressed it against my face, pushing my cheek into the floor. I began to whimper and he pushed the sole of his foot onto the corner of my mouth.

"Oh, Jeff," I moaned, and brought my tongue out onto the calloused bottom of his foot. He squashed me into the floor as I licked his toes, and put all five of them into my mouth at once, sucking voraciously.

He pulled his foot away and stepped down until he was at my thighs, and then slid one foot between my legs, forcing them to open. His foot went higher until the toes were at the opening of my cunt. I grunted and lifted my ass off the floor, serving him like a slave girl. I had begun to get very hot, and the controlled brutality he was exhibiting was starting to turn me wild. I spread my legs wider apart, and he pushed harder. pulled back, and then began kicking my cunt, slamming his foot into the soft tender lips of my pussy. It was painful and excruciatingly erotic.

"Like that, don't you?" he said.

"Oh yes," I groaned. "Harder, kick me harder."

Instead he raised his foot and brought it down on my ass. He pushed down, grinding my cunt into the floor, squashing my cheeks with the pressure from his powerful leg. Now I felt like a snake under a man's boot, and I wriggled and crawled and rolled around as he drove me into the ground. The galvanizing sensation of having his foot prod my ass crack was added to the thrill my clitoris experienced at being rammed so forcefully into the carpet, and I started to pump into the floor, my ass rising against his leg, and then being pushed down and rubbed into the ground. Once my humping motion had begun, he took his foot away. I heard a slithering sound and realized he was taking his belt off.

I went wild with anticipation, and when the first hiss sounded in the air I gasped before the leather landed with a loud thwack across my ass. He didn't hit me hard enough to damage me or to cut the skin, but only to make my ass red and tingly. He whacked my buttocks again and again, always in counterpoint to my fucking rhythm, until I was pumping faster and faster and he was whipping more and more rapidly, and in a moment my cunt contracted and released, and a flood of energy roared through me, the spasms exploding in my loins and rippling up into my belly. I yelled with the shock of orgasm and thrashed about wildly as I came with uncontrollable fury, my face deep in the nap of the rug, my tongue licking the carpet, my cunt spilling its sticky juices in a puddle beneath me.

I slowly subsided and lay there quietly, Jeff standing over me, tall, erect, brilliantly muscled, his lips in a thin smile, the belt dangling from his hand, his cock thrumming like a plucked guitar string.

Then, as I sighed and closed my eyes, his strong hands went under my body and he lifted me from the ground.

"Ooooh, Jeff, that was so good," I said.

"Just warmup, Julie," he replied. "Now we get down to the real practice session."

His habit of injecting football terminology into our fucking was sometimes disquieting. But any man who could kick my cunt, shove his toes up my snatch, make me lick his feet, and then whip my ass until I came, could, for the moment at least, be forgiven for small linguistic eccentricities. Or at least so it seemed as he carried me into what I thought would be the bedroom. Instead, we went through a narrow door and down a flight of stairs.

"What . . .?" I asked.

"A little surprise for you in the basement," he said.

We went into a large, well-lighted room that had been carpeted and was completely bare except for a collection of what looked like pieces of gym equipment. I wondered whether Jeff's penchant for athletic metaphor was going to lead to some form of absurd erotic exercise, but I was still tingling from the treatment

I had just received at his hands and was ready for anything he might have in mind.

He stood me up in the middle of the room and lifted my arms over my head. I looked up and saw a rope hanging from the ceiling. He wound it round my wrists and over itself until I was tied securely. Then he walked over to the far side of the room and began pulling on the other end of the rope, causing me to be raised several inches. He pulled until I was balanced only on my toes, my body stretched to its fullest length, thighs taut, tits jutting out, ass raised.

"Ever been fucked standing up?" he said, grabbing my bulging breasts in his huge hands and mauling them roughly.

My eyes widened in surprise. "No," I said.

Jeff walked behind me and went to his knees. He began to lick my legs, and moved his tongue slowly up to my buttocks. The skin was so tight that his licking sent unusually strong tremors through me. He worked toward the center, his mouth kissing the inside of my ass crack. He pulled the cheeks apart with his fingers and dove into the middle, his tongue darting directly into my asshole. I shuddered and tried to dance around, but I could not go far because I held such a precarious balance. He licked the length of the crack and again inserted his probe into the tiny puckered opening. It had the additional effect of shooting thrills of electricity into my pussy and I felt myself lubricating even more strongly than I had been. He had me growing frenzied again, the first drops of cunt juice oozing out from my already battered lips.

Jeff rose slowly, licking up my spine, and as he did his cock slid between my legs. I could feel its approach to my center, and wanted to spread my legs to accommodate it better, but was unable to get my feet any more widely separated. His great organ prodded at the space where my thighs joined, massaging my cunt and ass all at once. I tried to tilt my buttocks to give him better access, but again, I couldn't move.

Seeing my exertions, Jeff whispered, "That's the point honey; in the position you're in you can't do anything but stand there and take it. And I can go as slow or as fast as I want, and drive you crazy."

"Oh, do it," I said, "do it to me any way you want."

He bent at the knees and his cock came up at me from under. He pushed upwards and it started to sink slowly into my hole. I had never experienced any penetration as I did that one. Wanting to move, needing to respond, I was as though paralyzed. My muscles ached slightly from the strain, but the extreme posture had the effect of toning my entire body, making me more alert and sensitive to what was being done with it.

Jeff's enormous cock slid into me with tantalizing ease, an inch at a time. My frame shook with mounting lust, frustrated by my enforced immobility.

"Oh, Jeff, I want to move," I pleaded. "Untie me so I can fuck you back."

"Not a chance," he said, his voice showing a touch of cruelty, but the kind of cruelty that is mingled with a desire to provide a greater pleasure than can be found through conventional niceness. He continued to enter me, parting my pained pussy lips wider and wider, reaming out the furrows in my cunt, grinding into my cervix. I was effectively impaled, and could feel his curly bush brushing into the bottom curve of my ass. He was all the way inside me, all iron-hard twelve inches of him, completely buried in my throbbing twat. And still I could do nothing but feel him.

Jeff grabbed my hips for leverage, and began to stroke his cock into me with regular rhythm. He drew all the way out, the flaring crown lodged at the edges of my leafy labia, teasing me, and when I was gasping with anticipation, he slid it into me again, parting the inner lips, forcing the tiny central opening to stretch to its fullest capacity, and then ravaging the inner walls of my womb. At each end of his arc I cried out, a wordless yelp that was connected to my most primitive sexual core. I longed desperately to hurl myself on him when he plunged into my box, and when he slid out I tried to grab at him with my pussy, holding him tightly, and clutch him with my ass, making his cock a prisoner between the round, lush globes.

But my position allowed none of this, and as he said, I had to stand there and take it. Soon his movement grew faster, harder. He came up at me like a volcano erupting, thunderously and with great force. My sounds multiplied in volume, growing shrill and desperate, until I was emitting a single sustained shriek. I thrashed my head from side to side, the only movement I was capable of. My tongue found a life of its own and licked my lips and then lapped the air. It was as though I had to squeeze the entire expressiveness of my body into what I could do with my face.

Jeff was now fucking me in earnest, building toward his orgasm. I had never felt so used before, and while my body thrilled to the sensations, and part of me appreciated his inventiveness, I realized that our first sexual encounter after our separation had been laced with violence, both with the belt and degradation upstairs and now with the assistance of this mechanical device.

"Jeff," I called out, not knowing what to say.

But he took my cry for an indication that I was cumming. He held my hips more tightly and fucked me furiously, slamming in and out of my pussy, his cock rubbing the skin of my inner thighs raw.

"Yeah, baby," he yelled, "I'm cumming, I'm cumming now. Let's make it together."

I had been used to Jeff's riding off into his own explosion to the point of being utterly insensitive of me, but usually I was able to get off on his energy. But this time I was perhaps too clearheaded. The separation, the plane flight, the disorientation of a new place, the disappointment at seeing the house Jeff had found for us, the uncertainty as to whether I had done the right thing, and our sudden rushing into fucking without even taking time to re-acquaint ourselves, all combined to make me a little cranky. And now, tied to a rope in a basement while Jeff humped me furiously from behind, I was in no mood for dispensing largesse.

"This is creepy," said my mind even as my cunt was vibrating around his cock and bathing the shaft with love juices.

"Now!" Jeff shouted, and his body burst inside me, a series of sharp spasms, his cock hopping, his sperm spraying the inside of my pussy.

He stayed glued to me until his climax ebbed, and then he reached up and undid my ties.

"That was something, wasn't it?" he said, over my head, and not really listening for my response.

We fucked once more before going to sleep and after a depressing meal of t.v. dinners. The next day he had to be at practice, and except for glimpses of one another on the field, I wouldn't see him for another week. I slept fitfully and rose early to see him off.

"Well," I thought after he left, leaving me with the name of the man I was supposed to see about my new job, "here I am, living in a dumb suburb, with a dumb football player." I bit my lip when I thought of Jeff in those terms, and immediately tears of regret and self-pity came to my eyes. Perhaps I wasn't being fair. After all, he was terribly tied up in making a good start in his career, and he hadn't seen me long enough to make him very horny and thus a little insensitive. And, what the hell, I had enjoyed it well enough.

By the time I reached the office of the vice president who was to show me the ropes and get me started, I had decided to put my ambivalence on the shelf and pay attention to business. But a part of me had seen a nasty truth, and it would not be put easily to rest. I took a tranquilizer and tried to put all thoughts out of my mind as I entered the office of Roger Edwards, executive director of public relations for the team.

"He's a pretty cold fish," Jeff had told me, "but you won't have to spend too much time with him."

I gave my name to the receptionist and sat to wait, impressed by the richness of the decor. I leafed through a magazine and was lost in an article when I heard my name called. It was Mr. Edwards' secretary, a tall, elegant blonde in a simple black shift. I was slightly awed by her elegance, and when she said, "Mr. Edwards will see you now," I was struck by her British accent.

As I followed her subtly swaying walk, I began to feel a little nervous and foolish, I saw myself as a college dropout with hot pants for a football hero following him to his training camp and becoming a cheerleader just so I could get a taste of his cock once a week. It all seemed, from a certain point of view, horribly gauche, and once again the suspicion that Jeff, for all his prowess and surface intelligence was basically a clod started to gnaw at my mind. Shamefully, I felt embarrassed about being identified with him.

"Ah, Miss DeWitt," said a deep and cultured voice as I stepped into what at first glance seemed to be a suite of rooms. I looked in the direction of the voice, and took a small step back as a tall, slim, dark man of about forty-five, with perfectly barbered silver hair, and wearing an immaculately tailored suit came toward me. He wore a thin mustache and goatee, giving him a distinctly diabolical look.

"I'm so happy to meet you," he said, dismissing his secretary with a wave of his hand. He looked into my eyes, at my tits, at my crotch, down my legs, and then back into my eyes, letting me know that he had completely undressed me, and also telling me that he wanted me to know he had done it. The entire transaction took no more than two seconds, but it gave me a sense of how sharp he was. It was an extremely suave come-on, and I couldn't help but feel a little flattered, although I knew he had no interest in anything but my body. His approach also gave me a feeling I had been missing: it made me think of myself as a woman of the world and not a scatter-brained schoolgirl.

"I'm sure you could do with a drink," he said. "Why don't you have a seat while I make us a couple of martinis."

I had never had a martini in my life, but I wasn't about to mention that. "A martini will be fine," I said, feeling like an idiot.

He motioned me to a long low couch, and I sat on the edge of the cushion, my nervousness mixed with an anticipation that had to do with more than the job. He turned his back to me and took a good deal of time making the drinks. Finally, he spun around and started toward me, a glass in each hand. And when he looked at me his gaze went directly up my dress which was now above my knees. I pulled it down out of reflex habit. He saw that, saw me looking at him, and then he smiled. He was playing me like a fish, and I knew it, and was a bit miffed, but for some reason the anger seemed to be directed at myself.

He sat down next to me, handed me a glass, held his own up in indication of a toast, and said, "Well, here's to a new relationship. May it be profitable, educational, and entertaining."

I wanted desperately to say something clever, but all I could do was lift my glass in reply, and sip at my drink. Unhappily, I was distracted by the unaccustomed taste and the liquid went down the wrong opening in my throat. I sputtered and started coughing, and on top of that began to blush furiously.

Mr. Edwards lifted the glass gingerly out of my hand, put it on the table in front of us, and gently patted my back.

"My dear girl," he said, "do be careful."

I coughed for what seemed an eternity until the spasm subsided, but when I finished, his hand did not leave my back, but began stroking my spine between the shoulder blades, softly, easily, as though we were old friends and he was just exercising a gesture of warmth. I was less surprised by the rapidity with which he moved in on me than the acquiescence I exhibited. I suppose it was a relief to be with a man in total control of himself after experiencing Jeff's blitzkrieg tactics, but more than that, my decision to quit school and swing out on this larking adventure had started a process in me which did not end with Jeff. He started a process which he might not be great enough to encompass.

Finally, when I was calm again, he took his hand away, trailing his fingers over the back of my dress and momentarily caressing my neck, sending sharp thrills down to my crotch. He regarded me for a long moment and then said, "I understand that you're Jeff Arnheiser's *girl.*" He put an intonation on the last word which made me feel as though I had been described as someone's pet poodle. I wanted to protest but there was nothing in his words to protest against. I was indeed Jeff's girl.

"Jeff is a very nice *boy,*" he continued, again pitching his voice so that "boy" was emphasized and contrasted against its implied opposite: there was no doubt that Mr. Edwards was letting me know that he didn't consider Jeff a man. "He has a great career ahead of him, and *we* are hoping he will become one of our star ends."

That was the third time he had underlined a word and this time I had to react. "Who is *we?*" I asked, trying to sound nettled.

"Why . . . *us*" he said, waving his hand to indicate the luxurious offices, the building, and the entire multi-million dollar empire. "The owners, of course." I got a whiff of the wealth he represented and suddenly Jeff's forty-thousand-dollar-a-year salary shrank into insignificance. He leaned toward me confidentially and added, "You've made a major decision in following him here. A girl with your background would probably have done better to finish college. Perhaps when this fling is over you will see the wisdom of doing just that."

My face grew red, not only because he had put his finger on my secret doubt, but because he spoke in the same cool, impersonal tones my father would have used. "I don't see what my private life has to do with my coming here for a job," I shot out at him.

"Well, we've made a fairly substantial investment in Jeff," he told me, "and of course we made it a point to investigate the woman he suddenly took it upon himself to bring with him. He's a very impetuous youth, but we would prefer that he channeled his energy into playing ball instead of attaining cosmic orgasms."

"How do you know what kind of orgasms Jeff and I have?" I said, my voice almost cracking.

"He's been quite voluble in the locker room," Mr. Edwards said quietly. "There is probably not a person on the team who doesn't know your cunt with thorough vicarious pleasure."

I could feel my pulse pounding, and I was torn between an intense desire to run out of the room and to stay and hear exactly what else this man knew about me. And not only this man, but at least sixty-five others. Just how explicit had Jeff been?

"Above all else," he went on as he leaned back against the couch, "we are all committed to the concept of the *team*. We have specialized jobs and we have our star performers, but if we are to remain successful, we must all pull . . . or if you prefer, push . . . together. We can't afford to have any element among us which is too headstrong and individualistic. I am saying this not to demean you, but to disabuse you right away of any notions you may have concerning standards of privacy which do not apply in this context."

He reached over and patted my knee, and his hand rested there as he continued, "But I don't want to overwhelm you with too much too quickly. After you've been with us a while, you'll understand these things for yourself."

"Just what are you implying, Mr. Edwards?" I asked, aware that his hand was quite cool on my thigh.

"Call me Roger, please," he said. And then went on, "I'm not really implying anything you probably haven't thought about yourself. But for now, I really think we don't need to do anything but have you try on your uniform and tell you where and when to report for practice."

He went to the other side of the room, reached into a desk drawer, and took out a small package. "There's a bathroom over there," he said. "Put this on and let's see how you look in it."

"Here?" I asked, "Is that necessary?"

"Judging from what I have seen of your body, I'm sure you'll do just fine. But one of my prerogatives is to check out how our cheerleaders will look in uniform. You'll forgive me if I pull rank a bit and insist on it."

There seemed to be little else I could do, so I took the package and went into the bathroom to change. It was a stunning room, over fifteen feet long and almost as wide, with a sunken tile and black tile halfway up to the ceiling, with red velvet wallpaper above that. I took off my clothes and took stock of my situation. It was obvious that Mr. Edwards . . . Roger . . . was leading me rapidly and easily to bed. Something in me felt I should resist, but I couldn't find a peg to hang any resistance on. He was intelligent, good looking in a diabolic way, very affluent, and extraordinarily smooth, even more so than Manfred, the man who had relieved me of my virginity in so sophisticated a fashion.

I pulled on the bright red shirt with the team's name on it, wondering if I should be wearing a bra. My tits were seized by the clingy material and bulged boldly out, the nipples sharply outlined, even down to the small ridges in the aureole. Underneath went a pair of brief silk panties, and over that a small flare skirt that barely covered the bottom of my ass and cunt. I decided to leave my shoes off and walked out like that into the office, breasts swaying and feet bare.

He watched me closely as I walked across the space to him.

He was smoking a long cigarette rolled in black paper, and holding his martini glass. His eyes registered one long process of evaluation. He exuded a dry eroticism which made me feel as though I were dripping wet. I had never felt so naked in front of a man.

"You give promise of being very interesting," he said in an even voice.

"Christ," I thought, "can't he even give me a compliment without having it sound like a stock-market report?"

"Turn around," he said.

I faced away from him and let him see my back. I could literally feel his gaze inspecting my thighs, invading my ass crack, taking in the curve of my spine, drinking in my hair.

"Now face me," he said, "and raise your arms high over your head."

When I did it, of course, my tits were raised and thrust forward, making it appear that they were reaching out for him. His eyes glinted, and I saw his glance graze my nipples, jump to my flat belly, and rest on my crotch. The position had the effect of raising the skirt, and I knew that there was nothing between my cunt and him but a wispy bit of white silk. I knew that my bush was creating a black bulge between my thighs, and I felt my pussy quicken.

"Can I put them down now?" I asked sarcastically, my only successful attempt at equality with him.

"Of course," he said, and smiled, a humorless expression which did nothing more than to exhibit his long white teeth.

"Why not change back into your regular clothes," he said.

I went back into the bathroom and reversed the process, climbing back into my shoes and dress. I felt ravished, and tingled with an odd excitement. It was erotic, but not in any animal way. He had appealed to some deeper quality of female sexuality in me, a more cerebral quality. I realized that being fucked by Roger would be like taking a trigonometry lesson.

I went out and found him sitting behind his desk. The light poured in from the window behind him and he looked like a silhouette of himself. I walked over to him and he handed me a slip of paper. "This is the place you will go to tomorrow," he said, "and meet your fellow cheerleaders. They've all been on the team a while so they can fill you in completely, and tell you things from a woman's viewpoint. After all, a man can only go so far in his perception of reality."

All at once, I knew I would let him have me. My reserve, not too strong in the first place, simply dissolved and I saw that I was actually anxious to find out what this man could teach me. His obvious success, his perfect style, made me desirous to put myself in his hands.

He watched me for a long silent interval, then stood up. "That takes care of our business," he said. "But I imagine there are other areas of relationship we might profitably explore."

"What do you suggest?" I asked.

"Lunch first," he said, "and then a visit to my apartment. I have a duplex in the Sutter building."

I had only been to the city once before, but I knew the place he mentioned was one of Seattle's most chic highrises.

"Jeff will be in camp for the next six days," he added, "and in any case, you're not his property, are you?"

He flicked his intercom and said, "Miss Phillips, I'll be gone for the rest of the day." He held out his arm and said to me, "We'll go out the back way."

As we went down the elevator, he took the opportunity to casually and easily rub my nipples with the back of his hand, and when my mouth had fallen open in response, he put two fingers between my lips.

"We'll fill that delightful opening properly later," he said. I knew then that he was a sexual engineer, not a performer, and would remain absolutely calm while he aroused me to a pitch of screaming helplessness.

As we went toward his car I saw that it was a Maserati. Things were beginning to move very rapidly and were spinning off in unexpected directions.

"Roger, you've got class," I said as I climbed in the low-slung beauty.

"Class meets ass," he quipped as he got in and we drove away.

FOUR

When I arrived at the stadium the next day, I gave my name to the guard at the gate and was directed to the dugout at the side of the field. I walked past the lockers and several small offices, and finally arrived at a door that had "Cheerleaders" written on it. This was the space reserved for the women who provided the female counterpoint to what the men would be doing on the central stage.

I pushed the door open hesitantly and stepped inside, and the sight that met my eyes almost propelled me backwards. Three of the most ravishing women I had ever seen in my life were lolling about on couches and easy chairs in various stages of undress. One, a redhead with enormous tits and long legs was wearing only a pair of panties. Another, a blonde who looked as though she might be a professional swimmer, with a tight, trim body, small hard breasts, and an incongruously wide and soft mouth, was completely naked. The third, with brown hair almost the color of my own, wore panties and bra; she was almost six feet tall, and as I entered was idly rubbing her hand on her cunt, with the same ease with which she might be scratching her head.

The three of them stopped mid-conversation and all turned to look at me. I felt completely out of place fully dressed, and for an instant I checked an impulse to turn on my heels and walk right out of there. Their eyes were hard and humorous, holding the same look I had once seen in the glance of a successful and witty prostitute who had been a friend of my father's and often came to dinner to amuse us with her tales of the world of high society she serviced.

"Hi, I'm Sandy," said the blonde, standing up and walking toward me, her tits shifting as she walked. My eyes were riveted on her cunt, and I could see the full lips clearly underneath her patch of fine, yellow hair. I caught myself and abruptly looked up to greet her.

"Come in," she said, smiling, aware of my discomfiture. "We're pretty informal around here, as you can see. Take off whatever you like and have a seat."

I closed the door behind me and entered slowly, my eyes wide despite my desire to appear cool. "That's Marian," Sandy said, pointing at the brunette, who took her hand off her pussy and waved at me. "And that's Irene, our star redhead," Sandy continued. The woman leaned forward to smile at me, and her breasts moved ponderously to wave in my direction.

Sandy went back to sprawling in a large chair and I stood in the middle of the room, feeling awkward.

"Well, I'm Julie," I said in a weak voice.

There was a long silence, and then suddenly the room erupted in laughter, the three women falling over themselves in giggles. My spine stiffened and I unconsciously drew myself in for protection. But Sandy finally straightened up, her eyes twinkling, and held out her hands toward me.

"Oh Julie," she said, "you look like a pickpocket who's just been discovered with her hand in a policeman's pants. Come on, we're just folks."

Suddenly, the tension snapped, and I felt myself unwind. It had been a long time since I had been in female company, and I realized that my attitude was the same as if I had walked into a room filled with naked men.

"Do you always greet newcomers this way?" I asked, going to one of the empty chairs and sinking into it.

"It depends. We usually don't adjust ourselves in any special way when there's a knock on the door."

"What if it had been a man?" I wondered out loud.

"Well, he'd probably have an enormous hard-on by now," Irene put in.

Once again they glanced at one another, clearly sharing some joke that I was not yet privy to.

"We're the *cheer*leaders," Sandy said. "It's our job to see to it that the team stays in high spirits. And I don't know what makes a man happier than to have a whole slew of pussy lying around in the next room."

My temples began to throb. First Jeff, then Roger, and now this extraordinary scene. I wondered whether the women were expected to service the whole team, but I couldn't ask without sounding naive, and I decided to say nothing and see what happened.

"How about a drink?" Marian said, her voice low and throbbing. Without waiting for a reply, she went over to the small bar that graced part of one wall, and began mixing ingredients in a large shaker. Her ass wiggled as she worked, two extremely full and deliciously molded mounds framed by tight black lace panties. Sandy saw me looking, and asked, "Are you into women, Julie?"

I turned toward her, taken aback by her perception and her frank question. It seemed that the people on the team wasted no time on circumlocutions, but much of that had already been indicated by Roger. "Some of our ways may come as a shock," he had told me, "but after a while you begin to feel yourself part of a family. We are all highly dependent on one another, and we spend a lot of time in close physical proximity. Not the least of what happens on the football field is an immense accumulation of sexual energy and tension, and that infects all of us. So we have come to learn how to deal with it efficiently. We are not immoral people; it's just that our environment makes a certain adjustment of conventional morality necessary."

"I don't know," I said to Sandy. "I never have. I mean, I've never really thought about it."

"Stop seducing this innocent little girl," Marian said as she came back with a tray of glasses. I took one, sipped at it, and was delighted to taste a chilled daiquiri on my tongue.

"Innocent my ass," said Irene, now beginning to stroke her pussy lazily. "Not after the tricks that twelve-inch cock has put her through."

I could stand it no longer. "Does everybody know everything about everyone's sex life here?" I burst out.

"Everything," whispered Irene through her teeth.

"You're going to frighten her," said Marian, dispensing the last of the drinks and then coming over to sit on the arm-rest of my chair. She put one arm around my shoulders protectively, pulling me slightly toward her, causing my cheek to rest against the side of one bulging breast. She wore a net bra and the texture of her skin was palpable through the delicately scented material.

She turned to me and added, "You live just down the block from Jack and me, you know."

"Jack Karnovsky?" I asked. "Jeff mentioned that."

"Good," Marian told me. "We want to have the two of you over one night after Jeff is out of training and you've settled down a bit."

"Foursomes at the Karnovsky's," moaned Sandra in mock anguish, "what an introduction to Seattle."

"From what I understand," Irene purred, sipping her drink, "Julie's had her introduction last night."

"Oh, you mean Roger?" Sandy said cuttingly. "The last time I was with him he tried to talk me into letting his Great Dane fuck me."

"Did you do it?" Irene asked, her eyes glinting with excitement.

"I'll never tell," Sandy replied. "A girl's got to have *some* secrets."

"Aaiyeee!" I screamed suddenly, letting out a piercing yell.

Marian Jumped off the chair and the other two women sat bolt upright.

"What the fuck was that?!" Sandy said as I sat there with my fists clenched on my lap.

I smiled sheepishly. "I needed to break the pressure in my ears," I said. "I thought I heard Sandy say that one of the only secrets a person can expect to have around here is not letting anyone know whether she was fucked by a dog or not."

"Hmmm," said Irene, lying down again, "I suppose that's true. And it does sound slightly odd when you put it so clearly." She reached to the table next to her, shook a cigarette out of a pack, lit it, blew out a cloud of smoke, and said to the two other women, "Can it be that we've all become decadent without having realized it? I mean, are we the victims of a slow slide into irrevocable degeneracy?"

"Good God!" exclaimed Sandy in pretended horror. "How horrible!"

And once again the three of them burst out into laughter, only this time I began to see what the joke was, and like all real humor, it was the kind of thing that could not be explained to an outsider. One had to exist within the context to see why some aspect of that context, some specific viewpoint within that context, was funny. I found myself, if not laughing, at least grinning broadly. I was beginning to enjoy the company of these strange, brazen women, and to taste a vibration that I had never known was possible among women.

"Did you bring your uniform?" asked Marian suddenly.

"Huh?" I said, "oh, my uniform, yes, I have it here," I replied, fishing into my bag.

"Well, let's dress her up," she said to the others, and then, turning to me, added, "Then we'll go into the necessary but dull part of this job, which is practicing the routines we have to do for all the rubbernecks in the stands. We'll have about four hours of practice every weekday until the season opens."

"It's not that bad," Sandy chimed in. "You may be sore for the first few days from the jumping and stretching, but once you get in shape you get to actually enjoy the exercise."

"Not to mention flashing your ass and tits to all the boys who are trying to keep their minds on a dumb hunk of pigskin, and instead get erections thinking about fucking you that afternoon," Irene added.

"Do you remember the time Eddie was starting to throw a pass and your halter fell off," Sandy said to Irene, "and he got transfixed and six men piled on him at once and broke his arm?"

"Don't remind me," Irene said. I looked over at her and noticed that the crotch of her panties was sopping wet. During the entire conversation she had been quietly and methodically bringing herself off, and had probably had the world's most unobtrusive orgasm. Now her pussy juices were staining the cloth and dripping down into her ass crack.

"Come on," Marian said, "let's put on our battle gear and go out to face our master."

"Who's that?" I asked.

"Tony," Marian replied.

"Yeah, Tony," Sandy repeated, her voice indicating disgust.

"What's wrong with Tony?" I asked.

"He's probably a queer," Irene shot out.

"I don't know," Marian added. "We've all been trying to get into his pants for more than a year, but he just won't budge."

"Faggot," Irene said.

"Anyway," Marian continued, "he's the one who puts us through our training paces." She stood up and in an altered tone of voice said, "But let's get off uninteresting topics and see what you look like in your outfit."

"You're the second person in two days who's wanted that," I told her as I got to my feet.

"Oh, I'm sure that Roger ran you through his inspection," Sandy said.

"Where do I change?" I asked.

They all grinned. "Right here, honey," Irene told me.

The three of them came toward me, and in a moment I was surrounded by ravishing female bodies. "We'll even help you," Sandy told me.

And with that, her hands went to the buttons on the front of my dress and began undoing them, one by one. Marian and Irene stood to either side of me and started to pull the shoulders of the dress down. They took it to my waist and then let it drop, leaving me standing there in nothing but a pair of very brief panties. I felt a new kind of excitement, different from what either Jeff or Roger had aroused in me. My cunt tingled and my ass tightened and my nipples hardened, all usual reactions, but in addition to that I felt an overall throbbing that covered my entire body. My mouth was especially vulnerable to the sensation, and my lips fell open. My mind filled with an army of thoughts, but they were all too slight and quick for me to single out any one for comment. The most overpowering part of the experience was the smell, a mingled aroma of perfume, silky skin, and pussy secretions.

"My, what lovely boobs," said Sandy as she put her hands on my breasts, cupping the heavy orbs and lifting them slightly. Her thumbs circled my nipples and then rubbed the tips gently. I took in a sharp breath and my stomach clenched.

"And an ass to match," said Marian as her hands went behind me and roamed over my cheeks. I tightened my buttocks and she ran one finger down the crack, causing me to tremble and relax. Then she trailed the finger down until it was exactly opposite my asshole, and pushed in forcefully. I gasped and she pressed her entire hand between my cheeks, and grabbed my ass roughly.

Irene rolled down the top of the panties and then slipped one hand down the front, covering my hairy mound, lightly covering the pouting lips of my cunt. I tilted my pelvis slightly, thrusting my box toward her, and she smiled and let one finger probe into the center, entering the already moistened lips.

They all stroked and fingered me gently, not pressing, not insisting, not pushing the moment in any way whatsoever. I relaxed and let myself swim in the sea of flesh that surrounded me, feeling their tits rubbing against my arms and back, their hands tweaking my nipples and stroking my ass and teasing my cunt. At one point they brought their heads together and leaned against me until our hair made a single pool of contrasting colors, and we moaned and sighed and licked and kissed one another's mouths and cheeks.

I was being titillated almost past the point where I could sustain the energy swelling inside me, and in an instant would have brought my own hands up to begin caressing their bodies, for suddenly I was very hot to hold Irene's luscious tits and stroke Marian's lush ass and hold Sandy's hard athletic body against my own.

And it would have happened, except that there came a sudden loud knock on the door, one which almost scared me out of the shoes I still had not removed. I turned in the direction of the sound just in time to see a short, brawny man of about forty, standing no more than five and half feet tall, with shoulders that were as wide as Jeff's and a chest that might have been modeled on a beer keg. His face looked like a rock that had been eroded by wind, pitted and sharp-edged. And his eyes were pure black, and showed no depth or expression at all.

The other women just stepped back and seemed not especially perturbed to have been caught in this extremely revealing situation.

"That's Jack," Sandy said. "He's the head coach."

Jack stepped into the room as though he were stepping into a bar on a Saturday night with nothing more in his mind than starting a good brawl. He seemed not the least bit interested in the fact that four naked and near-naked women had been fingering and licking one another before his very eyes.

"I see you're breaking the new one in," he said, his voice like gravel. He turned to me and fastened me with those opaque eyes, and I immediately realized that he had a power that so far surpassed Jeffs that I was frightened just thinking about it. And that it was a power that had been trained and developed and honed to such a fine edge that he could take sixty-five male brutes and run them through bone-crushing exercises until they dropped from fatigue without so much as working up a sweat himself.

"You look like a nice girl," he said. "Have fun, but don't get crazy." And then swinging his gaze to the others he added, "Tony wants you outside in a half-hour." And with that he spun around and walked out of the room, leaving the impression that a rhinocerous had just thundered past.

"Whew," Irene said. "That man!"

"He scared me a little," I said.

"Well he should," Marian told me. "He's like an atomic pile, and when he explodes he shatters everything in the area. I've seen him pick up men twice his size and toss them around as though they were children."

"If he ever fucks you, be prepared not to use your pussy for a week afterward," Sandy said. "He's got a cock like a mule's, and as much finesse as a steam roller. He just throws you down, rams inside, and starts pounding like a jack hammer. And he goes on for hours and hours. I mean, literally hours. Until your legs ache and your ass is burning and your cunt is turning to farina. And all you can do is scream and scream, because he fills you with liquid fire. And after you've had your fiftieth orgasm of the night and think you're going to pass out, he really cuts loose and becomes a tiger, grabbing and swiping and scratching and thrashing around as though someone had shoved a poker up his ass. And when he comes, it feels like Niagara Falls cascading into your snatch."

"My, my," said Irene, "you sure do tell it pretty."

"But he's really very sweet," said Marian. "He's always solicitous and fatherly afterwards."

"Why on earth should I want to fuck him then?" I asked.

"Oh, honey," Sandy told me. "You saw his eyes, you felt his strength. If that man *wants* you, do you think there's any way in the world you're going to be able to say no?"

"And why should you want to say no," Irene put in. "A fuck like that is the experience of a lifetime. And what is there in life beside experience?"

There was nothing in her words I could put my finger on, but what she said sent a chill of terror down my spine. It was so dismal-sounding, so calculating, so *empty,* that for a moment I was gripped in an existential dread. She had unwittingly pulled the covers off my behavior, off the behavior of all of us, and the words we had found so amusing before, "decadent, degenerate," now returned to my mind with a more sinister intonation.

"What am I letting myself in for?" I wondered. I was learning a great deal very rapidly, but I couldn't be sure that I was assimilating it or whether it was assimilating me. Perhaps I was in the very process of becoming something, a someone that I might, in other moments, view with disgust and loathing. These thoughts, so sombre and far-reaching, did not, however, go very deeply, for they had to contend with the aroused lust that was pulsating in my body. And it seemed that that, for better or worse, was to be my primary guideline for the immediate future.

"Well girls, thirty minutes," said Sandy.

"Too bad," said Irene, "and we were just starting to get it on, too." Marian went over to one of the couches and flopped down on it. "Well, call me when it's time," she said and closed her eyes. Irene went over to the same couch, looked down at the other woman's inviting body for a moment, and then slowly and deliberately reached behind her and unsnapped her bra, letting the large soft tits fall in on themselves and spread to either side of her chest. She threw the garment onto the floor and then bent over and rolled Marian's panties down her thighs, over her knees, finally yanking them over her feet, leaving the tall woman completely naked. Irene stepped out of her own panties, and I got a glimpse of her red bush of hair before she first knelt and then lay on the couch next to Marian. The two women snuggled up close to each other and began running their tongues over one another's faces and their hands over one another's bodies.

Sandy looked over at me, her smooth white skin and shimmering blonde hair a picture of divine sensuality. Her mouth was open and her tongue running over her lips as she watched the other two. Then quite deliberately she walked over, her eyes never leaving Irene's rolling ass, stood next to the couch a second, and knelt down. She ran her hands over Irene's cheeks, then brought her face forward and buried her mouth in the dark musky ass crack, her tongue darting out immediately and diving for the small brown opening at the center. Irene moaned and thrust her hips back and parted her legs, allowing Sandy to lick beneath her asshole and into her very twat.

I watched the three of them for perhaps a full minute, at first feeling left out and then realizing that if I wanted in to the tangle, I need only go over and find a place to insert myself. I was turned on, but my mind was too jangled to deal with it, especially since it would be my first time with women, and to take on three such vastly experienced females, and all within the space of thirty minutes, seemed too much for me to handle.

I gathered up my uniform and headed toward the bathroom, thinking to just sit there and let my feelings settle. I went into the relatively large room, and was pleasantly surprised to see that it had a wall-to-wall rug on the floor. I closed the door behind me and was at once very glad to be alone. I had been starved for privacy for forty-eight hours without being aware of it.

I tossed the uniform onto the sink and sank slowly to the floor, lying luxuriously in the thick red nap. To my astonishment, I found myself looking at myself in a mirror that had been affixed to the ceiling. I smiled in amazement at just how thorough these people were in their pursuit of sensual pleasure.

What I saw staring down at me was a decidedly beautiful young lady, and I was pleased to note that I didn't measure up badly when compared to the stunning beauties whose groans were beginning to be audible through the door. My breasts lolled easily on my chest, full and round, the nipples two dark violet circles in their center. My waist flared in sharply above my hips, which were full and round. My legs pointed out at a forty-five degree angle from one another, long and shapely, the thighs not quite meeting at the torso, so that my cunt was lodged in a horizontal ledge which ran, when I stood up, parallel to the ground. The pussy lips protruded out from this ridge, and my cunt hair sprouted in wild dark profusion all around.

I ran my hands over my belly, around my hips, onto my thighs, finally joining them together at the edges of my cunt. I was extraordinarily randy from the attentions I had received, and could feel the first edges of frustration which signalled my need for release. I stroked my sore pussy, violently fucked by Jeff two nights earlier, and then put through a strange exercise by Roger the night before.

Roger had me quite hypnotized by early evening. A ride in a twenty-thousand dollar car, lunch in a superb restaurant with a charming and highly cultivated man, two hours on the top floor of one of the city's tallest buildings with a fifty-mile view all around and an almost sinfully rich decor inside, coupled with a constant edge of ironic erotic sensibility, is enough to turn any girl's head. And I had been in the mood to have my head turned.

When I was really primed, Roger had turned to me and said, "You won't mind if we dispense with the greater amount of the brutish preliminaries a man and woman usually feel the need to go through before they can enjoy what they truly desire from one another? Frankly, as you probably can guess, I have long since passed the stage where the crude activity known as fucking, with its train of concomitant emotions, palpitations,

ecstatic rushes, and erratic swings is of any serious interest to
me. My central desire at this point is unfolding and observing.
My major interest, in short, lies in provoking and watching."
He had regarded me for a long while and then added, "I should
like to use some equipment with you."

I had had difficulty in suppressing a giggle. "First Jeff and
his gym equipment, and now this," I thought.

But what Roger had in mind was somewhat more sophisticated,
and within a short time I was stretched over a curved board, my
head and feet back and my body arching forward reaching an
apex at my cunt. He had tied my hands and legs in a spreadeagle
position, so that I was totally wide open and thrust out.

For the following three hours it had been a bizarre mixture
of nightmare and daydream. On one end of the spectrum was
an episode in which he slowly crammed an entire banana in my
cunt and then slowly sucked it out, a process that had me hot
with the lust born of extreme repugnance. At the other end was
his strapping a long, thick, black dildo into my cunt, inserting
another in my asshole, and then throwing a switch which set
the two of them buzzing wildly. At first I was too shocked to
feel anything but vibration, but when the first impact faded, I
relaxed into a soothing sea of erotic balm. I could feel myself
let go down into my toes and up into my eyeballs. And upon
that came a re-localization of sensation, and I could feel the heat
building in my pussy and deep inside my ass.

The problem was that I couldn't cum. I was unable to move, and
the machines did not vary their tempo, so I was kept continually
at the edge of orgasm. After some ten minutes I turned to look
at Roger and found him regarding me with an amusement that
bordered on contempt.

"Would like to cum, wouldn't you, you obscene little cunt?"

His words were like a whiplash and I thought he would begin
to verbally abuse me, and that would lead to physical abuse,
which would lead to anything that would get me to orgasm! I
was dying to spend myself. But he said no more and did no more.
He smiled grimly and said, "I think I'll go bathe now. I'm sure
you will be able to take care of yourself. If you need anything,

call me. But . . . make sure you are willing to meet my demands if I bring you what you want."

He turned around and walked out of the room, leaving me literally hanging. I was able to stand no more than fifteen minutes more of the treatment and I began to call him. He merely taunted me and said that I didn't sound desperate enough. I cried out until I felt real tears starting to form. I was close to a pain threshold that was beyond the erotic. My whole crotch felt like it was filled with acid.

"Please, Roger," I yelled.

"Please what?" he asked.

"Please, stop this torture. I need to cum. Please, I'm burning up. If I don't cum soon I'll explode, I'll die."

"You don't sound really serious to me," he called back, and ran the water a bit more.

I found myself grunting to keep ahead of my anguish. My cunt shrieked, my asshole was a single mass of raw nerve endings. I needed to have those devilish machines pulled out of me. But before that, to have them thrust in further, deeper, from a different angle, to touch my trigger, to allow me to shoot off. I grew fiendishly desperate, and my voice was hoarse as I called out to him.

"Roger, I'll do anything. ANYTHING."

Finally, there was a long silence, and he walked out of the bathroom. He was wearing leather chaps open at the crotch, exposing his cock and his ass. He was bare-chested, and he carried a thin leather whip. His eyes were whirlpools of utterly composed and fanatic lust, and I knew then what the meaning of Satan was.

He walked up to me, looked at my trembling body with unabashed slavering greed, and, horribly, smiled.

"Yes, my dear," he said in that same maddeningly calm voice, "I do believe that now you will do anything, anything I ask, in order to be released. And not only will you do it, but you will find whatever button you have to press inside you to love doing it, to embrace it with total passion and abandon, so that you don't merely experience the act, but that you *become* the act." He paused, drew back his arm, and struck one long harsh lash across my thighs, the leather biting into the flesh and slapping across my open cunt. I stiffened throughout my entire frame and lept to within a fraction of the energy level necessary for orgasm, and just as quickly, I subsided.

"Yesss," he hissed. "I will bring you to the brink again and again, and before I am finished you will be drooling and slobbering and begging me to attain even greater depths of vileness. Won't you?" And as he asked the question, the lash struck once more, this time across my nipples, and I screamed at the top of my lungs as I was catapulted once more to the brink of climax.

"Oh, you foul loathesome bastard," I said out of a ragged mouth as I turned to face him, "please, please, whip me until I'm bleeding, unleash all your evil onto my body, please."

Roger snickered. "Really," he said, his voice assuming a sudden fey intonation, "I'm afraid you've gone somewhat overboard, Julie." And then he laughed, an ugly introverted snort that exploded in his chest and contorted his lips.

He reached over, undid the dildoes, untied my bonds, and threw me face forward on the floor. His whip began raining down on my ass and legs. I twitched and spewed gibberish under the blows.

"Start crawling," he ordered, "crawl into the bathroom, crawl on your belly into the bathroom, and we'll see how you like the actual taste of evil."

The vividness of what followed had begun to drag me into reliving the rest of the memory when I realized that I was no longer alone in the bathroom of the clubhouse. I opened my eyes and saw Sandy standing over me.

"Well, isn't that pretty?" she said, and I realized I was lying there with one hand on my right breast and the other halfway inside my cunt.

I blinked and grinned a little sheepishly. "I guess I almost dozed off," I said.

"Dozed, my ass," said Marian, poking her head into the door.

"Come on, you cunts," shouted Irene from the other room. "Shake your asses and get dressed, so we can go out on the field and shake our asses. Duty calls!"

I sat up slowly, reached for my costume, and tried to clear my head in order to go out for my first practice as a cheerleader.

FIVE

By the time I saw Jeff again, I realized that I had moved to a different level of understanding. I saw that he had served as the catalyst to bump me out of my monotonous grind at school and into the scarifying but terribly thrilling world of professional football. I knew that I still felt some fondness for him, and had no objections at all to fucking him again, but I was resolved to move out of the house he had found for us and set myself up independently.

The week had been exhausting. As Sandy predicted, I was sore from the unaccustomed exercise, but after a few days began to enjoy the exhilarating activity. Tony had turned out to be a rather unassuming and pleasant man, at least on the surface, and it seemed that the only thing that anyone could say against him is that he refused to join in any of the sex games that practically everyone else delighted in most of the time. He put us through our paces every day, showing us the routines, and then making us practice them until they were almost second nature.

The nights were something else. I accepted one more invitation from Roger. This time he tried to get me to suck his dog's cock, but I felt I wanted to draw the line somewhere, and I refused. He became peeved, and then ushered me out unceremoniously. I stopped into a bar for a drink to calm my nerves, and let myself be picked up by two college students who took me to their apartment and spent the night taking turns and doubling up on me and on one another. They were that new breed of bisexual which makes no distinctions at all in gender, and seems perfectly at home with whatever configurations it can conjure up.

As I lay between them, a cock in my ass and a cock in my cunt, humping furiously to engorge myself in both holes as deeply as possible, slamming back and forth on their stiff rods, feeling the intense heat generated in the thin membrane that separated pussy from anal canal, I knew that, for better or worse, I was following an arc of sexual activity which was shooting rapidly into uncharted spaces. The itch that I had felt in my cunt from the time I turned fifteen had grown into an almost unbearable ache, a yearning need to be rubbed and touched and stuffed. Manfred had busted my physical cherry, but Jeff had taken away my psychic virginity, the thing in my mind that had me thinking I was not free to swing out as far and wide as I wanted. My body was roaring with need, and my mind had acquiesced, and agreed not to manufacture any guilt about it, at least for a while. It was as though I had tacitly given myself permission to go all the way, and explore the erotic impulse to its core.

Each night after that I went hunting, and since I was young and randy and good-looking and wore clothes that flaunted my tits and outlined my ass, I had no trouble scoring. And by the time Saturday rolled around, I found myself wondering where I would go looking that night before realizing that that was the night I was to see Jeff. I suppose I knew that I would have a bad scene with him, but I was hoping to keep things light, to act sophisticated and sort of dance my way out of the entanglement with him without his becoming too upset. Of course, that was a fool's dream.

When he arrived, I had already cooked a smashing dinner and was wearing my shortest skirt and tightest blouse. I planned to feed him, ply him with drinks, and fuck him silly, and then casually mention that I thought it best if I moved in with Sandy, for companionship.

But as he burst into the house, I knew that I wouldn't have a chance to even attempt my plan. He was seething with anger, a rage that must have been building for days. His face was twisted and his whole body was tense with the threat of imminent violence. I blanched and became fearful for my very life.

He rushed across the kitchen floor and without breaking stride drew up his right hand and swung it through the air, clipping me backhanded across the face. The blow spun me around three times, sent stars shooting across my eyes, caused an explosive ringing in my ears, and finally had me crashing to the floor.

"You bitch," he yelled, "you slut, you scummy rotten cunt!"

The words poured down on me like fists. He reached down, grabbed my shirt, yanked me to my feet, and began slapping my face again, back and forth until I was screaming with pain and terror.

"Jeff, STOP," I yelled, "you'll kill me, Jeff!"

"I ought to kill you," he rasped.

"Why are you doing this?" I sobbed, holding on to him, forcing myself close to him so he wouldn't hit me any more.

He grabbed my shoulders, shook me harshly, and then threw me to one side. I caromed off the refrigerator, staggered back into the center of the room, and finally sank onto one of the chairs.

"Oh, you really can play the innocent," he said, his voice dripping with scorn. "You know what the word is around the locker room? They're saying that you let Roger Edwards piss on you in his bathtub."

I saw him standing there, his face beet red, and although I was literally horrified that he might really damage me, I couldn't help but see how ridiculous he was. He resembled nothing so much as a frustrated adolescent.

I laughed hysterically. "And what about you? Kicking me in the cunt, tying me up, whipping me. And what did you have planned tonight, to punch me to death. My God, after your brutality, Roger's little perversions seem the soul of tenderness."

"But you're *my* girl, not anyone else's," he shouted.

"And as far as locker room talk is concerned," I went on, recklessly, "who was it that told the boys how I suck cock, and what my pussy tastes like, and how much I like getting it in the ass? Who set me up?"

I could see that my words were getting to him, and he was losing his sense of righteous indignation. But I got carried away by my turning the tide of battle and rushed on. "And anyway, I'm not your girl or anyone else's girl. I'm not property. Nobody owns me, especially not you. And I'm going to pack my things and get out of this tacky little house and your tacky little car and your tacky little mind, and you can take all your repressed homosexual machismo and shove it up your ass. Or better still, go back to the locker room and have one of the boys do it for you."

I knew I had made a mistake when I saw what little intelligence had been left in his eyes go dim and be replaced by a look of sheer black brutality. I had wounded him too deeply for him to be able to deal with me rationally, and he was forced to revert to the mode of behavior which would give him back his ego, something that he valued, obviously, much more than anything that I might offer.

His face became a mask of violence, purpled with cruel lust. He regressed instantaneously back to a Stone Age mentality. which, given the fact that he was, after all, a football player, had never been too far beneath the surface to begin with. He advanced on me like a cave man, his shoulders hunched, his fingers curled, his brow thickened. He snorted through his nose and his mouth was a scar of menacing lupine pincers.

"All right," he said in a low hoarse voice, "all right. Go ahead. Do what you want. Fuck who you want. I don't own you. But before you walk out of here, you're going to have my brand on you. And for the rest of your life, you will always have my mark burned in your skin."

He stood in front of me, shot out one hand, grasped me by the throat, and lifted me to my feet. I gasped for breath. He brought his face to within an inch of mine. "I don't even want you any more, you little whore. So I'll throw you to the pack. But anyone who has you will always know that I was here first."

"What are you going to do?" I rasped.

He smiled, a hideous grin. "First I'm going to use your luscious little body, and then you'll see what I'm going to do."

It's difficult to describe what followed as fucking. Certainly, all the machinery and motion was present, but there was no meaning. Long before I lost my virginity, I had let myself be lost in the myth of love which has haunted us since the Romantic Period. There would be a man, I thought, and he would somehow be my *other,* my completion. We would complement one another perfectly, and yet he would be a bit stronger, a bit wiser in the ways of the world, while I provided a greater balance of stability, of home-sense, of—dare I use the word?—*spirituality*.

I knew I would be attracted on all levels: our minds would mesh, our bodies would merge, and our hearts would beat as one. And when we wished to feel and express the totality of our union, of our love, we would take to one another's arms, and shed our clothing, and give one another the rare gift of complete nakedness and vulnerability. Then there would be no games, no thoughts, no structure, but the simple unadorned flow of the life energy itself. And with that we would know rapture, and ecstasy, and passion, and finally, death itself.

Somewhere along the line between early teenage and age seventeen, I suppose I was infected with the modern illness which substitutes one model of reality for another without understanding that it is doing so, and thus invests us with a worldview that is not only less efficient but less aesthetically gratifying. In this way I came to view love as "old fashioned," even though I had not yet found anything as worthwhile to use as an operative paradigm. Slowly, I succumbed to my father's cynicism, my mother's indifference, and the general shabbiness of life in the twentieth century. And ultimately fell into the trap of divorcing eros from philos, and both from caritas.

The logical conclusion of this line of development now stood before me, a crazed demon that I had to take full responsibility for helping to conjure up. Once again I could only pray that his vehemence did not explode into the berserk, and that I came through with all my bones unbroken.

And yet, so much was I a slave to the pull of sensuality, that even as I stepped back in trepidation, my knees were shaking with muted desire and my cunt quivered in anticipation. I had a picture of myself, lips trembling, backing away, my eyes wide in horror, while my nipples hardened under the cloth of my blouse and my thighs flashed beneath the miniskirt. When I saw the gleam of lust in his eyes, I relaxed a bit, for it meant that libido had begun to take the reins away from mortido.

As he passed the kitchen table, he picked up a long wicked looking carving knife. I gasped. He lunged forward with his left hand and grabbed me by the belt. I was pulled tightly up against him, and grew weak as I was flooded with his powerful vibrations.

"Don't kill me," I pleaded.

"No, Julie," he said, "I'm not crazy. Just pissed off."

And with that he brought the knife between us and slid it under my skirt, yanked upward and cut the fabric neatly. It fell to the floor and I was nude from the waist down, my pussy suddenly shy in the light. He reached the knife behind me and slit the shirt down the back, and then pulled it off from in front. Now I had nothing on, and he was fully dressed.

He pushed me hard and I stumbled and fell on the cold kitchen linoleum. He stood over me and slowly unzipped his pants, and let his cock spring out. It was three-quarters hard and stiffening. As always, I was overwhelmed by its sheer mass.

"You're such a little slut," he said as he saw me involuntarily squirm on the floor. "Go ahead, rub your pretty little ass on the ground and get yourself hot. It'll save me the trouble of getting you wet. Come on, stick your finger in your slit and slosh it around. I want to hear your pussy gargle."

I fixed in my mind the idea that what was happening was not something I should identify with, that I could take the experience so long as I didn't let it wipe out my deeper and as yet untested sense of what sex is about. The reason Roger had so intensely attracted and then repelled me was that he was not satisfied with behavior, he wanted total commitment. The body was not enough for his jaded sensibilities, he needed to rape the soul. And yet, what was he looking for except what we all wanted: the totality of love.

Jeff knelt down between my thighs and watched with smoldering eyes as I slipped two fingers into my cunt and began sliding them in and out. The slim pussy lips parted around my hand, fluttering as I rubbed in and out, and by the third stroke, my fingers were already glistening with secretions. I brought my other hand around and took the lips of my cunt in my fingers and pulled in opposite directions, spreading the hole wide, letting him see the pink inner petals and the serrated tiny hole.

"This is cunt," I thought, "this is my cunt. And it has sent this mammoth of a man into paroxysms of jealousy and anger, and has now brought him to his knees."

My cunt parted like a great blind eye, sensitive but unseeing. I closed my eyes and let my cunt become the central organ of perception. It reached out its sensors, it quivered with radar vibrations, beaming out toward the beacon of his cock, and relaying messages of heat and proximity. My cunt could feel his cock approaching, knew when it moved in close, was aware of the angle.

"Julie," Jeff said in a strangled voice, "I . . ."

But the words didn't come, and for an instant I hovered on the brink of submission. I knew that if I wanted, I could *have* this man, could let him into me and let that entrance be the mark of possession. He would possess me, but I would also own him. And if he had been another man, a man I had never seen and didn't know existed, a man who brought to life the as yet unformed image of the one who was my true mate, I would have opened my eyes, and offered my lips, and given my heart.

But Jeff was not the one, and I knew that the pain and violence we had shared was simply the anger born of realizing that no matter how deeply we fucked, the primal connection would not be made.

Thus, with cold-blooded awareness, I rejected the implied request in his tone, and instead screwed myself into hardness and whispered, out of the corners of my mouth, "Come on, you cock stud, shove that hunk of meat inside me and stuff me with sperm."

There was a moment of skewed silence, and then he exploded, "You rotten whore, you slimy bitch, you cunt, you scum," and with that plowed his rod straight into the farthest recesses of my twat.

I gasped for air and my legs jackknifed high above my head. He drove mercilessly into the folds of my pussy, and his entrance was like a stab from a knife.

"Arghh," I moaned and brought my hands up to his shoulders. But he slapped them away. "Don't touch me," he said, "I don't want to touch any part of you but your hole. That's the only thing you're interested in, isn't it?"

His words cleared the way for him to rape me, and that is the only way to describe what happened. He would not let me enjoy a moment of it. Each time I veered toward pleasure, he turned me to one side, or tilted my legs at a different angle. He shifted his weight so he could bear down on me with full power, and his enormous cock, growing out of his powerful body, beat into me with a terrible rhythm. He slammed into my snatch, pumping furiously, driving my ass into the floor. He took his hands off the tiles and pressed them down on my breasts, letting the full weight of his upper body drive into my tits, squashing the round orbs onto my chest, grinding the nipples.

When he had punished me enough in that way, he pulled out and roughly turned me over, exposing my bare ass to his lust. I didn't think he would do what he did then, for he had not lubricated my asshole at all. But he guided the tip of his cock to the small opening, and then with a massive thrust pierced me clean into the bowels.

I screamed and fainted, never having known such a searing pain in my life. He pulled my hair and slapped my cheeks until I came to, and as I swam into consciousness my first awareness was of a gnawing burning between my buttocks, a fiery throbbing that went beyond anything I had ever experienced before.

When my eyes opened, he pushed my shoulders into the floor, rocked back on his thighs, and grabbed my hips with his hands. My ass was curved high, ravished and gaping. I imagined that this is what it would feel like to lose one's virginity to a man who didn't know how to be gentle, and while Manfred had parted my maidenhead with the most delicate ease, I felt I was now paying the karmic dues I had coming to me.

Jeffs huge hands tightened and he clasped me firmly, lifting my ass off the ground. And then he used it to masturbate with. Holding me lightly, he lifted and dropped and rotated and shifted my buttocks so that I did a dance around his cock, but no movement that I was responsible for. In one sense it was highly degrading, to have my bottom used simply as a hand to bring him off. But in addition, and partly because of that, the thing became very erotic.

As my sphincter muscles relaxed, I began to feel the glow of pleasure in the sensations, and could allow myself the laziness of just letting him run the entire number. I could hear him breathing more heavily, panting. He pulled me into him until his balls slapped against my pussy and his bush rubbed into my ass crack, the head of his cock prodding up to my belly, while the thick base of the shaft stretched my asshole to the limit.

"God but it feels good to have a cock up my ass," I thought to myself, "no matter what the circumstances."

But Jeff was determined to take his climax without imparting anything but pain to me. My cunt already ached and I knew that my anus would be bleeding and my tits felt horribly sore from having him squash them. There was really only one thing left for him to do, and he pulled out of me sharply, leaving me gaping like a landed fish, the sudden void between my cheeks throbbing with desire to be filled.

He put one arm under me and threw me over onto my back. I flopped over and in a flash he was on top of me, his knees into my armpits, his cock, smeared and steaming, pulsating over my face.

"Lick it," he ordered.

Involuntarily, I gagged, but that was precisely what he wanted, to force me into something repulsive. I clamped my lips shut, but his open hand swung down and slapped my right cheek with stunning force. My mouth flew open and my eyes watered.

"Now," he said, and tilted forward, bringing the besmirched prick to my lips. He pushed forward and it slid slowly into my mouth. He took each of my hands in one of his, and pinned my arms over my head. He leaned into me and started fucking my mouth. I tried to turn my face away but he was too strong, his rod like an iron bar prying my jaws apart, pressing my tongue down, opening my throat. The taste was acrid, the smell as rancid as spoiled butter.

"Now," he repeated, "you little cocksucker, you little tramp, take it in the mouth."

My lips flapped back and forth as he slid in and out of me, and his cock plunged more deeply into my throat. My legs curled and my knees hit against his back. My cunt opened and my asshole throbbed. He had done what he had wanted, reduced me to the status of open hole, and now he was taking revenge for what he felt was a terrible injury to his ego, but was really more serious than that, a refusal to accept him as my man.

"Fuck you . . . fuck . . . mouth . . . bitch . . ." he chanted as his ass flexed and he drove his hips forward ramming his hot rod down my throat. I began to gag because he didn't leave me time to breathe, and each time my stomach convulsed I could feel the thin vomit rising in my gorge. He was relentless, and kept pressing, until I was retching around his cock. At once he pulled out, leaving me gasping. To my astonishment, my tongue shot out and began to lap the air while my mouth made sucking noises. It was as though he had pressed a reflex button which triggered me into sucking motions. Following the James-Lange notion, the movement gave birth to the feeling, and suddenly I was hungry to have his cock in my mouth again. I reached up but my head could only come a few inches off the floor.

"Aahhh," I moaned, trying to lick the underbelly of his cock.

"Beg me," he said.

In reply I ran my tongue over my lips, wetting them lasciviously, and curled my tongue toward him, flicking it back and forth. I offered him a face of cocksucking salaciousness, silently imploring him to fuck my mouth and have it be all the dirty things that were going through his mind.

He released my hands and sat down on my tits, his hard buttocks flattening the soft squishy breasts into my chest. I reached my head forward, but he pushed it back. "If you move, I'll slug you," he said.

And then he wrapped his right hand around his tool and started jerking it back and forth. I watched with open eyes, seeing it tingle into super hardness, the crown flaring to its full hooded width and becoming purple with blood. My mouth took on a life of its own, hungry for the splash of sperm. I tried to cover the head of his cock with my lips, but he kept it a few inches away. Finally, I could do no more but to lie back, my head resting on the floor, my mouth wide open, waiting for him to cum. I could already taste the sperm, feel its pungent flavor on my tongue, smell its sharp aroma at the back of my nose. I pictured him spurting, great globs of semen shooting into the air and dropping into my mouth. My throat ached, and I swallowed in anticipation.

His face contorted and his chest tightened and I knew he was close to orgasm. He jerked more and more rapidly, his hand now flying, until he reached a peak. His spine stiffened, his head flew back, and he let out a loud wail as his buttocks contracted and his cock exploded. Thick white jets flew out of the slit in the head and splashed all over me.

The first volley sailed over my head and I moaned in disappointment, but then he began a second series of spurts, and the sticky drops fell on my forehead, onto my chin, and finally on my lips and onto my waiting tongue. As I gobbled the precious fluid, he continued to cum, now dribbling on my throat. I ran my hands over all the places he had splashed and scooped up the sperm with my fingers, and then sucked my fingers dry.

I don't know now why I reacted in that way, except that I had made the decision to take the experience on a purely physical level and let my body do what it wanted. I didn't know how I was supposed to act in terms of Jeff's scenario, but we weren't precisely being sensitive to one another's needs at that moment.

For a second, he slumped, and then his eyes brightened. He looked down at me and his face hardened. "That's the first part, Julie," he said. "Shooting all over your face and watching you lick it up, seeing what a *slut* you are. And now to make it official."

"What are you going to do?" I asked, suddenly worried.

He stood up, yanked me up by one arm, and then lifted me off the floor. He took me into the bathroom, stood me up, and went into the cabinet for a bottle of pills. "There's something I've learned in pro football," he said, "although the coach would kill me if he knew. I've discovered that you can make up for the energy you lose sexually by taking just a little amphetamine, and then there are tablets to help you sleep when you get wound up by nighttime. And these little sleeping pills are for you, Julie, just four of them, so you'll be knocked out enough to not know what's happening to you."

I tried to pull back when he twisted one arm behind my back. "You can take them willingly, or I can knock out a few of your pretty teeth and then shove them down your throat. Which shall it be?"

I had no choice, and I threw the four little pills onto my tongue and washed them down with a glass of water.

"What are you going to do to me, Jeff?" I asked, my voice subdued.

"I'm not going to do anything," he said, "but I have a friend who will."

"What?" I asked.

But he wouldn't say another word. He pushed me into the living room and told me to put on some clothes. I found a skirt and blouse and he watched as I put them on. I felt I had reached a base level of erotic despair, for overriding everything else was the certain sense inside me that I wanted more, that I hadn't been satisfied. And I know that that was just what Jeff had intended, to open me up and then turn me loose, thus giving me the liberty I wanted, but with his own peculiar twist.

I sat down and suddenly realized I was exhausted. The week's activities, the emotional and physical drain of the evening, and, I suppose, the sleeping pills, were beginning to work. I fought to keep myself alert, but I knew it would be a vain struggle, so I simply closed my eyes and let myself drift. I don't know how long it took, but within a short time I was foggy, bumping around in that pregnant state between sleep and waking. I heard Jeff making a phone call, but as though from a great distance. And then darkness descended, and I knew no more.

I had odd jumbled dreams, and a vivid flash of seeing two men standing over me doing something to my stomach. I remember disconnected sounds, and jabbing stabs in my belly, but I couldn't hold on to anything that was happening. As happens in such a condition, my thoughts merged with the symbols of the dream life, and the result was an incoherent stream of ideas and sensations which made no sense.

And the next thing I knew, strong sunlight was shining in my eyes, and Sandy was standing over me.

It took me a minute to clear my head, to figure out where I was, and to remember what had happened the previous night

"What . . .?" I said.

"It's O.K.," Sandy told me. "You're in my apartment. Jeff brought you here late last night."

I tried to sit up, but my body was one huge ache, and it felt as though I had stitches in my belly.

Sandy sat next to me and gently pushed me back.

"Let me guess," she said. "He found out about Roger, and you told him you were tired of him, and he went crackers, and worked you over. Right?"

I nodded my head.

"I thought so," she went on. "He carried you in here, tossed you on the bed, and said, 'Here, another piece of ass to be used by the team'." Sandy bit her lower lip. "I could swear he had been crying," she added.

"I didn't know I had got in so deep so fast," I said between parched lips.

She patted my hand. "But it's over now," she said. "You can stay here and rest up, and he'll cool down, and in a few days it will be as though it had never happened." She paused, looked at me, and said, "Do you think you still want to stay on as a cheerleader."

I blinked, and my eyes watered. "It's strange," I told her. "Everything is happening so fast. I don't feel like I'm in control of my life anymore. But it's gripped me. I mean, I feel as though I'm hooked on some kind of weird excitement."

"I know, kid," she said. "It's a lot of money and power and sex and glamor. But let it ride. If you're meant to take the trip all the way, then do it. You'll know when it's time to cut out."

"There's something," I said, "down here." And reached under the sheet to my stomach.

"It's a bandage," I exclaimed.

Sandy threw the sheet back and we looked down at my body. "I saw that when I undressed you," she said, "but I thought you knew about it."

"No," I replied, suddenly frightened. I looked at Sandy. "Will you take it off for me?" I asked, "I'm scared."

She reached down and gently pulled the tape off the skin, nipping the top edge of pubic hair. She lifted the bandage slowly and then looked down at what was underneath.

"Oh my God!" she said.

"What is it?" I asked.

I glanced down and even though the word was upside down to my vision, I could read it at once. In three-inch blood-red letters, rising up out of my bush, Jeff had had tattooed a single word.

"SLUT" it read.

I looked back up at Sandy, and for an instant we were at the edge of being horrified, but something clicked in our minds, and we turned the whole incident around, grasping it as something we couldn't afford to take seriously.

"Nice," Sandy said.

"I think that sums it up, don't you?" I replied.

"That Jeff really is a jerk," she added. "Everybody knows that the proper spelling for that thing is S-L-*I*-T."

"Oh Sandy," I said, halfway between laughter and tears.

She took my head and held it to her breasts and patted my hair. My arms went around her waist and we hugged each other for a long time. Finally, she moved back, tilted my chin up, and kissed me tenderly on the lips.

"Well," she said, "now you have a reputation to live up to. Let's have breakfast and you take a shower and then we'll rearrange the place so that there's space for both of us here."

I nodded and watched as she got up to go toward the kitchen. I had stepped on another rung of the ladder, but I wasn't sure whether my direction was up or down.

SIX

My father once said, in reference to the ending of his first marriage, that divorce is a form of death. That when a man and a woman form a bond, they create an entity, a gestalt, that is greater than both of them. And when they separate, each of the parts goes back to being itself; but the other thing, the living relationship, dies.

I suppose I felt that about what happened with Jeff, although we had had so relatively little with each other. After that night, I went about more than a little subdued. Yet, I felt lucky, for if we had continued and gone on to live with one another, that embryonic bond that had already formed between us would have developed into a tie that might not have been sundered short of murder, either physical or psychological.

But time worked its melancholy process, replacing pain with poignancy, poignancy with forgetfulness, and forgetfulness with new direction. The summer passed quickly, and I rarely saw Jeff except for fleeting moments on the field. During the day I went dutifully through my practice sessions, and at night I took up the erotic games which constituted the leit-motif of the cheerleaders' existence. Just before the first game of the season, I had been fucked by more than twenty of the players, in addition to several of the executive staff.

But the two who attracted me most strongly remained distant. Jack, the volcanically virile trainer, came to take a fatherly attitude toward me that was strangely disturbing and made me feel vulnerable. Partly because I was goaded by the other girls and partly because I was curious, I set a collision course with him, and finally managed to be lying on the couch in the dressing room wearing nothing but a smile when he barged in. It was almost evening, and no one else was around, and I thought that he would take the opportunity to do his much-vaunted number.

But he seemed totally impassive, and glanced at my body without desire or curiosity. Rather, he closed the door behind him, took a chair, and slid it under him, the back facing me so he could rest his chin on the top supporting rung.

"I know what you're trying to do," he said, his gravelly voice sounding almost tender. "But I'm not interested. You've been infected with this sickness, and you won't rest until you've fucked every man in sight, at least everyone except those rare few who still hold the marriage vows sacred. But I don't think that's really you. It looks like some sort of game." I must have shown some consternation on my face for he hurriedly added, "And I don't disapprove. I mean, you're doing what you want to, or need to. But it's just that when you get it all out of your system, or into your system, whichever it is, you won't end up like Sandy and the others. They're good people, and I like them, but they're basically whores."

"And I'm just a slut," I said, thrusting out my belly so the tattoo surged toward him.

"That's what you tell yourself. And . . . look, it's not my place to say these things, but since you offered yourself to me, I feel I should tell you what's on my mind. I hope you work it all out without damaging yourself, and someday find someone you can love."

"Thanks for the advice, *Dad*," I snarled, trying to sound biting, but actually I was close to tears.

He smiled, and stood to go. "O.K.," he said. "That's all I have to say." He turned and walked to the door, but before going out he added, "But if any of those jokers gives you any trouble, or tries to beat up on you, let me know, and I'll crack a few skulls."

After he left I almost succumbed to the sadness he had brought to the surface, but I bit my lip and determined that I would not let myself be washed down that particular stream. I hurled myself into an opposing mood, and went to the telephone to call Nick Johnston, a second-string tackle who had been trying to set up a scene with me and some of his friends. I told him I would be over that night, and that he could invite whomever he liked.

I showered, dressed, and kept talking to myself to maintain my sense of aggression and control. I was riding too high over too dangerous a ground to allow myself to slip. I had no one to catch me. I put on my tightest pair of shorts and a halter, piled into the Kharmann-Gia I had already made two payments on, and drove to Nick's apartment.

Waiting with him were Sal Tancredi and Joey Washington, both guards. Nick stood almost six feet eight inches tall, and weighed nearly two hundred and seventy pounds. Each of the other men was about six feet tall, but they must have been nearly three hundred pounds apiece. They all stood up as I entered, and I was staggered by what I had agreed to take on. I felt frail and incredibly tiny when faced by almost a ton of muscle and bone coupled with the coiled fury each had had trained into his body. I could see their eyes glisten as they raked my thighs and breasts with hot glances. And as I walked past them I knew they were devouring the back of my body, watching the way my ass swayed and shook, cupped tightly in the clinging shorts.

There was little point in extended preliminaries, since we all knew why we were there. The word was out that I was a hot bitch, a hungry twat. And, of course, my tattoo had made me nearly legendary. Sandy told me that the locker room talk had evaluated me as a wild cunt, who would take cock in the ass, down the throat, between the tits, in the hands, and was ready to wriggle, roll, grovel, beg, and suck anything from tongues to assholes.

We sat around for fifteen or twenty minutes, drinking quickly, and killing a fifth of vodka in no time at all. Nick and Sal sat on either side of me on the couch, while Joey sat cross-legged on the floor in front of me, his eyes rarely leaving my crotch. I was aware of the strange power that is inherent in a woman, or how I could mesmerize and hold captive these three neo-Neanderthals with the simple promise of letting them stuff my holes with their rampaging cocks.

The vibrations in the room got thicker and heavier, and it became difficult to talk. Even the fact that we were maintaining the pretense of polite company was highly electrifying, introducing a charged smuttiness into every word and gesture. My cunt went turgid and my ass seemed to melt. A deep lethargy stole over me and I let myself sink into the delicious space of surrender, knowing that they would take control, and I would need to do nothing but lie back and let them fill me with their extravagant energy. I wondered whether this was technically an act of vampirism on my part.

I slid down on the seat and rested my head against the back, and then, boldly, closed my eyes. The following few seconds of silence was filled with intimations of movement, and I could almost hear them nodding to one another, congratulating themselves on my being precisely what they had heard I was, an open cunt, ready to spread my legs at the merest invitation.

Then, abruptly, hands were on my tits and on my thighs. A sea of flesh broke over me, lips on mine, fingers tugging at my clothing. A tongue attacked my nippples as my shirt was raised over my head, and coarse knuckles pressed into my pussy as my shorts were tugged down my legs. I moaned and let myself sink into the vortex which had been formed by my self-abandonment.

"Wow, she's really a slut," said one of the men, "look at her."

"Yes," I thought, "look at me. Watch me writhe and claw the air. See my tits shake and my nipples wrinkle. Observe how my legs kick and how my cunt spreads. See my mouth purse and my tongue lick the air. Watch me go wild and thrash around on the floor. Do you want more? Let me turn over and you can feast your eyes on my lovely ass, that simple and mysterious shape which holds more power over a man than the wealth of the world. Is that enough? Does it drive you mad? Do you want to touch this wanton body? Run your fingers into my hot wet slit? Slide your tongues into my asshole? Pinch my nipples? Listen to me moan. Know that you can do whatever you want with me and let that thought inflame you. Are your cocks throbbing? Then put them where it will feel good. Bury them in my gaping pussy. Thrust them rudely and slowly into my asshole. Rub them on my tits. Cram them in my mouth. What else? Do you want to sit on my face? Do you want to whip me? Do you want to piss on me? Do it! Do all of it!"

As had so often happened during sex, I could find no way this time to make any connection between my feeling of abandonment and the actual abandonment of my behavior. Paradoxically, although I was experiencing inside myself the same thing that was going on outside myself, it was as though I had been split into two separate people, unable to communicate with one another. I imagine the cause lay in my inability to speak my feelings, and since words are the bridge between the interior and exterior life, when they are blocked a chasm opens in the person.

"Man, she's really a sickie," Joey said.

"Didn't I tell you?" Nick replied. "She loves it, she'll do anything."

"That's me they're talking about," I said to myself, "and in their eyes I'm a 'sickie.'"

They then proceeded to use me as the fulfillment of their fantasies and projections. It's almost impossible to describe how small I felt as they tossed me around and bent me into all sorts of lewd positions, holding me upside down and moving my legs to every conceivable angle so that my cunt would twist and gape and perform for their avid eyes. They threw me about as though I were a rag doll, and at one point two of them lifted me off the ground, bent me double with my forehead touching my shinbones, forcing my ass to its deepest curve, and then ran across the room with me, as though I were a battering ram. At the far end stood Sal, his cock stiff and pointed, and Nick and Joey swung me toward him and with a single careful thrust impaled me on his rock-hard rod.

I screamed as the huge shaft burst inside me, but the two men holding me shook me up and down, spun me over, and whacked me again and again against Sal's throbbing cock, giving it a massage with my ragged hole. It was obvious that the three of them were fixated at a level of adolescent homosexual horseplay, and didn't have the faintest idea of how to relate to a woman except as a surrogate hand to whack off with. And lacking the simple decency to do it to one another, they sought out female bodies to hide behind.

I suppose I got too far lost in my head because the boys began to grumble that I had become too passive in my body. The slightest hint that I was not flinging myself mindlessly into the fray would prove too threatening to their privacy, so they began to whip up a frenzy.

I was hurled onto the rug and Nick threw himself heavily onto my shoulders, pinning them with his knees, and grinding his buttocks down on my face.

"Lick it," he ordered, bringing his rough asshole to my lips. The force of his weight on me cowed me into submission and I curled up my tongue and slid it into the tight puckered opening, tasting the musky and rancid residue around the rim.

One of the other men seized my legs and pulled them high and wide, forcing my cunt open, while the third knelt at my parted pussy and attacked it savagely with his teeth. I tried to yell as he tore into the tender lips roughly, licking, biting, sucking. He blew into the hole filling it with air and sending me into paroxysms of strained pleasure, and then sucked out noisily, draining me of the injected air and the juices that had started to flow despite myself. But whenever I opened my mouth to shout, Nick pressed down harder, and I could do nothing but attack my lips to his asshole and suck voraciously, all the while slipping my tongue rapidly in and out.

The mouth at my cunt withdrew, leaving my twat sore and trembling, but what followed made that little more than foreplay.

"Let me do it," I heard Joey say, and then felt a pressure against the outside of my cunt. For a second I didn't know what it was, but then the sensations became unmistakeable: hard knuckles and fingers rolled into a fist were pushing slowly against my tiny opening.

"Shove it up her snatch," Nick said, "shove that fist all the way up that pretty little pussy."

The pain began to be excruciating as the grapefruit-sized fist inched its way inside me. I didn't think I would be able to stretch enough, but I had no choice. With all their weight and power holding me down, I was no more able to move than if a ten-ton truck had fallen on me. Nick pulled my legs more widely apart, almost cracking the tendons, and Sal squashed my face with his ass, while Joey stuffed my slit with his huge hand.

Suddenly, there was a sense of tearing, and I thought, "Oh my God, he's ripped my cunt." But at that moment I heard Joey exclaim, "Did it, I did it. Look at it. My fist is all the way up her snatch. Look at that pussy spread."

"Man," said Nick, "look at the way those lips grip your wrist."

"Fuck her with it," Sal said, "fist-fuck her good."

And with that Joey began punching my cunt with his fist, ramming it into the already ravished space inside, punishing my cervix and scraping the side walls. Then he started to rotate his wrist, twisting his fist around inside me. It was as though a wildcat had crawled into my cunt and was now freaking out.

My legs were released and I immediately tried to close my thighs, but that only had the effect of trapping the fist more tightly inside me, and I could feel its powerful bulk more strongly. Free to move my body, I began to thrash about, at first trying to wriggle away from the pressure of that hand, but very soon I realized that I was also trying to stuff it more deeply inside me. The pain was still very keen, but now that I had no fear of being torn, I could let the underlying pleasure come to the surface, and that was more than incidental. Having a three-hundred pound man with hands like hams shove his fist into my cunt and fuck my pussy with harsh strokes and twists was no mean erotic experience.

I began to grind my hips and thrust my pelvis up, fucking the hand that had been fucking me. I brought my own hands up to spread the cheeks that were pressed on my face, and sucked Sal's asshole rapturously as I worked toward climax on Joey's arm. Nick started in on my tits, pinching the nipples and sucking the globes into his mouth, using his teeth to punctuate the swirls of his tongue. And before I knew it, I had stopped thinking about what I was doing and what it meant and if it was some form of escape or degeneracy, and just let myself be worked over by three brutes, as I flung my mouth and ass and pussy and tits into full overdrive, retrieving my reputation as the dirtiest cheerleader on the team.

Then, abruptly, Nick pulled his hand out, the fist escaping

with a loud plop. I gasped, and Sal shit in my mouth. Moaning, gasping, spluttering, I turned onto my side, half spitting, half swallowing, appalled and thrilled all at once. More than anything, I had to have that thing between my legs again. His pulling out had left my hole more aware of its emptiness than it had ever been. My cunt felt as though it had been pulled inside out and was now lying like a punctured balloon against my thighs.

"Oooh," I moaned.

"She wants more," Nick said.

"Let me do her," Joey hissed.

"Unngh," I cried as I pushed my hips off the floor and thrust my cunt into the air.

"Oh, yeah, baby," Joey whispered, "I'm going to give it to you, going to shove my fist right up that dripping pussy."

He put his balled fist against my cunt and pressed, and this time I thrust against it, engulfing it in a single motion.

"Ahhh," I sighed as my cunt was once again stuffed far past its usual capacity.

"Look at her," Sal said, "with an arm up her snatch and her mouth all smeared with shit. Ain't she beautiful!"

"Fuck it," Joey said, "fuck my fist you hot bitch. Come on, push that pretty pussy all over my hand."

Their words enflamed me and I started to squeeze my ass tight and pump my hips back and forth, doing a fucking motion against the force of his arm.

Then Sal turned me over and bent me in two so that my cunt curved under and my ass turned up. And while Joey ground his fist in and out and around, massaging my cunt, and making me scratch the rug in an ecstasy of ravishment, Sal lowered his bulk down, brought his cock between my cheeks and sank it slowly into my asshole. I was almost paralyzed with sensation, being stuffed beyond my wildest dreams. And Nick completed the picture by lifting my head by the hair and then letting it fall, having placed his cock below my mouth so that as my face came forward, the stiff flesh staff would slide between my murky lips.

They fucked me like that for more than three hours, taking turns filling my holes, using their cocks and hands and feet, placing me in whatever positions they wanted, throwing me around whenever they needed, and in general using me as a rag to wipe themselves. And I variously loathed myself, or lost myself in orgasmic frenzy, or became indifferent to the process. But by the time they were finished, I could not stand up, and was barely able to raise an arm or keep my head erect. They had to dress me, and drive me back to Sandy's and my apartment. But by the time we had gone cross town they were horny again, and I had to blow each of them as they sat in the car, only their zippers open, their cocks erupting in my mouth one after the other, until my throat was clogged with sperm. Knowing they might not have me again, they took every last opportunity to feel me up, fingering my asshole and twiddling my pussy and kneading my tits as I sucked their cocks.

But finally, there was nothing left, and I dragged myself off to bed, grateful that the next day was a vacation, part of a three-day rest before the team was to play its first game on the road, in Denver.

By this time, I had come to feel pretty much at home with the idea of being part of the team, and was even learning a lot about the game by hearing different plays and kinds of strategy discussed all the time. But it wasn't until that first crisp autumn afternoon in the Denver stadium that the true excitement of the game struck me. Up to then, I had been involved in practice and preparation, not realizing that that was just a pale shadow of the real thing, both for the team and for the cheerleaders.

The sky was achingly blue and the temperature a zippy fifty degrees. The other three women and myself strutted up and down the sidelines, and drew more than a fair share of whistles and applause. I could even see some men signalling to me frantically, and I knew that I could make more than a small addition to my salary by being available to affluent men who got overly horny during a game. Sandy told me she had put away more than ten thousand dollars the previous year by judicious appointments with admirers in the stands. But I was too thrilled to think in those terms that day, and was having a ball flaunting my tits and showing my ass and causing an untold number of erective thoughts in the stadium.

Then the teams came charging out of their dugouts, and the crowd exploded, a deep surging roar that set my ears ringing. The sound swelled like thundering surf, and I rode down its foaming crest like a joyous surfer, letting it enter me until I could no longer distinguish the pounding of my heart or the throbbing of my pulse. I lept high in the air and out of the corner of my eye saw Sandy and Irene and Marian rising with me, their arms high and their legs bent at the knees, heels pressed into their buttocks. I grinned widely and let out a shout at the top of my lungs.

The four of us jumped again and again until I was breathing hard, and then we ran in patterns around one another, going through the routines we had so diligently practiced for three months, throwing up banners and doing bumps and grinds to the music of the team band. It seemed the most happy moment of my life, a period in which I stood totally out of myself, experiencing the true meaning of the word ecstasy. And when the two teams lined up for the kickoff, I looked at the Seattle lineup and my cunt throbbed as I realized that seven of the eleven men now standing there resplendent in muscle and uniform and determination had been inside me, that I had circled their backs with my arms, bit their chests, and sucked their cocks into my mouth and pussy. The whistle blew, the line moved forward, and the ball sailed high into the air.

From that instant on, all was pandemonium. I didn't have a moment's rest, but spent the time urging the crowd to cheer the team on, with Sandy, our captain, calling the routines which were appropriate to different situations. We appealed for touchdowns, we implored them to hold the line and block the kick. And in general exhausted ourselves, throwing our bodies into the struggle as heavily in our way as the men were doing in theirs. And always, behind us and in front of us and inside us was the sound, the perpetual roar, the song of animal excitement. The afternoon was like a long vigorous fuck, and when the final gun went off, with Seattle winning seventeen to six, I lept once more into the air and screamed in victory.

I must have been overly carried away by the moment because when I came down, I landed on the edge of my right foot and felt my ankle turn under me. A sharp stab of pain shot up my leg, and I almost fainted, my face going chalk white and beads of perspiration breaking out on my forehead. I lay on the ground writhing in agony, and to my surprise, the first one to reach me was Tony.

Something of a flurry of people developed around us, but he scooped me up in his arms and walked directly toward the dugout, went down the stairs and into the cheerleaders' dressing room without hesitation. I was amazed at how strong he was and realized that although he was at least six feet tall, his slenderness made him seem puny in relation to the physical monsters on the team, especially when they had all their gear on.

He put me down on the couch and went over to close and lock the door, telling the people who had followed us that I would be better off without a crowd of rubbernecks making me nervous. I was still a bit dazed and watched the whole scene as though through a fog. When the door was shut, he turned toward me and his eyes were blazing with anger.

"That was the dumbest thing I have ever seen," he shouted.

I couldn't believe my ears. I had thought he had taken me in to give me sympathy and instead he was pouring hostility on my head. I tried to prop myself up on my elbows to answer him, but the sudden shift caused the excruciating pain to pierce my leg again and I had to lie back down.

"How many times have I told you to be especially careful about how you land after a high leap? What were you doing all summer, dozing? Or have you had so many cocks down your throat that it's affected your hearing?"

My jaw dropped open in astonishment. Ignoring the pain, I sat up, and with tears brimming at the corners of my eyes I answered him. "Who the hell do you think you are?" I began. "It's none of your goddamned business what I do during my free time. And I might have a broken ankle, and you're standing there giving me lectures!"

"Your ankle isn't broken," he shot back.

"How do you know?" I asked, now almost sobbing openly from pain and chagrin.

"I'm in the business," he said. But as though relenting, he came over, took the ankle in his hands, pressed it, turned it back and forth, bringing me close to fainting again. "We'll have it x-rayed," he went on, "but I'll stake my reputation on the fact that it's not broken."

"Well, why did you bring me here?" I shrieked as he dropped my foot unceremoniously on the couch. "To give me more pain and deliver your opinions on my life?"

"I brought you here because I'm responsible for you, for all the cheerleaders. And because I was pissed off at your stupid stunt, and wanted to tell you that before everybody began showering you with sympathy."

"And you can't be bothered with any of that, can you? You . . . you . . . eunuch."

I hadn't intended to say that but I suppose that his cavalier attitude and rough treatment, coupled with his indifference to my come-ons during the summer, had built up a reservoir of resentment.

"What's going on in there?" said a voice from the other side of the door. "Open up."

"Fuck off!" Tony shouted.

He turned back to me. "Eunuch," he said. "Why? Because I haven't fucked you? Because I haven't volunteered to stand on line to take sloppy seconds and fifths and twentieths? I have no interest in the meaningless."

I wanted to scream, to protest, to fight, but the pain kept pulling me toward it, raping my attention. And his words were delivered with such cold precision that they cut down all my resistance. And on top of all that, he was right about my turning my ankle being a dumb stunt. He had warned us against that at least a few hundred times. I felt utterly defeated and simply turned my face to the back of the couch and began to cry, letting all my unhappiness rise to the surface and wash over me.

I must have wept for several minutes, and when I finished I felt drained and purged. I looked back toward Tony, a little embarrassed at having had him see me that way, but to my astonishment he was smoking a cigarette and staring off toward the far wall. From behind the door I could hear voices, one man saying, "What the fuck are they doing in there?" and another answering, "What else does that chick ever do man? It's probably a new kick, fucking with a broken ankle."

I was aware that Tony was hearing the conversation also, and our minds met in that realization and as though on cue he turned to look at me. His eyes were sad, almost moist.

"What a waste, Julie," he said in a low trembling voice. "You are so beautiful, so intelligent, so filled with life, and look at how you throw it away. And now you weep over spilled milk. What's the point?"

"I'm working my life out in my own way," I said, and was astonished to hear the tone of my voice. He was a man I had had no contact with outside of our practice sessions, and suddenly I was speaking to him seriously and intimately, without anger or bravado, but as one speaks to a friend or lover. "You don't know me, how can you say the things you do?"

"You don't know what I know," he said. "Just because I don't say anything or act out my impulses doesn't mean I don't observe and perceive and understand. I know you more deeply than you realize, and I feel things for you which would surprise you."

My head swam. It sounded as though he were on the verge of a declaration of love, this strange introverted man whom the other women presented to me as a challenge to our powers of seduction, and whom I tried from time to time to lure from his isolation. And I couldn't figure out where his words were coming from.

"Of course I noticed you when you arrived," he went on. "And when I first looked into your eyes, something happened to me, something that both excited and frightened me. I knew you were Jeff's girl, but that didn't matter, not until he began to show home movies in the locker room. And even then I wasn't disturbed too much, because it was not my place to translate your actions into my terms. But then it was Roger, and then Steve, and then Al, and now so many I can't keep count. And yesterday I was treated to the full detailed history of your debauch with Nick and his friends. And through all this, the feeling persisted, and grew, and at one point I knew that I wanted to take you into my arms and hold you and kiss you and tell you that I loved you, because I understood you."

"Oh, Tony," I breathed, overwhelmed by his torrent of feeling. And unconsciously I shifted my weight, let my legs fall open, and thrust my breasts forward in invitation.

But he merely curled his lip. "What does that gesture mean anymore?" he said. "You'd respond the same way with an orangutan. Your pussy is worthless. You've given it away too many times. And how can I kiss you, when I know you've pressed your lips against every cock and asshole that's been offered?"

My eyes must have shown bewilderment, because he went on, "Oh, I'm not a puritan. I don't care about the specifics. It's just that you're so goddamned indiscriminate, so tasteless, so . . . *vulgar.*" He took one step toward me and then stopped. The sudden movement had the effect of catapulting him out of the two-dimensional sheet in which I had been viewing the world and into a three-dimensional *thereness* which stunned me. He ceased being an image, and became a person, someone *other,* and that entity was thrust into my self-involved universe. I suddenly realized—I'm almost embarrassed to say the word— how handsome he was. Not in a movie star sense, but in his extraordinary maleness. And with that came the understanding that he had been training me for three months, and that I had totally underestimated how deep our relationship actually was. I was overcome with a deep sense of loss.

"Don't you see?" he went on. "It's not that I don't desire you, or haven't desired Sandy or any of the others. But that I hold desire to be so precious that I can't abide its being made coarse and cheap."

My gaze faltered and fell down the length of his body. To my amazement I saw that his cock was bulging in his pants. "Oh, Tony," I said again.

He put his hand on his cock and smiled bitterly. "This?" he said. "There's more to it than that, Julie."

Once more there was a pounding on the door, and this time Tony went over and opened it up. The team doctor was standing there, along with Sandy and the other cheerleaders and a few members of the team. They all rushed in at once, all speaking, all solicitous, and in a moment I was being comforted and examined and made a fuss over. But I didn't want any of them, I wanted Tony. I tried to call to him but he was already gone, and I bit my lip as I fell back on the couch.

"Does it hurt, baby?" Sandy asked.

And for the second time that day I started to cry. "Yes, it hurts," I said, holding her hand, but I wasn't referring just to my ankle, but also to a deep ache in my heart.

That night I dreamt of Tony. He stood before me naked and I knelt in front of him, his erect cock close to my lips. It began to throb, and he started to cum. But instead of sperm, hot scalding tears cascaded from its single blind eye.

SEVEN

The ankle wasn't broken, but before I was able to use it again, I had missed the following week's game. I began to understand the significance of what Roger had told me about the cohesiveness of the team; it was like being part of a large family. I was pampered, sent flowers, and reassured by everyone from the President to the water boy. I spent ten days back in Sandy's and my apartment, recuperating, and when I was completely healed flew from there to Los Angeles to meet the team for their third game. They had won their second match and had become the sportswriters' favorites to take first place in the league and go into the superbowl with the champions of the Eastern Division.

During the time I was laid up I had plenty of opportunity to think about my life and where it was heading. The encounter with Tony had proved to be profoundly unsettling especially since I received no word from him since. My feelings about him remained formless. I had always thought him attractive, but only as one of my potential sexual conquests. Now that he had revealed the deeper level to our relationship, one which I hadn't even been aware of, I didn't know how to think about him. It was difficult to differentiate guilt from desire, and I wasn't sure how much of what was troubling me was from my own sense of self or from the images he had imposed on me.

One afternoon, I stood for some time in front of a full-length mirror, examining myself to find what it might be in me that Tony had responded to. It was a foolish exercise, and yet what is time for but to experiment with? "What is it, Julie?" I said to my reflection. "You're obviously pretty and have a sexy body and a good mind, but you're not that much different from a thousand other women who surrounded you on campus. Jeff certainly had no trouble finding anyone he wanted to go to bed with him, yet why was he so taken with you? And Tony is turning out to be an extraordinary man who has at least three beautiful women chasing him; what makes him find you so special?"

I lifted my tits and pushed them forward, watching them swell, the smooth white skin bulging around my dark pointed nipples. "Is it these? These sacs of fatty tissue?" I brought my hands down to my cunt and parted the lips, exposing the pink interior. "Or this? This tiny wrinkled slit?" Spinning around I tilted my ass up and saw it in the glass, the twin round globes iridescent around the dark soft crack. "Or this? Evolution's practical joke?" I walked up to the mirror and pressed my lips against it, licking the glass with my tongue, making pools of mist with my breath. "Or is it my mouth they desire?"

I stepped back in consternation. None of that made any sense. Those were things that any woman possessed, some in a more aesthetically gratifying way than others, but on that level we were all interchangeable. Was it then some quality? Many of the men had commented on my wildness, my capacity for lustful frenzy. That had turned Jeff on, but Tony had relegated it to the category of the incidental. I remembered his saying that it had no importance if it became the plaything of every man who came by.

No, there was something that was more than the sum of my parts, and I could only call it my uniqueness, my individuality, my me-ness. In the way that the mirror could not see itself, so I could not be aware of that essential aspect which was so utterly myself that I must remain blind to it. Only another could see me in that space, and it was precisely the person who did perceive who truly loved. For he or she then called an entity out of its condition of formlessness, who, in a very real sense, created a conscious human being where before there had only been an instinctive functioning.

This train of thought brought to mind passages from various texts I had studied in my philosophy and psychology classes, and for the first time I realized that I might have done myself real damage by leaving school. While I believed that the experience

I was gaining on the team was invaluable, I sensed that I could derive more benefit from it if I had the tools of analysis to assist me, and the writings of people who had pondered life deeply to guide me.

As though we were in telepathic communication, my father sent me a letter which I received the very afternoon of the day I stood wondering about my life before the mirror. I had written him about my quitting school and becoming a cheerleader, and had mentioned Jeff, speaking about him as a lover, but had not gone into any details concerning my extraordinary sexual activity. His note was brief and, although acid in tone, comforting.

"Dear Julie," he wrote, "Asininity is a prerogative of the young. So is a sense of independence. Guard against early marriage, pregnancy, and venereal disease. Your mother, as usual, finds your vicissitudes too boring to comment on. Should you desire to return to the academic structure after this complex fling, we will honor our pledge to see you financially through your Master's. I have never offered you the false security of assuming that my wisdom is any greater than yours. I have simply observed more patterns than you, that's all. Should you falter, you will always have a refuge here. We are not effusive, as you know, but we care deeply for your welfare. Your brother has gone mad, but since he is expressing his insanity in a socially acceptable format, he is enjoying himself immensely. I find some slight vicarious titillation in imagining the orgies you must be attending. Remember that intelligence is the highest good, and the rarest accomplishment. Affectionately, Carl. P S. We shall watch the next Seattle game on television to see how well you have learned to leap."

My period of isolation and the knowledge that my family, if they did not precisely approve, continued to accept me as a daughter and would sustain me if things got too rough, restored my sense of well-being. I decided to put the incident with Tony on a shelf at the back of my mind. He seemed to show no inclination to follow up and I wasn't going to lay myself open to him in any way. I felt healthy and sane and looked forward to the further developments of the season. I didn't know what the future held, and that was exactly what I found so exciting. As far

as the notion that I was becoming the slut that Jeff had branded
me, I was ready to pursue that to its final conclusion. Already
it was apparent that this was a phase, and I knew that unless I
cycled through it completely, I would regret my timidity for the
rest of my life.

In short, I had integrated all that had happened up to that
point, and was ready for more action. I had no way of knowing
what that would be, and if I had had any suspicion of the horror
in store I might not have made my decision so jauntily. As with so
many things in life, I began a new round with enough renewed
vitality and sense of integrity to bring about an explosive erotic
evening. So delightful was it that it made me too sure of myself,
of my ability to control the forces which were already swirling
about my feet.

The team was met by a particularly tough Los Angeles squad,
and the ensuing game was punctuated with penalties and
fistfights. There were few fireworks as the players settled down
to a grueling ground game, each side rarely able to even churn
out a first down. That, coupled with my sense of pleasure in
being in Los Angeles again, plus the welcome-back attitude on
the part of everyone on the team, catapulted me into an inspired
cheerleader performance. I threw my heart into my movements
and shouts. And when, with four minutes left to play, our
quarterback called for a kick from our thirty yard line and
instead uncorked a surprise pass to Jeff, the crowd went wild,
lifting me up with them. Los Angeles was taken completely off
balance by the fake kick, and when. Jeff caught the ball midfield,
there wasn't another man near him. I screamed myself hoarse as
he hit his stride and began speeding downfield, bounding over
the earth like some mythical steed. And it was with a thunderous
roar in my ears that I watched him cross the goal line with what
proved to be the winning touchdown.

The final few minutes involved perfunctory play as a re-
charged Seattle defensive team came in to hold Los Angeles to
no gain. The gun went off as three of our line-backers swarmed
all over the opposing quarterback and smashed him into the
ground with the ball still in his hand. Since I had been fucked

by each of the men in that play I felt an especially personal thrill in the victory.

My ebullience was augmented when, as I was coming out of the dressing room after changing, I was approached by Larry Plains, the fullback, a gorgeous black with enormous shoulders and a waist almost as narrow as mine. He was called swivel-hips because of his ability to spin away from would-be tacklers, and I had had my eye on him for some time. Although I was not consciously prejudiced, there was still that part of me which wondered if and how a black man would be different in bed. And from the look in his eyes, I figured I was about to soon find out.

But he invited me to Frank Williams' house, to have dinner with Frank and his wife and three other couples. Frank was the star quarterback who risked so much calling the fake kick deep in his own territory, and as far as I knew he didn't fuck around at all. For an instant I wondered why Larry was inviting me to what appeared to be a staid evening, but decided that he might want to spend some time with me socially before fucking me, and that was enough of an oddity to intrigue me.

Frank and his wife had apartments in a number of cities so they could be, as Laura Williams explained, "at home wherever we go." Their place was surprisingly chic for what I imagined was a square couple. The dining room was sparse, and we ate out of bucketsful of Kentucky Fried Chicken, washing it down with a good red wine. The other couples were relatively strange to me, all the men forming that small percentage of the team which seemed to be, if not happily then at least, securely married. I was on nodding acquaintance with all of them, but had never met their wives.

The meal went cheerfully, with everyone recounting anecdotes of the day's play. At one point Larry slipped his hand under the table and stroked my thigh, and I breathed a bit easier with the feeling of being on familiar ground. After Tony, a man who wanted nothing more complicated than to slide his hard cock into my randy gap provided welcome relief.

After eating we went into the living room, which proved a real surprise. There was nothing in it but deep pile rug and large throw pillows. The lights were so low that it was difficult to make out another person's features at a distance of more than five feet. Music came from somewhere, a drum recording which sounded like Olatunji underwater. Given the texture of my life, I don't know how I could have missed what was happening, but so strong is the power of pre-conception that with my notion of these people as married squares I was completely blind to the purpose of the evening.

I sat on one of the pillows, resigned to another hour or so of chatter, when Melanie, the wife of Harvey Engram, sashayed to the middle of the room and began doing a slow bump and grind. For an instant I didn't perceive it as anything but a bit of spontaneous dancing, but in a few seconds her movements began to be more sharply defined. Her broad ass, caught in a tight velour dress, circled suggestively, while her shoulders shook back and forth, causing her full-bellied breasts to sway. I guess I still didn't understand until she brought her hands up and slowly peeled the dress off her shoulders, letting it slide down her sides. And before I could grasp the fact that she was stripping, her creamy and pink-tipped tits were totally revealed.

"Bravo," shouted Jim Reynolds, one of the other players.

I half-turned toward Larry, to confirm the suspicion that had formed in my mind, but I couldn't tear my eyes away from Melanie, who had now eased the dress down her thighs, showing the full bristling bush which covered her thick-lipped twat.

"What's the matter, Julie?" Frank called out, "your eyes are popping out of your head. You act as though you'd never been to a party before."

"But, all you people are . . . *married*," I said, the last word slipping out before I realized how foolish it sounded.

The laughter that met my remark, however, was good-natured, and Larry reached over and put his arm around me. "Honey, these people are all swingers," he said. "I thought you knew that." He looked at me for a moment and then went on, "You didn't think I was inviting you to just a dinner party, did you?"

I nodded. "I'm afraid I did," I said.

"Well, hell," Larry sang out. "I'm flat-out flattered!"

And once again the room rang with laughter. By now the

men had begun to remove their shirts and unhook their belts, while the other women were shrugging themselves clear of their dresses.

"It's O.K., isn't it?" Larry said in a low voice. "I mean, I assumed that you would be into it."

"You mean, with my reputation?" I replied a bit acerbically.

But I didn't give him a chance to continue, wanting to get the flow of the event moving. I had, of course, heard of the phenomenon of swinging, but had never given it any detailed thought, and now I was curious to see how these couples operated in their effort to have their cake and eat it too.

"It's O.K., Larry," I said. "I feel like I've just been given a surprise party."

To underline my words I pulled my blouse up over my head and flung it to one side, sitting there with my bare tits pointing out toward Larry's gleaming eyes. I saw him form the word "beautiful" soundlessly with his lips before he leaned forward and cupped each of my breasts in his two powerful hands. I looked down and caught my breath to see the stunning contrast of his jet black skin against my pale white flesh. The visual impact was even more thrilling than the sensations caused by his fingers rubbing gently over my nipples.

I must have become lost in reverie because I didn't notice that the others had all gathered in front of me, and I looked up to see eight naked men and women lying and sitting all around Larry watching him stroke my breasts. I think I may have blushed, for the moment was quite stark.

"Can we see it?" said Laura Williams.

"See it?" I repeated.

"The tattoo," she said, "we've heard so much about the tattoo."

"Fuck the tattoo," said Jim Reynolds, "I want to see that young pussy."

"Don't be crude," said his wife Karen, admonishing him as she might a schoolboy.

I began to reply but before I could say a word a dozen hands were at my waist, unhooking the button and pulling the zipper down and finally snaking the pants off my legs. They all pressed in close to see, and I heard a chorus of muted oohs and aahs as they examined the scarlet stigma rising like a flame out of my pubic hair. Someone whose hands had been fingering the letters ran his hands lower down and began tickling the edges of my cunt lips, causing me to squirm. But Larry dove in and pushed them all aside.

"My date," he said imperiously, "and I get firsts."

He had undressed and his body was even more commanding naked than it had been even with full gear. I had seen him run many times and wondered how it would feel to hold those churning hips in my hands as his cock plunged in and out of my pussy. In the dim light he looked like a smoke demon and I lay back almost in awe as he knelt between my thighs.

"We can help, can't we?" said Susie December, the wife of the fifth man there.

"Just leave me her snatch and you can do what you want with the rest," Larry said.

Laura Williams lay down next to me and began caressing one of my breasts, her soft hand stroking the firm flesh gently. "Don't feel picked on," she whispered after sliding her tongue in my ear sending shivers down my spine, "it's just that we've been together a hundred times and you're the new asshole in town. So naturally everybody wants a taste of you first."

They moved around me like a well-rehearsed theatrical group. Harvey put his cock in my right hand and Tom December put his cock in my left hand. Jim knelt by my head and slipped his half-erect cock between my lips. One of the other women began to suck my other breast, and the others positioned themselves in various spots, so that my belly was sucked and my ass fondled. Before long I was covered with attention, my entire body subject to one or another form of touch.

At first it wasn't specifically exciting, partially because everyone was so methodical and matter-of-fact, but the sheer volume, of flesh and level of energy wasn't too long in having an effect, and in short order I was beginning to lose my mundane sense of self to an identification with the erotic current, a tingling warmth which brought my skin to life and slowly burned more deeply into my insides. My breath came more quickly and Jim's cock swelled to full erection and he pumped it back and forth slowly into my mouth. I licked it with my tongue, wetting it, making slobbering noises, as with each hand I stroked the thick rods that had grown stiff with my fondling.

A finger went into my ass and I began to squirm, suddenly catching on to the erotic mood like a person climbing aboard a bicycle after many years and suddenly remembering perfectly how to ride. Tony's treatment of me and the ten-day period of solitude had removed me from a sense of sex, and now, with a grateful rush, I was recapturing it.

"Get the bitch hot," Larry whispered. "Get her good and wet and hot."

"The bitch," I thought to myself. "There it is again. That's all I am to him, to these people." And almost simultaneously with that idea, another voice popped into my head. "This is no time to get finicky," it said. "You're here to enjoy a friendly orgy. Be a hot little cunt and enjoy it."

I suppose I might have continued the argument with myself, but my body had a different perspective. It was going on without any need for approval from the mind. My legs were thrashing and my nipples getting hard and my cunt starting to drip. Everywhere there were hands or mouths or cocks or tits pressed on me. I was awash in a sea of sensuality, and my hungry flesh was drinking it in.

"What a sweet pussy," Frank hissed. "Look at that, Laura, isn't it pretty."

"I can hardly wait for you to fuck her," Laura replied. "And after you cum I'm going to eat your sperm right out of her tight little snatch."

It seemed odd to hear a husband and wife talk like that, but I suspected it was healthier in its way than most of what goes on between conventional couples. By this time I was highly enflamed, twisting my hips and thrusting my pelvis out. Everything was being touched except my cunt, and I was getting delirious with desire. Which is what I guess Larry wanted.

"That's it, baby," he said, "throw that pussy up in the air. Come on, give it here, push it out. Beg with it, Julie. I want to see your pussy beg for my cock."

I reached higher with my cunt, spread my legs wider, tried by

some physiologically impossible muscular trick to open the lips
by themselves, to offer an open hole to the prick I was getting
desperate for. At the same time, my mounting frenzy was
working itself out elsewhere, and I began to literally gobble the
cock in my mouth, sucking it into my throat, lapping it, teething
it gently. My hands were flying over the cocks I had curled my
fingers around, jerking them frantically. And my tits were aching
as two women sucked and licked them into they mouths. Now
two fingers were in my asshole and I was clenching my cheeks
to draw them in deeper.

"Fuck me," I moaned, my lips stretched around the bulging
base of Jim's hot cock.

"Fuck her," said Melanie, "give it to her. Shove that big black
cock up that pink twat."

"Yeaah," Larry said in a low growl, "Yeaah."

And he brought the tip of his cock close against the edges
of my cunt lips. I moaned when I felt it and fucked my pussy
harder into the air, trying to surround the silky crown.

"She's really hot," Tom said.

"Fuck her," said Jim.

"Fuck her, fuck her, fuck her," they all chanted.

"Fuck me, fuck me, fuck me," I groaned, my mouth stuffed
with throbbing cock.

And with that Larry let himself drop forward and sank
slowly and ponderously onto my body, his code slicing into
my cunt smoothly and surely. He entered for what seemed like
an eternity, going deeper and deeper until he was hitting the
farthest niche of my clutching vault. My cunt engulfed him
like a sword-swallower gulps down a shaft of steel. His entry
completed the circuit. I was totally plugged in. And with that, I
cut loose and let myself go bananas, writhing on the rug in that
strange room with nine people clustered round my body like
priests around an altar, carrying out some occult rite, a sacrifice
to a merciless god.

Now that other, more ancient language seized our beings and
we suffered a grand glossolalia of our bodies, fucking with the
same abandon which grips those who speak in tongues. The
only sounds were the rasping of labored breath and the moans

of ecstatic release and the quick chirping cries of climax. Jim spilled his seed in my mouth and I sucked his pulsing cock dry of cum, pulling on it with my lips until he had to force my head backwards to ease his tender prick out of my voracious grasp. He was immediately replaced by Tom, whose prong was ready to burst from the hand job I had been giving him, and I didn't miss a beat as one cock slid out and another slid in, the second easing in on the slippery coat of sperm that covered my tongue.

He must have been hotter than I thought for no sooner did his cock touch the back of my throat than he came inside me, spraying my mouth with his acrid juice. Almost like a wine taster, I could distinguish between the different flavors of sperm in my mouth as I swallowed the thick gobs of hot spunk lustily.

"What a fantastic mouth," Tom whispered as he pumped the last of his load down my throat.

"Let me have her," said Harvey, and as Tom slid his softening cock out from between my lips, Harvey thrust his stiff wide staff into the vacated space. Three cocks in a row spreading my lips, three cocks in a row fucking my throat, three cocks in a row being licked by my tongue! Both my hands were now free and I brought them up to the base of Harvey's cock and started jerking him off, bringing him to a climax as the head of his cock romped inside my hot cum-smeared mouth. The overall excitement of the group was so high that he was also at the edge of orgasm, and after a very brief flurry of strokes I felt the thick column begin to pulse and throb, and I opened my mouth wide to pull him all the way inside. I released my grip on the base of his cock and immediately he let loose, his pelvis twitching and the head of his prick exploding, shooting jet after jet of swirling jism on my tongue. I licked his cock lasciviously, and swallowed his cum greedily.

All this while, Larry was pumping steadily into my pussy. It was not that I had been unaware of him, but that the irresistible sensation of having three men, one after the other, cum in my mouth took priority over everything else. But now as I lay there, my lips raw and my throat rank with the taste and smell of so much sperm, two women still sucking my nipples, Larry started to move in earnest. He was propped up on his palms, his elbows locked, his huge shoulders twice as wide as mine looming over me.

"Now I'm gonna ride you, baby," he said, "gonna make believe you're a wall of defensive linemen and I have to screw my way through you."

I looked up into his eyes and saw nothing but a raging fire. I couldn't know for certain whether he was in his right mind or not. But when he started moving, it really didn't make any difference. His hips combined the erratic dips of a butterfly with the brute force of a rhinoceros. The sockets must have been hinged with ball-bearings, for it didn't seem that bone and sinew could produce such fluidity and range of expression. And the power was beyond all my expectations. Although not as tall or as heavy as Jeff, he had the fullback's gift of drive, that almost inhuman thrust which is necessary to break through a wall of three-hundred pound tacklers.

He rode endlessly, and after a while the others simply sat by the side and watched. The three men who had been sated weren't yet ready for another round, and Frank said he would fuck me next, "after the kid had loosened her up a bit." I hoped he had been joking, because I couldn't imagine anything heavier than what was happening. My legs were stretched to they limit, my feet high in the air. My arms went out to either side of me and my fingers curled in the thick rug. And Larry rode me with an unprecedented ferocity. His body flamed and fell and scooped and banged and raged. He slammed into my cunt a hundred times with unabated vigor, until my pussy lips felt as though they had been reduced to porridge. I could no longer feel anything but a roaring heat in my hole, a fire he kept stoking as he fucked me. After a certain point I realized that his capacity was greater than anything I had seen, and I started to let myself encompass the scope of his assault. I knew that if I allowed myself to reach for an orgasm in the same scale as the fuck he was proposing, I would blow out all my fuses. And in front of an audience to boot.

"What the hell?" I thought, and surrendered to the level of intensity Larry wanted me to experience.

Now the heat and tension really built, for each time he stroked into me, I quantum-leapt that much closer to orgasm. It was no longer simply a furrowing process whereby my pleasure came from having my pussy reamed out and battered; it had become a cooperative venture, in which I had to match his extraordinary power with my own capacity for opening and grasping, letting him explode into the deepest recesses of my cunt and then using my cunt to clasp him tightly as he escaped. In this way I was raised to a height of striving I had never considered before, and when I was pumping and wriggling and fucking with more abandon and lustiness and simple muscular exertion than I ever had, I felt the first surge of climax building inside me.

In the same way that a body-surfer will wait out the smaller waves and put himself in position only when a truly superior wave is seen, and is then awed and somewhat frightened because the wave that is now rushing in is far more powerful than he had imagined it would be in relation to what had gone before, so I felt that the orgasm which roared through my body would turn me head over heels and plunge me into the foam until I sputtered and swallowed and perhaps drowned, my body being pulled by the undertow to a salty grave.

I don't remember precisely what happened. Arms flailing, legs kicking, piercing scream, blood pounding, heart stopping, anus opening, tits flopping, fingers curling, cunt exploding. All of that and more. My mind an irresistible stream of colors and sounds, hallucinatory shapes and intimations of endless spaces. Pure ideas shimmering like crystals in sunlight. The entire history of life on earth recapitulated in an instant. Utter clarity of understanding, sharp and dancing perceptions. A sense of bliss, of eternal happiness, of kindness and joy. Christmas bells. The entire vast and mysterious universe spinning in the center of my forehead.

And then a gradual re-adjustment, a focusing back on the ordinary reality, the mundane level of awareness. Back on the planet, in the year, in the city, in the room, in my body, and feeling Larry's cock slither out of me like a snake darting from under a slimy rock.

"Oh," I said, encompassing everything. It was a moment when I would have given anything to be with a person, anyone, who had some inkling of the profundity of my experience, who would authenticate that what I had just felt was something special, something . . . real.

But when I looked around all I could see were hideous grins. I'm sure that they were all good people and all meant well, but they were so distant, so strange, so removed from my intimate self, that when they smiled all I could see were baboon death masks.

"Wow," Laura Williams said, "she really is the hottest little piece of ass I have ever seen." She turned to her husband. "Come on, Frank, you fuck her. Put a load up her snatch. I want to suck her pussy so bad I can hardly hold myself back. But I want to eat your cum."

"Why don't you eat this while you're waiting," said Tom December. His cock had become hard again, and he was staring at Laura's mouth with a salacious glint in his eyes. He held his cock in one hand. "Come on, Laura," he urged, "wrap your pretty lips around this while Frank fucks the slut."

She was already on her hands and knees and she turned toward him, walking on all fours, her eyes heavily lidded, her mouth hanging open. I saw her ass sway as she moved away from me. Harvey had begun to screw Karen in the ass, and the others were beginning to arrange themselves in new positions and combinations. I knew I was in for an all-nighter.

Frank Williams lowered his bulk over me, and curling one arm under my belly, flipped me over. "Lift your pretty little ass in the air," he said, "I want to fuck you from behind."

I didn't think there was anything left inside me, but the minute he slid his cock into my dripping pussy, I knew that I had to regain my orgasmic balance. I had flown very high, and now I was going to get very low. I put my head on the floor and began to grunt like a sow as he plowed into my insatiable hole.

EIGHT

The season began to gather momentum, taking on a life of its own, with a logic and direction which obliterated all other rhythms. The state of the world, wars in distant lands, poverty and restlessness in the nation, the promptings of my heart, all fell into dark shadows as the fierce light of victory blazed more brightly in our eyes. The team had not lost a game, and our collective mood was that of an army within sight of the citadel we were marching to capture. Winning the league championship, and the superbowl, meant fantastic bonuses for the players, and up to five thousand dollars more apiece for each of the cheerleaders. In addition, the prestige meant bigger crowds, and higher fees for television coverage, so that the entire operation would be bathed in an overflow of opulence. In addition, of course, there was the simple animal excitement of coming out on top. And for several weeks I forgot everything else except the great drumming excitement that filled all our days.

As so often happens when one is totally involved, I became wound up with an extraordinary tension. I wasn't aware of it until one afternoon, in the Chicago dressing room, for no apparent reason I began to tremble and weep. Sandy came over to comfort me and asked what was wrong. To my surprise, I spilled out a tale of confusion and unhappiness, feelings I had not even been aware of. I told her of what Tony had said, and how used I felt after the party at the Williams' apartment. And confessed that along with a sense of ebullience I was being slowly filled with a deep disgust at myself.

"I'm all right as long as I remember that this is all a process I'm exploring and don't identify with it," I said at last when my sobs had subsided. "But what with all the pressure from the season and the sex scenes I keep getting into, I can't help but crack sometimes I guess." I smiled weakly and added, "I'll be all right."

She patted my cheek and said, in that delightfully brisk way of hers, "Sugar, all you need is a little vacation to get you out of this rut. God, it's a wonder we don't all come down with the heebie-jeebies. But most of us have been around a few seasons, so I guess we're used to it. And I'm afraid that this is nothing. If the team keeps winning, by the time we reach the end of the season the tension will be enough to stun you."

I don't know whether it was the unaccustomed tenderness, or the fact that Sandy really seemed to understand my vibrations, or perhaps a deep and long-standing desire on my part, but when I put my head against her chest to bask in her warmth, the initial feeling of friendliness gave way to a warmth which I was all too familiar with. Something stirred in my cunt, and my lips went slack, not just with relaxation but with the first stirring of desire.

I suppose she felt it too, and now that I look back on it I'm certain that she had been patiently waiting for me to arrive at that spot. What made the moment so lovely was my awareness that if I had never reciprocated, she would not have thought any the less of me or treated me more coldly. Her desire for me was clean, offered in a genuinely passive way, for me to respond to or not. And all of this without an overt gesture on her part since that first day when I walked into the dressing room and was almost swept into that vortex of female sensuality.

Sandy held my head in her hands and lifted my face toward hers. Her eyes were shining and filled with such a limpid amiability that I all but melted on the spot.

"Listen," she said, "we play back in Seattle next week. We can fly to San Francisco and spend five days there before the game." She paused, kissed my lips lightly, and added, "just the two of us. We'll get a real fancy hotel room and eat champagne and strawberries for breakfast and paint the town red. And . . . not let a man anywhere near us." She looked deeply into my gaze. "O.K.?" she said.

"O.K.," I breathed. I knew that she was inviting me to have

a brief fling with her, and that we would sleep together and make love and go to movies and in general behave like lovers. And at that instant, I could conceive of no more lovely thing in the world to do. I got very excited, almost like a teen-age girl, and hugged her tightly. "Oh, Sandy," I exclaimed, "just to do nothing but enjoy ourselves and have fun. What a treat!"

"And no pressure, and no talk of football, or of dark brooding trainers with saturnine restrictions in their words."

I laughed at her description of Tony, and impulsively I kissed her, just joyfully at first, but as our lips blended into one another, my mouth parted and her quick pink tongue touched my own, sending strange lava-flows of desire down into my belly. I had had peripheral sexual contact with women, the most radical being Laura Williams' ravenous sucking of my cunt after her husband blasted his sperm into me, but I had never been directly involved; it had always come about as a result of our mutual contact in relation to a man or group of men. This confrontation with Sandy challenged something in me, and while my body squirmed, my mind experienced its own form of cerebral lust, a raunchy curiosity to understand myself in this new context.

Sandy broke contact just as my hands were going toward her breasts. "Not here," she said. "Let's wait until we can spread out and take our time. I dig you an awful lot and I want our first time to be right."

In response I smiled my gratitude, and we disengaged and set immediately to packing our bags. The rest of the team was catching a flight directly to Seattle, and as we were ready to leave, Marian and Irene waltzed in, having joined in the locker-room celebration after the game.

"Boy, that's fast," Marian said.

"We're splitting for San Francisco," Sandy told her. "We need a vacation."

"Oh, what a great idea," Irene chirruped. "Maybe I'll come too."

"Sorry," Sandy said, "private party."

The two other women exchanged arched glances. "Well, pardon me," Irene intoned in her best imitation of a catty voice.

The four of us looked around at one another and all burst

into smiles. In a second we were all hugging in the middle of the room. Marian turned then to embrace me. "I'm very happy about this," she said. "I think it will really help you to get your head straight."

"Not to mention her quim," Irene purred.

She was so obviously good-intentioned that I had to hug her, despite the seeming sharpness of her words. We exchanged kisses all around, and before I could fully digest the implications of what was happening, Sandy and I were in a cab to the airport, and then in a plane heading toward that jeweled and exotic city, the place where the cataclysmic hippie movement was born. As we winged west through the dark sky, Sandy's hand slipped between us and her fingers intertwined with mine. I inclined my head toward her and we smiled at one another as we slipped into a light and relaxing sleep.

When we landed it was eleven o'clock, and the night was delightfully warm. We got into a taxi and Sandy surprised me by suggesting we go to North Beach before finding a hotel. "I'd like a drink," she said. But when we arrived on the garishly lit main drag of Broadway, she steered me into one of the topless-bottomless bars. "It's owned by a friend of mine," she explained.

Inside, we were among the only women in the crowd, while the stage held three naked lovelies doing their bumps and grinds. A burly affable man made his way toward us and embraced Sandy. He turned out to be the owner, and announced that drinks were on the house.

We sat and watched the show for a while, consuming three vodka martinis apiece, and the alcohol and ambience combined to make me more than a little itchy. My thighs felt as though tiny ants were nibbling at the soft flesh. The women were all slim and very sexy, and as I watched their bobbing tits and gyrating pussies, I kept reminding myself that I would soon have my mouth buried in Sandy's cunt, while her fingers explored my own. I guessed that this very reaction of mine was one of the reasons she had taken me there. As the show progressed, she began to stroke my thighs under the table, and I responded in kind, loving the feel of her firm legs beneath her short skirt.

Then, for the second time that night she surprised me. "Like to dance?" she asked.

"Huh?" I said thickly, slightly drunk and a little turgid with swollen lust.

"Mac usually lets me get on stage and do a number. Usually I do it just for kicks and to see if there's anybody interesting in the crowd, but tonight it'll be for you. But I'd love it if you joined me."

"Why not?" I said, looking out over the sea of piercing male eyes, imagining what it would be like to have them focused on me. I had become used to the nature of exhibitionism, and was ready to take it to its next logical step. Sandy made a gesture to the owner and when the act finished, he bounded up on stage and made his announcement in a loud voice.

"A real treat tonight," he boomed. "Two cheerleaders from the Seattle team, and one a dear old friend of mine"—he winked lewdly to approving chuckles—"will grace us with a special performance. Come on girls." And with that the small combo struck up a Latin beat.

Sandy took my hand and we made our way to the stage, all stares on us. I clambered up, almost stumbling, and suddenly found myself practically blind, powerful spotlights beaming down on me.

"Take it off," a raucous voice shouted.

The music increased its tempo, and with a glance at one another, Sandy and I started peeling off our clothes. The crowd started stamping and whistling, and in a few seconds I was stark naked on the stage of a nightclub in San Francisco, a roomfull of howling men at my feet. For a second I was paralyzed, and then the music penetrated my consciousness. Forgetting everything else, I threw myself into the rhythm of the dance, breaking into a kind of mambo shuffle. Keeping time preoccupied me for a while, but once I had the feel of the movement, I let myself go and just enjoyed the freedom of swimming through air, supported by the beating drum and thrumming guitar. I glanced over at Sandy and my heart leapt into my mouth. She was beautiful! Tits already covered with sweat jiggling back and forth, her ass trembling with each step, and the furry mound over her vulva bristling as she lifted and dropped her legs. It took a moment for me to realize that I must look exactly the same, and suddenly the stunning power of the scene hit me. I was shaking my ass to a crowd of men who were probably already erect, and only the thinnest fabric of social convention kept them from stampeding onto the stage and fucking us on the boards. With the knowledge that I was safe, I began to enjoy my cock-teasing dance. I lifted my breasts with my hands and offered them to the audience. I ran one hand between my thighs and rubbed my pussy. I turned around and shuffled from right to left, letting my cheeks wobble and shake.

The roaring in the crowd increased and men started pounding on the tables. The music hit a faster beat and a small frenzy developed. Suddenly we were out of time and space. This might have been the Coliseum in ancient Rome or an Aztec sacrificial altar. It was what it was and everything else besides. I spun around and found myself facing Sandy. We grinned at one another and started dancing to each other's movements, advancing and retreating, coming close and touching nipples and then backing away while our hips pumped forward. It was the sublimation of sex and the prelude to sex. The vodka stirred my blood and the raw lust of the crowd raped my brain and my body leapt free of restrictions and launched into a wild orgiastic explosion, as I leapt and threw my arms about and stomped on the stage and emitted fierce cries. It was an extraordinary purgative and I wondered whether Sandy had planned this also. I took everything that had been troubling me, all my fears and self-doubts and burned them in the acid of corybantic ecstasy, reviving the archetypal power of archaic priestesses who celebrated secret rites to gods unknown to men.

This was the antipode of the literary lesbianism which had come to form my stereotyped understanding of woman's celebration of herself. It was the spirit of the huntress in the hills, and my vision filled with eruptions of blood as I hurled myself into the climax of the dance. The audience, the music, Sandy, my life, all the sex, the doubts, all burned and dissolved in the final whirling conclusion as I spun around and around, arms flailing, tits flying, cunt gaping, until the world exploded in a single triumphant chord, and I lay on my back, panting, staring up at the twinkling stage lights, the adulating roar of the audience cascading over my ears.

I suppose that if I had been alone I would have gone on, as everyone was urging me to do, and caused such a vortex of seething passion that the whole place would have been drawn into my orbit. There would have undoubtedly been a gangbang, with the men taking me and all the other dancers in the place, and I would have easily made the front page of the *Chronicle* the next day. But Sandy helped me to my feet, gathered up our clothes, and spirited me into the dressing room.

I flung myself onto a couch and closed my eyes until everything stopped spinning. When I looked up, Sandy was watching me with undisguised desire. One of the other dancers was standing in the corner, putting on eye shadow. "That was real pretty, honey," she lisped, "but it's not an easy act to follow."

"Let's split," Sandy whispered.

I nodded, and we dressed, and within minutes we were in our third taxi of the day. It was one of those nights when the world seems unhinged, to have lost its mundane regularity, and is no longer bothered with revolving around the sun or spinning on its axis, but has burst loose into outer space. It seemed that all convention, all law had been suspended. I was flushed with an extravagant euphoria, and felt lifted high above all humanity. I looked back on the Julie that had been weeping over her troubles just that afternoon, and from my Olympian height was able to pity her and dispense largesse. I had been catapulted into a different state of consciousness, and while I was the same person I had always been, I now, temporarily, had access to a wider range of energies.

"I feel so high," I said to Sandy.

"That's what a vacation is for," she replied. "For five days you have no name, no history, no attachments. Everything is flow, everything is climax. It's time to blow out all the gaskets and let your system wax out to its fullest. So when you return to the other world, you are invigorated and refreshed."

"Oh Sandy," I said, "I'm so randy for you."

"Me too," she whispered. "Soon now."

We took a room in one of the smaller hotels on Nob Hill, barely able to contain ourselves to go through the ritual of signing in. I let her handle all the details, and after what seemed an eternity we were in the elevator, and finally in the room, the busboy having dropped our bags and handed us the key. Sandy and I looked at one another. She was ravishing, and my desire for her was unabashed and total. As she suggested, I didn't even try to relate the moment to any other context in my life, but wanted only to experience it fully, to drain it of its juices.

Sandy glanced at me and her eyes glittered with cold intelligence. "For five days we love each other, nothing held back. And after five days, we become friends again. All right?"

I sobered long enough to accept the full meaning of her words. I knew exactly what she was saying, and was happy that she was taking the onus of defining our relationship upon herself.

"Yes," I breathed. "And now, now, I want your mouth," I said, the words spilling out of me as I ran across the room to her. I flung myself into her arms and our lips melted into a single opening while our tongues sent slithering thrills through mingled saliva.

For a long long time I was lost in the discovery of the beauty of a woman's body. Of course, I knew that women, including myself were beautiful, but mostly through reflection in men's eyes. But now I could taste and touch and smell that incredible loveliness for myself. Sandy and I shrugged off our clothing as we kissed, our hands flying from clasps to zippers to stretches of exposed flesh. We embraced and caressed, danced and stumbled, an unceasing torrent of lustful vibrations buoying us along until we found ourselves naked, sprawled across the double bed.

I didn't know what to do first. My mouth was on fire with the long complex kiss we held, my hands filled with Sandy's fullness, holding one firm conical breast, pressing it against her chest, tweaking the nipple into erection, while running my other hand over her twisting buttocks, stroking her high curved ass, running my fingers into the spreading crack. Our cunts were pressed against each other, and we pumped our hips furiously, straining for contact, my clit pounding against her pubic bone, my cunt lips tickled by her hair.

We rolled over and over, legs thrashing, tits squashed into one another's breasts, our mouths seeking voraciously to devour the entirety of the other. There was a sudden shift in rhythm, and without a word we began to revolve around one another's bellies, like two hands on a clock, our tongues parting unwillingly but continuing their agitated licking, now over shoulders, arms, tits, thighs, and finally, to the desired target.

With a groan I flung my face into Sandy's crotch, drinking in the deep smell of her juicy cunt, feeling her hair scratch my cheek. Her legs parted and her pussy lay revealed, black-rimmed and wrinkled outer lips, opening to coral curves within, and ending in a deep pink serrated bud: the hole of her hole. I curved my fingers around the edges of her twat, and stared in fascination as it parted. I was almost dizzy from the rich pungent aroma of cunt, and my mouth watered in anticipation of the feast it was about to enjoy.

I had not realized how alluring and mysterious a cunt was until then. Beneath it, the lower curves of her asscheeks provided the frame, while the insides of her long muscled thighs gave support, like two pillars holding up a temple. Above, her sloping belly. And in the center, beneath its mat of furry hair, the soft gash itself.

"Unngh," I moaned, and brought my lips to the core of her cunt, pressing my mouth against the already moist pussy. My jaws trembling with weakness, I curled out my tongue, and almost swooned as the acrid juices covered it. I tasted, and decided that it was the single most fantastic thing ever to hit my taste buds, at once rich and subtle.

I could control myself no longer. I lunged into Sandy's cleft, sucking and licking and nibbling. I was buried in cunt and wanted to stay there forever, drinking from that eternal fountain. I remembered all the men who had gone wild between my legs, and at those times I was so taken with my own pleasure that it did not occur to me what theirs might be. Now, in retrospect, I received the vicarious pleasure from all the times I had been eaten, thinking what a wonderful thing it must be for someone to slurp-worship my twat.

The thought was obviously spurred by what Sandy was doing at precisely that moment. As I burrowed deeper between her thighs, fucking my tongue as deeply as I could into her juicy hole, pressing my lips tightly against its lips and sucking all the juices from its folds, she was doing exactly the same with me. I was so involved in the feelings coursing through my mouth that I did not at first notice the sensations in my cunt.

But now they started to reach me. Sandy had taken my clit between her teeth and was grinding it gently. This brought me so close to the edge between pleasure and pain that I shook with tension. My thighs were clamped tightly about her head, and my ass quaked as orgasmic tremors shot through me. The jolts of electricity went up my spine and into my brain and out my tongue!

The esoteric meaning of the sixty-nine position dawned on me: this was the snake swallowing its own tail, the current of cosmic unity. It wasn't me doing her or her doing me, but a single unified action in which there was no distinction between individuals. It wasn't to be my orgasm or her orgasm, but a single spasm in which we both felt the same surging conclusion. This meant there could be no manipulation, no trepidation. We would both have to surrender to the flow and let it decide when and where we surfaced.

I let all my thoughts go and become one with Sandy's body, my mouth glued to her cunt, giving it intimate messages with lips and tongue, breathing into it, kissing it, speaking to it, while my cunt opened to her mouth, sucking in her tongue, tingling to her teeth, spending juices for her throat. My breasts were crushed against her thighs and hers against mine, while my hands fluttered again and again over the marvel of her perfectly shaped ass. I parted the cheeks and traced one finger down the crack to the small anal opening. It was already slick from the secretions and saliva that had trickled down between her thighs. The whole space from cunt to asshole was a swamp of woman-smells, a pool of thick sticky fluid.

My finger went in easily, and her tight asshole clutched it firmly. I pushed harder and soon was buried up to the third knuckle of my middle finger, and was wiggling it around, and thrusting it in and out, teasing her asshole as I lapped her pussy with broad strokes. Her finger went into my ass, and her hands pushed my cheeks inward, crushing me to her face.

Locked like that, we began to ride. With mounting pelvic thrusts and raunchy slurping sounds, we ate one another's pussies like thirsty women drinking water. I got lost in the welter of sound and motion and growing excitement. We were both cumming, that was clear, and there was no doubt but that we would cum together. Our long friendship, the shimmering night, and our impassioned fervor in the hotel room had worked us to a pitch of complete complementarity.

Our legs kicking and sliding across the sheets, our tits rubbed sore against one another's thighs, our fingers in each other's assholes, our cunts and mouths in utter communion, we skipped like a rock skimming across the water into a series of light staggering orgasms, exploding . . . sailing . . . exploding . . . sailing . . . exploding . . . sailing . . . eight, nine, ten, eleven times, until we finally subsided, and like a stone sinking in a pond, leaving a trail of overlapping concentric circles at each place we had touched, and deep ripples where we ultimately sank.

We lay a long time without moving, side by side, our mouths still fastened to one another's pussies, our hands still inside each other's assholes. I had become a total blank, a simple movement of breath, without sensation, without thought.

"This," I thought, "is peace."

And right upon my thinking it, Sandy stirred. She disengaged herself gently and rolled to the edge of the bed. She reached down to the floor, and I heard the clasps of her suitcase snap open. I didn't know what she was looking for, but her ass was so inviting I couldn't resist the temptation to do what I did next. Snaking over, I placed my mouth on the back of one of her thighs, biting firmly. Sandy gasped. I licked the bruised spot and worked my way higher, trailing inwards toward the black center where her thighs met. I glanced up and her buttocks loomed like vast hills. She spread her legs slightly and I could see between her thighs: the puckered anus, with the skin around it purple from arousal, and beneath that the gaping cunt, its crown of hair wet and straggly from pussy juices and my own saliva.

I licked the bottom of one of her succulent globes, and then dove over her rump and into the crack, my cheeks inside the spread of her cheeks. I slid out my tongue and touched her asshole lightly, causing her to squirm. I pushed forward, now bringing my lips against the tiny hole, kissing it passionately, loving its shape and taste and smell. She arched her hips and pushed back, grinding her ass into my face. I returned the pressure, hurting my mouth against the bottom of her ass crack. My tongue probed further and penetrated the arcane orifice, swirling into the hot musky canal. Sandy groaned and brought her hands back to part her cheeks further, giving me greater access to the bud at the center. I shot my tongue in as far as it would go, straining it at the root, and then pulled back, and pushed in again, fucking her asshole with my tongue. I twirled it again and drew all the way out, and then began licking the crack with long broad strokes, starting at her pussy and covering her asshole. I licked her like a dog until she was moaning steadily and audibly, and then I turned on my back and slid under her, pulling her on top of me so that she sat on my face.

Now she threw her full weight into me, and I lay back passively, my mouth open, my tongue extended, as she rubbed her bottom all over me, covering me with her cunt and asshole, grinding my head into the bed with her lust-induced rhythms. She worked more and more frantically until she was lost in another climb toward climax. I brought my hands between my legs and thrust four fingers into my cunt, plunging them in and out, sloshing into the wet center and rubbing my clit frantically. Sandy grabbed my hair and held my head in a fixed position as she rode my face, fucking my mouth with her cunt, and suddenly her motion became spasmodic and I knew that the Greater Force had overtaken her, and her gasps of climax filled my ears as her pussy juice filled my mouth, and within seconds afterwards I was kicking my legs in the air as I fingered myself into my own orgasm.

Sandy climbed off me and reached down to the floor by the side of the bed. When she straightened, she held a long, thick violet dildo in her hand, shaped like a cock. She leaned over and kissed me, but I could tell that she was just beginning to get warmed up sexually, and was ready to really swing out into something wild. Her eyes held a glint of humor laced with an erotic wickedness. I didn't know what she had in mind but I was ready to go wherever she wanted to take me.

"Do it," I whispered.

I thought she was going to use the dildo to fuck my cunt—which she later did—but at first she had another idea. She brought it against my lips and pressed it gently to me. At first the obscenity of taking that rubber phallus in my mouth repulsed me, but it was the very salaciousness of the act that propelled me forward. I opened my mouth and she slid the big cock inside. I ran my tongue over the tip, feeling the slick surface and tasting the unmistakable tang of rubber. It was beautifully sculpted, and even had a hole in the tip.

I ran my tongue over the hole, and Sandy pushed it more deeply inside of me. It slid down my tongue and nudged the back of my throat. It was bigger than any cock I had ever sucked and it filled my mouth completely.. I began to get off on the sensation of being stuffed by the lewd dildo and the image of myself lying naked with this immense artificial cock jamming my lips.

Still looking down at me with a glint in her eyes, Sandy knelt over my head, one knee at each of my ears, and lowered herself until the other end of the dildo was at the top of her cunt. She pressed down further until her weight was slightly pushing the cock into me. And then she rose a bit, lifting the rod with her so that its flaring tip was just past my teeth.

"Plug up the hole with your tongue," she instructed.

I suppose I knew what she was about to do, although I didn't articulate it to myself. I curled my tongue and pressed it against the hole in the tip of the cock. And then I heard the sound, the low hissing, and I saw her stomach contract, and realized that she was pissing into the tube.

I could taste it with the very tip of my tongue and could feel its heat through the rubber against my lips. She went on a long time, pissing into the hollow cock, until it seemed completely full.

"Now," she whispered, "it's all up to you. Take away your tongue and you can drink as much of my piss as you want. Do you want it? Do you want it?"

I moaned and I trembled and I closed my eyes. The cock seemed so huge and hot inside my mouth. My jaw felt it couldn't hold its tension any more. My tongue was tired. I was sinking into a dreamy lethargy in which I would not be able to examine what I was doing. I was putting my critical faculty to sleep and letting my basest instincts take over, that part of me which revelled in wide erotic surrender.

"Mmm," I whimpered, and let my tongue fall away.

Immediately, the hot salty liquid trickled into my mouth. It was tangy on my tongue and soon filled my cheeks. I couldn't breathe unless I swallowed, and to swallow was the final degradation. And that is what I was there for. So I gulped and Sandy's piss burned its way down to my stomach. I grasped the tube with my lips and sucked at it like an infant at a tit, licking the head of the wide rubber cock, sucking at the hole, sucking the salty urine into my mouth, and swallowing it greedily.

"That's it, baby," Sandy crooned. "Yessss," she hissed. "Drink it, drink it, drink my hot piss. Drink it, Julie, drink my piss."

And when I had drained the entire tube and lay there gasping, Sandy came over and pressed her open lips to mine and licked the whole inside of my mouth.

"Now I want yours," she said.

I put my arms around her back and sighed, "Oh Sandy, I want to do everything. *Everything.*"

"We will," she reassured me. "This is just the foreplay. We have five whole days to really get it on."

Then she eased me off the bed. "Let's go into the bathroom," she said. "I want to lie in the tub while you squat over me."

NINE

The week I spent with Sandy had a double effect. On the one hand it opened me even further erotically, for she brought me so far out and then peeled me so thoroughly, that when we returned to Seattle I was little more than a naked vibrating cunt. Any man or woman with eyes to see could have had me for the asking. But the experience also strengthened my growing dissatisfaction with impersonality in my sexual encounters. It's true that when our fling ended Sandy reverted to simple friendship, but during our days and nights in San Francisco, I wasn't just a body to her. I was the unique thing called Julie Ann DeWitt. And as we returned for the next game, I resolved that I would try to effect some kind of rapprochement with Tony, the man who had so roundly condemned me for my promiscuity.

That did come about, but not as I imagined, and only later, after the terrible party when the team won the final game of the season and assured itself of participation in the superbowl. I made it my business to run into Tony one afternoon and after some awkwardnesss we went out for coffee together. His manner was very reserved, even though I could read the flicker of desire in his eyes.

"Don't you fuck at all?" I asked him as we talked.

"I haven't for about eight months now," he said. "In fact, you're the first woman who has even vaguely interested me."

"But why?" I asked. "I mean, why such a long time, and why me?"

"I told you," he explained. "A thing is made precious by its rarity. If I were to fuck every woman who was ready to open her gap for me, my cock would fall off in no time at all. I don't want to be the anonymous stuffer, the hunk of meat that gets used to compensate for a woman's lack of inner identity. And why you? I frankly don't know. If I try to analyze it, it's hopelesss. All I know is that my instincts point me toward you."

"Well, why don't we do it?" I said.

"Because you haven't finished your trip yet. You've understood how empty all that dumb frenzied fucking is, but you have one level of hunger that still hasn't been satisfied. And until it is, you'll be edgy with any man you make it with. When I get my cock into that sweet slit of yours, I don't want to run into any barriers. Oh, I know there aren't any physical blocks. At this point you could probably fuck an elephant without discomfort. But I won't abide any emotional cheating, or intellectual shallowness. If I am to have you, I want the totality of you. What's the point in possessing a woman if one only gets part of the goods."

"Aren't you embarrassed to be talking about possession?" I probed.

"You mean because of the so-called liberation of women?" He laughed. I wanted to reach out and hold his hand. His smile pierced my heart. His eyes looked into my soul. I barely knew him. Yet he seemed to have penetrated my very depths. I wanted desperately to love him. But he kept his distance. "A woman is, of course, free," he went on. "And when she gives herself, that is a free choice. But having made that choice, she is then possessed by the man. He literally invades her body. He burrows into her belly. He plants his seed in her deepest channel. After they disengage, naturally, he no longer possesses her. They regain autonomy. And she is free to make her next choice. To accept him inside her again, or not. Or perhaps to take another man. Or a woman. And the man has his yes and his no. And while my body says yes to you, Julie, my mouth says no. I don't want you now because you aren't really free. You are still obsessed. And when that final demon has left you, I will take you in my arms."

"And then?" I asked.

"That's as far as we can know at this moment," he continued. "The chemistry that flows between us shall determine the shapes we assume."

I could have sat and talked with him for hours. Not only

because it was the first real conversation I'd had with a man in years, but simply to be sharing his vibration, drinking in his face, soaring on the sound of his voice.

But he stood up abruptly. "Well, I must leave now. I'm glad we got this chance to talk," he said.

"But can't we . . ." I began to protest.

He fixed me with a stern stare. "I think I've made myself very clear, haven't I?"

I nodded in acquiescence and he turned quickly and walked out of the cafeteria. Subsequently I tried to remain celibate, but that made me too nervous. Tony was right; he had seen what I had known since the beginning: that I was working out some karmic cycle and could not rest until I had seen the end of it. I was afraid that if I fucked anyone else again, Tony would be turned off, but then I realized that he already knew in detail everything I had been doing all year, so nothing I did now could shock him.

So it was that with a sense of randy resignation I re-entered my pattern of activities. Practice one day a week, a game on Sundays, and the rest of the time given over to one or another form of erotic gameplay. It went that way until the end of the season, when the gun went off signalling that Seattle had won the game and the division championship, that hell broke loose.

The terrific tension that had been building all year, the balance between surging toward final victory and staying calm enough to play each game as it came, finally burst after the gun that signalled the end of the season. The fans swarmed out of the stands and roamed over the field, shouting, screaming, lifting players onto their shoulders. Three men rushed at me, picked me up bodily, and threw me into the air. They were good-natured enough, but when I landed in their arms, more than one hand grabbed my ass and squeezed my tits. But such was the exuberance of the moment that I didn't mind, and in fact squirmed around a bit and let them enjoy their lusty feels. For more than an hour the stadium was a sea of sound and movement. The other cheerleaders and I finally managed to escape into the dugout, running the gauntlet through lines of men whose lust for victory had mingled with desire for our bodies.

If I had thought the dugout would be a refuge, I was soon disillusioned. The place was packed with players, drinking champagne and emptying bottles of the foaming brew over one another's heads. Reporters shouted questions and television cameras wormed their way through the wall of tightly packed flesh. I bumped into Jeff, and for the first time since our horrible breakup we smiled at one another, the team's triumph dissolving all residual tension. He caught me in his arms and crushed me to him, my tits pinched by the equipment he still wore under his jersey. His hands cupped my ass and his mouth covered mine. I returned his kiss heartily and pushed my pelvis into his crotch.

He finally released me and whispered, "See you later," before I was swept away, spun off by the tumultuous activity all around me. A hand caught my arm and I found myself looking up into the face of Roger Edwards, who had not said a word to me since I had refused to suck his dog's cock.

"How does it feel, Julie?" he shouted above the roar, "the sweet smell of success, eh?"

I was becoming so euphoric that I even had a kiss to spare for Roger, and as my mouth went on his, his tongue darted between my lips. At the same time he squeezed one of my tits, and then moved away quickly, leaving me gasping.

From time to time I caught a glimpse of Sandy and the other cheerleaders weaving in and out of the male giants who dominated the relatively small space. Some of the wives were there, including Laura and the other women I had "swung" with. I looked for Tony but couldn't see him anywhere. Every three minutes more champagne was poured into my glass. And the room soon became a dizzy whirl of overheated vibrations and flashing glances.

The mood was definitely orgiastic, although it never occurred to me that there could be any actual sexual activity in that space. When I thought about it at all, I imagined that I would wind up with a bunch of the men and a couple of women at someone's apartment, fucking until dawn. But more time passed than I knew, and without my being aware of it, the camera crew slipped out, along with reporters, and everyone else who did not belong in one way or another to the team. How it occurred

I will never understand, but a moment arrived in which I was the only woman left in the locker room. I had been drinking and flirting and kissing and dancing about, lost in the general uproar, and I guess Sandy and the other cheerleaders made their own connections and were whisked away to different pads.

My first clue as to what was happening came when I glanced toward the opening of the dugout and saw that the doors had been closed. The radio was still blasting out a succession of harsh rock songs, and many of the men were still shouting and horsing around. But the crowd had definitely thinned, and a subtle change in the ambience crept over the space. More of the players were following me with their eyes and my ebullience lost some of its edge as I realized that I stood in the center of the locker room, dressed in my tight shirt and very brief skirt, while more than forty men gradually stopped their random celebrating and began to focus on me.

They ranged from fully dressed, complete with shoulder pads and uniform, to wearing nothing but jock straps. The place smelled of booze and raw animal sweat. They were still covered with dirt from the field and they resembled nothing so much as a small army that had just spent a month in the trenches. And I appeared as the first woman they were setting their eyes on.

Nervously, I began to back toward my dressing room, but as I moved sideways I bumped into Rick Folsom, the center. I looked up at him and saw the unmistakable gleam in his eyes.

"Where you going, Julie?" he said, leering.

"Uh, just going to get dressed," I said in a low voice.

"Got to get undressed first, don't you?" he taunted.

"Well, yes," I mumbled," I was intending . . ."

But I didn't get a chance to finish the sentence. "The least we can do is help you get undressed," he said in a loud voice. And then pitching his voice so that it covered the whole room, he added, "The least we can do is help Julie undress, can't we boys? In appreciation for everything she's done for us this season."

"Please," I said. The moment could have been overwhelmingly erotic, but as they massed and moved toward me, the only sensation I could feel was fear. There were at least forty of them, and they weren't in a gentle mood.

"Please what?" John Carrol said as he stepped toward me. He was one of the men I had fucked during the year, and he had found his special form of enjoyment in hearing me beg for his cock. I knew that he was reminding me of that.

"This can't be happening," I thought, and tried to picture what might come to rescue me. But I knew that the stands were long since empty, and that no one would be coming through those locked doors.

Rick slipped his hand under my shirt from behind and began to hoist it above my shoulders. I tried to push it down, but two men sprang forward to help him. In an instant seven or eight of them were holding me, grabbing me by the ankles and wrists and waist. I kicked and twisted, but it was of absolutely no use. Ineluctably, they got what they wanted, and I moaned as my shirt was ripped from my body, exposing my bare tits to their eyes. Quickly, my skirt was unhooked and my panties yanked off, and then I was naked, my cunt visible and accessible to the entire mob of lust-crazed football players.

As a sage cynic once observed, part of being raped is getting fucked, and while I dreaded what was being done to me, I can't deny that I responded to the intense massive erotic charge that was being poured into my pussy. Their eyes seemed to smolder and their faces were distorted into masks of sensual cunning. All their innate brutality rose to the surface, and I was aware that if they went berserk they could easily rip off one of my limbs without noticing.

I decided to follow my father's advice, which was to make the best of any situation. Resistance would breed violence and faced with more than eighty times my body weight in the form of a gang of huge fierce men, I realized that my best hope lay in surrender.

So I stopped struggling and let my head fall back and relaxed my stomach. I gave them the Julie that existed in their imaginations, the slut whose label was indelibly marked across the top of her pubic hair. I didn't know if my body could take the punishment it would receive, but I had no choice.

"That's better," one of the men said. "You know you want it."

"Come on," another voice shouted. "Let's fuck her."

One of the cots from the cheerleaders' dressing room was brought out and I was tossed on it. I landed with legs apart, my tits flopping wildly. Not an instant passed before they were all over me. I felt like the victim of an automobile accident lying in the street while a crowd milled around to rubberneck at my body. Only they weren't content with watching.

Hard rough hands gripped my tits, pummeling the soft flesh and pinching the tender nipples. Fingers pulled at my cunt lips and poked insolently into my ass crack. A cock thrust itself between my lips and began fucking my face rapidly. Another cock slammed into my twat and started ramming in and out with pounding strokes. From the sheer impact of all that flesh, my cunt got wet and lubricated the stiff pole that ravaged it.

"Oh yeah," hissed the man fucking me. "She's getting wet. She's getting hot."

The excitement must have been too much for him for he came almost at once, and I could feel his cum splashing inside me. Another took his place immediately. And once more my pussy yawned to take a savage prick inside itself. The man above me came in my mouth, forcing his cock into my throat so that it spurted down the tube and into my belly. I had to swallow to keep from choking. And again, no sooner had he finished than another took his place, sliding his thick cock on my slippery tongue.

Some were sucking my tits, biting the nipples, causing more pain than pleasure. I groaned but the sound was stifled by the pole of meat stuffing my face. Calloused fingers dug into my ass as a third man started to fuck me, the second having already deposited his sperm in my cunt. My cheeks were pulled apart and a finger rudely thrust into the asshole.

"I want to fuck her butt," a rough voice said. "Hurry up and finish so I can have her ass."

Almost more than the specific actions of the men who were fucking and feeling me, I could feel the urgency of the others, the almost two score who pushed in from behind, watching with avid looks as I was split apart, my legs held high in the air. I could feel their eyes ravishing my bruised tits, lapping at my pussy, boring into my ass, hungering after my mouth.

"Tits and ass and mouth and cunt," I sang to myself as they humped me into oblivion.

I was rudely shocked out of my inner reverie by a hard slap across the face. "Come on, you bitch," someone rasped. "Stop playing dead. Start pumping that pussy."

I didn't move and I was slapped again, hard enough to bring tears to my eyes, and then the hand hit me in a regular rhythm, back and forth, until I was sobbing.

"Hey, man," someone said, "Let's keep it friendly."

"Shut your hole," the first man said, "I want to see this cunt get hot."

I couldn't take any more of the beating so I began to pump my pelvis back and forth, and to roll my hips around on the cot. The movement sparked something in me, and I felt the first rushes of genital pleasure as the fourth man mounted me and started his ride. They were all cumming quickly, probably due to the white-heat intensity of excitement in the room. For so many men to gang-bang a pretty young girl must have roused all their archetypal modalities of male sexuality.

After a while I lost count of numbers and lost track of time. I don't know how many entered me, or what hour it was. It occurred to me that when they finished, those who had gone first would be ready for seconds. My mouth was a pool of semen. It caked on my gums and lodged under my tongue and stuck to the roof of my mouth and splashed up my nose. Men came in my mouth and on my lips and all over my face. My tits were a single shriek of agony as they were pummeled and slapped and pinched and mauled by immense hands.

A dozen times I was turned over, sometimes to be fucked from behind, but more often to have my asshole split and reamed. I cried out at first but by the third man my anus was as loose as my pussy, and they fucked me there with total ease. I was stood up and bent over, rolled to my side, made to kneel, and screwed from every conceivable angle.

As the thing hit full stride, I could not remain passive even if I had wanted to. So much energy, so much power, so much consistent and terrible penetration in all my openings had weakened a final wall of reserve, probably the spot Tony had mentioned. And I knew that this was the moment when I would have to break through once and for all, to irrevocably take my fill of sexual excitement so that it would no longer drive me.

I started to move with the men fucking me, humping my cunt into the succession of cocks that entered me, sucking on the pricks that slid into my mouth and tonguing them avidly. When I was fucked in the ass, I bucked my hips back and slammed my buttocks into the thighs of whichever man was behind me, clamping my muscles tight and draining his cock dry.

In short, I let myself go wild. I became a mindless, moaning, gurgling spasm of sexual frenzy. I flailed about, shaking my ass violently, licking my tongue up to lap whatever was placed there, cock or asshole or foot. I grabbed cocks with my hand and jerked them back and forth with total abandon, giving all the handjobs I had never given as a teenager, forgiving myself for all the boys I had left hanging after a night of heavy petting.

The sounds that came from my throat were something that no animal could ever make; the howls of a human who had rescended to a level below beasts. I didn't care anymore, didn't care if I died. This was the logical conclusion of my decision to follow Jeff, and I would live it to its fullest. I begged, I bleated, I crawled. And still they came, their livid cocks piercing me again and again, until I was little more than a twitching rag doll, fluttering aimlessly to each intrusion.

But after a while, I noticed a change in the tempo, and realized that there weren't as many men as there had been. I heard showers running in the distance and figured that some were washing and dressing and leaving. I was as one drugged, and my thoughts were sparse and foggy. One more man came in my mouth, perhaps the thirtieth load of sperm that had exploded on my tongue, and the next cock that went into me was limp. I started to suck it and a thick stream of hot piss shot down my throat. I spluttered and coughed but he held my head to his crotch until he had emptied himself entirely.

One of the men had taken off his belt and was whacking me steadily across the ass.

"What do you want?" I screamed. "Do it, take it, do whatever you want. Kill me, fuck me, kill me, fuck me." My voice was a hoarse wail that echoed off the metal lockers.

And still the number of men decreased. One muttered, "Jesus, this is really sick," his voice tinged with disgust as he went.

I thrashed about howling for more. I had drained a platoon and was now hitting my own stride. I had leaped over the hurdle of my own fear and was soaring into free space. I spread my cunt with my hands and hurled my challenge. "Come on! Aren't there any more? I thought you were men."

Another man mounted me, his throbbing cock plunging deep into my pussy, hitting bottom causing me to bend in two. He put his arms behind my knees and pushed my thighs to my chest, exposing my ass and cunt in their most vulnerable position. He rammed into me again and again, sending bolts of pain into my belly as the friction from his rod had my cunt swarming with flashes of heat. Although my cunt was wet, I was experiencing a rather dry eroticism. Sensations were there, and movement was there, and pleasure was there, and even climaxes occurred, but every aspect remained separate from every other. I was in a state in which extreme clarity and heavy grogginess co-existed with equal impact.

Finally, he came inside me, and released my legs. I lay back on the cot waiting for the next onslaught, but nothing happened. I opened my eyes and saw that the dugout was almost empty. Two men were standing by their lockers and putting on their clothes, and only one person remained over me: Brock Reynolds, one of the half-backs and the only man I had spurned of all those who had made a pass at me. There was something so evil about him, so inhumanly degraded, that even at the height of my debauchery I would not put myself in his hands, Sandy had warned me against him saying, "He's not just a pervert, baby, but a real sadist. The kind that will go after you with a razor blade." And now I was alone with him, lying naked and spent under his raging eyes. I tried to call out to one of the other players, but he put his hand over my mouth and forced me to lie still. I didn't even have the strength to try to push his hand away.

He waited until the others left, one of them calling out, "One last piece, eh Brock?" And Brock called back in a voice that chilled my spine, "Yeah, *one last piece.*"

When the dugout was totally empty he took his hand away and stared down at me. His eyes went over my face, caked with sperm, over my tits, showing black-and-blue marks, over the tattoo on my belly, and finally to my raw and ragged cunt. He smiled, his lips like pencil lines.

"Well, what are you waiting for," I said, "why don't you fuck me and get it over with?" I hoped my voice carried the ring of bravado I wanted to hide behind.

"Fuck you?" he said. "Do you think I'd put my nice clean cock in that stinking hole of yours? Not a chance. But I'm going to give you something better. Something that's going to make you forget every cock you've ever had."

It was then that I looked down at his hands. He was holding a football. For a second I didn't make the connection, but when I realized what he intended, I started to scream in sheer raging terror. But he merely reached across and slammed the back of his hand across my mouth, sending stars through my brain and almost knocking me unconscious.

"Not here," he said, and reached down, slipped one arm under my waist, and tossed me easily over his shoulder. I moaned and felt blood trickling from the corner of my mouth. He walked slowly and steadily to the end of the dugout, bent down to pick up some rope, kicked the doors open, and stepped out onto the field.

The stadium was completely empty and totally silent. The night air held a bitter chill, and the stars burned brightly in the black sky. The park was without light, and we moved like ghosts over the hard ground, gliding past the chalk lines which marked the five-yard intervals. I wondered if there was anything I could do, but at once understood that it was hopeless. Not only because I was alone and in his power, but because I was reaching the final act, the ultimate destination of the road I had chosen when I left school.

Brock stopped at the goalposts and tossed me onto the cold earth. I lay in a twisted heap at his feet, while he towered over me, his uniform still on, the padding making him seem grotesque and enormous.

"You rotten cunts," he said. "Always strutting your asses around, driving me crazy with your pussies, pushing your tits under our eyes. You're all the same. And when you get what you want, you drain a man of his strength, you suck the sperm out of him and leave him weak. And you're never satisfied. You'll drag one man down and then move on to the next." He looked down, and then deliberately spit on me, the glob landing between my breasts. "Forty men tonight," he went on in a harsh throbbing voice. I could hear a lifetime's pent-up emotion in his chest and realized that I was not only a specific target, a woman who had rejected him, but a symbol for all the women he had known, probably beginning with his mother. "And after all that fucking, all we have to show for it is soft dicks. While you're all bloated with our cum. Vampire. Cocksucker." He spat on me again and kicked my ass, his rubber cleats cutting the skin.

I realized that this was the personification of my demon, my counterpart. The same lust that had driven me to such excesses was taking him to the ultimate conclusion of his own insanity, and the awareness filled me with a strange calm that stilled my fear.

He tied a length of rope to each of my wrists and then secured the end of each to one of the vertical bars of the goalpost, so that I lay on my back on the ground, my arms pulled wide. He returned and stood in front of me. His eyes were narrow slits of hate, and in a flash I understood that this was the same look, modified to one degree or another, I had seen in the eyes of every man who had ever fucked me. This was the final curtain I needed to part, to make the absolute distinction between those who would use me and those who would love me. It was a simple lesson, but earned with terrible struggle, and one which I was not sure I would survive.

For already Brock was kneeling on the turf, placing the football between my legs.

"Spread," he commanded.

I parted my legs very wide, and lay there, awaiting what my destiny had prepared for me.

He placed the tip of the football at the opening of my cunt,
and began to press it in slowly. At first I yielded easily; my cunt
was extremely slack from all that fucking. But past a certain
point, it seemed to have reached its mark of maximum entry.
Brock pulled my pussy lips apart with his fingers, stretching
them over the smooth leather. And then he pushed some more.
The ball sank in another inch, and now I was convinced it could
go no further.

He continued his pressure and I felt my cunt spread still more.
I lifted my head and looked down. It was only a fourth of the
way in. And already I felt as though I were bursting my seams.

"It's like childbirth," I told myself. "Don't panic. A baby is
just as big when it comes out. The cunt can stretch that far. Don't
tense or he'll tear you in half."

His face was a single point of concentration, his eyes riveted
on the spot where my cunt grasped the ball. He put his shoulders
behind the next push, and jammed the spheroid yet another
inch into me. I felt as though I were being pried apart. My pussy
ached, and still he drove forward. The ball oozed in yet another
fraction of an inch. The image of a boa swallowing a large pig
went through my mind, and I giddily thought that somehow I
would have to unhinge the joints of my mouth to take it in. But
my mouth was the snake's mouth, and the snake's mouth was my
cunt. I was becoming delirious with the strain.

Brock spun the ball around, trying to screw it inside me, but
that did nothing but burn the insides of my cunt lips.

"Brock," I pleaded, "Don't."

It was as though he were deaf. With a fanatic single-mindedness
he thrust the ball harder into my snatch. My legs could stretch
no more. I began to bleat in anguish.

"Stop that noise!" he screamed. "I can't stand it, stop that
noise. Stop doing that, leave her alone, leave my sister alone."
His voice rang out in the huge empty arena, and I knew that
he had flipped out. Some excruciating scene from his past had
superimposed itself on the reality, and he was no longer in touch
with even a shadow of the actuality in front of him.

He looked down at me and in his eyes I saw nothing but the
distorted flame of sheer madness.

"You *enjoyed* it," he accused. "You *wanted* him to do that to you."

And with that he lifted his right foot far behind him.

"Wait," I screamed, "I'm not your sister."

But he was beyond hearing, and he swung his leg in a long driving arc, smashing his foot into the exposed tip of the ball, propelling it with explosive force deep between my thighs.

A sheet of black pain flooded my entire body. My breath left me, and I jerked like a puppet suddenly yanked by its strings. I soared backwards, as far as the ropes tied to my wrists would allow, lilted physically from the ground by the power of his kick.

I landed on my back, hitting the earth heavily. I could not keep my eyes open and something kept tugging at my brain, pulling it into unconsciousness. Brock leapt up and down, shouting "Touchdown, touchdown," in a crazed voice.

And finally I passed out, tied to the goalposts, naked on the playing field, caked with dried sperm, the word *slut* tattooed on my belly, and an entire football, a thick, long spheroid of taut leather, lodged completely inside my cunt.

TEN

I awoke to the sound of temple bells and Buddhist chanting. I opened my eyes and found myself lying on a very low bed in a large cheerful room. One entire wall was glass and opened onto a vista of distant mountains. It was a clear blue day and the sun seemed to be directly overhead.

"It must be about noon," I thought.

I tried to move and found that my body was a vast complex of aches. Easing myself slowly, I slid another pillow under my head so I could half sit up. I lifted the sheet covering me and looked down on my body. Black-and-blue marks dotted the skin. My breasts especially seemed a mass of bruises, and when I brushed a finger over my nipples I shuddered with the memory of pain. I could almost see the thumb prints embedded in the pink tips.

From the next room the deep rumble of a single monotonous chant rose and fell, interspersed with the clacking of beads and the ringing of a small bell. I could smell the faint aroma of incense.

"Where the devil am I now?" I thought.

I slid my hand down and tentatively touched my pussy. It seemed intact. I slid one finger inside, and realized that it had been coated with a soothing balm. The membrane was extremely sore and tender, but the organ was resilient and firm. I realized that I had been bathed, dabbed with antiseptic ointments, and bandaged in several spots.

I took a deep breath and was surprised that despite everything else, basically I felt healthy and refreshed. I was warm and comfortable, and filled with that joyous sense of well-being that comes after a high fever has broken. I was clean, not only outside, but in my soul. I had been purged; I knew that as sharply as the reality of the strong light that poured in through the window.

I drifted off to sleep again, dozed for a few moments, and when I awoke again the sounds from the next room had stopped. I slid back a bit more to raise myself to a sitting position, deciding to wait to see what happened.

Within a few minutes, the door opened. I looked over and saw a tall thin man, dressed in a *yukata,* the informal kimono that Japanese wear around the house, walking toward me. He was carrying a tray holding two huge tumblers of freshly squeezed orange juice and two mugs of steaming coffee. The apparition was so startling that for a few seconds I didn't recognize who it was, but then his features suddenly snapped into place and I gasped with surprise.

"Tony," I breathed, "it's you."

"I trust you slept well," he said in an easy conversational tone as he knelt by the bed and placed the tray on the floor next to me.

"What are you doing here?" I exclaimed.

"Why, I live here!" he replied. And then with a playful smile, added, "And what, may I ask, are *you* doing here?"

"I don't know," I said, my eyes wide with wonder.

"Well, I do," he answered, "and as soon as you drink your juice I'll tell you."

He handed me a glass and I sipped the delicious chilled pulpy juice down, feeling its revitalizing power fill my body. I was amazed at how good I felt.

"I got an insane phone call from Brock sometime around midnight," he said. "He was shouting, 'I've killed her, I've killed her.' It took me ten minutes to sort out the story, but when he told me what had happened, I rushed over to the stadium and found you where he had left you. For a minute I was afraid you really were dead, but I realized that it would take more than a forty-man gangbang and a football kicked up your snatch to do you in."

His tone was teasing, and I wondered how he could be so lighthearted about such a terrible occurrence. I glanced over at him, a little embarrassed that he had seen me in such a state, but his eyes were steady and warm. It seemed that nothing could ruffle this man.

He picked up his cup and sipped at his coffee, staring into space for a long time. For the first time since I was a child, I could hear the quality of silence; not merely the absence of sound, but the vibrant vitality of the creative void itself. It was as though Tony had entered a profound meditative state, although there was nothing about his posture or facial set which indicated anything but simple reflectiveness and relaxation.

"This may seem odd to you, Julie," he said at last. "but I want you to see something." He went into a drawer of the low table next to the bed and pulled out a stack of photographs.

"You know, when I saw you there, it was something close to a mystical experience. You had reached the bottom of the pit of degradation and had become so grotesque that you transcended categories altogether and emerged as a creature of unearthly beauty. I took these because I knew that such a moment could never occur again."

He handed me the pile of photos and I leafed through them slowly. They were all Polaroid snapshots, taken with a flash, and all portrayed me, from a dozen different angles and from far away to extremely close up. He was right. Unconscious, twisted, dirtied, tied, naked, beaten, I presented a picture of such complete surrender that an eerie beauty was born. I saw myself as some kind of sacrifice, the slaughtered virgin on the altar of professional football, and even the white goalpost served to augment the image, rising ghostlike and symbolic over my shattered body.

The last photo was difficult to make out for an instant, and I studied it intently before seeing that it was a shot of my cunt, the tip of the football protruding obscenely from between the horribly stretched lips.

"What are these for?" I asked.

"For me to look at from time to time," he said. "And for nothing else or no one else. They have a meaning for me that I won't try to explain, even to you. But they provide the key I've been looking for ever since I met you, the understanding of why I am so powerfully drawn to you."

"Tony," I protested, "you mean that you found me in that brutalized state, maybe dying from internal hemorrhage, and instead of cutting me loose at once you took the time to snap all these photographs of me?"

"Well, I didn't take the pictures at once," he replied. "I had to go to my locker to pick up the camera." And with that he laughed, obviously enjoying some private joke.

"What's so funny?" I said, my voice rising.

"Oh, the obviousness of things," he replied. He took out the pack of cigarettes that was stuck in the sash around his waist, lit one, and commenced staring into space once more.

"Tony," I said, "what's happening?"

"I'm afraid I don't know," he told me, blowing out a cloud of smoke. "I'm not too much different from you. Some years ago I graduated from college, and joined the Marines. There I received an education that made me rethink everything I'd learned to date. I was stationed in Japan, and had the good fortune to meet a master of erotic arts. At the same time I was introduced to certain meditation techniques. When I got discharged, the job as trainer and coach presented itself to me. I had come to the conclusion that the healthiest—both physically and psychologically— way I could earn a living was to do something that involved the vigorous use of my body. I have no worldly ambitions as far as career is concerned; my real work is of a different nature altogether. And so I've been working for the Seattle team, and living my life, and doing a lot of travelling off-season. I'm really quite content."

"And how do I fit in?" I asked.

"That's curious," he said. "I've been aware for some time now that I need a mate, someone to complement me. Also, someone to make love with. And since I realized that whoever she was would be chosen for me by the same Force to which I have surrendered the rest of my life, I have been waiting for a sign. And as I told you, when I saw you, I knew that you were probably the one."

I shook my head in wonder and disbelief. He sounded so certain of himself, so confident, that I felt there had to be a flaw somewhere.

He must have read my thoughts for he went on, "I don't

expect you to understand all at once. In fact, I'm just learning about it myself, what it's like to live by faith. You have no idea how chagrined I was when I began to find out what you were up to. The orgies, the violent sex, the perversions. Again, I have nothing against any of that as an activity in itself, but that you were so indiscriminate had me doubting my intuition. And then I started to see that you were being prepared, you were being taken through a complete cycle of a certain kind of abandonment. That, in a word, you were being *trained,* by destiny, to exorcise all the residue of false sexuality that everyone in this society is heir to. And then I knew that I had only to wait, to have patience until you were clear, and came out the other side. And then we would be free to find one another."

"If that's a declaration of love or a proposal of marriage," I said, "it's the least unromantic one I've ever heard."

"You have no conception of true romance," he shot back, an edge to his voice. "You still think that romance is a feeling; you don't understand that it's a worldview, a sublime discipline, a path that very, very few can follow successfully, and one laid with more traps than the mind can imagine."

Despite the act that he was melting my resistance with every word, a resistance not to him but to the vision he was creating before my eyes, I tried to hold my ground, even though in my heart I was fiercely certain that he was speaking my deepest, most secret fantasies.

"Well, what happens now?" I asked, attempting to rise to sarcasm, "do I just fall into your arms or do you have a detailed blueprint which will tell me how to behave?"

He put out his cigarette, stood up, unwrapped the sash, and let his robe fall to the floor. He stood before me completely naked. And he was extraordinarily beautiful, with a body like a dancer's, slim, the muscles long and pliant instead of knotted tightly. He was covered with a very fine down, except for his chest where a thick patch of black hair erupted, and the triangle between his thighs, the mat of curly brown pubic hair. His cock was soft, and hung full and curved from his crotch. Even in that state it was thick and long, succulent, as though filled with juicy pulp. The crown flared out in violet grandeur, impassive and hooded. His eyes shone with a strange light, and for a moment I thought I was in the presence of a god.

"What you have seen up to now," he said in a measured tone, "has been merely the personality. Now you are looking at the body. And soon you will see the essence itself. And then you will know what to do."

He walked around to the other side of the wide mattress, sat down facing me, and folded his legs. His hands pressed down on his knees, palms toward the ground. He took a deep breath, and his gaze went inward. I don't know quite how to explain what took place, but it was as though he disappeared. He was there, and yet he wasn't.

I watched him for perhaps five minutes, my heart racing. And then he returned his gaze outward and pierced into the space behind my eyes with his glance.

"I can instruct you in techniques, and I will, slowly. But more important than that is the structure of our flow. The movement must begin with you; you must have the impulse, you must initiate. And I will serve as the unmoving point around which your dance takes place. I can be no more than the focus." He paused. "Do you understand?"

"You mean I'm the one who gets on top," I said.

Tony laughed, a deep, warm, reassuring sound. "Yes," he said, "although the position can vary. Later, we can lie side by side, in equality. And on rare occasions we can enter the animal mode, with me providing the thrust. But the central idea, and the one which will form the basis of all our erotic activity, will involve your being the one who decides the time of our union."

Something tugged at my brain. "Wait a minute," I said, "what if I don't want to get into anything with you? What if I put on my clothes and walk out and never see you again?"

"I do not own you, I do not hold you, I do not control you. I am the self-contained. Again, I tell you, the decision to come or go, to join or pull apart, is completely yours."

I sat up, throwing the sheet off me, disregarding the twinges of pain. A current of anger had begun to run through me. "You've got it all figured out, haven't you?" I said. "You've come to your conclusions and now you think you can get me to go along with your game plan."

Tony raised one hand, palm forward. It was a gesture that meant *stop,* but I recognized it as one appearing on Burmese statues of Buddha. "I have to keep reminding you," he told me, "that I desire nothing. I have revealed to you everything that I am. And now you must decide whether you are in accord with that or not. There's nothing personal in any of this."

"That's just the trouble," I exploded. "It's all so fucking impersonal. You act as though I were a figure on a diagram instead of a person."

"What you identify as person," he replied, "is just your separative ego. That's as relevant to your true identity as that sign across your belly."

His remark caught me up short, and in that moment of abrupt stillness, I realized that I had become quite aroused. It was not a specifically erotic feeling, for it had none of the sharp focus of lust. But my entire body surged with energy and my mind crackled with alertness. I found myself moving toward Tony without having had any conscious desire to do so.

"How is this different from any other trip?" I asked, slightly maddened by his imperturbability. "I mean, what you're telling me sounds very grand, but in effect it's just another offer from a man, isn't it?"

"Well, I'm a man and you're a woman," he said drily. "I suppose that that aspect of our interaction has to enter in at some level. And, of course, you're free to view things from any angle you desire. For myself, if I'm going to assume any viewpoint at all, I prefer it to be the loftiest possible."

He seemed unassailable and as I watched him I pondered the many aspects of the confrontation. Having behaved in a scrupulously gentlemanly manner, having spoken to me with only forceful honesty, having rescued me from the dangerous situation of the previous night, knowing all about my record of debauchery and overlooking it as lightly as he might a trivial bad habit, this man now sat naked before me and offered me a relationship in which our erotic life would be led solely by my impulses. And beyond all this, I would have absolute freedom to come or go as I pleased, whenever I wanted.

And at once I saw the subtle trap of his disclosures. For if I began to taste the heady froth of such a relationship, I would never be able to settle for anything less. And since it would be nearly impossible to find another man who operated consistently on that level, I would find myself bound to Tony.

"But this all implies marriage," I said.

"I'd rather call it mating," he replied. "The connotations of the other word are too misleading."

"And how would we live?" I went on. "Where? What kind of life style? Would you expect me to chant with you and become a Buddhist or whatever the hell you are?"

Before the words left his mouth, I knew what he would say. "I expect nothing," he told me.

Almost like a commando attempting a last-ditch effort to find a chink in an enemy's defenses, I went for his cock. I had climbed to such a pitch of generalized excitement that I needed to give the energy some form, and as a cloud of electrons will be polarized and release their charge in a single sizzling bolt of lightning splitting the sky and striking whatever object is unfortunate enough to rise sufficiently above the ground to attract the jagged thunderbolt, so the electricity in and around my body gathered at the base of my spine, rose up the s-curved column, and shot out of my tongue. I fell forward very slowly and my head dropped into his lap where his turgid cock met my already sucking lips.

"Now we'll see just how cool he is," I thought as I curled my tongue under his prick and took it into my mouth.

For a few minutes I tried every cocksucking trick I knew. Licking, nibbling, sliding the shaft down to the base of my throat, biting the tip gently. I rolled around on the bed as though groveling before him, giving him full view of my ass. I rubbed my tits against the sheets, stoking the fires of my own desire. I held the base of his cock with my hands and jerked it back and forth, stuffing him inside me.

Tony got hard very slowly. His cock came to life like a sleeping man gradually waking into consciousness. It was as calm as he was, and I knew that he was allowing the pleasure I gave him to seep into his skin. There was no grabbing, no haste. no urgency on his part. All that came from me. Which, I recalled, is how he had said it ought to be.

While I tried to resent finding myself in the position I had fought against, I could not deny that I experienced a dimension of erotic enjoyment I had not known before. I felt, amidst my growing arousal, a sense of vast space, of endless time. It was as though what was happening was not just a limited act, with a beginning, middle, and end, but an ongoing process, a general movement which was proceeding eternally and of which we were merely the momentary symbols.

I lost myself in my reflections as I let my body do its ritual, and before I was conscious of its occurrence, Tony's large, beautifully sculpted cock was stiff and throbbing in my mouth.

I feasted on its length and shape, treating my tongue to the textural smoothness of the flaring crown. I buried my face in his crotch, letting the phallus slide deep into my throat. I licked its veined underbelly, and covered its taut skin with glistening saliva. Unhindered, appreciated, I lavished love upon the rigid principle of creation.

I pulled back and looked up into Tony's face. His eyes were lidded, seeing me but not staring. His gaze was as impassive as if he were watching a sunset, and filled with as much of a sense of wonder. His body was still. I ran my hands up his chest and was barely able to feel his heartbeat There was not a whisper of urgency in the coursing of his blood.

I slid up his torso, flowing the movement of my arms. My hands went around his neck, my legs curled behind his buttocks. And with a small easy movement, I covered his cock with my moist and tingling cunt.

As he slid into me, as I lowered myself onto him, a low sigh escaped my lips. He filled me totally, perfectly. The inside of my cunt was sore, but all my stiffness and pain faded to the background. I leaned my head against his chest, my breasts pressing into his ribcage, and tightened the clasp of my legs and arms. I embraced him totally, and opened deep inside myself as he penetrated into my core.

We sat like that for a very long time, not moving, until our breaths became as gentle as those of a sleeping infant. More than any superficially sexual sensation, I felt a deep and abiding completion, a joining which held intimations of a real union. Everything else—thoughts, emotions, the structures of mundane existence—melted and ran off my soul like ice yielding to the mid-day sun. I entered a state of awareness which soared beyond all words, beyond all meaning, a gentle undifferentiated bliss which in truth had nothing to do with my much-vaunted individuality.

To speak would have been blasphemous, and so I remained silent.

Then, something stirred. I can't even give it a name or a reason. Simply, suddenly, there was movement. It manifested in my body, but was not only physical. I neither wanted nor did not want to move; the impulse was an imperative from a source far deeper than I could conceptualize. At first slowly, and then with mounting rapidity, I began my dance. My arms began a pattern in the air, a serpentine slithering through space. My shoulders rotated, and my chest swung back and forth, the right and left sides in rhythmic alternation, causing my breasts to sway. My hips rolled, forming figure-eights along the dorsal plane, circles along the lateral. With that, my buttocks churned across his thighs. And all of this centering finally in my cunt, which had become a turbulent sea of incredibly complex gyrations, swarming over the cock which pierced it like a hundred waves of ants sweeping over an immense log on the forest floor.

The movement found its necessary expression, and once established, began to increase in range and tempo. I started to spin into a state of transcendent awareness, losing myself like a dervish in the dance. I climbed higher and higher as the spirit of exhilaration seized me in its soaring spiral. Shivers shot through my flesh, my nipples felt like burning coals, my ass sang in an ecstasy of abandon, and my cunt grew dizzy with delight, rejoicing in its heat and wetness and scintillating sensation and, above all, in its utterly unique and totally detached intelligence. It felt itself at last as the complement and complete equal to the organ which had usurped supremacy so early in life and assumed control of the direction of my being. The cunt finally arrived at the understanding that it was its own brain.

A roaring swept through me, an effusive unfolding; my body flew into a vast consuming convulsion and I thrilled throughout every fiber with the overwhelming orgasm. The climax went on for minutes, and subsided slowly, leaving me pumping my pelvis spasmodically into Tony's cock.

Once again we became quiet, and I slid back into the silence, the unity, the state of undifferentiated awareness. I held him loosely, simply feeling him, his strength, his solidity, his unshakable centeredness. And when I had lost all sense of being separate, when there was no longer an "I" in my consciousness, the movement began again, and again swept me through the many stages of the dance, until I soared into orgasm, a climax which did not have the abrasive quality of an explosion but came rather as the rapid fluttering of wings seen just before a seagull lands upon the water.

The cycle repeated itself countless times, and although the physical manifestation was almost the same in each instance, the tone of each phrase uncovered a new modality, pointed to a different dimension, a deeper aspect. It was obvious that the process was open-ended and infinite. I don't know how long we went on. I didn't become tired, for it seemed that no energy was lost. Instead it passed back and forth between us, with each passage providing another purification of the erotic vibration, until the act was a single sustained hum.

There came a point at which I suddenly knew that we had finished. Tony said nothing, remaining still and silent as he had throughout, although I never for an instant doubted his total and intense participation. It was, again, a signal from some source I could not identify which, as it were, tapped me on the shoulder and suggested that I bring the movement to an end. I lifted my face, kissed Tony on the lips, and gently raised my body, sliding my cunt off his rigid cock.

We sat facing one another for a long time, his cock slowly sinking back into its lax downward curve, and my body's functions returning to their normal moderate speed. The veil which had surrounded us parted slowly, and mundane reality re-asserted its mood. I stretched, and realized I was ravenously hungry.

It was only then, as I regained a sense of my usual level of awareness, did I get a sense of just how far out I had been.

"Tony," I said, "that was . . ." I didn't have the words.

"Yes," he said. "I've never experienced it so totally and for such duration. But it bears out the textual descriptions with amazing accuracy."

I was dumbfounded to hear the man with whom I had shared such an extraordinary afternoon talk as though we had been demonstrating some proposition of theoretical physics. "Textual descriptions!" I shouted, returning to my ordinary level of emotional reality with a sharp bounce, "were you fucking me or a book?"

"To be precise," he said in his calm voice, "you were doing the fucking. I merely provided the stage upon which the dance could take place. In addition, it must have occurred even to your obstinately contrary mind that what has been occurring for the past five hours does not fit into any of the categories of personality."

"Five hours!" I said. I turned and looked out the window. It was dark outside. "Have we been fucking for five hours?" I asked. "No wonder I'm so hungry." A spurt of sentimentality gushed through me and I batted my eyelashes coyly and said, "It was wonderful, Tony."

"Good God," he said, uncoiling his legs and rolling off the bed. He stood up and bent over to massage his thighs and knees. He peered up at me, smiled warmly, and went on, "Just my luck to find my Shakti and have her turn out to be a Betty Boop devotee."

He rose to his full height, and held out his arms. I rose off the bed and went to embrace him. He held me tightly, his arms pulling me toward his hard chest.

"Ooh," I sighed, "I was beginning to think you didn't have any feeling at all."

He stepped back, held me at arms' length, and let his gaze roam over my face. "Feelings are just things we have, like noses and fingers and ideas. We can enjoy them and express them, but they can never, in themselves, be the cause of anything lasting. It's not that I don't have feelings, but that I don't give them any special importance."

"Not even love?" I asked.

"Love is the purest form of energy available to a human being. What we did on that bed was an inkling of that truth. In fact, sex is itself a meditation on love, no more, no less. Love is the supreme manifestation of the Force which sustains all the forms of creation. It is, and does not take an object. You and I can enter the field of love together, but it is misleading for me to say, 'I love you'. I may love, and you may love, and if we merge our fields of energy, then we love together. The love which attaches to a specific person is only a shadow, an example, of the universal love of which everything is but a symbol."

My eyes were sparkling and my heart was full, and yet my mind resisted. "I can agree with all that as an idea," I said, "but it has no meaning unless I can feel it." I put one hand between my breasts. "Here," I added.

"My idea, and your feeling, and our bodies. This is the triangle which lies at the core of creation. The greatest mistake a man can make is to insist that a woman think as he does; the greatest mistake a woman can make is to insist that a man feel as she does; the greatest mistake a man and woman can make together is forget that each needs the other's body to complete the circuit of energy in which bliss is found."

He dropped his arms and stepped back. "Are you as hungry as I am?" he asked, abruptly changing tone.

We went into the kitchen and prepared a very late breakfast of eggs and home fries and toast and fruit. I found myself moving about the room as though I had lived in the apartment a long time.

"What do you think—excuse me, feel—about moving in with me?"

"I don't know," I told him, pouring hot water over the coffee grinds. "It sounds silly to say after what we've been through, but I barely know you."

I realized that I had matured quite a bit since impetuously taking Jeff up on the same offer.

"I need to think about it," I added, "but in my heart I want to say yes."

"There's no rush to decide," he said.

We ate slowly, and in silence. At one point, one of the hundreds of questions that had been racing through my mind came to my lips, and without considering, I asked, "Did you cum, Tony?"

He laughed, the same open expression of simple pleasure, and again, it seemed to point to a joke which was utterly private to him alone.

"I didn't ejaculate, if that's what you mean."

"But aren't you frustrated?"

"Not in the least."

"I don't understand," I said, for perhaps the tenth time that day.

"I'll give you a couple of books to read," he told me. "It's too tedious to explain without your having some rudimentary knowledge of the concepts I'm involved with."

I wanted to press him further, but he stood up. "There's a program on at seven I don't want to miss," he said.

"Television?" I asked.

"It's another form of meditation," he said.

I suppose my face must have registered annoyance, for he added, "Please don't have any preconceptions about me, Julie. I don't want to perform for you, nor explain overmuch. Learn about me as I am."

"But it seems So odd. After what we shared today and all your talk of exalted states, how can you do something so . . . so *bourgeois?*"

"I'm very bourgeois," he said. "I had a very conventional middle-class upbringing, a standard education, and I work at a rather routine job. I'm just an average man. Enlightenment does not stand outside history, and spirituality is nothing more than accepting one's true nature, in all its sublime *and* banal manifestations. Despite the fact that I am in touch with a deeper reality, in the way I live my life I am very, very ordinary."

"And what shall I do while you're watching the tube?" I asked, sounding peevish and not really liking myself for it.

"I don't know," he said. "Do the dishes, maybe, or come and watch with me, or . . . whatever you like."

"Or maybe I'll return to my place," I flung at him.

"Please don't threaten me," he replied softly. "I won't fight with you. I have no desire to dominate or be dominated. I'm bored by that kind of challenge. Of course, as I've had to remind you a number of times, you are absolutely and unconditionally free. So you can do what you wish. But if you remain at the level of infantile intimidation, what you get in return won't be very interesting."

"That's very high-sounding," I said. "But the fact remains that you want to have your cake and eat it too. You want to stay wrapped up in your world of private fantasy—excuse me, *vision*—and not have me disturb you at all, and yet you want me to climb aboard your cock and fuck you silly. Pardon my crude language, but that's the bald truth of it, isn't it? You're just like any other man. You want your piece of ass when you want it, and otherwise you don't want to be bothered."

"You're merely reformulating, in your refreshingly saucy language, the basic contradiction which defines male and female. It is my mind and your feeling locked in tension with each other. And it is only in our bodies that that duality can be resolved. I'm no more happy with that polarity than you are; but there it is, it's one of the givens of creation, and all we can do is deal with it intelligently."

"Which means your way," I shot out.

"It's the way I've chosen, but it's been in existence for at least five thousand years. I really can't claim that it's *my* way. When our bodies are joined, we complete the triangle. When they aren't, we must remember not to let the inherent contradiction become antagonistic, nor pretend that it isn't there. We must know how to be neutral, to let one another *be*."

He frowned for a moment, staring at the wall over my head, and then he added, "We can't possibly solve all this right now. And there's no point in getting so intense we wind up tied into knots. I'm going in to watch television. You can join me, or make yourself comfortable in any way you like. And if you really want to leave, I'll drive you back."

"Oh, I wouldn't want you to miss your program," I snapped, wondering why I was being so nasty.

"I'm sorry that this has to happen, Julie. Believe me, I don't relish pain and negative emotions. But if this is who we are right now, then it must be borne."

"Mr. Generosity himself," I said, my voice dripping with scorn.

Tony came at me with total deliberation. He took three steps and was standing less than a foot away. Without breaking stride he drew back his right hand and smashed it open-palmed across my face. I half-fell off the chair from the impact.

"I've asked you for nothing," he said, his face a mask of controlled anger. "I've been honest with you. I probably saved your life. And this afternoon I gave you some inclination of what real sex could be. On top of this I have offered you my apartment, and have tried to remain reasonable while you have lacerated me with anger, sarcasm, and threats. All this after I allowed myself to become vulnerable to you. You have behaved like some debased and vicious criminal. And now you demand, with an arrogant toss of your head, that I somehow entertain you, that I have no right to do what I want but must provide for your whimsical desires, as though I were a court jester and you a queen. It's not like that, Julie, and whether you have been chosen for me by destiny or not, if you can't exhibit at least a minimum of simple, decent human concern, then you can put your rags back on your shoulders and crawl back to the animals who used you and discarded you last night."

With that he turned sharply on his heel and walked into the next room.

I sat for a long time, a swirl of mixed feelings and inchoate thoughts, my body still throbbing from our extraordinary fucking, my face burning from his slap. I felt paralyzed. To leave at the moment would have been heartbreaking, to stay painful. If I fought to maintain my integrity, Tony and I would be at one another's throats. If I submitted, I would despise myself eventually. Despite the fact that this relationship came couched in a vastly different vocabulary, offered a highly sophisticated eroticism, and promised total individual freedom for each of the partners, underneath all that the same old man-woman mechanics were at work, tapping out the same message: you can't live with the opposite gender, and you can't live without it.

I got up and walked toward the next room, uncertain of what I would do. But as I reached the doorway, Tony stepped up to the same spot, coming from the opposite direction.

"Tony," I said, "why is it so difficult?"

"It's not difficult," he said, cheerfully, "it's impossible."

"Then what are we going to do?"

"Well, I'm going in to get a soda and then watch the rest of this program." He kissed me on the forehead. "I won't be your father, Julie. I suffer from the process easily as much as you do. I have all I can do to keep myself together in the face of life. I can't save or rescue you."

And in that instant I did understand. I had been nagging Tony because unconsciously I expected the man to take the lead, to give the answers, to come along on the white horse. And yet if he had done so, I would have hated him for condescending to me. And throughout all our changes, he steadfastly refused to play that part, and kept reminding me that I had to find my own source of salvation within myself.

I looked up at him and smiled, and in our exchange of glances we said all that had to be said, for that crisis at any rate.

"Let's get some soda," I said. "And go watch television. It must be a fantastic program to pull you in there with such force."

"It's an old-fashioned love story," he said, "about a man and a woman and their choice between romance and marriage."

"Oh," I replied, "a comedy."

But although we sat contentedly on the couch, holding hands and sipping our cokes, looking for all the world like any pair of newlyweds caught up in one another's vibration, a separate center had been born within me, an unsleeping eye. Without being able to pinpoint the precise second, somewhere during the year I had lost my innocence, and sometime during the night I had become aware of the fact.

I glanced over at the man sitting next to me, his face a show of shadow and light. Never had I been so close to a man, and never so distant at the same time.

I turned my head and watched the screen, wondering

about the future, ready to open myself entirely to life, which had become something terribly real, fierce, vast, awesome, as necessary and as alien as the mysterious chasm between woman and man, the abyss which alone makes union possible.

About the Author

MARCO VASSI was, without a doubt, the foremost erotic writer of our generation. Praised by Norman Malier, Kate Millett, Saul Bellow, and Gore Vidal, he was not only the ultimate sexual explorer, but a literary craftsman whose own life experiences became the stuff of his fiction—expanded, of course, by a grand imagination and a full sense of the absurd.

Tragically, Vassi died from pneumonia after he had contracted AIDS.

OPEN ROAD
INTEGRATED MEDIA

Open Road Integrated Media is a digital publisher and multimedia content company. Open Road creates connections between authors and their audiences by marketing its ebooks through a new proprietary online platform, which uses premium video content and social media.

In Touch
The Vassi Collection
Volume VII

In Touch

Marco Vassi

OPEN ROAD

INTEGRATED MEDIA

NEW YORK

Copyright © 1993 by Marco Vassi

ISBN 978-1-4976-4079-5

This edition published in 2014 by Open Road Integrated Media, Inc.
345 Hudson Street
New York, NY 10014
www.openroadmedia.com

in memory of
Bill Clark

In order to make a revolution,
we must have time to dream.
- Rick Shoblad

Introduction

Were the Sixties put on earth so that Marco Vassi could happen? Or was Marco Vassi put on earth so that the Sixties could happen? To read his classic works of erotic fiction and his masterpiece of autobiographical fiction, THE STONED APOCALYPSE, is to realize that the man and the era were created out of the same fire and primordial elements. It is not, however, enough to say that Marco Vassi was a child of his age. It could just as accurately be said that the age was Marco Vassi's fantasy, a fantasy so intense and compelling that it is impossible to read any of his books in one sitting: one must either jump into a cold shower, relieve oneself sexually, or go for a long contemplative walk to reflect on the profundity of his insights into human behavior.

Vassi had done many things before he became a writer, but writing was not one of them except for some translations from Chinese and critiques of manuscripts submitted to a literary agency where he was employed for a few years. He had also tried numerous identities on for size as he acted out and lived out the experiences that were to pour from his mind like water raging over the spillway of a dam. When in the late 1960's " Fred" Vassi announced that he was embarking on a journey, his friends knew that it was not to a place but to a state of mind.

The state of mind was what came to be known as The Sixties, and anyone seeking to live in that state must enter it through the vision of the author of these works. In cartographic terms it was a journey from the East Coast to California, a trip that resonates with meaning for every student of The American Experience. Speaking metaphorically, however, it was a trip into the heart of life, love, laughter, horror, and sweet pain. Fred Vassi came

back Marco Vassi, having recreated himself in the name of the
intrepid voyager to the ends of the known world hundreds of
years ago.

Heart fecund with all that had happened to him, he started
writing the work that was eventually to become THE STONED
APOCALYPSE, a book that captured in coruscating words what
others of his generation were capturing so brilliantly in music.

With no source of regular income he tried his hand at what
were then popularly known as sex novels, a genre of tame
pornography that pandered to the fantasies of repressed males
still mired in postwar inhibition. With the wide-eyed innocence
and self-deprecating humor that characterized every venture he
undertook, he showed them to me, his friend and a fledgling
literary agent. He merely hoped to raise a few dollars with them.
I told him that they were the most incredibly arousing works
of erotic literature since Henry Miller, and arranged for them
to be brought out by Olympia Press, Miller's publisher. Critics
and reviewers confirmed my assessment. What distinguished
his books from the rest of the pack was the application of Vassi's
intelligence. He knew that the mind is the most erotic organ of
all. He termed this fusion of mind and sex organs "Metasex."

For Marco Vassi, the liberation of sexual emotions, paralleling
the liberation of so many others in the late 1960's and early 1970's
promised a new age of beauty, love, and honesty, and he lived
his vision to the hilt—quite literally. For a long while it seemed
to him impossible that this vision did not rest on the bedrock of
reality.

But, in the words of Robert Frost, nothing gold can stay.
The bloody hand of Vietnam and the corrupt fist of the Nixon
presidency crushed the fragile beauty of the flower generation.
The unbridled commercialism that became the 1980's captured
and exploited the butterflies of Woodstock, enriching half of
them and killing the other half with sex, drugs, and rock and
roll. Finally, the horror of a new scourge, AIDS, visited death
upon the bodies of those who had dreamed of eternal love,
irresponsible fun, and self-realization. It was then that Marco
Vassi awoke from his dream of The Sixties. When he did, the
virus had entered his blood. The first malady of any consequence

to come along, in this case pneumonia, conquered his defenseless immune system and made short work of him.

Marco Vassi's body died, but not the body of his work, which lives again in these new editions. Like a rainbow over a bleak landscape, his dream of The Sixties shimmers above the depressing, sordid, and tragic decades that succeeded his. And ultimately, it triumphs over them.

Richard Curtis

1

"How unhappy do you have to be to kill yourself?"

"What makes you think she's unhappy?"

"Why else would she be committing suicide?" The two policemen spoke in whispers, but their sergeant heard them and shot a glance over his shoulder to silence them. The offenders did their best to look chastened until their superior turned his head again, and then winked at one another.

They were among a dozen policemen, two doctors, a building attendant and four reporters who were crouched and standing some fifty feet from the edge of the still unfinished helicopter ramp on top of one of the World Trade Center buildings. They had been summoned because of a report that a woman had smuggled herself into the huge glass mausoleum and made her way to the roof. A Port Authority helicopter pilot had spotted her and sent out the alarm.

She stood perfectly still and was stark naked, her opalescent skin glowing dimly against the black sky. She faced west, looking out over the Hudson River to the plains of New Jersey, now a vast smoldering conglomerate of ugly cities, sterile suburbs, and mile upon mile of oil refineries, dying marshes and garbage dumps.

A fifth of a mile directly below her, New York gave its nighttime show. A hundred million lights. Cars winding among streetlamps. And a panorama of windows. Here and there the flashings of fire trucks and ambulances, their sirens barely audible. The whole an incredibly dense heap and spread of gaudy display made somehow terrifying by its underlying pattern, the notion that the awesomely unnatural creation was not the product of an insane demonic force but the result of intelligence.

The woman trembled slightly in the chill breeze, her long hair stirring about her shoulders. Her dancer's body was a sculptor's dream. Not yet thirty, she seemed to arch up from her calves into deeply muscled thighs which flared into hard buttocks and thinly padded hips. Her breasts were small, like champagne cups. She stared straight ahead of her, and what the men behind her could not see was that a soaring sweep of sparkling awareness had captured her eyes.

It was a bizarre tableau: the nude and superbly balanced woman at the edge of that shattering precipice and the heavily clothed and armed men unable to get near her. Each attempt on the part of the latter to inch closer was met by a minute but intimidating tensing in her leg muscles. One of the doctors had been talking to her for almost an hour, using most of the standard approaches he had been taught were effective in such instances. But the thing he wanted to say most and, who knows, which might have been most successful, caught in his chest.

Tom Madden, M.D., twenty-eight years old and starting to taste the first disillusionment with his chosen profession, had been fighting the stirring of an erection from the moment he laid eyes on the woman who seemed intent on killing herself. The combination of the extraordinary danger of her situation, coupled with his own fascination-fear of heights, joined his male lust that found tremendous potential in such a beautifully formed and trained body. These mixed with an idealistic desire to save-the-damsel-in-distress and, perhaps, then marry her and take her to his laboratory where she would keep him endlessly delighted with arcane erotic uses of bunsen burners and beakers whenever he was not preoccupied with alleviating the sufferings of humanity.

"Please don't jump," he was saying. "Whatever's bothering you can be worked out. You have a whole wonderful life ahead of you."

"Don't jump," he wanted to say, "Don't smash that tentative body on hard concrete. Let me caress those upturned breasts, lick those taut thighs, press myself into the hot hole that opens into your belly."

For Marsha Seligson, however the voice of the man behind

her, the silent appeal of those behind him, and the totality of everything she had been taught, been made to feel and understand, had passed into the realm of illusion. The sheer scintillating drop that fell off just three inches from her toes, and the throb of the city upon the pinnacle of which she stood, were aspects of a dream. They had imposed upon her once too often, and she made the simple decision not to accept the world of common reality any longer, the domain where each kiss was paid for by a cut of loneliness, each kindness by a twist of forgetfulness . . . the world of hard edges and raucous sounds. She was moving into a space where nothing existed except her secret wishes, her most private perceptions, unchallenged by the brute interference of others whose sensitivity had been so blunted that they could no longer distinguish hunger from food. She had sprung into an alternate universe, one of light and fragile wonder, the realm of dance.

She'd come to the city eight years earlier, filled with a humming hopefulness that here, the dance center of the world, would be where her latent talent would blossom into its violet flowering. At first she ran from class to class, sampling each approach, each idiosyncratic idea. But in the near decade that followed, she discovered only one true teacher who, unfortunately was himself so tortured that his tiny studio on West Seventy-second street became more often the scene of his acting out his inner anguish than a place where he helped his students find their own centers. With a mane of silver hair, bristling eyebrows, and eyes like those on a blind man, he spoke with such certainty and exuded so powerful an animal vitality that Marsha had been mesmerized for three years. The rest of the men and women she worked with were either trying to build their own careers, using young dancers as material to work out their choreography, or phonies who had picked up some technique and were attempting to make a few dollars instructing those who were too naive to see through them.

The city had taken its toll in other ways, with the strident tone of living, the noise, the dirt, the struggle to pay the rent, the affairs which were stamped in a single mold of expectation and futility, the string of dingy apartments. Marsha had finally taken to seeing a therapist to cure the ills which flourished only because she lived in a place which made the existence of therapists possible and necessary. That too proved to be little more than another straitjacket, one more pair of alien spectacles through which to view herself.

And then something in her had snapped. She looked backward over her life and saw that there was no returning to innocence and the studied peculiarities of small town survival, for that had been scoured out of her. Looking into the future, she saw nothing but a continuation of the current dreariness and frustration. She had wanted only one thing in life—to dance, and now it appeared that everything in creation conspired to keep her from that single, simply joy.

She had made no conscious plan, used no terms to define her decision. Somehow, she was guided to the spot where she sensed she might at last be free, and there eased herself into a state of feeling in which what she did had a logic without any consequences outside her personal reality, a reality which everyone else in the world would call fantasy.

Now, she turned to the doctor who was still cajoling her and gave him an odd smile. Then, one hundred and ten stories above the earth, at the very brink of a soul-shrinking height, she raised her arms into the air, came up on her toes, and slowly, with radiant precision, began to dance.

When the phone rang, Lydia Stone and Fred Fenwick had been discussing the nature of illusion and reality. They were standing on Lydia's small terrace overlooking Central Park when Fred leapt up to the top of the three foot railing and balanced himself on the nine inch cement runner. Lydia caught her breath and looked away. The street lay twelve stories below them.

"From this height," Fred said, his arms spread wide, his torso jerking back and forth to maintain balance, "even the raw confusion of the city can appear to be a dream. Down there, a half million people are locked in their cars, negotiating the streets like robots, snarled in idiotic traffic. Each is a universe of frustrations and ambitions and needs. But from here, the combined effect is a web of dancing light."

He did a small turn on the balls of his feet and jumped lightly back onto the terrace floor. His tall, thin frame, perfectly set off by a pair of hand-made slacks and a silk sport shirt, vibrated with an electric vitality. Except for a certain fullness in the face, he might have passed for a double of his namesake, Fred Astaire, some thirty years earlier.

"Illusion . . . reality . . . it all depends on the point of view, doesn't it?" he said.

"But whose point of view, that's the question."

They were continuing a conversation that had been at the heart of their relationship since they had first met two years earlier. At that time, Lydia's therapy practice had increased both in quantity and the amount she felt free to charge, and she had moved to her current location, a spacious six room apartment with a terrace over Central Park West. Fred Fenwick was a writer for one of the daytime television soap operas, and they were introduced at a cocktail party.

"Fred, this is Lydia, your counterpart," the host had said. "You make a living with fantasy and she peddles reality."

It was one of those gatherings which seems to have no point except to shuffle the karmic deck to see what sort of new hands might be dealt out to those bored or foolhardy or horny enough to plunge into the mix. Lydia had found the tall writer immediately fascinating. His blue eyes combined a frankness and openness with a hint of some obvious but very subtle joke. It had been almost two months since she'd been fucked, and all at once she suspected that the drought might be at an end.

But Fred's opening line made her wonder. "A therapist?" he said when she told him what she did for a living. "One of the misery merchants."

The phrase had rankled, and she found herself defending her work, something she hadn't been guilty of since her graduate days. But as she went on for a full five minutes tracing the history of therapy back into the practices of primitive tribes with their shamans, and bringing it up through religion with its ritual of confession, and into the scientific age, she noticed that he seemed to pay no attention to her words. Instead, his eyes roamed over her body, with that same intriguing combination of honesty and hidden humor, until he had taken a complete inventory of every inch of her. She sizzled in her black sheath dress, a small fury battling with a bristling lust.

"Are you interested in any of this?" she finally exploded, trying to lace her tone with sarcasm. But being barely five feet tall she had difficulty in bringing about the desired effect.

"Of course, I'm interested," he told her, "but not in that stale rigmarole that's pouring forth from your exquisitely shaped mouth."

For the first time in her adult life, she had actually blushed.

"Look," he went on, "the world's a mystery. Every once in a while some ape who may be a bit more clever than those around him might pick up a clue as to what's going on . . ."

Then, to her amazement, he passed one hand in front of his eyes and mumbled, "But this isn't at the highest level of understanding," and then smiled to himself and added, "Oh, what the hell, it's good enough for the occasion."

He re-focused his eyes on her and continued, "Well, that's no big deal, but if the ape wants to cash in on it, to make a living out of the fact that he or she has caught on to some trivial knack, such as being able to get people to talk about themselves, then the justification and jargon come in. Then come the degrees and official organizations. But intelligent people know that's all a lot of crap. Just because you got a Ph.D. piling up bullshit, don't expect me to fall for it."

She literally could not catch her breath. It was not what he said, although that was enough in itself to wind her, wiping out as it did in a single sweep every single rationalization she had ever formulated in her life. But more than that was his manner, a no-nonsense certainty which had such a ring of conviction that it left no room for argument. Even as she was being swept away, however, she made a small but deadly resolve that one day she would crumble this man's infuriating and utterly irresistible sureness. For the moment, the slight dampening between her thighs took precedence over all ego considerations. She smiled her best social smile, straightened her back, and struck a pose intended to convey to anyone watching that she was having a polite conversation with a charming stranger, and not being slapped back and forth across the ideology with offhand wrist-flicks from a man who seemed to hold her and her entire profession in disdain.

He reached through her posture and took her arm and whispered, "Come on, I know much better things to do with such beautiful lips than to listen to them spout platitudes."

He took her to his West Village duplex where, as though they had both memorized a script, they loped through an entire seduction, with a full complement of music, wine, grass, and long, delicate foreplay, until she was trembling with need and, to her astonishment, begging him to do whatever he wanted with her body.

Their relationship had, as these things do, mellowed and taken refuge in pattern. All their subsequent talk was one or another variation on the first conversation they had had, with Lydia still trying to get him to admit that therapy had real and lasting effects on people's lives, and Fred airily replying that he preferred his soap operas on television and not in some tedious psychological milieu.

"The world is the unknown, the unformed, the uncreated," he would tell her. "The sense we make out of it depends entirely on the perception we have of it. Most of us have accepted the common world view, and so we muddle about at a level of consciousness no higher than that of the *New York Times*. Now, we all want to break out of that conceptual straitjacket, and the way we do it is through fantasy. And the therapist merely sells one form of fantasy, that's all, a rather inferior form at that."

Their lovemaking almost invariably followed a pointed discussion and they used the heat of their bodies to melt the tension generated by words. Both were sophisticated enough to realize after a while that the content of their conversations were much less important than their function, which was a kind of foreplay. Fishes twitched and cats yowled and birds strutted and people talked.

Now, they walked back into Lydia's living room, with her going toward the ringing phone and Fred following at a close distance. His stunt of jumping onto the edge of the balcony had slightly unnerved him. It wasn't something he'd planned to do, but once the impulse had seized him, his body acted for him.

He watched Lydia as she moved. She was wearing a pair of yellow hip huggers which set off her full thighs to their most splendid effect. Usually, when working, she wore loose dresses for fear of offending her patient's images of what a therapist should look like. To complement her slacks, she wore a sheer, black blouse that clung to her torso and outlined her bra-less breasts. They jiggled as she walked, the tiny nipples like bullets in the cloth.

Fred snuggled up behind her and began to run his hands over her ass cheeks, but the expression on her face as she listened to the voice on the other end of the phone stopped him. He watched her for a full minute until she hung up.

"Bad news?"

"It's Marsha," she said, "a woman I've been seeing. She's at the top of the World Trade Center building, threatening to jump. The police found her purse and it had my name in it. They want me to go over and talk to her."

"Of course," Fred said. "I'll go with you."

"Would you please? They're sending a car right over."

They put on jackets against the chill autumn night and went down the elevator to the street where a patrol car, its lights flashing, was just pulling up. They got quickly into the back seat and were sped down the West Side Highway to the twin towers. Lydia put her head on Fred's shoulder.

"I saw her just two days ago," she said.

"Was she upset?"

"No more than usual."

"Did she mention suicide?"

"Oh, they all do, at one time or another."

Realizing that her comment might appear cynical under the circumstances, Lydia bit her lip and added, "I mean, it's part of the way they have of releasing tension and self-pity."

"What did you tell her?" he asked.

"I gave her the recommended response."

"Good God, do therapists have a standard reply for suicide announcements?"

"It's a well known fact," Lydia told him, feeling somewhat sheepish now, "that people who want to kill themselves just go ahead and do it, while those who talk about it are looking for sympathy. So when she said she was thinking that life wasn't worth living I said . . ."

She broke off and stifled a sob in the handkerchief she had clenched in her hand.

"What . . .?" Fred prompted.

"I said, 'Well, if you're going to do it, do it right. Why don't you jump off the tallest building you can find'?"

Fred burst out laughing, a loud rhythmic guffaw. "My God, that's rich," he said. "That's so outrageous I wouldn't dare use it on one of my soaps. No one would believe that it could be real."

"It's not funny," Lydia snapped.

"It's not anything but what it is," Fred told her. "You can laugh or cry or view the entire thing with cosmic indifference."

"Sometimes I think you don't have a heart," she said.

"And sometimes I wonder whether you can tell the difference between real feeling and sentiment."

They arrived at the building with a screech of brakes, and were whisked into the mammoth lobby and up a fifth of a mile to the very top of the building.

"Up and down, up and down," Fred intoned. "First we were looking down at the world from your apartment, then we became part of the sea of trumped up humanity clogging the streets, and now we zoom up to the skies again, perhaps to watch someone take a long glide to the bottom."

"Oh stop it," Lydia rasped.

"Some people got no respect," one of the policemen said, casting a sympathetic glance at Lydia.

When they stepped out onto the roof, they were frozen in their steps by the sight that greeted them. Marsha was dancing at the very edge of the building, leaping, gliding, striking poses of great solemnity and beauty. One of the policemen was playing a haunting melody on a harmonica. And far overhead, a helicopter hovered, kicking up the chilly air over the entire surface area of the roof. An occasional flash bulb from a reporter's camera threw the scene into stark relief.

The young doctor who had been trying to talk Marsha back from her decision came over and introduced himself to Lydia.

"Why in God's name is that man playing a harmonica?" Lydia almost screamed.

"Well, when she started to dance, I thought the best thing would be to humor her. Obviously, she's lost all touch with where she is and I thought that music might intensify her fantasy and make it possible for us to sneak up on her.

"And?" Lydia asked.

"No," the doctor said sadly, "she's sharp enough to be aware when we begin to creep forward."

Fred, who had taken several steps forward to gaze with rapt attention at the dancing woman, turned suddenly and remarked, "She's not lost in any fantasy. She knows exactly where she is and what she's doing."

"Who the fuck are you?" the doctor said, annoyed.

"He's a friend of mine," Lydia told him.

"Well, I'm not sure he's authorized to be here," the man in white went on, still petulant.

"My credentials are in my brain, not on some dimwit sheet of paper, *doctor*," Fred told him. "Now why don't you step out of the way and stop trying to act important. You've already proven your complete impotence in this matter."

The doctor and Fred squared off to face one another and Lydia slipped away to walk toward the wildly dancing woman. As she went she turned to the policeman playing the harmonica and told him to stop. He looked at her over his cupped hands and his eyes indicated that he had absolutely no intention of listening to her.

"That woman may lose her life any second now," Lydia told him in her most guilt-producing tones. "And I'm sure you don't want to share in the responsibility for that."

The policeman took the harmonica away from his lips which had curled into a sneer. "What are you, a cop?" he asked.

"All right, Reilly," the sergeant called out. "Enough of your lip! Just do what the lady tells you."

With a toss of her shoulders, Lydia marched forward until she was within twenty feet of her patient.

"Marsha," she yelled across the windswept plain, "it's me Doctor Stone."

Marsha stopped with an abrupt snap and swayed slightly. Lydia clutched her stomach with the realization of what lay just behind the young woman's heels.

"Don't come any closer, Lydia," Marsha said. "I know you. You're going to try to sell me your reality again. You're going to try to convince me to be unhappy."

"No, no," Lydia cried out. "I want you to come to your senses and discover what true reality is."

"*Your* reality," Lydia snapped. "I know all about that. I pay you to tell me what's real and I get unhappy and you get rich. I've had enough of that. You can call my world a fantasy if you like, but it's where I want to live. Here, I decide what's true and what's beautiful. Not you, and not anyone else."

"Good for you," cried Fred who had walked up behind Lydia.

Lydia spun around.

"How dare you," she snapped. "This is *my* patient."

"*Your* nothing," Marsha said. "I don't belong to you. I'm my own person. I live my life and I make my decisions. And if I make a mistake, that's no one's business but mine. I know what's beautiful and what's ugly. I don't care what you call reality."

"Right on," one of the policemen called out.

"I'm with her," another chimed in.

"You men keep quiet," said their sergeant.

All over the roof, a general unrest broke out. The ancient problem of authority versus freedom erupted, posed in its most pointed question: does a human being have the right to take his or her own life? It was made complex by the interlocking series of roles that were being played by doctor and policeman and therapist and would-be suicide. But in each of the minds of the people there, no matter how dimly, the essential issue of individual liberty was at stake.

Suddenly, Lydia was confused. She felt she had an obligation to save Marsha's life, but she knew no way to do that except by convincing the other woman that her current reality—dancing naked at the edge of the tallest building in New York City—was merely a fantasy and should be put aside.

But for what? What was Lydia offering as an alternative? Some vague notion of what sanity and health were? She was sophisticated enough to know that a large part of her job was helping people to adjust to a world that was perhaps not fit to be adjusted to. Yet, everything she officially stood for, all that she had been trained for, told her that she must persevere in her way of doing things. Even though there was something in Marsha's terrible beauty at that moment which told Lydia that the dancer had discovered some source of energy which might be forever closed to the logical mind of the therapist.

"This is no time for me to be caught in an ambivalence of values," Lydia told herself, and yet each attempt she made to speak to the other woman lacked conviction.

"There's no single reality," Fred whispered. "The world is open-ended and infinite. Only our choices define what is real. And it is wrong to take anyone's choice away from them."

Behind them, the policeman started his tune once more, the sad melody changing the mood of the night. The helicopter wavered and flew higher, then veered off to land at a further distance from the scene.

"Don't you see?" Marsha keened. "Don't you see that I am happy now?"

And with those words she ran the length of the rooftop, skipping, leaping, pirouetting, until she reached the far edge, and then with a leap that would have done credit to Nureyev, she jumped joyfully from the lip of the building.

Everyone on the roof gasped, practically in unison, and after a split second ran to the spot from which the girl had leapt. When they reached the edge and looked down, she was still falling, circling, spinning, her arms and legs kicking lazily, as though she were sky diving. But there was no parachute, just a naked body, head and limbs and torso sailing through the air, hair blowing, ass clenching, cunt gaping.

"And nothing and no one shall ever change this moment for me again," was the last thought which went through Marsha's mind as she hit the pavement and her body broke, and splattered, and flew into a hundred pieces, to finally return to the infinitesimal atoms from which it had been put together.

2

When the doorbell rang at ten o'clock the following morning, Lydia wasn't sure she could handle what was coming. After Marsha's leap into space, the entire crew that had been on the roof rushed down to see the result with that tingling admixture of fear and ghoulish curiosity which accompanies disasters. Lydia had been astonished to find that the sight was not as gory as she had expected. The fall was so great that Marsha's body exploded upon impact and hardly any of it remained in any kind of coherent whole. Even the blood and guts was minimal.

"It's almost as though she disappeared," Lydia had whispered to Fred.

"She did disappear," he told her. "She stepped off into a separate reality which we, from our granite viewpoints, might call a fantasy. I don't doubt but that she still exists, somehow, somewhere."

"Why, I never expected you to be religiously sentimental," she replied, amazed at her ability to make conversation. Then the walls of the building blurred before her eyes and she swooned into his arms.

He had taken her to her apartment, run a hot bath for her, and when she was completely relaxed, lifted her out, dried her, and laid her gently on the bed. Then he massaged her muscles and tendons until she was as limp as a freshly killed carcass. Smiling to himself, Fred mounted her and entered her slowly, his cock as sensitive as a tongue, his steady, even movement not exciting her but rather filling her with a throbbing energy that imparted a sense of vitality without disturbing her drowsy state.

"How odd," she thought, "to be being fucked so shortly after I watched a woman leap to her death."

Fred had fucked her for well over an hour, in total silence, and from time to time she actually dozed off, soaring into delicious dreams of flying, and then descending to consciousness, only to find that the man above her was still invading the deepest recesses of her body with insidious sensuous awareness.

Neither of them approached the slightest intimation of orgasm, and finally he picked her up and rolled her onto her side. For a long time he lay next to her, and they did nothing but breathe deeply and sink more comfortably into the mattress, soaking up the sweet caress of gravity. Then he slid slowly up toward the headboard until his crotch was level with her eyes. His cock was erect again. Her lips fell open naturally and he moved into her without tension. He filled her the way a mother's breast fills a baby's mouth. And she sucked him in precisely that way, gently, lovingly, sleepily, almost absentmindedly. He put his hands on the back of her head but didn't need to guide her, for she was following an instinctual rhythm that had more intelligence than either of their mechanical minds might ever muster.

When he came, the cream spurted onto her tongue and she swallowed his nectar succulently, allowing it to trickle out and over her lips. She was already asleep as the last drops oozed down her throat.

But the following morning crashed in upon her with as much jittery confusion as the night before had produced solace. Fred had already left and she lay alone in bed, the alarm buzzing nastily. It was a quarter to nine and her first patient was due at ten. She rose, went to shower, and shook her head when for a few seconds she couldn't open her lips. They were glued together with dried sperm. By nine fifteen she was getting breakfast together, and when the doorbell rang she had just put the finishing touches on her makeup.

Her patient was Mrs. Nora Norwood, a thirty-six year old housewife who had come to her with a standard marriage complaint several months earlier. For more than a year she had not experienced orgasms with her husband. The first four years of their marriage, she reported, had been idyllic, and they had carried on like newlyweds almost all the time, except for those periods when the normal load of emotional problems and other pressures put them off their feed. But then, gradually, she had noticed a falling off of desire. She didn't love her husband any less; if anything, she cared for him more. And their sex life had not deteriorated; they remained imaginative and inventive. But somehow, a certain element of passion had evaporated. What Mrs. Norwood called "the magic" had dissipated before her very eyes.

There are many explanations as to why these things happen. The most pessimistic states simply that the flow of energy which provides the juice between two people dries up because the constant repetition of the same smells and textures and movements creates a state of boredom in the brain. Thus, while intercourse becomes more dimensional and human, it loses the edge of raw desire which activates the more primitive and exciting centers. Another possibility is that the pure erotic drive is overlaid with ancillary concerns having to do with running a household, raising children, and so forth. Also, hidden resistances and rigidities, unnoticed during the first flushes of erotic involvement, begin to make themselves felt and take prominence; that is, the neurotic personality overcomes the early attempts at putting on one's best possible manner.

Lydia took the first four or five sessions to test the most obvious possibilities. It was clear from the first that Mrs. Norwood was not frigid. Nor was there any major psychological malfunction. The factors of boredom, routine, staleness were present, but did not provide sufficient explanation for the inability to attain orgasm. At the end of the second month, Lydia took the case to Doctor Monroe, her control therapist.

The old man had listened gravely, thought for a long time, and then asked, "What about masturbation?"

"She doesn't," Lydia told him.

"That might open a few locks," he replied. And had refused to comment further.

Now, Lydia opened the door and ushered Nora Norwood in. As always, she was taken with the woman's freshness and glowing exuberance. She had no children, and since her husband was a

highly paid executive, she spent most of her day lolling about the
house, or going to yoga and dance classes and immersing herself
in the bowels of beauty salons. She had a maid to shop and clean,
and except for her inability to make that small connection which
climaxes the sex act with a series of convulsive shudders, she did
not have a problem in the world.

She was a bit more than five and a half feet tall, with close-
cropped, jet black hair. Her cream-white skin did not have, nor
did it need, a trace of makeup. She wore a transparent white
blouse which almost totally revealed her slightly overlarge
breasts, and a pleated black skirt which, on any other woman
would have appeared unfashionable. But Mrs. Norwood's style
was such that she could carry clothes few others would consider
wearing, and make her outfits appear ultra chic.

Lydia closed the door behind her and walked after her patient
as she went into the office where therapy was ordinarily done. It
was appointed in classic non-intrusive style, with beige walls, a
brown rug, two Eames chairs, and a low coffee table.

Lydia's basic approach had been low keyed. She did little
more than act as a sounding board for the patient's feelings.
The theoretical underpinning held that the individual had the
solution to his or her own problems within the self and required
only to exteriorize the condition for the confusions to become
clarified. It was a technique which, as with all others, could be
powerfully effective in the hands of a skilled practitioner and a
parody in the hands of a nuts-and-bolts therapist. In the trade,
the following story had gained currency as a wry comment on
the approach.

A patient walks in and tells the therapist that he feels like
jumping out a window. The therapist says, "Ah, you feel like
jumping out a window . . ." The patient then says that he is
going to kill himself. The therapist nods with empathy and says,
"Ah, you feel like you are going to kill yourself." Whereupon the
patient takes a running leap and hurls himself out the window.
The therapist walks over, looks down to the sidewalk, and says,
"Ah, splat."

Lydia had worked in that manner for a few years before she
came under the influence of a Reichian who had convinced her

that no progress toward health could be made unless the tensions which are locked into the muscles were directly attacked. This led to a year of experimentation with psychophysical techniques and finally culminated in an approach whereby Lydia synthesized several classical methods.

It was while she was deeply into exploring that approach that Lydia had met Fred and his first reaction had been to mock what she was doing.

"It's all so formal," he told her. "Instead, take a housewife, give her a Valium and a glass of Scotch, and plunk her down in an easy chair in front of the tube, and then feed the collective fantasies of the nation directly into her subconscious. It's cheaper, easier, and free of all the rigmarole you indulge in. Soap operas are much more honest than therapy, because they don't pretend that each individual's tacky little melodrama has any more value than being merely an idiosyncratic manifestation of the national mentality at any given time. The soap opera provides precisely what your therapy does: catharsis."

"But what about integration?" Lydia argued.

"Does it make people relate their fantasies to their reality in such a way that they change?"

"Nobody changes," Fred sneered. "Sometimes we feel better, sometimes we feel worse. Sometimes we get ideas that we're going somewhere, and most of the time we realize that life is just a march to the grave. Therapy is a lie because it promises something that can't be given."

Fred's ideas had unsettled her, but there was nothing she could do but continue as she was, trying to find meaning in her work, even though, in her most honest moments she had to admit that all her therapeutic expertise really seemed to have no effect on anyone's life at all.

Nora Norwood kicked off her shoes, unbuttoned the top of her blouse, and lay down on the thick rug, assuming the position with which Lydia began her sessions. It was common practice for her to let her patients lie still for five minutes, to collect themselves, before beginning to bring them into a state of heightened body awareness. But Nora noticed something different about Lydia's mood this morning and she sat up.

"Is something wrong?" she asked.

"I had something terrible happen last night," Lydia said. "A patient of mine committed suicide."

Nora brought her hand over her mouth.

"That girl that jumped from the World Trade Center building? The one on the front page this morning?"

Lydia nodded.

"Oh, how terrible," Nora said. And then, seeing the look on Lydia's face, added, "I hope you're not blaming yourself."

"Well, what if you went home this afternoon and slit your wrists after spending an hour telling me how unhappy you were. Of course, in a sense there is nothing I could hold myself responsible for, but on another level, I would wonder if there was anything I might have done, or said."

Nora lay back down. "My problem isn't all that serious," she said.

"Neither was Marsha's," Lydia told her.

"What was it?"

"She couldn't find any meaning in her life."

"And you think that's not serious?"

"It's nothing that doesn't afflict all of us. Even you. Your lack of orgasms isn't anything more than an inability to make a connection with yourself at a deeper level."

"Whew," Nora replied, "that's quite an interpretative leap."

"Well, let's see," Lydia told her. "Let's do something about getting you an orgasm and discover what it is that you uncover along the way."

Nora lifted an eyebrow and shot an edgy glance at Lydia. "Just what do you mean, doing something about getting me an orgasm?"

"When's the last time you masturbated?"

"Oh, good Lord, when I was fifteen, I think." Nora smiled. "Then I discovered that men served the same purpose but with a great deal more scope."

"Perhaps now that you are temporarily blocked in relation to what a man can do for you, you might try to rediscover your capacity to give yourself what your husband can't."

"Really!" Nora exclaimed, her voice registering mock shock.

"Really," Lydia replied. "What do you have to lose?"

Before Nora could respond, Lydia began the ritual of getting the other woman relaxed.

"Uncross your ankles," she said, "and put your arms out at your sides. Now, roll your head from side to side and release some of the tension in your neck. Close your eyes so that your attention gets focused inside your body. We've done this enough times so that you can do most of the work yourself; just let my voice help you along."

Nora let out a long sigh and her entire frame visibly relaxed. "It's extraordinary," she said, "no matter how often I do this, during the intervening week I always forget how incredibly delicious it is just to let go."

"You should do this for yourself at home," Lydia went on, "but let's not get distracted by talk. Keep the sense of opening going on. And begin to get into your breathing. Not just the actual breath which enters your nostrils, moves down your throat, fills your lungs, pushes your diaphragm and swells your belly, but the *sense of breath* that seeps into your shoulders and arms and legs, the feeling of life-giving energy which floods your whole body."

Lydia watched for several minutes as Nora sank more and more deeply into a trance, and when she gauged that the other woman was totally receptive, she went on, "Find some spot in your body that calls attention to itself, some sensation, and let that grow and develop. Let it move through you until it reaches the point where you can give it a name, and then let that name blossom until it flowers into a fantasy. And when the picture is firmly fixed, let me know what it is that's happening."

Nora's frame shuddered, she took a deep sigh, and then began to speak. "It's the same," she said, "I am lying naked in a strange hotel room. A man I've never seen before is standing over me, his face contorted by a kind of evil desire. He's actually gloating. He leans forward and pinches my nipples with his fingernails. It's painful, but still bearable. The sensation makes me squirm. I am twisting and writhing on the bed. I know that my legs are kicking and parting and he can see my cunt. I know that my cunt is spreading wide and he is peering down into the center of me. He pinches harder and I start to moan. He whispers all sorts of vile thing in my ear."

"What things? Say them."

"'Slut, cunt, whore, bitch, tramp.'"

As Nora recited the litany, Lydia smiled, something Nora could not see. It always amazed Lydia that the moments of greatest shameful eroticism produced the most banal vocabulary.

"'You hot hole, you slimy twat, you piece of ass . . .'" Nora went on. "'You love it, don't you? You love having strange men shove their hands up your snatch and put their pricks in your mouth, don't you?'"

"Answer him," Lydia prompted. "Let yourself say whatever comes to your lips."

"Fuckfuckfuckfuckfuckfuckfuckfuckfuckfuckfuck," Nora chanted over and over again. As she said the word her body began to move in a new way. Now she was pumping her pelvis into the air, twisting her thighs, and her hands had moved up to grasp her breasts.

"What's happening now?" Lydia asked.

"The scene's changed," Nora told her. "I've been picked up by a taxi driver, a huge, burly, greasy man with thick lips and calloused hands. He takes me to his garage where he parks his cab. He pulls me out and throws me over the fender of the car, face downward. Then he hikes up my skirt and pulls my panties down. My ass is completely exposed. Behind him are a dozen more men, all like him, fat, ugly, sweating, chewing cigars, licking their lips, their eyes blazing with smoldering depravity. And I am so clean, so tender, so fragile. They can't believe they have such a prize in front of them. A sensitive wealthy lady who has let all her cunty animality break through. My legs are kicking in the air, my mouth is crying for cock, my tits are crushed against the hard metal. The first man enters me brutally and after a few harsh jabs he fills my precious cunt with his hateful fluid. And when he is through, the others come on, endlessly, shoving their cocks in my cunt, in my ass, in my mouth. Their sperm is coating me, their hands are tearing at me, and I'm . . . I'm . . ."

"What?" Lydia urged, "What?"

Abruptly, Nora rolled over onto her stomach, taking in actual physical reality the posture she had assumed in her fantasy. Her hands now went between her thighs, pulling up her skirt. Finally, they reached bare flesh and her fingers slipped beneath the edges of her panties and slid into her juicy cunt. Lydia watched as Nora twitched on the rug, her ass contracting, her mouth opening and closing.

"Yes," Lydia urged, "Do it, do it!"

Nora cupped her cunt and ground the palms of her hands against her clitoris. "They're fucking me, fucking me . . ." she groaned as she ground her pubic bone down into her own flesh and caught that elusive spark of electricity which triggers orgasm. Then, as Lydia watched, Nora climaxed before her eyes, shamelessly finger-fucking herself to conclusion.

There was a long, long silence in the room. Finally, slowly, Nora rolled over, and looked up at Lydia. Her face was flushed and open, her eyes sparkling.

"My God," she whispered, "what have I done? I've let you watch me masturbate."

"So you have," Lydia replied, and noticed that she was breathing hard, and experiencing a familiar warmth and moistness between her own thighs. "But don't be too upset. It's a first for me too. After all these years of sharing people's most intimate thoughts and feelings, this is the first time I've ever been this naked with anyone."

A deep musky scent of female secretion pervaded the room and both women noticed it at once. They looked at one another, glanced momentarily away, and then looked back, smiling warmly and somewhat sheepishly.

Then, in an action that shocked the therapist more than it did the patient, Lydia cupped the other woman's chin in her hand, pulled her face toward her, and kissed her tenderly on the lips.

"There," Lydia said, "I've done something shocking too. Now, let's talk about what happened and see if we can make some sense of it all." The two women went into Lydia's kitchen where they sat over coffee and cigarettes and tried to sort out the morning's events.

"I want to steer us away from the sensationalistic aspects of what happened," Lydia said, "although believe me I found the experience as exciting as you did, including the definite lesbian overtones to my reaction. But our task is to try to link your failure to attain orgasm with your husband to the material we unearthed today. Do you have any openers?"

"Yes," Nora replied, blowing out a cloud of blue smoke. "The degradation aspect. I suppose I'm as well versed in the women's liberation literature as anyone, and the degradation theme is one that men have imposed on us for some time. What puzzles me is why I seem to go straight to that to find excitement."

"What about you and your husband? Do you get into any of that at all?"

"Oh, just the usual married stuff. He spanks me sometimes, and pisses on me in the shower, but it's all so . . . *normal*, if you know what I mean. The actions themselves are not important; the crucial element is doing it with a man who despises me, or rather, despises my womanhood."

"Have you had any actual experiences along those lines?"

Nora shook her head. "I lost my virginity to my college sweetheart. I fucked one other man before meeting Ralph, my husband. And that's about it. And I don't think I'm repressing anything. I enjoy straightforward, loving sex. Then why does this other stuff excite me so? This isn't the first time I've had this kind of fantasy, you know."

Lydia remembered. The first time she had taken Nora on a fantasy trip she had been surprised to find the well-groomed woman rolling around the floor screaming like a cat in heat, having visions of being gang-banged by an entire football team. She had explained it to Nora in rather classical terms. "Nothing to be alarmed about," she had said. She advised attempting to integrate her breathing exercises with her fantasies and bring that to the fucking she did with her husband as a means of snaring the elusive orgasm. But over a period of time it became apparent that it was not a question of bringing two separate modalities together, but one of choosing one over the other. Today's experience had driven a wedge into Nora's psyche.

"I'm afraid I don't have an answer for you," Lydia replied at last. "I think we're dealing with dynamics which transcend our usual categories of thinking."

Nora nodded. "It's as though the fantasy is exerting a pull far stronger than anything reality has to offer. I mean, I know that I'm supposed to consider warm and adult sex with my husband as the mature means of expression my eroticism and that the rest of this stuff is just neurotic underlay that has to be gotten through. But in a strange way, I feel that diving into my fantasies, especially with the energy I build up from masturbating, is offering me a real alternative, something to rival what I might have from conventional sex."

Lydia massaged her forehead with her right hand. "I think that's what Marsha discovered last night. She saw that the world of so-called reality is nothing but a prejudice which has been handed down to us by our society, and that beyond that bubble of perception is an infinite and mysterious universe of possibilities which we can step into any time we want to. The only trouble is that that discovery destroyed her."

Nora shuddered. "And me? Do you think it could destroy me?"

"I doubt, it. But it might end your marriage. At least, it might end the marriage you now conceive of. You might have to bring Ralph into this area of knowledge and see if you can find some way to share that journey into the unknown."

"I have a suspicion that that's a place one can only go alone," Nora said.

"You may be right. But at least we can hold one another's hand. We can do that much for one another. Maybe that's all we can do." She paused, lit another cigarette, and went on. "But the thing is not to get trapped in the fantasy. You see, I'm sure that the fantasy is just another false perception. And while it may be the doorway into the infinite, it would be foolish for us to get trapped in that doorway. What we did today gave an indication of what's possible. But it's only the beginning." She looked up at Nora and smiled ruefully. "That is, if you want to continue."

Nora reached out and stroked Lydia's cheek. "Just try and stop me," she said.

"As far as the degradation business is concerned," Lydia continued, "I wouldn't make too big an issue out of that. I suspect that our fantasies will shape themselves around whatever socially conditioned myth we happen to be carrying around with us."

Nora shook her head and sighed.

"Nobody ever told me therapy would be like this," she said.

Lydia didn't answer for a few seconds and when she did her voice was serious. "It isn't. I think what we're doing is the first step beyond therapy. I think we have begun to enter the realm of magic."

3

Her body had become the music. Blood, bones, skin, hair, lost all definition as parts of a physical whole and were transformed into variations of rhythmic, raucous sound. The ordinary dulled distinction between inner and outer worlds evaporated in the heat of the insistent, dogmatic rock which left no choice but for whoever became susceptible to its spell to abandon the daily dualism of thought-ridden existence. The universe was experienced as the meaning of the word used to describe it . . . universe: one turn, one twist, one idea, one poem. Cutting through the music itself, the dimly discernable lyrics slashed at the tendons of the mind, reducing the conditioned patterns of the brain to conceptual porridge. They took all the pious and opaque hypocrisies of civilization and set them happily on fire. Lydia, now at once animal and angel, was driven into a frenzy of jungle lust which was indistinguishable from the purest meditative perception.

She was drunk and stoned. She was high on abandon. She was surrounded by more than three hundred people, all bound together in a mounting orgiastic frenzy. Many of them were naked, most in outlandish costumes, capes, scraps of organdy, face and body paint, leather jock straps. Lydia herself had nothing left on but her jeans. Her shoes had been flung off an hour earlier, and when her blouse had become so drenched with sweat that it was plastered to her skin, she had ripped that off also.

Now she danced with the euphoric transport of a dervish, her legs trembling with an energy that springs from the cosmic life force of which each body is but a momentary reflection and flares forth when one has gone beyond the six stages of exhaustion. Her tits bounced and flew as she moved and each slap of flesh against flesh seemed to whip her into an even more eruptive state.

She had lost sight of Fred some time earlier, and she roamed the floor in narcissistic solitude, finding herself changing partners continually, if the kind of dancing they were doing even admitted of the concept of partner. Rather each was a flake of brightly colored stone in an undulating mosaic of everforming chaos. At times Lydia would be with a man, acting out in pantomime the most scintillating erotic scenarios, perhaps dropping to her knees, her head lolling, her tongue lapping, as the stranger pumped his pelvis at her face. Another time found her with a woman, wrapped in an ecstasy of kinesthetic stridency, building higher and higher levels of tension until the two of them flew into one another's arms, their breasts crushed, their mouths merged. Again, and she was one of a group of five who had formed a circle, acting out a complex tribal dance which discovered its own structure as it went along. Time and eternity played sixty-nine, with each temporal crystal attaining immortal significance, and endlessness infusing itself with amusement at its own expense.

Lydia was at the wildest discotheque in Province-town. On the Friday after she had seen Nora, she met Fred for lunch and told him of her experience.

"I'm a little frightened. I became a therapist because I wanted to explore the depths of the human experience. But I really had nothing going for me except a random sprinkling of insights and a head stuffed with theories. But now that I am beginning to taste the terrible knowledge that everything which exists is nothing but a momentary whimsy bubbling to the surface of the essential mystery, I am filled with both horror and boundless excitement. I mean, consider our choice. To shuffle about the safe routines of the common social perception or to leap into the unknown."

Fred had yawned.

"You remind me of a friend of mine," he told her, "a man that keeps re-discovering the wheel. I give him credit because he insists on his originality, his insistence on finding out for himself. But then I see him as a total shmuck because he wastes so much time coming to things he could take as part of his cultural heritage, and go on from there. It's like the Primal Scream nitwits who don't realize that their discovery is nothing but a reformulation of a truth that's been understood for thousands of years.

"And now you come along with your patient's suicide and a woman who's learned that it's fun to masturbate in front of an audience, and think that you've descended into life's deepest meanings."

He sat back in his chair, gazed at Lydia for almost a full minute, and then went on, "I think I'd like you to meet some people."

They'd made the five hour drive in a rented car, Lydia's mood lightening as the city fell behind them, the dense concrete concentration of New York opening into stunted and sprawling suburbs, then into open stretches of land, interrupted-every now and then by a smaller city, a New Haven or a Bridgeport. And by the time they'd covered the length of the Cape itself, and reached the ocean, faced with the flesh-colored dunes, and she'd smelled the ocean air, her entire Manhattan existence had come to seem some kind of dismal prison term.

The town itself shocked her. Commercial Street, the main drag, leapt at her with the crowded vulgarity of Coney Island, with thousands and thousands of people doing little more than rubbing against one another, working out some primeval herd instinct that the denizens of human civilization consider quaint in other species but do not recognize in themselves, and mask with oblique terminology, referring to parties, ball games, rallies, church-going and other rationalizations for carrying out the dictates of biology. The street was a mile-long strip of bars, restaurants, souvenir shops, bookstores, clothing boutiques, and quick-food shops.

Fred took her to his friends' place, a large subterranean apartment which looked like a museum, loaded with art deco pieces, feathers, broken mirrors, fantastic costumes hung carelessly on hooks. The scene could not have been designed, but could have reached its condition only through a process of accumulation. And yet, on closer inspection, it proved to be functional, efficient, continually gratifying to the senses with its colors, different textures and. motifs, and faint smells of incense, marijuana, and body oils.

Within an hour, Lydia had met more than a dozen people, who bustled and wafted in and out in various states of consciousness. Men who looked like women, women who looked like drugged peacocks, people whose gender was totally indeterminate, and all of them involved in utterly unconnected and yet oddly harmonious activities. Somehow, food got cooked and the floor was swept and it was possible for some to sleep while others talked or listened to music. And at one point Lydia heard, the sounds of fucking coming from behind a screen. Fifteen minutes later she saw two young boys and a woman with nose rings saunter out, all smiling and sweating and naked.

"Lydia, this is Reginald," Fred said when a dark man with a full mustache walked into the place. "It's basically his apartment."

Reginald wore skin-tight velour pants and a tattered, transparent Indian shirt. He had black coal under his eyes and a trace of lipstick on his full mouth. His right ear was triply pierced and carried a gold hoop, a diamond-tipped stud, and a hanging silver crescent. His body possessed that mixture of suppleness and rigidity often found in certain types of homosexuals, men who have resolved their entire psychophysical ambivalences into a fixed posture and then become comfortable within that frame. His walnut brown eyes did a quick scan of Lydia's face, seemed to register a definitive impression, and then he smiled.

"Well, basically I pay the rent," he said.

"Lydia's a therapist," Fred said. "She's studying the relationship between fantasy and reality."

"Wow," someone behind them said. Lydia looked over her shoulder and saw a black man, short and stocky, doing pushups, looking back at her. His eyes rose and fell as he worked himself up and down from the floor, and gazing at him gave her a feeling of vertigo. She knew she was being mocked, but somehow the tone was kindly.

"Really, Fred," she said, "I don't think it's necessary to go into any of that." In that milieu, her words and diction sounded stilted and strained to her ears.

"But that's precisely the reason we came here," he told her.

"You see, they are living out, in their rather baroque fashion, some of the so-called discoveries you think you are making. He turned to Reginald and related the stories of Marsha's suicide and Nora's masturbation."

"But that's confidential material," Lydia blurted out, and then put her hand over her mouth. In this atmosphere, the notion that what someone did with her or his body could be private emerged as a grotesque joke.

"Don't you know . . ." said the man doing the pushups, "that we all . . . do the same . . . thing? I mean . . . there's just so . . . many things you . . . can do with . . . the human animal . . . And what makes . . . people uptight . . . is thinking they . . . got something special . . ." His phrases came out in spurts, in time with his exercise.

"Well, that's both too fast and too simple," Reginald said. "The woman is from a different culture. Treat her as you would an anthropologist. Let her look around, pick things up at her own speed. And please, don't put her on. This isn't a pigpen."

Lydia retreated to a corner and tried to become invisible. For over an hour she did nothing but sit and look, attempting to make sense out of the kaleidoscope of impressions she was receiving, the comings and goings, the hierarchical structure she felt had to be there, the ultimate purpose of it all. She worked with calm, feverish commitment to fit this reality into the context of her own perceptual structures. And after a while, she hit upon her first insight.

"They have no time distinctions," she said to herself. "Or rather, their sense of time has to do with their individual biological clocks and not with the clocks on the wall." She looked around and saw that there were no clocks on the wall and that no one wore wristwatches. They had, as far as is possible, reduced time to two variables, the variation of dark and light.

The next thing she noticed was that there was very little overt interaction. It was something like the psychotic wards she'd visited during her internship. But with a difference. These people were not withdrawn and apathetic; rather, they seemed interested and involved. But she couldn't tell with what. On the one hand, there was continual movement; concurrently, the environment kept being taken apart and put back together. But she couldn't find the connection between what the people did and what got done as a result. She put it together in a second formulation—the people were communicating with some other language besides speech, something even more subtle than body language.

Even as she thought that, however, Fred came up behind her and whispered, "Telepathy."

Lydia almost fell from the chair.

"I was watching you," he continued, "and could tell you were trying to figure out how they operate. It's a process of telepathy. They have learned how to be sensitive to one another's auras, so that they can *read* one another directly, without having to go through the cumbersome process of communication."

Lydia turned to him. "But how did they arrive at that? What are the techniques? Why, if that can be studied and understood, it would revolutionize therapy."

Fred laughed. "Don't you understand? Psychotherapy is a very low grade of behavior, the crude effort by a moribund society to pump life into its walking corpses. When you arrive at a state of pure mental interaction, therapy has all the appeal of an oil tanker. You won't get anywhere if you try to translate this reality into your categories. What you need to do is to change your categories to encompass this reality."

"But from another level," Reginald said, sliding up beside them, "we are just a bunch of sick, drugged, sex freaks living on the decaying edges of a decadent civilization."

Lydia looked at him with surprise. Reginald smiled.

"Reg's a Ph.D. He took his doctorate in history at Columbia ten years ago, and it's left him with the habit of switching contexts."

"But which is real? I mean, for you?" Lydia asked.

"I choose from whichever frame of reference allows me to move through the flux of creation with as much pleasure and meaning to myself and as little damage to others as possible," Reginald replied. "Isn't that what having flexibility of intelligence is all about?"

"Have you no sense of an Absolute?" she asked.

"You sound a little like the fish who went in search of water," Reginald told her. "We *are it.*"

"Then, according to you, Marsha's jumping off that building . . ." Lydia began.

"Was just one way of looking at things," Reginald continued. "To judge it as reality or fantasy, as sick or healthy, is to indulge in low-level—excuse the term—psychological masturbation."

"I can see what you mean," Lydia said, "and in fact I'm beginning to understand its implications through some of the work I'm doing, but it's frightening."

"No more so than that first day when you realize that your mother is just a little old lady living in the Bronx and no more capable of keeping you from dying than anyone else."

Lydia shook her head slowly and fell into silence.

The two men drifted off, and the evening moved with startling rapidity after that. First the grass, which she was offered with amusement and diffidence and tried out of bravado. She'd smoked marijuana before, but not been aware that it had been a mediocre grade shared with people whose level of awareness was relatively low. Now she was toking on a murderously strong strand from the mountains of Peru among people whose idea of a good time was to go stark raving mad.

After her second joint, Lydia was reeling, trying to catch her astral breath, while her physical body had developed into a switchboard of hot and cold flashes, tremors, hallucinations, and landslides of insight. She sat like someone just strapped into an electric chair, her spine rigid, her hands grasping the ribbed arms of the wicker chair.

When Judy approached her, Lydia could not be certain for several seconds whether what she was seeing was an apparition or not. A tall, skeletally thin blonde wearing a sequined bikini pulled up a stool in front of her and proceeded to lay out an array of make-up utensils.

"Want to make you look Venusian," she purred, and for the next forty-five minutes worked on Lydia's face with the intensity of an artist at her canvas. She plucked, stroked, rubbed in creams, drew lines, applied swatches of color, drew tiny designs, glued on bits of colored glass. And when she finished she held up a mirror, and Lydia found herself gazing into the face of a stunning serpent goddess, utterly alien, other—worldly, and irresistibly beautiful.

"Me?" she mouthed with her lips.

"I see your soul," Judy said. "I make your face look like your soul."

Fred returned and stood over Judy's shoulder, beaming down like a proud father.

"What's happening?" Lydia asked.

"A party," Fred told. "A perpetual awareness that reality is only fantasy's special case. The courage to let go all the safe little moulds of perception you've been programmed with."

"This is *my* doorway," Lydia said to herself, her words not audible to the others. "For Marsha, it was the leap; for Nora, the masturbation; and for me . . . what?"

She felt as though she were about to lose her virginity. Despite her cerebral sophistication and growing understanding of the limitations of her intellectual orientation, Lydia was still caught in the habit pattern of trying to think through what was happening a few beats after it happened, instead of seizing on a single existential attitude and letting everything take place within the embrace of that one posture. If she were to analyze the condition formally, she would remark that the split was between Western and Eastern ways of thought, or between that of artists and that of scientists.

Yet, the ambience and the grass and the wine worked their way with her. Lydia's mind kept slipping notches, so that each time she tried to focus to figure out what was going on, she was in an entirely different world than she had been five minutes earlier. After several hours had passed, she couldn't know that if the woman she had been when she walked into the place would be able to recognize herself. For, viewed from the outside, Lydia was a stoned freak, painted and smiling and moving with the same lassitude that the others had exhibited when she first began to observe them. Viewed from within, she had been converted, and had entered an exalted state of tribal consciousness.

From there it was but a series of consistent steps to the point at which she was dancing barefooted and half naked at three in the morning, losing herself in the orgiastic abandon of the night.

Fred suddenly loomed up out of the stroboscopic flicker of bodies and put his arms around her waist.

"Come on," he said, "we're going."

"Where?" she yelped.

"To a party," he told her.

"A party! For God's sake, what's this?"

"Warm-up," he said, and swept her out.

Going out into the street provided a case of the cultural bends. Fred threw a jacket over her shoulders which barely protected her from the chill night air. But what struck her was the incongruity of the houses and shops, not to mention the people, with what she'd been experiencing. Again, she hadn't realized how far she had been carried down the stream of dissolution until she tried to measure her present state with what she'd previously considered to be normality. Now, the entire edifice of her civilization appeared as a monstrous block against the flow of life. The movement inside the dance parlor had been liquid, warm, sinuous. Out here she could see the crystallized anti-life tendencies of the ordinary world. Square houses lined perpendicular streets. People moved with an unconscious self-consciousness. The cars rolled past like deformed beetles, ugly and noxious, great wasteful carriers emitting poison gas. It was as though humanity were a single lovely body and civilization a straitjacket choking it slowly to death, a constraint constructed of time-clocks and rules which served the abstractions of finance rather than the eternal and infinite pulse of life itself. This was the reality, she suddenly saw, that she had been attempting to get her patients to adjust to. This was the reality which she had taken as a measure of health.

A thousand glimmerings gathered over years of work coalesced into a fierce illuminating flame. She understood that *neurosis was merely an unsuccessful attempt to protest the morbidity of the prevalent and triumphant worldview of a crippled species.* People who were considered normal were almost always those too feeble to fight against the closing coffin lid that perpetually threatened to smother them. Neurotics were people who struggled but failed to get free, and were stuck in one or another of the tunnels that promised to lead out of the prison. Psychotics were those who had chosen pain as the only valid protest against the blindness of humanity. And only the artists of living somehow got out to the other side, into a space where the throb of life suffused inner awareness and external functioning in such a way as to create a seamless lifestyle which was at once pragmatic and fantastic.

Lydia's thoughts carried her through the night like a flying carpet, and before she realized how far she had moved in terms of her time/space matrix, she was inside the house where the party was being held. The scene blasted her clear out of her introspective reverie, almost singeing her eyelids with its heat and power.

Some forty or fifty people were present. Most of them were already lying down so that most of the movement she perceived involved rolling and sliding instead of walking. More than half were naked. The lighting was a combination of candles and flashlights propped up at various points on the walls. All the necessities of an apartment seemed to have been jumbled into a single large space. A kitchen sink sat next to a velour couch. A shower stall stood by an ornate desk. Rugs and linoleum and hardwood floors merged into one another, and one corner held an eight-by-eight square of black earth and sand. The ceiling alternated wooden beams with plates of glass through which the stars could be seen. There were no walls on the section that contained the toilet equipment, so men and women peed and shit in full view of everyone.

When Lydia walked into the room, a spotlight went on, flicked over the floor, and settled right on her. For a few moments she was blinded, and Fred whipped the jacket from her shoulders. Suddenly, she was standing in front of a horde of total strangers, tits bare, while a wave of applause and whistles broke over her.

"What . . .?" she started to say.

Then everyone became quiet, and a slow drum beat began in the far corner of the room.

"You're the star," Fred said. "The stage is yours. So, begin the dance."

She glanced over at Fred and did not recognize him. The

lighting, the drugs, the heat in his eyes, all conspired to sculpt his face into a demon's mask. "Perhaps that's his soul," she thought, remembering how Judy had painted her own face to match what she had seen inside.

"Na . . . ked . . . na . . . ked . . . na . . . ked . . . na . . . ked . . ." A chant began and picked up in volume and intensity in time to the ominous beat of the drum.

"Take off your pants, Lydia," Fred suggested.

"I can't. This is insane."

"It's all right to tell your patients to let themselves go, but you won't do it yourself, will you?"

Suddenly, Reginald was standing in front of them.

"We've all seen pussy before, doctor," he said. "Believe me, it's not prurient interest that's motivating us. We just want you to get it on."

"Either this is the sickest thing I've ever been involved with, or the most liberating," Lydia said to herself.

"Or just the silliest," Reginald added, reading her mind.

"And what have you got to lose, except your pants?" Fred concluded.

Not even bothering the give a dramatically appropriate shrug, Lydia stooped forward and peeled the sweat-drenched jeans from her thighs. A chorus of hoots went up when her ass was revealed, and when she finally stood up straight again, wearing nothing, the drum began to speed up, to be joined by another, until the room was filled with the deep thrumming of African rhythms.

Lydia closed her eyes and practiced on herself the technique she had been using with her patients. She began to allow her breathing to assume a consciousness of its own, aware of the vital air as it filled her lungs, her belly, and then the idea of breath going into the rest of her body, mixing with her blood, making her one with the universal prana. She did not dance, but rather let herself be danced, led by the throb of human flesh against taut dried animal skin stretched over vibrating wooden tubs.

Her pelvis rocked gently, her hips swiveled, her breasts shook, her patch of curled black pubic hair thrust itself forward.

"Can I really be doing this?" she wondered, "shaking my cunt at this mob?"

Now her feet lifted and she started to cover ground, her arms joining in the general movement. Like a falling body accelerating in its sweep toward the earth, her dance gained momentum independent of her volition or thought. And so, physically liberated, her face a mask of a previously unrecognized soul, she exposed herself to herself and allowed the world to watch.

Then, in the middle of a gesture, a bizarre psychic occurrence froze her in place. She had not merely a vision of, but a complete sensory identification with Marsha at the moment she had jumped from the edge of the building. For an instant, she felt as though Marsha's soul had seized her own, that the spirit of the dead woman, haunting the ether, had taken possession of her very faculties. Terrified, she opened her eyes, but instead of a room filled with lolling orgiasts, she saw New York City spread before her, and realized that she was actually looking through the brain of the woman who had killed herself four days earlier. Her skin swelled with tiny bumps as she felt the cold night air flicker in from the north. The moan of a mournful harmonica filled her ears.

And then she was falling . . . falling . . . falling . . .

The people at the party perceived nothing more than what seemed to be a strange dance: the naked woman slowly building to an erotic tempo, beginning to leap from the ground in a cunt-splitting arc, and then freezing as though she had turned to marble. But at that instant, the impact of what she was experiencing flashed through the collective consciousness of the room, and as one person everyone there suddenly was grasped by an unaccountable sense of hideous gaiety. They stared at her with the tense stillness and silence of a rabbit paralyzed by the coiled power of a snake.

At which point Lydia screamed at the top of her lungs, a rending, piercing cry which shattered the spines of everyone who had been mesmerized by her transmogrification.

Pandemonium blew three great blasts on its pipes, and the entire sea of bodies broke in a wave of surging flesh.

When Lydia came to, three men were fucking her. Reginald

had wrapped himself around her from behind and was filling her ass with his hefty cock. Fred had taken her cunt for himself. And a third man, someone she didn't recognize, was slipping his semi-erect penis in and out between her flaccid lips.

Next to them a boy of about sixteen, his eyeballs almost white with heroin, was mumbling in a hypnotic chant, "Fuck the dead, fuck the dead, fuck the dead."

4

"Do you think a cow has fantasies of being an eagle?"

Doctor Monroe turned from the window where he had been
following the unintentionally humorous self-importance of a
helicopter buzzing across the panoramic view he commanded
of the city from the sixty-seventh floor of the Chrysler Building
where, for twenty years, he had maintained his practice. It
was, in the eyes of his profession, an odd choice of location,
but he maintained that the building was "the most beautiful
example of religious architecture in America," contending that
since finance was the true guiding mythos of the epoch, the
skyscraper had replaced the cathedral as the dominant form of
collective aspiration. He had a singular passion for the building,
daily relishing its extraordinary detail, down to the inlaid wood
panels on the elevator doors and the silver scallops at its peak.
The Empire State Building he considered majestic but pedestrian,
and for the World Trade Center towers and all the other glass
and aluminum boxes which had sprung up during the boom of
the nineteen sixties he had such great contempt that he refused
even to discuss them.

He was a spare, almost brittle man in his early seventies, a
bit over six feet tall, with close-cropped white hair and a pencil
mustache. He was never seen wearing anything but three-piece
suits. He had been an intimate of all the great pioneers in analysis
and therapy, having worked with Freud, Jung, Adler, Reich,
Rank, and Krug. One shelf of his library held thousands upon
thousands of letters to and from them, including his latest brief
correspondence with Laing, in which he called the explosive
psychiatrist "a psychotic chauvinist."

It had always been difficult for Lydia, given Doctor Monroe's imposing background, elegant personal manner, and massive academic credentials, to gain anything approaching a sense of equality with him. Invariably she left his office feeling like a little girl who had been either scolded or praised by her father. She both idolized him and struggled to free herself from that mixture of transference and objective reverence which kept her transfixed. The simplest thing would have been to stop seeing him, but she couldn't take that as anything but defeat at this point. And when she made her ambivalence known, he retreated into a noncommittal attitude, letting her have the burden of decision.

She'd introduced him to Fred a year after she began her affair with the writer, anxious to know how these two men who formed such a great influence in her life would get on. It is almost a truism that those who are closest to us rarely appeal to one another since our friends and lovers reflect disparate aspects of the total range of our personalities and introducing them to each other often involves a violent clash of colors. As she had feared, the two men disliked one another at once. Their lunch date ended with Fred's calling Doctor Monroe a boring old fart, while the older man noted that since Fred's head was up his ass it would be difficult for him to know whose farts he was smelling. It was the first time Lydia had heard Doctor Monroe use a vulgar word, and she took it as a measure of Fred's influence that he was able to ruffle the venerable therapist. Oddly enough, there had been no real verbal contention, and the surface conversation had been congenial enough. But the men reeked with the rippling aggression of stud stags tangling horns over a doe in heat. Afterwards Lydia had returned home alone and almost immediately torn off her panties and masturbated to a rapid, shattering climax.

"I'm sorry," Lydia was now saying. "I'm a bit fuzzy today. What about cows and eagles?"

Doctor Monroe settled himself in his chair and regarded her with volatile amusement. "After the weekend you described, I'm surprised you are even conscious, much less alert."

Technically, the man was her control therapist. It was his

function to listen to her problems concerning her work with her patients, and to make recommendations, to point out where she might be losing objectivity, or missing an aspect of the total picture. But over time, the distinctions between herself as therapist and herself as person blurred, and often they ended up talking about her without any reference to her patients. This afternoon she had walked in and simply spilled out the events of the previous two days.

After she had awakened to find three men fucking her, she had become hysterical, not only because of the bizarre circumstances but because she still felt the residual vibration of having been inhabited by Marsha's ghost. Her thrashing and screaming had been taken as erotic frenzy, and within seconds a mammoth orgiastic horror show pitched its tents on the pegs of her torment. It had gone on for hours, until every person in the place was sated, had stopped twitching, and Lydia had been definitively defiled.

She and Fred had returned in deep silence, too stunned to speak.

"In some ways," Lydia replied, "the weekend provided the most massive injection of awareness I've ever experienced."

"Please don't confuse stimulation with awareness, nor imagery with consciousness," he told her. "All that happened was your own projection of supposed meaning into an otherwise purposeless event. I think that your fascination comes from the fact that you can't decide whether or not you enjoyed it and, more, whether or not you'd like to repeat it."

Lydia nodded. He'd yanked the covers off her psyche once again, and with an effortless flick of the wrist.

"My earlier question," he went on, "has to do precisely with this issue. As far as we can tell, no other life form experiences discontent with the limitations of its structure and function. A dog does not yearn to be a fish, a tree has no hankering to become a bird. Only the smug ape, the human being, persists in searching for ways to break through the membrane of its inherent limitation. We do this through drugs, of course, through the orgy, through almost all the artifacts of our civilization which are not strictly utilitarian. And finally, most insidiously, we do it through art."

Lydia groaned inwardly, for she knew what was coming. Each person, no matter how intelligent or sophisticated, contains within himself or herself the capacity to be a crank on one subject or another. For Doctor Monroe, it was art. He loathed literature, painting, music, sculpture. The only forms he admitted were architecture and dance, and these he saw not as art but as primary expressions of the organic human being. Even there, however, he could draw strange lines, and contended that dance was valid only as communal ritual; the minute one involved an audience, the form became decadent. And he had been heard to mention more than once that even living in caves was a sign of degeneracy, contending that the species made its first mistake by coming down out of the trees.

Today, however, he surprised her by saying, "But I don't want to get into all that. I bring it up just to remind you that the entire weekend, with its experiences and insights and complexities can be understood quite simply as an attempt by a number of people to pretend that they are something other than people."

"But isn't that attempt the very thing which defines progress, evolution?"

"Evolution?" he repeated, his forehead darkening. "You mean the idea that everything began lower and is becoming higher? I'm surprised that you still have that sort of nonsense knocking about in your brain. Do you think that the planet has produced any life form more perfect than the tree, more burningly beautiful than the hawk, more precisely engineered for survival than the roach? Humanity is merely one of an endless variety of possible life forms, no better or worse than the rest. It is only our insufferable vanity which has us placing ourselves at the crown of creation, confusing cleverness with consciousness, greed with intelligence."

He rose from his chair in a swift singular motion which belied his age and began pacing in front of the picture window.

"You're a therapist, Lydia. And I am not suggesting that you limit the range of your behavior. Go to as many orgies as you want. But for God's sake don't let yourself be led down a primrose path of fantasy. You are exhibiting dangerous tendencies. One of your patients commits suicide, and you wonder whether jumping off a building doesn't express some arcane truth concerning the nature of semantic reality. No! Jumping off a building is just jumping off a building. A human being falls a long way to the earth and her body is smashed beyond all comprehension. And she may have been wrapped in a delusion which made her last moments euphoric, but don't translate that into a notion that she was somehow perceiving a reality beyond the common view. Then, another woman comes in and masturbates in front of you and finds it highly exciting. She's bored with her husband and indulges in a bit of hanky-panky, complete with therapeutic approval. Well, she could get the same thing in a whorehouse, except it would cost more and lack comforting rationalizations."

"It's a shame he and Fred didn't like each other," she thought, "sometimes they sound so fucking alike you would think they were reading the same script."

Doctor Monroe turned toward the city again. For several minutes he was lost in thought. These were the times she liked him best, for he alone among all the people she knew was able to pause in the middle of a conversation to consider what was being said, to reflect on it, to ponder the implications of a question. Of course, she was sure that half the time he did that he was only striking a pose, building a certain effect on his listener. But still, it was an impressive and refreshing mannerism.

Finally, he faced her again and walked over to sink once more into his deep chair. The office was very large, more than twenty by twenty feet in area, but it held only a rug and two chairs so that all attention had to be focused on the people in it and, when the drapes were drawn, the presence of the city.

"The view gives me perspective," he liked to say. "When I get too far into a tunnel vision of my patient or myself, I look out and realize that there are several billion people on the planet, and at any instant millions are dying and being born, laughing, sobbing, starving, fucking, praying, killing, and carrying out their parts in the vast pattern of life in the universe."

They gazed at one another, woman and man, teacher and student, therapist and therapist, human being and human being.

They assumed all the roles necessary to continue the business of busyness while their biological clocks ticked relentlessly away. But beneath all that, what was happening? From a galactic viewpoint, two less than microscopic flecks of stuff were fluttering about making noises at one another. And, peculiar as it seems, taking one another seriously. Because no matter how insignificant the individual life is from the perspective of any other level, to the individual everything else totally and eternally revolves around the self.

"Look, Lydia," he continued, his voice softer, "my approach is a non-approach. I've tried all the systems, known their founders, watched their results, and after a relatively long lifetime have come to the conclusion that nothing changes, nothing can be changed. A therapist can only be an empty vessel. In the old days, we would have been confessors. People come to us and bare their souls. And the single biggest trap we need to avoid is coming to imagine that this process imbues us with any special power or faculty. Oh, we can suggest, occasionally interpret, point out an aspect, and, if the situation calls for it, lend a shoulder to cry on, or give a reassuring embrace. And none of this requires elaborate theory or formality. It's simply finding a strong, flexible center to relate from, and allowing the other person—the patient, if you will—to experience his or her storms of impacted personal drama which will, hopefully, after a while, spend their fury and leave the soul at peace."

As he spoke, his voice became golden. "This is *his* vision," Lydia thought. "While he stands there disputing my ideas with his words, he becomes the living reality of what it is I've been trying to show him."

The moment slipped into one of those oblique corridors of interaction where two people seem to regard one another through eyes that have nothing to do with any of the physical organs of the body. It was akin to the hypnogogic state, that twilight realm between wakefulness and sleep when untranslatable truths are revealed. It was this very condition that Lydia strove for in her sessions, for she felt that that kind of mutual awareness allowed for more penetrating communication than was ever possible through direct interchange of words. She had shied away from the concept of telepathy, because of its occultist overtones, but since the experience in Provincetown she had been converted to the idea that mind-to-mind contact was not only possible, but constituted the essential language of the species.

Fantasy, she now saw, was nothing more than the warehousing of information which could not be telepathically shared.

Doctor Monroe floated down off the cloud of visionary grandiloquence which had pushed all the buttons in the pleasure centers of his brain.

"So you see," he went on, "the more you *do,* the less you *accomplish.* All your private researches into fantasy, and fantastic reality, and socially conditioned perceptions, whether you use meditative techniques or erotic excess, are nothing but admirable. But their result must find you a more dimensional, more balanced, and, above all, more transcendent human being. Otherwise you become one of the vulgar little mechanics like Janov or Lowen, sticking your fingers into people's mouths and your dogmatic ideas into their minds." He waved his hand violently in the air. "Stay away from that, stay away from it. It's only a masked form of violence."

Lydia stood up abruptly and walked to the window. It was her turn to think things through. Doctor Monroe fell back into his chair, lit a cigarette, and puffed contentedly. He enjoyed his sessions with Lydia. They provided precisely the proper edge of tension which allowed for the fullest expression of the interpersonal game. They'd been working together for four years. After the end of the second year, he'd fucked her, arguing that when a man and a woman work together they build a certain tension that must be resolved erotically or they will begin to get on one another's nerves. It had been a lovely and courtly night, and he had asked if she minded getting on top because at his age he couldn't stand too much strain. The next morning they parted cleanly and no reference was made to the event again.

Now he wondered whether they might not be ready for another fuck. As he grew closer to dying, his world view simplified, and he sometimes viewed his entire education as one long distraction from appreciating the basic pleasures of being alive: good eating, hearty drinking, lusty fucking and sound sleeping. He would have liked, in a way, to tell Lydia precisely that, advise her to drop the absurd notion that we have to understand why we do what we do, and just go ahead and enjoy it. But that would be interfering with his own credo of non-interference. Besides, what was applicable to an old man might not be right for a young woman. He was certain that her present experimentation was healthy and he wanted to encourage her, but at the same time warn her not to be precipitous for she could do real damage to people who made themselves vulnerable to her. The masturbation incident with Mrs. Norwood was potentially quite dangerous. He knew how most people require some authority to tell them what to do, when to get up, where to work, what to believe. What was Hitler, after all, but a man who evoked a racial fantasy in a people and then set them to acting it out? He knew Lydia had no evil intentions, but as much harm could come out of ignorance.

Doctor Monroe watched her. The shapely calves disappearing under her full skirt, the pinched waist, the pert breasts, and the utterly lascivious mouth, all inspired in him an abstract lust. He experienced very little active desire any longer, but could still remember the taste of erotic need on his tongue, and realized that if he were younger, Lydia would be a true torment to him. He recalled the soft resiliency of her buttocks under his fingers as she straddled his thighs and urged her cunt onto his twitching rod. She had been so serious! Had tried so hard to do it right! He was aware of the whopping transference she carried, and of his own equally powerful counter-transference. It was important that she see him as just a man, and he had justified his behavior by reasoning that fucking was the royal road to the conscious mind.

"By Jove, it *would* be delightful to ram my prod into that juicy young snatch," he said to himself, and decided that for this occasion he would use the same rationalization as he had used the last time.

"It's not even scratched," he argued.

Lydia turned slowly.

"Maybe there's something to it," she said. "On the other hand, if you see someone about to get hit by a car, don't you try to pull them out of the way? And what about the people who have such a low energy level that they can barely speak without constant prodding. I suppose what I'm asking is, to what degree is a therapist a doctor, or even a savior?"

"Ninety-five percent of all the people you will ever see are suffering from some form of dietary deficiency, even though they may be overfed. Most have no healthy exercise for their bodies. They are weighed down by pollution, noise, anxiety, the fear of nuclear war, threats of starvation, unemployment, not to mention the routine wear and tear of relationship in a competitive society. They wear restrictive clothing and don't even know how to sleep properly. Their entire civilization is out of kilter. And they have practically no contact with their biological rhythms. Now, what are you supposed to do? Clearly, one wants to do everything, to solve the total world problem at once. But how much is possible? At best, a human being can hope to bring some order and light into his or her own life, and if that much is accomplished, perhaps to illuminate the way for others. But to meddle . . . why, that's monstrous."

"And what about Marsha?"

"What about her? If someone wants to commit suicide, what can you do? Keep a twenty-four hour guard?"

Doctor Monroe looked at her steadily, his eyes half-hooded. While the rational portion of his mind had been listening to her and speaking coherently, the sexual center had begun to throb with a deep booming resonance.

There are moments between a man and a woman which don't require much explanation. Times when the lips fall open and leave a sentence half finished. When the eyes start to glow with an ancient flame. There are a number of ways to understand such times, but the simplest is probably the truest. It is then that the god Eros enters the space, and what had simply been an interaction between two people now becomes a hallowed ritual, the dance of a god whose spirit ruled half the earth. The visitation of the god can be ignored, or misinterpreted, or taken as a private triumph of seductive charm. But if we can see through all those devices to the vibrant reality of the god, then a great grace is given, and those so honored can taste immortality for a few brief hours, grow heady on the elixir of eternal life, and know such beauty that the human heart bursts in its attempts to encompass its own rapture. The god is capricious, and visits when and where it wills. One can cajole or pray or demand, and sometimes meet with a response, but the most ecstatic of all experiences is feeling the sudden embrace from behind.

"I . . . suppose . . . you . . . can't . . ." Lydia said. Her words fell from her lips like sweet sticky drops of nectar from a freshly sliced pear. Her diction was slurred. She spoke very slowly.

"Then, learn to be, and let what happens happen. Listen, absorb, grow steady. That's your only responsibility, your only possibility." As Doctor Monroe spoke he slid down into his chair. He seemed to shrink and fade and disappear. His body was thin, very thin. He gave off a strange light.

"Does . . . that . . . end . . . the . . . session . . . for . . . today . . .?" she asked, her words catching the molecules of the air like oar tips cutting the water.

"Be hot cunt," he said.

"All right," she replied.

She walked toward him, hips swaying, breasts lolling softly under the cloth of her dress. Both hands massaged her belly and she undulated as she moved, as though she were a belly dancer daydreaming with her navel. She had heard the call also, and was surprised at that, for her last erotic encounter with Doctor Monroe had been essentially psychological, an exercise of the body to work out the needs of the emotions. This time, however, there was more of the mood she had experienced in Provincetown, a sense of being captive to a force larger than they were. Of course, on another level, she saw herself as a woman of thirty-four about to fuck a man of seventy-three, a man with whom she had a long, complex, and not always clear relationship. But that level was dry, abstract, in the face of the passionate god who called her to worship.

The sun was setting over her shoulder, crashing in through the window of Doctor Monroe's office set high above the city. The entire space was boiling with light, the great red ball itself booming into the room as it hurled fierce rays through the plate glass and sizzled the air with radiance. The old man squinted and could barely make out Lydia's figure as she slowly peeled off her clothing. She stood out in total relief, her body a black silhouette. He discerned now a lifted thigh, now a curving breast. He leaned back more deeply into his chair as the naked woman loomed over him.

It seemed that this single moment, this precious instant, was the culmination and reward for a lifetime of labor. He sat in the center of his working space, where he had seen thousands upon thousands of people, where he had pondered and plumbed the depths of the human psyche, where he had rejoiced in his ability to help, and despaired over his helplessness in the face of human suffering.

In the next room stood his books, and his collections of letters, and the photographs showing him with an arm around Freud's shoulder, throwing snowballs with Reich in Maine, playing chess with Jung. He was at the height of his career and life, universally venerated, liked, respected, one of the few who had gone through the entire course of modern analytic and therapeutic history without making bitter enemies. And now, his favorite student, his most cherished follower, his psychologic daughter, was pulling his zipper down, bending over his thighs, sucking his wrinkled cock into hardness, and then lowering her luscious nakedness onto him, her feet on the floor, rocking on her buttocks, enveloping him in warmth, filling the room with the melancholy aroma of female secretions.

What more could he desire? His mind danced in delight, his loins trembled with pleasure, and his hands roamed delicately over the soft and sensitive flesh of Lydia, the darling of his eye.

The sun struck directly through the window. From far away he could hear the howl of sirens, of fire engines. He could feel their height above the street, and their immense distance from the globe of fire which now grilled the room with heat. The whole universe swung as nonchalantly as a feather falling through space. He knew that the totality of what he felt and thought at that instant had to be the most any human being could expect from life. All the days of his years passed before him like a sweeping mosaic . . . the loves . . . the friends . . . the early period as a student in Austria, the flight from the Nazis, the struggle in America in the thirties, and then the gradual accumulation of fame and fortune.

Lydia moved with more cutting urgency. The sun whipped her back and she started to sweat freely. Doctor Monroe's face was bathed in light, a radiant red-orange, and his silver hair seemed aflame. His eyes were closed and his lips curved into a faint smile. His cock throbbed between her thighs. She felt only waves of pleasure, none of the sharp edges that indicate orgasmic climax. She had no sense of coming, but only to ride like this forever, to mount her father-figure teacher-guide and gallop slowly home into the sunset.

But he moaned gently, his jaw fell open, and his thighs quivered. He sat up straight. Then, the wet pulsing in her cunt, and the awareness of his sperm filling her. His eyes opened for a split second, he looked at her oddly, gasped, and sank back against the chair.

For him, the climax had begun in his loins, but moved quickly to his chest. As his cock spurted and his mind tingled, his heart swelled with warmth as rushes of love fell like a series of small waterfalls. But the warmth was suddenly transformed into a stab of heat, and then into a searing lance of white-hot pain. It seemed as though the rays from the sun and the electricity from Lydia's cunt and the fire in his chest were all one thing, one single bolt of pure energy.

"I'm dying," he thought as he came.

Lydia sensed the sudden and radical change in him and instantly leapt back, his sperm dribbling down her thighs, cooling rapidly.

His face was grey and his eyes opened slowly. He had trouble focusing, and stared feebly into the light of the sinking sun.

"The sun and I die together," he said.

"Oh, Doctor Monroe," Lydia said.

"Please, my dear, after all this time and at such a moment," he gasped, "surely you can call me by my first name."

"Edgar," she whispered, "Don't . . . you can't . . . die."

"I hadn't planned on it," he said, and then caught at his chest with one hand.

The spasm passed and he inclined his head slightly, beckoning her forward. She knelt next to his side, and held one of his hands to her breasts.

"Tell me," he said in a low trembling voice, "how should I view my death now? Is it real, or is it a fantasy?"

"How can you . . .?" she began.

"Now," he hissed, "is the most important time. Look into my eyes. Listen to me."

She leaned forward.

"I'm at the very edge between the two worlds, and I can tell you something you can't know until you reach this spot yourself. Listen to me."

"Yes, Edgar, yes," she said, and came to within an inch of his face.

Then, his lips curved into an imbecilic grin while his eyes raged with unbearable wisdom and in a strained, cracked voice he began to sing . . . "Row . . . row . . . row . . . your boat . . . gently down the stream . . . Merrily . . . merrily . . . merrily . . . merrily . . . Life is . . . but . . . a . . . drea . . ."

He never pronounced the final consonant. He died with his lips parted. Lydia stared at him a long time, tears flowing down her cheeks. Then, she got to her feet and, unaccountably, began to smile.

"You old bastard," she said out loud. "The whole thing's been a joke, hasn't it? And you never told the punch line."

She dressed rapidly, wiped Doctor Monroe's cock clean, put it back in his pants, and zipped him up. Then she called the police.

The next day the *Times* ran a lengthy obituary in which it was reported that the venerable therapist had died of a heart attack while in the middle of a session with one of his students, and noted that he passed away while doing his work, which had been the keynote of his entire life.

5

Lydia brooded over the city. It was a pus-grey day in late November, the air smirking with a sudden chill, the sky invisible through the sheet of pollution particles which aged the air. She wondered how it was possible for anyone to find anything approaching health in such an atmosphere, and was reminded of the experiments done with rats during her undergraduate days. Put a large number of rats in a crowded space and they begin to develop all the symptoms of human neurosis: hostile aggression, apathy, perversion. The term for it was behavioral sink, and that was precisely what New York looked like that morning, the bottom of a sink in which someone was washing out dirty mops.

The funeral had been that morning, and Fred had gone with her. She had told him about how Doctor Monroe had actually died, expecting him to turn the incident into a bit of black comedy with a quip or a one-liner. She herself, when the police had arrived and were bustling about the office, had thought, "Jesus Christ, can't I just get laid anymore? It's always turning into some kind of melodrama." But Fred had instead become silent and concerned, and then said something which frightened her.

"Look, Lydia, you know the scene in the old horror movies where the mad scientist's assistant turns to the doctor and says, 'There are some things that human beings should not tamper with.'? Well, I'm beginning to feel a little like that with you. I don't know what's happened to you since that girl jumped off the tower, but you're accumulating weirdness the way a vacuum cleaner sucks up dust."

The cold wind had whipped around her legs as the small knot of people watched quietly while Doctor Monroe was lowered into the ground. He had requested in his will that his funeral not be turned into a circus, and only his friends were there. No one from his family attended and Lydia discovered, after all the years she had known him, that the old therapist despised all his relatives.

"Please," she told Fred as they walked away from the grave, "you're not going to blame me for his death, are you?"

"It's just that you're beginning to have the look of someone possessed," he said. "And maybe you'd better just cool it for a while. Take a vacation, get some fresh air and hot sun. It will burn away the morbidity."

The very word "sun" sent a shiver through her. She would never forget the eerie orange light which seized the room just as Doctor Monroe died. Then, a second later, the sun had dipped behind the shoreline of the Hudson River, and a darkness immediately enveloped her.

"I'm not deranged," she said in a voice too loud, for several of the people walking next to them turned their heads to look at her. "You were there the night Marsha jumped; you know something extraordinary was going on. And I don't care how much it's rationalized afterwards, what that woman did had a special meaning. And as far as what happened in Provincetown, that was all on your instigation."

"I know," he replied, "that's why I feel partially responsible and want to help you out of this funk."

"Who are those two?" one of the women walking behind them whispered.

"She was with him when he died," another replied.

"Looks like a hussy," the first one concluded.

Lydia and Fred overheard the exchange and smiled at one another, and then fell into a pseudo-respectful silence. He had not said anything further that morning but after they parted, he to his office and she to her day's roster of patients, she reflected on his words. In less than a week she had been involved in two deaths, an orgy, and an incident of explosive voyeurism. And now the man who more than anyone else had goaded her to break out of the straitjacket of reality orientation was hinting that she might be going off the deep end.

She did feel the speed at which she was moving, but it had none of the reassurance of a train barreling along its tracks. Rather it was like a runaway bus careening down the highway, swaying and lurching, the driver almost certainly drunk. She, she realized with a start, was the driver! All her life, especially her professional life, Lydia had been the soul of caution, never intruding, never even suggesting too strongly, but merely listening, accepting, acting as a feedback machine, doing little more for the patient than amplifying what she or he already felt. Now, it was as though she had gone berserk, chasing after a goal she could only dimly perceive, much less define. And as always in life, clarity was a function of distance. The closer she involved herself in her pursuit, the less detachment she could manage. She had no criterion for judging whether she might be right or wrong any longer.

The doorbell rang and she broke away from her moody contemplation on her life and from the hypnotic appeal of the massively depressing day.

It was Edmond Morrison, a man in his early forties, who had come to her several months earlier with a problem of impotence. For the previous twenty years he had lived a rather carefree bachelor life, getting his fair share of sex, usually through brief encounters but occasionally by an extended affair. He had never considered marriage. Until he had met Julie, a schoolteacher who had managed the rare trick of not letting him fuck her, while keeping his interest lively. They had dated for two months before she acceded to going to bed with him, by which time he had grown inordinately fond of her and come to know her in a dimensional way. They'd talked about their respective childhoods, met one another's friends, shown photographs of their parents, and, in short, gone through the entire paraphernalia of middle class courtship. But when the moment came for him to take her in his arms, he found he couldn't maintain an erection. They tried a dozen times, each one ending in failure, until, in desperation, she had buried her head in his crotch and tried to suck him into hardness. His response was extreme: he hurled her away and burst into a fit of anger, screaming that he couldn't allow her to do such a nasty thing.

It was shortly after that that he'd gone to see Lydia. Her work with him had been unpromising. He was a handsome man, dark skinned, with black eyes and modishly styled pepper-and-salt hair. A successful electrical engineer, his clothes showed exceptional good taste and the investment of a good deal of money. But like all articulate and educated people, he tended to be very glib about himself, putting forth analytic explanations for his condition before he was able to contact his actual feelings. Lydia knew what he needed—it was necessary for the man to make a connection between his perceptions and his emotions—but she didn't know how to accomplish that. Doctor Monroe had given his usual advice: "Heavy empathic feedback; reinforce even the smallest show of feeling. But under no circumstances attempt to draw him out, for that might precipitate an explosion for which you really might not want to take the consequences."

She had been patient, non-directive, but even the most thorough relaxation and breathing explorations had produced nothing but tenuous cerebration. Today, with all the ambivalences of the past week plucking at her mind, Lydia decided to move forward. From one viewpoint, what she planned to do was not very drastic, for therapists all over the country were taking it upon themselves to re-program their patients, involving them in everything from muscle-tearing massage to immersion in pools of warm water. Lydia had nothing more drastic in mind than giving Edmond Morrison a small push, and not even from a very high place.

He seemed dejected as he entered, and removed his jacket and shoes, loosened his tie and belt, and lay down on the floor without saying a word. She let him relax for a few minutes and then asked, "Ed, how long have you been coming here?"

"A couple of months," he replied.

"Do you feel these visits have done you any good?"

He shifted his eyes to look at her for a few seconds to see if there was a hidden trap in her question.

"Well," he said, "I feel a little hopeful every time I arrive, and every time I leave. But otherwise, I don't think I'm any closer to solving my problem than I had been before I started seeing you."

"Good," she said.

He looked at her with surprise.

"What I mean is, I'm glad you're so clear about what's been happening, because that's my evaluation also. And quite frankly, I feel that we could go on as we have for years, or you might try other therapists, and still not see through the dynamics of your condition. Oh, you'd certainly be able to understand it conceptually, and I'm sure you could talk on it for hours even now. But to have that block inside split apart . . . that's the issue."

She let herself down to the floor until she was sitting next to him. "Today, I'd like to try a technique that some people call guided fantasy. And all that means is that instead of working with your body and waiting to see what sort of fantasy material is released, I'll sort of help you along, give you little nudges."

"Sounds harmless enough," he said.

"I don't know," she said. "Under ordinary circumstances, it would be, but there's a very strange energy gathering around me these days, and bizarre things are taking place. This may sound a bit crazy, but I feel as though destiny has suddenly decided to use me as the agent for something spectacular."

Her words created an odd tingle in his loins, one which mixed apprehension with eroticism. It was as though she were suggesting something disreputable, naughty. He glanced at her with appraising eyes, something he had never dared to do before, thinking it improper in their relationship. What he saw now impressed him. She no longer wore the rather shapeless dress which had been her trademark, but a pair of form-fitting hip huggers that clasped her round thighs and even emphasized the slight bulge of her pubic mound. A sleeveless blouse revealed a slim torso which supported smallish but very firm breasts and—he now noted with wonder—the nipples of which poked clearly out into the thin fabric. It astonished him that he had not noticed all this as soon as he walked into the room.

"You've changed," he said, somewhat lamely.

"Yes," she told him. "And so has your inability to see me in certain ways."

"What ways?"

"With desire, for example."

Lydia was startled to hear her words. What she said couldn't be considered anything less than a straightforward erotic ploy.

"Why am I doing this?" she wondered. "Do I feel any desire to get it on with this man, or am I just being reckless?" It was astounding how quickly she was leaping levels.

Edmond looked intently at her face as it melted before his eyes. First the sharp-edged mask which was his conditioned perception of the therapist. Then the young and sensuous woman beneath that. Then the wise lady who could guide him into himself. Deeper still, he saw the teenage Lydia, with her pimples and plans. And then, the almost terrifying features of an utter stranger, someone, he realized with a start, he did not know at all.

"Close your eyes," she told him.

His lids flickered and lowered. At once, his breathing became deeper.

"Now, try to let all your tension flow into the floor. In this position, gravity becomes a friend instead of an enemy. You don't have to use a single muscle to support yourself. In fact, you can let your muscles be massaged by the pull of the earth. Sink into it, sink into the arms of Mother Earth."

She spoke slowly, evenly, her voice low. She was like a woman lulling an infant to sleep, and also a snake charmer, weaving a web of music around the head of a cobra, dancing with her flute, mesmerizing the serpent with sound and movement until it responded to the slightest flicker of the master's eyes.

"In this approach," she went on, "the key word is surrender. You are to give up all your tension, all your resistance. Melt into the floor, and melt into yourself. Pretend that the floor is quicksand, and that you are being sucked down, pulled into the wet enveloping darkness. Go into a space where there is no time, no differentiation, but only an all-encompassing forgetfulness, a loss of every sensation except your breath, an end to all experience except emptiness."

She watched him closely. His breathing had become deep, regular. His face had lost all its wrinkles. He began to look very, very young. This was the condition of pure receptivity, and now she faced the most difficult part. It was now that she would try to suggest something to him to begin his fantasy machinery, to start the journey into his psyche to find out where he might be blocked. It would be a voyage into the dark for, while she might foresee some of the general responses possible, she had no way of knowing what his specific reaction would be.

In the past, at this point, she would have given him a neutral image, such as standing on a beach or walking through a woods. Now, however, she gazed at him a long time, trying to get some vague glimmering of proper direction. Then, all at once, she smiled. She had seen it.

"Can you see yourself as a Viking?" she asked.

He was quiet a long time, and seemed to be struggling with something. A small frown formed on his forehead. And after several minutes he reported, "I can see it. I have on a silver breastplate and helmet, a shield, and a huge sword."

"Fine. Where are you?"

"I'm stepping off a boat. I'm with a small raiding party. We're going to attack a small village."

"Good," she said. "What happens next?"

The process was beginning to get exciting. She felt like a potter at her wheel, except that instead of clay she was using the psychic energy of another human being to create shapes. There was something godlike about it, and small warning bells went off in her mind, trying to warn her to be careful. But the pull forward was too strong, too compelling.

Ed began to shift about on the floor. She noted that his breathing was getting more rapid, more shallow. His face had regained most of its tension.

"I'm rushing into a hut. There's a woman there. She's nursing a baby. She's young, perhaps only twenty, and wearing just a skirt. Her breasts are round and gleaming and filled with milk. I . . ."

He broke off, his body stiff with resistance, unwilling to continue.

"Go on," Lydia urged. "Follow the fantasy."

"She looks up at me," he continued. "Her eyes go wide with fear. She tries to shield the baby and to cover her breasts. The nipples are still dripping. She tries to move away from me. She seems more naked to me than any woman I have ever seen. I have burst into the very core of her intimacy. And now my cock is rock hard, stiff, hungry."

"What do you do?"

"I step forward. I'm laughing. I pull the baby from her arms and . . ."

Now he froze into a grotesque contortion, his fists clenched, his jaw locked, his spine rigid. Every muscle in his body was under intolerable strain.

"NOOOOOOOOO!"

Like a dam bursting, the tension exploded and he let out a loud booming scream, a sound that shook his entire frame. He began to roll about on the floor, his fists pounding the rug.

"Keep going," Lydia whispered, but even as she said it she wondered, "Good God, I hope I'm not pushing him into some realization about himself that will damage his psyche."

"I . . . I . . . throw the baby against the wall," he continued, gasping. "I throw it hard and ruthlessly, not caring whether I kill it or not. The mother tries to go to it, but I strike her with my sword. I cut her arm deeply, and suddenly there is blood everywhere. The sight enflames me. I grow wild with lust. I fling myself upon her. I suck her tits, drawing the hot milk into my throat. She struggles against me, and then, magically, my cock is out. I yank her skirt away. I am still sucking her breasts, drinking the delicious honey of her body, and at the same time pushing my cock into her, probing her belly, slipping between her thighs, and finally finding the hole. She is wet! I can't believe that she is aroused. Her baby is dead and her arm is half cut off and a savage is gnawing at her nipples, and yet she responds. She groans when I enter her. Her face is a mask of hatred and still there is desire in her eyes. Her movement is as much into me as against me. I feel her slick cunt walls pulling at my cock, her ass pumping, and then I am coming, shooting into her. Suddenly, everything becomes everything else. Her milk squirting into my mouth is my sperm spurting into her cunt and both are the blood that is covering our bodies with wet heat. And I am putting the seed of a new baby into her to replace the baby I have killed. Her face keeps changing. I see the face of every woman I have ever fucked, the face of Julie, and now it becomes the face of my mo . . . my moth . . . my . . . no . . . not her . . . not my mo . . ."

Ed sat bolt upright, his face covered with sweat. His body was trembling, his hands clenching and unclenching, and his eyes were pried wide open as though he had just looked upon a definitive terror.

"Ed," Lydia said softly.

He put his hands over his face, and to their great surprise, started to sob, great heaving gasps that seemed to burst from his heart. He cried like a little boy, without reservation, without shame, without embarrassment, letting a lifetime of buried feeling well to the surface.

Lydia watched the child emerge through the consciousness of the man, and a deep warmth suffused her chest. She had done it! She had forced him to make the connection.

When the crying stopped, and he took his hands away, his eyes were pools of amazement.

"Was that me?" he whispered. "All that violence and horror and pain and brutality. Can that really be what's inside me?"

Lydia ran a hand through her hair, sighed deeply, and began to explain to him what had happened. She knew that her interpretation would be off the cuff, but thought that that's what she should give him, without any theoretical shenanigans.

"All of that . . . ugliness," she said, "is what lies between your surface personality and your true nature, which is one of simple affection. All of the years you spent fucking women were a function of the superficial self. That's why you were such a successful cocksman, because you had everything in control. But when you met Julie, she touched something deeper in you. And when you started to respond at that level, you had to go through all your negative feelings. And you became frightened of facing them, so you shut yourself off. And since we can't cut off one part of ourselves without that affecting all the other parts, the erotic impulse was also corralled, and thus your impotence."

"But I can't believe all that is inside me," he said, reaching for a cigarette. He lit it and smoked for a few seconds. "I know I'm not a bad person."

Lydia realized that he hadn't understood what she had told him. So she tried again, from a different angle. "We all have that inside us," she said. "It's the disease of our civilization. We see its results either when we act it out, and become murderers or rapists or just generally hateful people, or when we suppress it and pretend it isn't there, at which point we become dull and empty and lifeless."

"But then what can we do with it?" he asked, finally seeing the point.

"Just feel it," she told him. "Go into it and touch it and don't be afraid. Then your feelings, your deeper feelings, will be released, first the tears, and then the joy, and finally the simple peacefulness that lies at the heart of everything."

She paused for a few moments and then went on. "The structure of your fantasy is incredibly clear. The baby at the woman's breast was you, the old you, and you had to kill that baby in order to make a new one. Cutting her was destroying the false image you have of women in order to avoid facing the fact that you have been defending against seeing your mother in them. When your mother's face did emerge at last, you fell apart. But by then you had already planted a new seed in her belly, thus fathering your new self. And what you found most astonishing is that even though you were being murderous and brutal the woman still desired you, which expresses your feelings of being unworthy as a child for all the erotic desires you had for your mother and couldn't communicate. And then to learn that she reciprocates those feelings, why that is truly traumatic."

Ed shook his head. "You make it sound so simple."

"It is simple, once it's understood. But even as dramatic as today's session was, it's going to take time until you can weep freely, and then integrate those feelings into your total self. And even more time before you are operating completely out of your core, and able to love Julie and give her a baby and fuck her like you wanted to fuck your mother, all at once."

Lydia lit a cigarette for herself, blew smoke, and thought for a while. "You know," she said finally, "I'm beginning to see that once we free our fantasies, they will take us anywhere we want to go. But not just in our heads. They will tell us what we need to know to live well, like fairy tales or parables. And they can change our emotions, and our perception of reality, and even the nature of reality itself. It's strange and wondrous and magical, and the whole process excites me and disturbs me terribly."

They were silent for a long time and then Ed cleared his throat.

"I have something very embarrassing to say," he told her.

"What better place or time?" Lydia said.

"I'm very aroused."

For a second she didn't grasp his meaning, and then she glanced down and saw the erection tenting his pants.

"It feels like it will stay hard forever," he remarked. "What do I do with that?"

"Call Julie, I would say," she replied, but even as she spoke she knew that that wasn't what either of them had in mind. She had to admit to herself that her arousal paralleled his. She hadn't paid any attention to her state because she had been swept up in maintaining her therapeutic distance, and lost in trying to think through the meaning of his fantasy. Yet now, she could feel the unmistakable moisture dampening her inner thighs, the telltale wrinkling of her nipples through the fabric of her blouse. Suddenly, the whole structure of their situation fell away, and she was a woman, coming into heat, and he was a man who seemed ready to tear all their clothing off.

"What if we were to reverse the roles?" Ed asked. "What if I were to ask you to lie down and get into your fantasies. What do you think you would come up with now?"

Lydia chewed her lower lip and stared down at the floor. All at once she felt like a blushing teenage girl. Once the barrier of her role as therapist had been let down, she realized that she was totally vulnerable to the actual feelings and needs that motivated her as a person. On the one hand, this gave her a sense of heightened reality; but on the other, she no longer had any firm ground to stand on. She wondered what therapy was anyway, this highly artificial situation in which one human being assumed a stance of superior wisdom in order to supposedly help another human being with problems which the first person might be harrowed with in his or her own life. Yet, without that distance, false as it might seem, people would not reach the point that she and Ed were at now.

"Therapy is like Wittgenstein's ladder," she concluded. "Once it's been used to get one to the second floor, it can be thrown away. Therapy is a tool, no more, no less."

She looked up at Ed, and saw that he was leering. He had taken her yielding silence for acquiescence and was now relishing fucking her. Or, from the look in his eye, raping her. A flurry of perception flipped through her, and she saw the situation from a score of viewpoints at once, including the scenario in which she emerged as an object of degradation, preying on people's vulnerabilities to slake her ever-growing lust, like a vampire with an insatiable hunger.

She thought she heard a rustling in one corner of the room, and she glanced over to see what it could be. A spasm of paralyzing horror gripped her as she saw the face of Doctor Monroe forming in the air, his ironic gaze taking in the entire scene.

She didn't have too much opportunity to remain in that condition, however, for Ed was already coming toward her, his hands reaching for her breasts. Something in his manner, something in the way that what she had intended as a serious experiment in therapeutic relationship had degenerated into erotic tawdriness, disgusted her. But she could not move. The specter of Doctor Monroe held her in thrall, and her own lascivious vibration put her cunt in control over her mind.

Her thoughts vacillated between psychological rationalizations and the brute reality of her condition. She was alternately working on the edge of an erotic revolution, breaking down the walls between patient and doctor, and at the same time being nothing more than a randy woman who was using her therapist's role to have people come to her office and pay for sex, either to masturbate in front of her, or as it seemed would happen now, to fuck her.

She struggled with the conflict, all the while listening to Doctor Monroe's ghastly chuckle, while Ed pushed on relentlessly. She felt his hot breath against her cheek, his tongue in her ear, his fingers at her nipples. A certain loosening took place in her belly and her thighs parted slightly, giving him access to the rapidly secreting slit between them. She could already smell her own secretions beginning to fill the space.

His frantic hands slid down her stomach and one cupped her cunt while the other made its way behind, covering the crack of her ass. She was clutched tightly, and found herself squirming in his grasp, rotating her pelvis to rub more energetically against his palms. Then, he seemed to have ten arms. He was stroking her and prodding her and taking her clothes off and unzipping his pants all at once. They rolled around the floor, puffing and wrestling and humping like college students on a babysitter date.

Lydia was now practically naked, her blouse thrown to one side, her slacks down her legs and hanging on to one of her ankles, her panties literally torn down the middle and discarded. The lithe, lovely and intelligent therapist was writhing on her own rug and her patient of a few moments earlier was mauling her indiscriminately, his salivating tongue laying wet swatches on her breasts, his teeth nipping her nipples, his hands insinuating themselves into her cunt and asshole.

"Oh, you hot little bitch," Ed moaned. "I knew it, I knew you were a slut. Under all the fancy talk, you're just a hot cunt just like all the others."

She both reveled in and was horrified by his words. They simultaneously inflamed and frightened her. For she was, in a sense, what he said she was. But at the same time her whole effort had been to help him with his feelings about women. With an inspiration born of desperation, she tried a dangerous stratagem.

"Just like Julie, eh? Is your little Julie like this? While you try to turn her into a virgin, is she somewhere right now with some man sticking his cock into her quivering quim?"

An insane rage flashed into his eyes, and he reared back and slapped her hard across the mouth. At once she tasted the metallic tang of blood. For an instant she feared he might go berserk and really hurt her, or even kill her, but instead he grabbed her hair and yanked her head forward, pressing her face against his crotch.

"Suck it, you therapy whore," he said.

"Oh Lord," Lydia thought. "It's going to be another one of *those*."

"I'm glad you explained it all to me, Lydia," he said. "Now that I'm clear as to where the different aspects of my behavior come from, I can choose which level I want to work from. And right now, I'm digging all the horrid, icky neurotic shit in the middle layer. So put your cunt mouth on my hot prick."

She felt the throbbing length of hard flesh push itself between her lips and slide along her tongue. Ed pumped his hips into her face and his cock lodged in her throat. But it was a temporary stay. She couldn't breathe and the gag reflex set in. She started to vomit. He pulled out, gave her a second to catch her breath, and then shoved in again. Again, her stomach lurched as her throat constricted and convulsed. Ed was on his knees while Lydia lay on her belly. He held her face up by pulling her hair, and he fucked her face with hard, almost vicious strokes. He looked down with an expression of gloating delight. Here was his therapist, an educated and stunning woman, her mouth around his rod.

Something in Lydia snapped and she gave way to the erotic manifestations and movements which complemented the action she had been conscripted into. Her ass rotated as she pressed her pussy against the floor. It's interesting that certain motions, abstracted from an erotic context, serve no purpose but to allow the body to free itself of certain inhibition tensions, and have come to be judged erotic in themselves.

"I've got a cock in my mouth, and I'm pumping away like a nymphomaniac trying to have an orgasm, but I swear this isn't sexy," Lydia said to herself.

Then her whole body was racked by spasms, and even as she felt herself beginning to throw up, the one thought that caught her was that Ed would be viewing this as a quintessentially erotic scene.

He pulled his cock out, and before he could thrust it in again,

Lydia vomited, spewing up the contents of her stomach over Ed's thighs.

"Son of a bitch, that's wild," Ed said as he ejaculated.

He came for a long time, still twitching after his seed was spent, and when the excitement passed away, he let Lydia drop. She fell as though unconscious and lay without moving. Ed looked down at her and shivered.

He rose slowly to his feet and backed away. He made his way to Lydia's bathroom, cleaned himself as best he could, went back to get his shoes, and walked quickly, nervously out of the apartment.

Lydia lay in a yellow stupor until she was revived by the screams. They came from far away at first, and she didn't connect them with herself. But as she focused, opened her eyes and looked around, she saw Marie Jorgenson, her next patient, standing in the doorway, terror carved into her features.

Lydia sat up slowly, shook her head, and then spoke, slowly and calmly. She was smeared with blood and sperm and vomit, her body naked, an expression of sparkling bemusement, a second-cousin to madness, lighting up her face.

"What's wrong. Made," she asked. "Haven't you ever seen a fantasy come to life before?"

6

As the city sank deeply into the grey of winter, Lydia collapsed further into herself. More and more she stayed at home, leaving only rarely, having her food delivered, going from apartment area to office area and back without varying her routine a lot. She had never felt more alone, even though she was surrounded by people during much of her waking day. Fred was staying away, showing a faint and vague disapproval of her consciously chosen mood.

Doctor Monroe was dead. And there was no one else in the world to whom she could bring her doubts and insecurities. The incident with Ed had unnerved her, but she had nowhere to go but forward. Or was it downward? Once a person is embarked upon a course which is totally involving, taking in a sense of identity, as well as function, the whole of reality changes. Everything from one's friendships to one's relationship with the Absolute undergoes a subtle and terrible transformation. It is like going to a foreign country, and staying for longer than just a visit. Soon, one starts to absorb the language, the tempo, the nuance of the people. But all the while, back home, life is moving at its usual pace and the people there are sharing common experiences. Then, abruptly, one returns and finds that he had become an alien, a pleasantly welcomed but intrinsically distant stranger. The attitude of everyone one knows is something like, "Well, we're glad to have you back, but don't expect us to drop everything; we've been struggling with our lives while you've been traipsing off." And then one realizes that one must stay in one's own home for as long a period as one had been away in order to re-acclimate, and still, after all that, forever have missed that slice of contextual time, forever be just a little out of step.

So it was with Lydia. Her colleagues seemed removed, and she did not know whether reports of what she was doing were reaching them or not and affecting their feelings about her, or whether she was projecting her own unease onto them.

One afternoon she had run into Casper Gemini, a man with whom she had had shared one drunken night at an American Association of Humanistic Psychologists' convention in Chicago when the two of them had absorbed almost a fifth of vodka and then gone swimming naked in the chill waters of Lake Michigan. Afterwards, when he had fucked her on a slab of rough concrete, she could not distinguish her tremors of passion from the shivers of cold that seized her body in a continual attack. The following morning she awoke in pain and ran to the mirror to gaze in astonishment at her back which was a plain of scratches and cuts and abrasions. The skin from her buttocks to her shoulders did not have a single square inch which had not been cut or ripped or rubbed raw.

Since then they had run into one another at parties, meetings, and on the street, and shared the chummy camaraderie of people who have been through a war together. But at their last encounter, there had been something strained about his attitude. When she smiled at him, he returned her greeting with a small scowl before putting his face back into its mask of usual neutrality. From then on, as they sat and had coffee in the Oak Room of the Plaza, he had appeared friendly enough, but she was convinced his manner was forced. And when she tried to swing the conversation over to some of the latest developments in her work, he had actually turned his eyes away and stared over her shoulder.

"I said, I'm beginning to explore some interesting aspects of fantasy," she repeated, compelling him to pay attention.

"The way the world is today, reality is unreal enough without trying to get fantastic about it," he replied, still not looking at her.

Lydia felt a chill of apprehension course down her spine. She leaned back in her chair, sipped at her coffee, and lit a cigarette, all the while studying Casper's face. He had the air of a friend who had to tell you something unpleasant and wishes you would go away so someone else could give you the news. Finally, the tension between them became like that between two lovers on the telephone, when he is in a distant city and she is lying in bed being fucked by another man. He suspects the truth of the situation and she is balancing herself between guilt and self-assertiveness, and both are talking about oblique trivia. Lydia stubbed out her cigarette and blurted out, "What the fuck's going on, Casper?"

Still without meeting her eyes he said, in a rapid monotone, "Look, Lydia, I like you, and what you do with your patients is your business. I'll just tell you that Ed Morrison went to see Harry and told him the whole story of your little trip together."

Harry was Harry Saunders, a man who, despite the fact that his peers considered him a trifle absurd, carried enormous prestige in the therapeutic community.

"Harry has muttered something about having you brought before the Licensing Board," Casper went on. "I personally don't think it will come to that, especially if you lay low for a while. Which might not be a bit of bad advice."

"I'm sure that's precisely the advice the medical community of his day gave to Freud," Lydia replied, her voice trimmed to elegant tautness with irony.

"Maybe you're right, and maybe the price experimenters have to pay is running the risk of having their careers ruined. And if you believe in what you're doing strongly enough, then my blessings on you. It just all sounds like you're into a strong regressive cycle and aren't doing anything more creative than playing with shit, your own and other people's."

"Maybe it's only that," she told him. "But how am I supposed to find out if I can't even talk about it to any of my colleagues, even those who are supposed to be friends?" The accusation in her words did not go unheeded and the man looked away in embarrassment

"I'm sorry," he said at last, "but not me. I have a large mortgage and an unproductive wife to support, not to mention three leeches who are passing themselves off as human beings claiming to be my children."

Lydia looked at him with disbelief. Almost fifty, running to fat, his hair thinning, his glasses slipping down his nose, the play of fear in his eyes, he gave all the appearance of a cornered rat.

"And this is a man who is supposed to be dedicated to helping humanity," she thought.

Casper intercepted her glance. "I know what you're thinking," he told her. "But consider the other side. You are into something very, very dangerous. The idea of using fantasy is, of course, as old as the Greeks. But the point is to allow the fantasies to illuminate, not to direct or control the reality. You seem to be urging your patients, if what Ed says is not too grossly exaggerated, to act their daydreams out, and even joining in yourself. Now, you've already got one suicide, and the suspicious circumstances surrounding old Monroe's death . . .'

Lydia's eyebrows shot up.

"Oh, there have been rumors. The word is that you and Monroe were fucking when he had his heart attack.' He lowered his voice. "Frazier has a friend who is a drinking buddy of the Coroner's, and he told him that Monroe had dried vaginal secretions around the base of his cock."

Casper leaned forward and took Lydia's hands in his. "I know, it's all very hypothetical and rumorish, but little by little a noose is being slipped over your head. Now, with this Morrison incident making the rounds, a lot of people think that maybe you've flipped, or . . ." he lowered his voice, "that you've been cursed and are carrying some kind of jinx."

"And the response to all that is for everyone to turn their backs on me?" Lydia said, almost shouting.

"There's potentially big trouble in all this," Casper told her. "Lawsuits, loss of license, criminal charges. Anyone who gets too closely associated with you will get splashed with blood if you ever come under the axe. And please don't think of it in terms of cowardice. Because I *would* fight if it were something that *I* believed in. But why should I risk my career for some idea of *yours*, something that may not be more than an acting out of your residual neurotic structure? I mean, you may be heading for the edge of a cliff. So why should anyone follow you?"

"How about preventing me, if that's what's really happening?"

"Well, you know you can make an appointment with me anytime, Lydia," Casper said, using a tone on her that she had used countless times with others. In an instant she saw through the infuriating smugness of the therapeutic guise, and she felt retroactively ashamed for all the people she had treated with such professionally polished and camouflaged disdain.

In a startling moment, the entire therapeutic community appeared like a cloud over Casper's head. She saw thousands upon thousands of timid people, lost in books and theories and techniques, hiding from the brute reality of life. Refusing to consider any phenomenon which didn't fit their neat little models, discounting everything from diet to politics to celestial influence. Oh, a few had been able to broaden their horizons a bit, but even at that they remained pitifully limited. She suddenly realized that if one took a therapist to the fullest development of his or her powers, one would finally emerge with nothing more esoteric than a simple intelligent human being.

"Therapists are professional retards," she thought, "using other people as stepping stones in their own development or, worse, as rungs in a ladder for their scramble to the top of their self-aggrandizement. And it's probably true that a whore has more honesty than anyone with initials after their name."

Since that afternoon with Casper, she had become more and more of a recluse, sinking into her work and thoughts and researches, worrying from time to time because she was becoming someone she didn't fully recognize, but also finding herself gradually suffused with a new sense of strength, the kind of confidence which arises when one has the liberty to do what one pleases within the context of what one believes to be right. It was as though Doctor Monroe, and all the tradition he represented, had become a surrogate parent, a sort of giant amorphous superego which had gradually suffocated her, to the point where she had been afraid to live according to the dictates of her own conscience. Now, she reminded herself daily that she was not doing anything but attempting to learn, and she had warned all her patients that she was as much in the dark as they. She might make mistakes, but that was part of understanding.

Interestingly, the more she got into her new approach, and the more she told her patients that she was only experimenting, the greater the number of applicants she received. Fred, before he disappeared, cynically remarked that one often finds lines outside of movie theatres and whorehouses. But she had heard the unmistakable ring of jealousy in his voice, and wondered whether he was jealous of the people she had intimate contact with, or of her freedom itself. It led her to speculations on that peculiar biological reflex which has as its purpose and basis the production of children but which has been distorted into a social form, generally given the name marriage. In its context, two people play out the drama learned from their parents, with the result that one will find grown adults worrying about being home later for dinner or staying out all night, just as they did when they were teenagers.

"Through marriage, we turn ourselves into our own parents," she thought, and shuddered at the hideousness of the process.

Lydia looked down at the nighttime city remembering that it had not been too long before, on a night like this one, that Marsha had taken her final bow, and shortly after that that Doctor Monroe had gasped and ejaculated his last. She glanced down at her watch. It was almost eight o'clock, time for her group therapy patients to be arriving. She considered the last phrase, taking each word in turn. "Group." A cold term for a communion of people. "Therapy." A stiff and formal expression for the attempt by people to become more human. "Patient." So reminiscent of the hospital, indicating people who have been ill and are now quietly waiting to recuperate.

She shook her head. Someday she would have to clean out the whole broom closet of psychiatric jargon. And she was smiling to herself at the notion when the doorbell rang, realizing that a psychologist without his fancy words would be revealed as just another person trying to make a living selling ideas.

And what is an idea? An itching in the brain, a flurry of electrons along pre-patterned channels, an occasional explosion in an area not yet touched in a particular human being? Why is thought considered so remarkable, when it is absolutely trivial in relation to such functions as breathing, circulation, and digestion? There is no one alive but feels his or her fancies as precious and unique, so why does a conceptual elite become able to sell visions to a world that is hungry for bread?

"Why is it," Lydia wondered, "that they've monopolized concepts? Can it work the same way with us as in the auto industry? There's the Big Three: Freudians, Behaviorists, and the new Humanist Wing. The classical analysts, of course, have been King of the Mountain for some time, harping on the direct transmission of pure technique and rationalization and charging the most outlandish fees, sometimes as much as a hundred dollars an hour for a forty-five minute hour. The Behaviorists, carrying the prestige of academia and experimental psychology, along with the bias of being an American-based movement, have snared the big posts in the national psychological organizations and set much of the tone of the official publications. The third large segment, of which I am supposedly a member, started as a true alternative, spurred by such things as Esalen and the psychedelics. But now they've solidified into their own kind of authoritarianism, and have drawn their own lines about what they will and won't allow. Theoretically, they're open to anything, but in fact any given individual can be as persnickety as the most hidebound Freudian."

The doorbell rang again, driving the whirling thoughts out of her head. The people who entered came in on a cloud of euphoric pandemonium. There was Nora Norwood and her husband Tom, who had finally decided to join his wife in what she had convinced him was the key to saving their marriage. Behind them came John Abbot, shrouded in hair. Followed by a dozen or so of the ones who had found enough value in Lydia's approach to commit themselves to its process. They were chattering and laughing, like schoolchildren on a picnic. Some of that, Lydia realized, was nervousness, for the sessions had been getting heavy and they were apprehensive about what might be coming, but much of the behavior reflected simply good feeling.

"It feels like a family," Lydia thought, and as soon as the word came into her mind she saw that she had latched onto an idea which brought together a number of seemingly unrelated pieces in the puzzle of trying to figure out just what she was doing.

Lydia led them into her office where the men set about moving all the furniture to the walls. Lydia pulled the drapes and locked the door. What they would be doing involved a high level of sensitive adjustment, and for that absolute physical security was necessary.

When everyone had quieted down, standing in a semicircle with Lydia as the focus, she spoke in a very low voice.

"I've been giving a lot of thought to just what it is that's happening with us," she said. "As you know, I no longer think of myself as a therapist, and if I had to give myself a label, I would say I was a medium. And not a perfect medium at that. It seems to me that we are all trapped in history, forcing ourselves to keep pace with what the general consensus of humanity says is possible at any given period. In a sense, we can't escape from time. Any person or group of people that goes too far too quickly will draw attention to itself and most likely be destroyed, either by bombs or by tourism. But why must we muddle along, pecking at the bars that confine us? Why can't we at least blow a hole in the wall of the prison of history—and I mean the history that's written into our bodies and minds—and find ourselves an open space to live in? That's what's been happening to me, and it has been incredibly thrilling and also very scary. Most of you have experienced the same thing in some of our private sessions. Our groups have gone slowly however, and mostly because I think we are all afraid of what might happen if we all opened up simultaneously."

Lydia's breathing had become shallow and rapid. She was building herself up to something, and groping for the articulation of what that might be. When the words came out, she was as surprised as anyone else in the room.

"I think that tonight we should work in the nude."

A few sharp gasps punctured the skin of attention in which the group had been wrapped. The people looked around at one another, as though seeing themselves for the first time. Their clothing, taken for granted, put on each day with no reflection as to its meaning, considered merely as protection from the cold or ornament for the body, now hung on their bodies with all the ominous significance of a metal shield raised to protect against an enemy lance. There have been many definitions of what distinguishes human beings from other animals, and one of them might be: we are the only animals who wear clothes. This because we are the only animals who insist on living in climates which our bodies cannot survive in without the use of clothing, and because we are the only animals who consider the genitals shameful or glorious or private or almost anything beside what they actually are—merely organs of the body.

Seeing the response of mixed caution and anticipation, Lydia added, "If there is anyone who really strongly objects to doing this, I'm ready to listen to what he or she has to say. But I'd prefer it if we could just step over our inhibitions and get to the other side all at once. I think that until we're all naked, our feelings about being naked are merely academic."

"You start," said Eileen.

Eileen was a Columbus Avenue prostitute who had read *The Happy Hooker* and become enlightened about her profession. She had since set about trying to rid herself of guilt for the kind of work she had chosen to do, something that began with economic necessity and blossomed into a real vocation. She was one of those rare whores who felt that just because she was being paid didn't mean she couldn't enjoy herself and have as many orgasms as she liked. Her popularity was enormous, for most men are so insecure that they are less interested in their own pleasure than in making an impression on a woman. Eileen was a little over five feet tall, black, with a body that had all the fascination of a snub-nosed revolver. She had sought Lydia out and been seeing her for more than six months before Marsha's suicide had spun the therapist off on her new path.

"I'm for that," added Robert Madison, a high school teacher, a man of thirty-five, almost six feet three inches tall, and built like a halfback. He now kept order in one of the roughest schools in the city simply by his menacing presence.

"I've had more hard ons than I can count thinking about our dear therapist's ass," he said. "It would be a treat to finally see what lies between those well-packed legs."

In reply, Lydia unbuttoned her blouse, slowly slipped it off, and stood before the others bare breasted and slightly breathless, her nipples wrinkled with embarrassment. She swallowed and then bent over to loosen her slacks and slide them down her thighs, until she stepped free of them and emerged without a bit of cloth on her body. She looked very tiny standing there, her breasts and pubic hair poking out like burial mounds on a plain of rolling hills.

"It's such a small thing," she said, "to stand naked, and yet, to be here like this in front of you feels like the beginning of a new way of being, a fresh start to civilization."

"Or the start of a nudist colony," said John Abbot from the depths of his hair. He was a musician who had not gone a day without some form of psychedelic drug for more than three years. The process had left him permanently detached, and his manner had evolved into one of lofty cynicism mixed with street earthiness and humor. After flipping his line out into the center like a cigarette butt, he peeled off his leather vest and pants.

"More than that," Lydia said, regaining her sense of direction. "In a nudist colony everyone gets naked and then pretends not to be influenced by that. They sell themselves the myth of naturalness. But the opposite is true. For us, to be naked is to be unnatural. And that's the first thing we have to confront . . . our awkwardness, our embarrassment, our small, muted excitements. Also, in a nudist colony, the people seem to forget that they have uncovered precisely those things that clothing is meant to hide. They walk around not noticing their refusal to confront the cocks and cunts flashing in the sunlight."

She looked around. With varying degrees of alacrity, everyone else had begun to undress. Some of them made jokes, a few looked as though they were in church, the rest tried to be noncommittal. They all looked to her for clues, but she purposely did nothing.

"Don't forget, this is an experiment," she said. "I can dictate the conditions, but I have no idea of the result."

The next five minutes passed in comparative silence as each person made his or her peace with the changes going through the group. Confronting one another without the shield of clothing, with its subtle distinctions of rank and prejudice and inverse narcissism, the people shifted psychic gears continuously to find the right tempo of relating. Some of the men, Lydia noticed, were sucking in their stomachs, some of the women surreptitiously checking degrees of breast sag in comparison to one another, a few shrinking into themselves by pulling their thighs tight, while one or two gazed with open erotic interest on the scene.

"I want to thank you all for being so brave," Lydia said. "We are involved with one of our most pervasive taboos, one which strikes at the very animality of our being. Just for us to get this far is astounding. If someone told me six months ago that I'd be standing naked before a dozen of my patients, also naked, I'd have said they were crazy. Yet here we are."

"When's the party start?" John Abbot asked in a raspy voice. He was massaging his cock and looking around with a leer. His pantomime was greeted alternately with scowls and smiles, but Lydia took the incident as an opportunity to begin the workshop.

"Each of us will have a different fantasy to go with this situation, I'm sure," Lydia said. "Maybe the best way to deal with these various visions is for us all to get down on the floor and disengage our bodies and let our hidden aspects become manifest."

It was a process they had all experienced before, so everyone went very quickly into the basic meditative position of their approach. Lydia had discovered that while the cross-legged sitting posture had gained great vogue since the time of Buddha, it was by no means the only, nor even the oldest, technique possible.

Now Lydia gazed around the room. Seven men and five women lay in front of her. She had never seen so many naked people in positions of such relaxation and vulnerability before. She tried to go over her usual check points: the rate and depth of breathing, tension points in the face, residual twitches in the muscles. But she couldn't keep her eyes off the cocks and cunts. What she felt was not specifically erotic, but a sort of prelude to excitement. She realized that her body was letting go its own tension.

She recalled a theory put forth by one of the orgonomists

who followed Reich, that all the ills of society began during the Ice Age, when we were forced to put on clothing and formed the distinction between private and public parts. The simplicity of the animal disappeared. The brain which had become capable of imagination because of the enlargement of the frontal lobes found fertile ground for fantasy as soon as the genitals were covered. This gave rise to a curdled sensuality which soured every human endeavor since. It was an absurd theory, but the peculiarity of thought is that it conforms to any given reality, and the most intelligent people can accept the most idiotic rationalizations if the wind is right.

"Let all time and space fall away," Lydia heard herself saying, and as in the best of all her workshops, she spoke more to herself than to the others. Shaw once defined a poet as a person who speaks to himself and allows others to overhear, and Lydia's relaxation and fantasy monologues, at their best, constituted poetry.

"Now there is nothing between your self and yourself. All your badges of identify have fallen away. Your ages, your relationships, your clothing . . . even your genders have all become the accidents of existence. All that remains is the breath, the flow of air in and out. This is the rhythm of all creation, of everything that *is*. And as you breathe, be aware of the fact that it is not simply your breath, but the breath of everyone in the room. The molecules in your lungs will be expelled in a second and become part of the air that someone else takes in. Realize that we are all tiny flickers of temporary awareness within the body of the huge organism of life on the planet, and that this body is the most minute cell in the infinite and eternal Consciousness of which life is but a crude reflection. We are in communion with plants and birds, fish and insects. Everything alive is pulsing with breath. Everything alive is one life, one Awareness."

As she spoke, she could feel a change in the vibration of the room. Not only the physical differences, although those were clear enough. The breathing had become very deep, and bellies rose and fell all around. But the feelings liberated by the breathing and relaxation were rising to the surface and coloring the atmosphere as clearly as dye in a vat of water. Nora was crying silently, tears coursing down her cheeks. Ralph was gritting his teeth in resistance. And here and there a sigh escaped, or a groan.

"Without any sense of the individual 'I', allow what you are to express itself," she continued. "Whatever your feelings or thoughts or desires, let them be. Try not to hold on for, remember, there is no one there to hold. We are temporary and tiny, tiny and temporary, practically illusions in the great cosmic mirror. Even on our small planet, we are a young and perhaps doomed species. And each of us is a most insignificant member, an insignificant, tiny, and temporary fragment. All our judgments and attitudes about what we do and how we are are the most trivial ego projections imaginable. Be anonymous, be free."

Lydia let them lie for five minutes, not saying anything. She walked around the room and examined each person closely. For one she might press her hands on the chest to loosen constriction, for another she might massage a thigh. She lifted heads and pulled arms and in general behaved like an engineer working on a complex and very sensitive instrument. Also, she was a bee going from flower to flower, carrying the smell and taste of one to the other, inseminating.

"When there is nothing left but a sense of breathing and pure sensation, then let that find its own expression," she said when she had finished her rounds and was again standing in the center of the rough circle. "You can begin with sound or movement or both, and find out where the impulse takes you."

For several minutes there was little activity. A few people just stretched their fingers or toes; someone yawned. But slowly, a larger pattern emerged. Lydia was familiar with this phase of the work. If she had let it go unhampered, sooner or later everyone would more or less roll into a fetal position, make various noises, roll around, indulge in a bit of touchie-feelie, and come to a sitting position, looks of imbecilic satisfaction on their faces.

But once again, she decided to tamper. She went over to her stereo and put Olatunji's Drums of Passion on the turntable. She was quite aware that she was injecting a mood into a space of high receptivity, but she wanted something specific to happen.

"It's not therapy," she said to herself, "there's no point in holding on to that ridiculous cover. It's more like theatre, but much more risky than that."

"I don't know what it is," she muttered out loud, "but I want some action."

Who knows how the revolutionary is born? Discontents, insights in small increments like electrical impulses along a nerve until a certain charge is built at the gap and suddenly the spark jumps and the neuron snaps and thought is translated into action. But this is the province of everyone. Why do some people one day decide to risk everything, their liberty, their health, even their lives, to take the one action which puts them in direct tension with the basic entropy of society? Up until that instant, Lydia had walked the edge of serious transformation, but had remained within tolerable limits. Nothing that had happened so far was irreversible because it had remained on a one-to-one basis. But now she was going to inject an entire group with an unknown element. As she put the needle on the record, she held her breath.

The people responded gradually as the throbbing rhythm took possession of the space. Their movements were tiny at first, and guarded. But within a few moments they started to stretch out. They caught the infectious mood and began to twitch and roll about on the floor. Lydia herself started a slow shuffle, her hips rolling, her breasts jiggling. Some of the others got to their feet and began to dance, flinging themselves about in response to the demand of the insistent drums. Most of the people still had their eyes closed, following the logic of their inner impulses.

But just then, Judy Bachrach went wild. She let out a wild scream and tossed her head insanely back and forth, causing her long silky hair to whirl about her head. She flung her arms out, flexed her legs, and leaped high into the air, and when she landed she started to dance with a manic intensity. The others all opened their eyes to look at her.

John Abbot was pumping his pelvis into the air and grunting. Nora was wailing. And when she took the entire room into awareness Lydia realized that there were thirteen naked people going wild to the jungle savagery of booming drums.

When the keynote of liberty was struck, everyone in the

room gave vent at once to a wealth of suppressed feelings. Anger, fear, violence, shame, lust . . . all emerged in pure form, without the distorting covers of language, clothing, and social role. And because the expressions were pure, they were beautiful.

For an instant Lydia was overwhelmed by the raw power that had been unleashed. Naked men and women were throwing themselves about in total abandon, yelling, crying, whispering to themselves, their bodies flailing in time to the swelling music. It was a primitive spectacle, totally innocent. The scene might have been defined in a variety of ways, and a hundred interpretations given to it, but all would have fallen short of the sheer energy of the life force that had been released.

Lydia danced around and through the others, her body taking on a thin coating of perspiration. If she had gone over a waterfall in a barrel, she could not have experienced a greater din, a more saturating chaos.

"This is what Marsha saw," she thought. "We are in the state where reality is the same as fantasy. Each of us has gone into our sense of ourselves as animal or angel or killer or god, and in doing that, thrown away the clothing and the petty social identity and so entered a different space, a dangerous space, a space in which we are aware of the wonder of our strength and beauty. Why, if we were to pick up spears and run into the street now, we might conquer the city."

Lydia suddenly saw why it was that barbarian tribes overthrew old cultures, because the civilizations got tired and mired in a humdrum common reality, while the barbarians still felt the pulse of unfettered life running in their veins.

She didn't know what made her do it, but she ran over to the wall and threw the switch. Suddenly, the room was pitch black.

"That's the last barrier," she cried. "Now we are in the heart of chaos. And there is no truth except what comes from inside."

The bodies found one another. Like living magnets they were pulled to that which called them most truly, forces which had nothing to do with any of the usual markers of the senses, including thought. For their minds had gone beyond rational categories, and they were blind and could hear nothing but the infernal music of the jungle and their own cries. They leapt into the embrace of their most basic nature, being informed by smell and touch and taste, impelled by nothing except brilliant and voracious desire.

And so it was that someone leaped next to Lydia, sniffed loudly, reached out and grabbed her, ran hands over her breasts and down her belly to her thighs and ass, and then pulled her close, covering her cunt with a hot questing mouth.

The music left the track and the bodies collided and coalesced, beginning in twos which fell to the floor, rolled, met with other coupled bodies, blended, until every person in the room was part of a single mound of pulsing, twisting flesh and all distinctions were lost.

Now nothing existed but sound and movement in the dark. It may have been like the first consciousness the universe ever had of itself, an empty and unconnected impulse reaching out. Skin slithered over skin and hands groped parts and tongues licked whatever was in front of them. Fucking and fingering took place and the mass began to give off the aromas of sweat and sperm and vaginal secretions and saliva. The line had been crossed and the people had entered the realm of orgy, the finite return to the cosmic erotic state. The fragmented egos had melted into simple sentience. The stiff bodies had flowed into writhing life forms. The rigid social roles had collapsed into a single feeling—action that subsumed all possible identities.

But in the midst of it, Tom Norwood, having climaxed in an unidentified orifice of an unidentified person, and suffering a sudden overpowering spasm of disgust, staggered to the light switch and threw it on. At that precise instant, the record ended. And the transcendental experience was abruptly thrown into the most stark and negative judgment. It suddenly became a grotesque group-grope, a wallow of middle-aged people on a therapist's rug in a musty apartment off Central Park West.

Everyone froze.

"Whew," said John Abbot. "Cat's got a strange sense of drama."

Torn between the need to continue to individual and group climax and the terrible presence of Tom Norwood who glowered like an Old Testament prophet trying to whip them with his eyebrows, they blinked against the harsh glare.

Nora Norwood was lying on her belly, Marie Jorgenson's cunt against her mouth and Robert Madison's cock in her ass.

Tom began to tremble with what he considered to be a justified rage.

"Get up out of there, you slut!" he ordered.

Nora winced, and for an instant seemed that she would respond, but some deep slow change flowed through her and her entire attitude was transformed into the opposite of what would have been her conditioned response.

She raised her head.

"No," she said.

"*SICK!*" he screamed. "This is sick. You're all sick. Nora, come with me."

"No," she repeated simply.

"You get your whore's ass out of here right now and come home with me or our marriage is finished," he threatened.

"Then it's finished," she told him. "I'm not moving."

"All right," he said, his jowls shaking. He walked over to where his clothes lay and began dressing rapidly. "But don't come back," he went on. "I mean, don't even try to get in the front door. I'll pack your things and put them in storage and you can get them when you want. But I don't ever want to see you again."

"But Tom," Lydia said. "You were just as much a part of this as she was."

"You hypnotized me," he charged. "You hypnotized all of us. You call yourself a therapist, but you're only a madam."

"I've been telling you all along that what's happening isn't therapy," Lydia protested.

"I'm sure the police will be interested in your little scene, *and* the psychological association."

He turned to his wife again. "Well, are you coming."

At just that instant, however, Nora was squirming slightly to readjust the angle of Robert's cock in her asshole. The gesture was all the answer anyone might need.

The scathed husband backed slowly out of the room, raking everyone with beams of hatred and, in a symbol of futile defiance, turned the light switch off once more as he went through the door. The room was plunged into darkness again.

"Mmm, that's better," Eileen murmured as she slid her mouth over John Abbot's cock again.

"Lydia?" Nora said.

"Yes?" Lydia answered.

"Can I stay here? Can I stay with you?"

For an instant Lydia thought Nora was asking if she might stay for the night, or for a while until she found another place to live. But something in the other woman's voice told her that something deeper was happening.

"What do you mean by 'stay'?" she asked.

"I don't want to go back to the old way. Not just to Tom, but to the old civilization. I mean, you're my family now, my real family. I want to live through my fantasies all the time. I think I'd die if I had to go back to the world of dumb reality. I want to create a new reality, with you." She paused. "With us," she added.

"Wow," John said, half in response to the wet warmth of Eileen's tongue as it licked his cock, and half to the full significance of what Nora was saying.

A fist of fear bunched in Lydia's stomach. Suddenly, she had become the leader of a new tribe, the founder of a different culture, a twentieth century matriarch. The fear was all the more paralyzing because it was in response to a real stimulus. She had blundered and wormed her way into a position of enormous responsibility, and it was now impossible for her to go back either. She and Nora were wedded. And she knew there would be others. Some of the ones already in the room, and more she had not even met yet.

The fear exploded and in its place there arose a shimmering vision. The deep and ineradicable hope which exists in every human being for a beautiful world suffused her entirely. The notion that it was possible to create a society which would not degenerate into stupidity or staleness or violence or fatal lassitude came to her as a form of knowledge. Suddenly, she *knew* that it was possible.

"Look," Marie said.

Lydia's body was encased in a low, shimmering light. Her aura had begun to glow.

"Of course," Lydia said. "Of course you can stay with me."

Her voice was golden, mellifluous.

"What about me?" Eileen asked.

"And me?" John added.

"And the rest?" Lydia asked.

"I haven't come yet," Robert said. "I don't want to make any decisions until I come."

"All right," Lydia said, laughing. "Let's finish the orgy, and then we can talk."

7

The fountains murmured continuously as the waiters moved about on the thick rug, their footsteps silent, their manner so calculatedly unobtrusive as to constitute a minor art form. Perhaps thirty people were having lunch, but the space was so wide and the atmosphere so still that each table seemed cut off by itself, an island of casual interest. The restaurant was based on the premise that those who could afford to pay extravagant sums for the privilege of initiating an imitation of royalty would overlook the essentially mediocre cuisine and the callousness—camouflaged as poise—of the help, and consider themselves participating in some form of chic.

Lydia studied the menu with distaste. It offered a series of French dishes which amounted to little more than several kinds of meat smothered in several kinds of sauce. But she had agreed to have lunch with Fred and felt that voicing her repugnance for the artificial ambience would be impolite.

The rationalization she was using in her work was that no one was being forced to attend, so their presence implied a certain agreement with the ground rules of the scene. She reasoned that she owed the same respect to The Four Seasons. She could stay outside and criticize its blatant vulgarity, but if she went in she owed the place a certain minimum of civilized response.

As she peered at the menu, Fred watched her. He had stayed away from her for a month, hoping that when he saw her again she might have come to her senses. He felt a measure of responsibility for the direction her work and life had taken, for he had spent two years mocking her therapy fetish and goaded her into breaking out of what he called "the context bag." His taking her to Provincetown, he judged, helped push her over the edge of her faith in therapeutic justifications. He was convinced that she was trying to emulate what she'd seen that weekend, and getting herself more and more deeply into a conceptual quagmire.

Fred had always seen fantasy as a mode of escape. There comes a point in every man's life when the raw, grey truth of physical existence becomes the inescapable parameter of whatever else he might think or feel about the universe. The splendor of the galaxies, the thunderous brilliance of the sun, the surging mystery of creation itself, might all provide pleasant, exhilarating or terrifying moments during the daily round, but they could not remove the sting of mortality from a man's consciousness. When that awareness became intolerable, one could skew one's angle of perception and change one's attitude in such a way as to blunt the edge of knowledge. And if one did it consistently enough, a basic philosophic attitude slowly crystallized.

He reasoned that the religions of the world were nothing more than taking a specific fantasy and defining that as the primary principle of reality, and then living out that principle through the fluctuations of life's changes. Each age developed its own idiosyncratic myths, and the myth which concocted the most high-blown phraseology, or commanded the most persuasive teachers, or allied itself with the dominant political movement, emerged supreme for that era. Buddhism, Christianity, Islam. And in the twentieth century, a gap had opened in which a series of contending world views fought with one another to become the major model for the world-system which was forming and would hit its stride in the following century.

Of course, the dominant myth was never recognized until it had peaked. Catholicism, for example, did not seem anything special to the peasants of the eighth century; it was simply the way everyone looked at things. It was only at the start of the Renaissance, when a new myth was struggling for supremacy, that the church became a self conscious entity, grew into a horrid vehicle for oppression and torture during the Inquisition, and finally degenerated into a pathetic toothless tyrant several hundred years later.

Fred's deepest feeling—and he rarely admitted how serious he was about it—was that theatre, not communism, formed the essential myth of the era. That movies had changed the consciousness of the world, and that television was completing the process. His notion was that a housewife watching a soap opera was performing a metaphysical act, in the same way as a Jew going to Temple, or a Jain walking barefoot into a Mosque. The soaps took the raw reality of daily life, codified it, amplified it, and fed it back to the source from which the material originated. The myth of the twentieth century, he reasoned, is the banality of existence, the despair felt by the species as a whole upon the final and total acceptance, of the fact that we are merely a strange kind of monkey, perhaps the newest experiment of Nature, and no more privileged and probably less long-lived than either the dinosaur or the cockroach. That we probably have a lower consciousness than trees or lizards, that we live on an insignificant hunk of rock circling a middle-aged star, that we are really nothing special. And the medium of that myth is television, the metatheatrical instrument par excellence.

He had tried to show this to Lydia, to point out how therapy was an unhip effort to do the same thing, a process that was limited, expensive, and overlaid with suffocating theoretical horseshit and a mountain of rationalizations born of ontological insecurity. He had been pleased when she began to break out of that mold. But she had gone too far, had misunderstood what he was saying. She had tried to take the therapeutic myth and hype it to a new level. This bordered dangerously on political radicalism. And if Fred knew anything, he knew that any attempt to thwart the machinery of history was doomed to end violently. He felt that Lydia was being carried away by an orgasmic hysteria, and allowing herself to be committed to a way of action that he was certain she would eventually disavow, but perhaps too late to escape having damaged herself and others. She seemed to have lost the sense of irony he felt was the only attitude an intelligent person in the twentieth century should display. Irony, he thought, was to the twentieth century what piety was to the tenth.

He glanced at Lydia as she made faces at the menu. He knew she was offended by the restaurant, and he shared her feelings.

The dimension she missed was the ability to be amused by the place, to see it with a certain detachment. He was able to *float* through the environment, and this quality of floating was at the heart of successful fantasy evocation. He considered it absurd to lock oneself into a room with a group of people and pretend to be sharing a fantasy when one could not perceive the fantastic in the day-to-day reality.

"Have you decided yet?" he asked.

She put the menu down.

"Fred," she asked, "why this place?"

"Well, I haven't seen you in a while and I thought I'd bring you to a posh restaurant."

He smiled his most disarming smile, but she remained unaffected.

When he had called her, he half hoped he would find the old Lydia, the slightly stuffy therapist, filled with stifling ideas who, once she took her clothes off, became an uninhibited animal, someone he could still tease, and slowly bring around to his way of thinking. But as they had a drink in her living room, and she told him what she'd been doing, he became increasingly discouraged. The nude groups had been bad enough, but now she had five people living with her. He couldn't believe she was actually starting a commune!

"It's so square," he had said.

"What about your friends in Provincetown?" she replied.

"All the difference in the world," he told her. "Those people come together out of a pattern of individual liberty. Your group is put together by insecurity and fear."

She had refused, at that time, to discuss it further.

The waiter glided up and waited silently by their table, exuding a pressure for them to respond to his presence. Fred looked over at Lydia questioningly. She squinted, pursed her lips in thought, and then very sweetly said, "I'll just have a cheeseburger." Then, turning to the waiter, added, "With a slice of raw onion. And please bring a bottle of catsup."

Fred grimaced but said nothing.

"How's the veal today, Arthur?" he asked.

"Quite good, sir," the waiter replied, dancing in his composure.

"As good as the cheeseburger, Arthur?" Lydia asked in a mincing tone.

"Please, Lydia," Fred said.

She looked down.

"You're quite right," she said. "I'm sorry." There was no point in being unkind to the waiter.

"Bring me the veal," Fred went on, "And bring the lady a cheeseburger." The waiter and Fred exchanged a fragment of a glance, the implicit male awareness that it was often necessary to treat women as though they were rational creatures capable of understanding language but that that should never lull a man into thinking that he was faced with anything more remarkable than an alien creature which had learned to mimic human speech.

"One veal and one *hamburger au fromage*," the waiter repeated.

Lydia and Fred sat in silence for a minute, sipping their drinks. He was dressed in a three piece suit. Lydia had on the slacks and blouse that had become almost a uniform with her. Her hair was slightly tousled and she wore no makeup. They made an odd pair, and only the conditioned politeness of the people who frequented the place kept them from being stared at.

"You know that this place is utterly absurd, don't you," Lydia said.

"That's precisely why I brought you here. I thought your sense of the absurd needed some sharpening. I thought it might give you some perspective."

"On what?" Lydia asked. "For the first time in my life I feel that I am acting like an adult, taking responsibility for my own actions and thoughts and feelings. And maybe what I'm doing is a mistake. And if you would, you might give me feedback to help me. But to dismiss my entire work as wrong is the grossest oversimplification, and you know it."

As Fred watched her, a slow heat began to spread through his chest. Her eyes were flashing and her mouth curling in anger; her excitement aroused all the latent lust that he'd been putting on the shelf for the month he'd forced himself to stay away from her. He x-rayed her as she sat, and realized that he knew every pore of her body, from her pale pink nipples to the crispy turn of her pubic hair. There was hardly a thing they had not done together, and he could, if he concentrated, recall the pungent taste of her cunt's secretions, the musky smell of her asshole, the deep sandalwood aroma of her armpits. He had seen her on her knees sucking his cock, on her belly with his prick in her ass, lying across a bed as he plunged again and again into the marshmallow melting of her yielding snatch. They had kissed and stroked and pinched and fondled one another for hundreds of hours. And talked and laughed and explored the recesses of the city's collective psyche in its museums and bars and theatres and clubs. For an instant, he saw that they had been courting a long time, and now wondered why the thought of marriage had never occurred to him.

"Because it's climbing that damned cliff," he thought. "Tied to one another with a rope, exhilarated up the first easy slopes, ecstatic when the first dangerous shelves are passed, bored during the long monotonous stretches. And then there always comes that instant when you've worked your way up the face of a sheer rock face. Half way up, you realize that you may not make it. And there's no turning back. And you wonder how in the hell you ever got there. But it's too late. There's no way out of marriage except divorce or death. The price of being born is dying, but no one has a choice about whether they want to start the life trip. The price of marriage is taking on another life form which has to suffer its own death. But in that case there is a choice."

"What are you thinking?" Lydia asked, breaking into his reverie.

He smiled. "I was thinking that there are much better uses for a mouth like yours than spouting platitudes."

For a second she was angry, and then remembered the reference. It was the first thing he'd ever said to her. A flash of fondness ran through her and she felt the impulse to run her fingers through his hair and pull his head to her breasts. It was only then that she saw how far she had progressed in the previous few months. Fred had been a man who could make her squirm with uncertainty, and now he appeared as little more than a charming boy, the product of his empty way of life.

She reached across the table and took his hands in hers.

"Look," she said, "what I'm doing is no longer in my control. I don't want to sound like a revivalist about it, but I really believe that I have plugged into forces that are greater than ours, than those ordinarily available to human beings. I don't know how to say this without sounding like a fanatic, but my only commitment is to truth. It has always been that, of course, but in the past I wasn't so sharply aware that living by the truth requires immense courage and risk. I'm through with being concerned about earning a living, or maintaining a reputation, or building a career. I only care about discovering what is true. And this impulse began with Marsha's suicide, with the sudden understanding that reality is more than what we are told by our scientists and philosophers. It's greater than anything the human mind can imagine. I guess I've always had that in the back of my mind or I wouldn't have become a therapist. And I suppose that the message of the psychedelic teachers and the gurus is the same, only I have been too immersed in my theoretical structures to hear it. But I've found my own way now. And you were one of the people who gave me the important clues. In many ways, I wouldn't be here now without you. So I don't really understand why you have become so negative about my work."

"Because I think it's taking you someplace that is potentially fatal. When I spoke to you about fantasy, I meant that you should change your inner attitude, alter your way of seeing things, get looser about your approach. Reality goes on without us, you know. The great swings of the galaxies, the shifts of the continents, the sweep of evolution, the birth and death of the sun, and even the convolutions of history all are vast schemes that are beyond our control. My argument with you is that you got stuck at that level and let it wear you. down. I simply wanted you to look at creation the way a child looks at a toy. And to step into a state of awareness which floated over all that terrible, implacable reality which the culture defines for us. Do you understand? Fantasy is the way to beat the reality game, but you're perverting that.

You're trying to infuse fantasy into reality to change what *is*. And that's a form of pride, as well as a futile exercise."

Fred was surprised to find himself breathing hard. He had become carried away by his impassioned appeal and he was aware that his voice had carried to the rest of the restaurant. He was not even sure that his words made sense. Terms like fantasy and reality were so slippery, forming as they did the ground upon which all other definitions were based. But that ground was drenched with Marsha Seligson's blood and Marsha couldn't stand easily on it. Fred felt secure about his own position but he was thrown off balance trying to hold Lydia up. She continued to show a seemingly obtuse unwillingness to see the difference between fantasy and myth, and between myth and reality, and had come to a muddled synthesis in which she was somehow equating fantasy and reality.

He settled back in his seat and lit a cigarette, his hands sliding out of Lydia's grasp. The murmur of the huge fountain which sat in the center of the restaurant washed over him and soothed his vibrations. And in a few moments, the waiter returned, wheeling a large chrome cart loaded with covered dishes. He sailed up to their table and halted, and then with practiced gestures uncovered each of the plates and slid them onto the table. Lydia looked down at a white and blue bone china dish which held a tiny hamburger. She glanced up at the waiter.

"I asked for a cheeseburger," she said.

"The *fromage*, Madame, is *inside* the burger," the man said in clipped tones.

Lydia frowned to keep from giggling.

The waiter finished placing the side dishes of vegetables on the table and rolled away, his cart squeaking slightly.

"Oh, it's so ridiculous," Lydia said when the man was out of earshot. "This whole scene can't be real."

"Come on," Fred cajoled. "It's just a middle-brow restaurant with pretensions. Don't tell me that it's really upsetting you."

"Oh, not just the restaurant. The whole thing. The city, the civilization. It's so stilted. I mean, that waiter, all those people there eating like well-programmed robots, are no different than the people I see in my office."

She leaned forward, her body stiff with excitement. "Don't you understand?" she began, using the very phrase that Fred and Doctor Monroe had so often stopped her with, "I have entered a different state of perception. When I look at people, it's not just their clothes or their body postures or their identities that I see. I look into their very hearts and minds, and perceive the fantasies, the desires, the ability to drop all the conditioned states and emerge as free beings. Nothing in this society impresses me any more. It's all moribund, miserable. And a place like this restaurant is the worst of all, so far removed from anything truly human and alive that I don't see how it can exist at all."

"Oh God," Fred exploded, "you're getting just like every other utopian crank I've ever met. You sit in the middle of the most powerful city in the world, fed by the totality of the entire civilization's technology and resources, and you go into this whining number about how meaningless it all is. What do you think you're gathering around you but a bunch of overfed, super-saturated neurotics who are happy to jump at the chance for orgies and sensitivity sessions and fantasy acting-out? It's the kind of crowd you get in response to a *Voice* ad, hangers-on and losers who haven't got enough of a center to create a life for themselves. The whole situation is putrid. I remember one group therapy session I attended years ago before I got to know better. Some dismal woman was on the hot-spot with everyone firing questions at her and demanding that she be 'real'. And finally she seemed at the edge of saying something but couldn't get it out. And they harped at her until she yelled, "All right. I'll tell you what I'm thinking. I'm thinking: would any of us be here if we had anything at all more interesting to do tonight?' And that's it in a nutshell. Urban ghosts haunting the night looking for some form of life and finding nothing but ghouls like themselves."

To Fred's astonishment, when he looked over at Lydia, tears were trickling from the corners of her eyes. He was taken aback.

"Hey," he said, "hey, what is it?"

"I was thinking of Marsha," she told him, "who finally found a way out of her misery. And of all the others, who slide into lives of unhappiness at low boil, who become greyer and more cynical and deadly and who die without ever having lived. And I don't care what you say, someone has to do something, no matter how crazy, no matter how feeble, no matter how neurotic it seems. Because we can't keep going the way we're going, living in this . . . this . . ."

Lydia stood up and raised her arms to take in the entire restaurant, with its fountain and carpets and polished furniture and expensive food and waiters in tuxedos. And at the top of her lungs, she finished her sentence.

"In this SHIT!" she yelled, causing forks to drop and heads to turn and officious types to begin walking toward her.

But she turned rapidly and strode out of the room looking neither to the right nor left.

Fred stared at her for a few seconds and then jumped to his feet and ran after her, their food still sitting on the table. As he passed Arthur he pressed four twenty dollar bills into his hand and rushed on. Lydia was already on the street by the time he reached the door. She was moving very quickly, and he almost lost her in the crowd.

"Lydia," he shouted, "Lydia, wait."

He caught up to her on Lexington Avenue and took her arm from behind.

"Please, Fred," she said, stopping and turning to face him, "I don't want to fight with you. I just think that I've moved into a different world than yours and I don't see that we have anything in common any more."

"Lydia, this is insane. We've known each other for more than two years. We've made love a thousand times. We are in love."

As he said the last words, they looked into one another's eyes, sharing a glance that set them to rocking on their heels.

"Yes," Lydia told him, "I do love you. But that means something far different to me than it once did. Love for me used to mean tension, the struggle between my autonomy and the man's will. Now it means sharing, the ability to enter a common space together. I have a purpose now. I don't exist as a reflection or an extension of a man. I'm my own woman. And I have my own destiny and vision to fulfill."

Around them the traffic belched and ground its gears and

honked, the thousands of cars and busses and cabs transforming their drivers into slaves of the machinery, and reducing the hundreds of thousands of people who walked the streets into mere obstructions to the flow of metal. Men and women rushed past them, hurried, harried, clutching bags and briefcases. It was controlled pandemonium, the ultimate in focused anarchy, the city a great center where millions pursued separate goals in the context of a ruling abstraction called progress.

Fred held Lydia by the arms. He closed his eyes and breathed deeply. He didn't recognize himself.

"I want you to marry me," he said.

She did not reply for a long while. They stood so still that even the ordinarily tunnel-visioned passersby glanced at them, some wondering if this were a scene from a movie and casting about to see where the cameras were. Lydia was breathing heavily. What Fred had just asked were words which, if she'd heard them three months earlier, would have transported her into a heady euphoria. But now they sounded like a declaration made in a foreign language. She simply didn't understand them. They were totally outside her current context. After having plunged with her newly formed family into waters of oceanic eroticism and multi-dimensional interaction, this offer made as much sense as giving a stale biscuit to a woman who'd been feasting on fruit and nuts.

"I'm afraid," she said slowly, "that I couldn't even think of something like that with anyone who is outside our group."

"What!?" he replied. "Outside your *group*!"

"Why, yes," she said simply.

"God, you sound like some idiot fanatic. Don't you see what's happened to you? You've committed the classic mistake, you've divided the world into *us* and *them*, the grisly beginning of all crusades."

Lydia shook her head slowly.

"You're responding to the words," she said. "What's really happening is that I am forming a family, a real family. Call it a tribe if you will. But I've found something that I can only call a religion. Not the tired old orthodoxy, but a real connection, something with actual juice in it, something that gives meaning to my life and the lives of those who have decided to join with me. And that's my primary responsibility, to the group that has learned to share its fantasy life, to make its most secret and cherished dreams come true."

"Come true how? Where? You're nothing but parasites, just like the rest of us. Living off the surplus of civilization, enjoying its benefits, and then putting down its substance. What makes you think you're so special? How are you different than anyone else? There are forty million housewives who turn on their TV. screens and enter into an electronic communion far more pervasive than anything you could even imagine. And you crawl around a dark room and grope one another and give it a fancy name. Lydia, please, you're more intelligent than that."

"Or is it that you just can't stand the idea of me groping anyone else, or anyone else enjoying my body?"

He glanced down at his shoes. Lydia felt a mixture of scorn and tenderness for him.

"Maybe you're right," she told him. "But I can't help but see you as anything but an outsider. Everything you're saying is destructive. You're not telling me anything positive. Don't you think we're sophisticated enough to see ourselves in the light you portray us? But so what? What is our alternative? Back to the routine, off to work, and the dictates of the culture and then nodding out in front of the tube? I don't want to put down the way you earn a living, but please don't become an apologist for a dumb way of life."

Fred stepped back from her. There was something of the old confidence on his face. He grabbed onto the handle that he had been looking for, the way to attain the position of dominance. It was not that he wanted to force Lydia into a submission so much as needing to have the more comprehensive expression. It did not even matter to him whether what he said were judged more complete or profound by her or anyone else, so long as he could rest in his own estimation of his words.

"All right," he said. "If you're serious, you have to get out of the city. You have to go somewhere and be totally self sufficient. You have to grow your own food, heal your own sick, bury your own dead. You have to get out of Egypt and go find your promised land. And if you can do that, without getting ingrown and convoluted, then maybe you'll have some justification for thinking that your way has produced a real change in the human condition. But so long as you remain here, living the parasitic existence the rest of us wallow in, then you're not doing anything but jerking off."

She put her hands on his shoulders. "Fred, will you come with me . . . with us?"

"Huh?"

"Come to one of our groups. Meet the others. Join the fantasy work. Get naked with us. Live with us. We really need someone like you, someone with your mind and even, yes, your cynicism. You could be so valuable. And we could be together. That might be a real marriage."

He looked at her as though she were a panhandler who'd just casually asked for twenty dollars.

"What? Leave my work and go live with a group of insipid . . ."

But he let his words trail off. He didn't want to say that kind of thing to Lydia any more.

"Don't you see?" she said. "I'm one of those insipid whatever-you-want-to-call-us. I don't define myself apart from the family any more. I'm committed to all of us." She paused, cocked her head, and asked. "Why did you ask me to marry you? Was it a pride thing?"

"Perhaps," he admitted. "And a last grasping at straws. I feel you moving away, and that was some kind of crazy attempt to grab you back."

"But you can have me," she said hurriedly. "And in such a beautiful way. Instead of feeding flatulent realities to bored housewives, you can help us bring a rich fantasy to life, to make a vital dream come true. Think of it, a tribe of people in which our inner life feeds the outer, in which the unconscious structures the cultural forms, in which the horrible split of western civilization . . . of all civilization . . . is finally healed."

As she spoke, her face began to shine, and her eyes glowed with a violet radiance. Fred involuntarily stepped back. Even her voice had a ring, an echo to it, which made it sound as though she were speaking in a large empty cave. The vibrations emanating from her enveloped the two of them and the scene around them seemed to fade from their senses. The noises, the tempo, the cascade of visual impressions, all disappeared and only Lydia remained, calling to him, calling from a great height, beckoning him to climb, to mount up, to fly.

For a period out of clock time, Fred was mesmerized by the apparition, but then the totality of his conditioning stepped in to sweep him back into the world of his patterned perceptions. The line between the actual and the hallucination is a matter of choice, and Fred decided that what he had just seen would be relegated to a bizarre quirk of consciousness. He shook his head briskly, straightened his spine, and stepped into his posture of jaunty indifference.

"Well, it's all very brave new world, I'm sure," he said, his voice a trifle cracked but close to the proper tone of amusement he wanted to feel and project, "but it's not at all my cup of tea, really. I mean, the notion of me standing naked in front of your gypsy army of therapy rejects boggles even my ordinarily wide spectrum of possible behaviors. So, I'll mosey on off back to decadence and wait for you to give me a call, as soon as you are off this kick."

"Or until you realize that you are the one on a kick, you and the entire culture you're choosing to remain part of. And then you can call me."

They stepped back from one another with that edge of smiling hostility which masks all potentially messy sentiment when two people break up.

Then he turned sharply and dove into the stream of bodies that flowed around them.

Lydia watched him until she could no longer make him out from among the thousands of others who were swept down the concrete funnel the people and automobiles used as a street.

8

Her whole life was changing, and yet nothing appeared other than it had been. Lydia was beginning to learn that merciless lesson about which Fred had warned her: that reality moved on unheeding of the efforts of human beings to alter it. No matter how exciting her work, or how extraordinary her experiences, each day found her one day older than the last. The earth turned with mammoth indifference to the feelings of the creatures who crawled and walked and flew and swam upon its surface.

"Life," someone once remarked, "is a disease of matter," and there were times when Lydia felt the power of the statement. Like the protagonist in Herbert Read's *The Green Child*, she began to develop an affinity for the solidity of dense physical reality, seeing the soul as the restless villain in the drama of existence, the vagabond adolescent that wouldn't accept the fact that everything that is, is limited. She did not articulate it as such, but the law of opposites was making its power felt. The more she and her group involved themselves in out-of-body experiences, the more their bodies seemed to acquire a gravity and magnetism which removed them from the common understanding of reality. In a word, as far as most other people were concerned, Lydia and her group were becoming weird.

After a particularly explosive session, such as the one in which Richard Carstairs watched his wife transmogrify into a snake goddess through the intensity of her fantasy and then go into a three hour fit of trembling withdrawal in which he could do nothing more than whimper for her to have mercy on him, Lydia wondered whether any communication with the world outside their circle was even possible any longer. To them the incident had been strong, but not particularly strange or upsetting. To an outsider, it would seem that they should all be in an asylum.

"It may really be what we need," Lydia thought more and more often. "Fred said we'd have to go somewhere, become self sufficient. The day may come soon when we'll have to find an asylum."

The tenants in her building were beginning to look at her askance. The odd looking people trekking in and out, the screams and wails that seeped out through the thick walls, and the general sense of revolution all combined to tear the curtain of invisibility which every New Yorker holds as the real First Amendment.

She often spent hours sitting on the terrace, gazing down at the city. Just a few hundred years earlier, a blink in evolutionary time, Manhattan had been a pleasant island, wooded, with deer and small animals of all types, with fresh streams and gentle meadows. Indians had lived there for thousands upon thousands of years, close to nature, suffering perhaps the same difficulties that faced all life forms, old age, disease, sorrow, and death. But in the process they had not tampered with the beauty of the place they lived in. They were still in touch with The Spirit of the Earth, and although they fought and killed, fucked and laughed, they remained strong and pure and honest and clean. Then the Europeans arrived, bringing with them the rotting shreds of their decayed culture, and within a few brief centuries had fouled the rivers, covered the earth with concrete, destroyed almost all the wild life, and polluted the very air. And then to compensate for all that, generated a civilization which operated at a level of manic intensity or crippling depression. She sometimes tried to picture what it would be like for an Indian to be lifted off the Manhattan of four hundred years earlier, suspended in a time capsule, and plunked suddenly in the heart of midtown. He would have to go stark raving mad at the horror that had overtaken the place. Or else, plunge into the corruption in order to keep his balance. He would have to swim in the alcohol, the drugs, the tawdry eroticism, the idiot superficiality of commercial thought, the dreary mechanism of compulsory education, the greed, the lusting after paper, and the generally deadening routines of a people who have lost touch with what it is to be human in the widest sense.

And there seemed no chance of the situation's changing for the better. The whole world was infected with the sickness of size and noise and garbage. The population grew larger, the weapons of destruction more ghastly, the quality of life more shabby, and the very language itself had lost almost all its meaning. It was easy to blame the Pentagon, or the capitalists, or Madison Avenue, or any other phantom reality one might choose, but it was too late for all that. The only chance was to escape it. But to where? There was certainly enough land left where a group of people might make a new home, but how long would that last? And if the air was being poisoned, if the radiation belt around the earth was in danger of losing its shielding power, if the oceans were dying, what did it matter where one went?

At such times Lydia uttered deep sighs that threatened to burst her rib cage, and on occasion she might walk to the edge of the terrace and peer down, asking herself the question, "How unhappy does a person have to be to commit suicide?" She treated herself to that fantasy . . . the momentary teetering at the brink, the sudden letting go, and then the falling, the long gliding dive into space. What thoughts at such an instant? What feelings? What insights? And then the concrete. Would there by any pain? Perhaps an instantaneous and total blasting of every nerve ending in the body so that the last moment of life comprised the summation of all suffering? Or perhaps an immediate unconsciousness, with awareness bursting free from the quick corpse to dissolve in that realm from which it arose before it had coalesced to haunt a human body. And what was awareness, then? She, like most people, tended to think of it as a thing, a substance, something that entered the self at the moment of conception and left at death. But perhaps awareness was a myth, a prejudice of the organism, an illusion.

At such times she might weep and call out for Fred or Doctor Monroe. Yet she knew that neither could help her even if they were there. She had chosen the path of individual struggle for truth, and she had to face these feelings alone. It was one thing to wave her magic fantasy wand and develop an image of herself as a matriarch of a new tribe. It was another to find the depths of strength inside herself so that she didn't get discouraged, didn't lose a revivifying cheerfulness.

All the words of wisdom, the teachings of the ancients and the moderns, when stripped of their symbolism, personal poetry, and historical trappings, devolve to a single message. And untold billions have been led astray, looking for answers to a question no one has ever been able to formulate, all the while disregarding the immediate reality of their lives. Is there enough food? Do we have shelter? Can we clothe ourselves against the weather? Can we maintain our health? These are the only real questions, the only valid issues of life.

And it is in the paying attention to those problems that happiness is found. If we do our work and reap the reward of our labor, there is nothing more for us on this planet. The rest . . . the pleasures, the speculations, the voyages, the games, are merely toys. And the structures of the society which supposedly exists merely for us to be able to help one another attain the necessities, the monkeybar of civilization with its status roles and power roles and symbolic gratifications, have swollen to such monstrous proportion that a large majority of the people in the world go to bed hungry each night. And the leaders and teachers through all the millennia seemed to accomplish nothing more than to lead those people down one or another blind alley.

As she went more deeply into her explorations, Lydia was finding that the fantasy work, as exciting as it was, could be a deadly trap if one element was missing, and that element was nothing more mysterious than her ability to keep her own eyes fixed on a vision, and to sustain that in face of the tendency on the part of the others to fly off into states of euphoria which were inevitably followed by depression. And they had begun to look to her, either consciously or subliminally, for that kind of direction and support, like children who play without fear because they know that a wise parent is watching over their welfare. When her mood became black, the others easily succumbed to despair. If she radiated hope, their faces would light up and they would throw themselves into the work with renewed vigor.

Now the night had turned bitter cold, yet Lydia dreaded

returning to the apartment. There were moments when she hated the sight of the faces that surrounded her all the time. In the first flush of enthusiasm, when Nora had moved in, Lydia let four others share her apartment. And for a week or so it had been lovely, what with re-arranging the furniture and having company all the time and, of course, the mass smugglings in bed at night. But it soon began to pall, and Lydia found herself yearning for simple solitude, for a space around her and, more cogently, inside her. She sometimes saw her fantasy approach as a Frankenstein's monster, for she rarely had any internal privacy, since she was committed to the idea that all should be revealed all the time in order to make the inner be realized in the outer world.

Like so many people who choose a course of action, Lydia found herself swept along into areas she was not sure she wanted to be in, or could even handle. The speed of the journey was often frightening. More than once she looked into a mirror and did not recognize the person she saw there.

The voice inside her, the voice she had identified as her truest self for as long as she could remember, no longer spoke to her, or when it did, she did not respond. Her former self was like an ex-lover one meets on the street by chance. There is memory, and echoes of fondness, but essentially the other is a stranger, more so than any actual stranger could ever be.

She hugged herself against the cold, and wished for a moment that she could talk to Fred, to have his warm irony blanket her in her loneliness, to take some of his strength to sustain her through the periods in which she had to dredge up every bit of reserve energy she could to maintain the optimism necessary to keep the group from collapsing or flying apart.

That had been relatively easy when she still had the role of therapist to bolster her. But after discarding that to enter into a more flexible relationship with what were once her patients and were now her family, she was left with nothing to rely on but her raw, inner resources. When conditions had thrust her into a position of almost unbearable responsibility, when she became guru and mother and friend all at once, she discovered that her burden of social image had added new subtleties to itself. At times she recalled Fred's admonition that she was dealing with a group of rootless neurotics seeking a tit to suck, and no matter what she did they would drain her dry.

It was a Tuesday night and Lydia was lonely. The apartment was filled with members of her growing community plus others who were being drawn into the vortex, and she couldn't stand the idea of even talking to one of them. She let herself back into the apartment and went very rapidly to the bathroom which led off what used to be her bedroom but which now served as the communal sleeping room. She and the others had had a meeting and agreed that the first rule of any community would have to involve each person having his or her own private room to sleep and work in. But her present place didn't allow for that necessity, and everyone was getting a bit frazzled by the continual rubbing of elbows and clashing of psyches.

Once inside the bathroom she latched the door behind her and lay down on the bathmat next to the tub. She was close to tears but didn't want to give way to them. She clenched her fists against her mouth and let out a silent scream. Never had she felt so alone in the world as then, when she was surrounded by people who voiced their affection. There was still some block inside her, an inability or unwillingness to let go. This despite the fact that her power had never been so full, nor her ability to swing loose into different emotional levels so advanced. She was sure that she was very, very close to some ultimate breakthrough, some final snapping of the essential tension which defined her rigidity. And the closer she got to liberation, the more the negative elements resisted. There would have to be some kind of explosion, she knew. Otherwise, she would remain in this kind of seesaw conflict, or drift off into a superficial spaciness which might be comfortable but entirely unsatisfying.

"It's the old civilization," she thought, "the fist of the ancient culture that's holding my heart tight." She wanted to go into the living room to be with the others, to let them know how she was feeling, but she was frozen into her resistance.

And then the realization hit her. Her community had become another form of tyranny. The same tyranny that had been the molding by her parents and teachers, for which she had substituted the tyranny of her profession, and then Doctor Monroe, and finally Fred, was being played by her own creation. She had lost the ability to be capricious, to be contradictory, except in the highly ritualized moments of their group fantasy explorations. This was the evil, the fact that any social organization almost immediately assumes a weight and life of its own and forces its members to conform.

"But it's insane to be imprisoned by my own . . ." she started to say out loud when the face of Doctor Monroe appeared before her, and his voice filled her ears. "The minute you begin eliciting fantasies, suggesting images, you are doing nothing but using others to fulfill your own inadequacies," he had said just before he died. And now that process was wreaking its damage.

Lydia stood up, turned on the light, and washed her face. Then she spent half an hour fixing her hair and making up her eyes and mouth. She did this instinctively, mindlessly, seizing upon the most palpable handle available for pumping up her ego. To complete the impulse, she went into her wardrobe and picked out her most scintillating dress, a pale blue sheath which clung to her with the indifference of silk. Over it she put her mink coat. Silver-lamé pumps completed the outfit.

Then, looking as though she were going to a function halfway between opening night at the opera and a transvestite ball, she took a deep breath and stepped boldly into the living room.

From her present state, the others looked like a pack of scraggly ersatz beatniks and failed back-to-the-farm enthusiasts. She raked the room with a cold stare, causing all conversation to stop. In one corner Robert had talked a woman of about twenty-five, someone new to the group, into taking off her blouse and bra, and was sanctimoniously massaging her tits as he poured the verbal debris of the New Age rhetoric into her ears. Nora had mesmerized two men and seemed ready to pull them into a threesome at any moment. And all around, the hopeful victims and the cagey predators eyed each other, the former wanting to be destroyed without being hurt and the latter entertaining visions of roaring brutality. John Abbot, who along with his clothes, had moved in nearly five hundred books on the occult, was sitting cross-legged on the living room table, pointedly being superior to it all and quietly waiting for someone, anyone, to sit at his feet.

"It's a madhouse," Lydia murmured.

Her presence galvanized the room. Like animals who had been lying in their cages daydreaming of jungles leaping to attention when the attendant comes with food, the people dropped their poses and activities and focused their awareness on Lydia. In that instant, she saw to the heart of what had been bothering her. It was that they all looked to her for clues, waiting to be defined by her reactions. Having started the process, she now wanted to fade into it, to become just another member of the body. But like it or not, she was its head and so possessed responsibility for the functions of speaking and thinking.

"Why are you all stopping," she said, her voice strident. "Do you think that I have some special message for you, some answer from the mountain top, some new game to entertain you? Haven't you—" she paused, shook her head and went on—"haven't *we* learned anything? Are we going to fall into authority structures with all that we know?"

They gazed at her like children who are being admonished but don't know what for.

"Who are these people?" she asked herself. "What are they doing here? Why are they in my home, eating my food, sleeping in my bed?"

The room began to go flat before her eyes, appearing two dimensional, and the faces of the people melted, lost their shapes. Everything seemed ringed in black. It was as though she had suddenly fallen into a nightmare. The guiding perceptions that she had been raised with, which formed the common pool of human definition of reality, was no longer operative. She had discarded that. And what was to have been her new mode, the transportation of fantasy into that world, was on the verge of becoming a weird travesty. Nothing was happening that hadn't happened before; the major difference was that now she had no guidelines with which to judge and handle it. She was totally awash in the chaotic vibrations, and the room and the people and the very structure of her life swam before her and through her and the next thing she knew she was lying on her back on the living room table staring at the ceiling.

At first she thought something was wrong with her eyes for the light seemed to be flickering, and then she realized that she was surrounded by candles. Her body was laid straight out, her arms stiff at her sides. She still wore her mink coat and shoes. All around her rose and fell the low murmur of voices. She tried to shake loose from the web of immediate confusion to sort out specific aspects of the scene. She could make out sobbing and whispering and, in the background, a monotonous chanting. The smell of incense and flowers choked the air. She blinked several times to clear her head and tried to move. But found she couldn't. It was as though she was paralyzed. She went to speak, and couldn't open her mouth.

Fear shot through her, first sending a harsh tingling through her limbs and then churning about in her belly. She cast about for some explanation, any conceptualization that would describe her situation in such a way that her mind could make peace with it. A score of possibilities reared up like frightened horses and started to stampede down the ravines of her consciousness before she took hold of the reins of speculation, drew in the runaway herd of malevolent images, and rested in a settling dust cloud of fragmented doubt. Taking a deep breath, she reached down into her psyche and chose a single conclusion with the care of an archer picking the best arrow from his quiver.

"I'm dreaming," she said to herself. "I must have fainted. The last thing I remember is the room going black. I must have passed out, and now I'm dreaming."

She recalled that the most successful nightmares convey the most chilling sense of reality, and so she expected that she wouldn't be able to find the same in the dream. Yet, she would try. For years, when she was a teenager, she had trouble falling asleep. She would lie in bed thinking, feeling herself, saying over and over, "In a few seconds I won't know I'm here. I'll still be here . . . my body will be here . . . but I won't be aware I'm alive." And as she sensed herself falling asleep, she'd jerk up in bed and force her eyes open, doing that again and again until, suddenly, she woke up and found that it was morning.

In later years, during her early therapy, she'd seen the whole process as an early cognition of death and a fighting against the inevitability of ultimate unconsciousness. She told her therapist how she was plagued by a peculiar form of nightmare. She'd find herself in a perfectly normal setting, going through mundane routines, until something very small but very striking, such as a clock's not being on the mantle where it belonged, would trigger an explosion of unbearable terror, and she'd start to struggle to escape, fighting to remove herself. While that was happening in the dream, the person on the bed would be whimpering and moaning, trying to punch her way into consciousness. Sometimes the experience revealed seemingly endless layers, as when she would think she was awake, but only be dreaming that she was now lying on her bed after just having surfaced from the nightmare. But when she attempted to move, the same paralysis afflicted her and once again she'd struggle and moan until she dreamed that she had awakened again, but by now be sitting up in bed, relieved at being out at last. But then she'd sense the presence of someone or something else in the room, someone or something coming toward her in the dark. She would try to scream, but find her vocal cords paralyzed. And still once more understand that she was still dreaming, and fear that she would always be dreaming, never to emerge from the countless dimensions of the nightmare world, until, with an effort of will that flowed from her toes and sucked strength from her entire body, she *would* scream, this time bursting through, waking herself up, and discovering herself lying on her back in her bedroom, screaming and screaming and screaming, until the lights went on in the hallway and her mother came flying into the room, clasping her to her breast, rocking her, and sighing over and over, "It's all right, it's all right, it was only a dream."

Yet the memory of those nights haunted her through the years, and after she had completed the bulk of her therapy she told herself that she understood the process and therefore was no longer vulnerable to it. When she first began to explore the question of fantasy in relation to consciousness and what is normally termed reality, however, those incidents came up for re-evaluation, although she had been unwilling to delve into the darker implications. For to open oneself to one's fantasy life meant not only discovering the latent joyousness and liberty which is strangled by the confines of civilization, but tampering with the hidden demonic forces that lay coiled at the roots of existence.

"So," she now thought, "it's happening again. Another one of those dreams."

Yet, there was something about her present condition which inclined her to think that she was really awake. She recalled the anecdote of the old Taoist rational lunatic Chuang Tze who noted that he fell asleep and dreamed he was a butterfly and now didn't know whether he was a man who had dreamed he was a butterfly or a butterfly dreaming he was a man. Lydia tried to roll her head around but found that it was bound tightly. That was the odd note. In her dreams, the paralysis had always been without an obvious cause. Now however, she could feel the ropes and tapes holding her. Her ankles, calves, thighs, waist, torso, wrists, elbows, chin, and forehead were all tied to the table. She was pegged as firmly as Gulliver in the land of the Lilliputians. And the reason she couldn't speak was the strip of surgical tape over her lips. Her back itched and she was sweating.

She moved the only part of her she could, her eyes, but couldn't make anything out. The flickering shadows and highlights on the ceiling, and an occasional movement along the periphery of her visual field, were her only clues. She took another deep breath and tried to sort out the sounds at another level. The audio resembled nothing so much as a scratchy recording of some jungle ritual recorded on a cheap tape recorder by an anthropologist. It had the same roughness, the same communal energy. But what was the ceremony? The tone was one of sorrow, and the mood was somewhat depressed.

Then, with rapid shifts of figure-ground perception, the picture snapped into focus. The scene was a funeral. The people around her were mourning. And she was the corpse

She would have smiled in relief except for the tape which kept her lips immobile. Now it was clear. She had fainted just when she was on the verge of heaping a tirade on their heads, and while she was unconscious they had worked up the fantasy of her death, taking her attack on their over-dependence to its logical conclusion. If there were any truth in the notion that they were draining her by being unable to find their own centers of energy and enthusiasm and direction, they would bury her and find out how they fared using her as a totem instead of as a living guide.

A fluttery elation tickled her chest. This was a vindication, somehow, a feeding back to her of all the energy she had poured out. Also, it allowed her to be totally passive, something she had been finding impossible for months. At the heart of the entire bondage and submission exercise which has begun to attract so many people is nothing more complicated than this desire to be helpless in the hands of someone who will bring pleasure and caring.

"Luckily, I'm with people who won't hurt me," Lydia thought.

But even as she was thinking that, the sounds around her subsided and from the corner of her eye she saw John Abbot standing next to the table, facing the others, his back toward her. He waited a few moments until there was complete silence, and then began to speak.

"It's difficult to know what to say," he began. "We all knew her, or thought we did. But somehow, when someone dies the way she did, we are always left wondering whether we ever got to see more than the mask. Nora found her, and thought she was sleeping. Then she found the bottle of pills on the night table."

John paused and seemed to be sniffling. When he spoke again, there were tremors in his voice.

"Why did she kill herself? How can we ever know?"

"Good Lord," Lydia thought, "they've imagined me a suicide."

"She left no note," John went on. "I'm sure all of us have examined our memories and consciences to ask whether there was anything in what we said or did, or didn't do or didn't say, which helped push her over the edge. She was a woman struggling with the final contradiction, one foot in the cultural world and one foot in the world of becoming. She was torn between a desire to discover a way out of the straitjacket of the traditional civilization and a hunger for the false freedom it offered. Just before she killed herself, she had dressed in the style of her previous values, and was gone for twenty hours. When she returned, it was obvious to all of us that she had debauched herself hideously. We can only imagine that she despaired of ever breaking loose from the appetite for what the world calls reality, or of ever committing herself fully to the communal fantasy that has become our new reality. She saw us first as her patients, and then as her children and followers, and finally as her burden. She couldn't do herself what she was trying to teach us to do, which is to plunge into the most painful portion of our perception to emerge purged on the other side. She tried, perhaps more than we can understand. But somewhere inside her she must have judged herself a failure. She couldn't face us with that, and so she killed herself."

"Oh, I can't believe she's gone," a woman's voice wailed. To Lydia it sounded like Nora.

"Well, she is and she isn't," John continued. "The body will decay and be buried. So much for reality. But she has taught us to go beneath the surface of things, to find a world within ourselves which is infinite and eternal. It no longer matters what happens to any of us as individuals. For the dream we have liberated now carries us in its arms. We now exist beyond truth, beyond love, beyond beauty. These are only the steps that lead up from the tomb of reality into the fields of fantasy, the realm beyond all definition. It is where language loses its content and becomes pure form, where form loses its outline and becomes pure potential, where potential sheds its dynamic and becomes pure awareness, where awareness discards its consciousness and becomes what the great mystics have tried to point to."

"Sweet Jesus," Lydia thought, "they've made a god of fantasy. I've really created a band of fanatics."

She tried to feel horrified about that, but the sensation would not come.

Paradoxically, although she was tied to her table in her living room while a score of people held a mock wake for her, she felt more in touch with herself than at almost any other time in her life. The situation was the living proof of what she was trying to work out: that in going to the farthest extreme of fantasy, one touched an entirely different reality. The thing she kept reminding herself was that this was *real*. The best way to put it into sharpest contrast was to imagine what would happen if the door suddenly burst open and a dozen policemen and reporters rushed in, perhaps led by Fred who would be "trying to save her from herself". The happening would be viewed as a freak-out, as an orgy, as a witches' sabbath, as a far out therapeutic experiment, as avant *garde* theatre, and, in fact, as anything but what it actually was, which was *life*.

Incongruously, she remembered the feeling she had had as a child when the family gathered for a holiday and everyone got a bit drunk after dinner. With the ties so strong, and with everyone knowing everyone so perfectly, their sore spots and foibles and grace points, they could become more and more boisterous, more crude, more intricate, more down-home than most alienated people would think possible. A stranger walking in would have seen only what passed for fighting and off-key singing and earthy erotic innuendo. But when everyone is kin, the human drama is just that, a drama, with no persnickety intellectual building a fancy theory over the raw fact. Similarly, in her living room, Lydia felt totally relaxed, at home. Even though the razor-thought that they might serve her up as a human sacrifice to meet the standards of the fantasy sizzled through her brain from time to time.

"As a farewell to the vessel which held Lydia's spirit," John was concluding, "we are going to pay our last respects to her corpse. I guess none of us wants to go so far as to cut her up and make a soup out of her, but neither do we desire anything so abstract as a wafer to serve as a symbol. So, since she's been dead for less than an hour and the body's still warm, we can say goodbye to her in a way that would have pleased her immensely."

Lydia watched as John leaned over her after he finished speaking. His hands came up toward her face. He was holding a strip of black cloth. She could not protest as he placed it over her eyes and fastened it around her head. And then everything went dark. She now could not move or speak or see.

In a few seconds, she felt her coat being parted. Then her dress was lifted. And she heard the thin sound-slivers of steel against steel as a pair of scissors snipped off her panties. It was then that she knew what they were going to do.

"This is the body of our beloved, dead Lydia," John said. "We have all known its countless delights when she was alive. And we can pay her no greater homage than to re-create the ritual of sex now that she is gone."

Lydia felt the bonds around her legs being cut and then her legs being spread apart. It was the single most vulnerable moment of her life, to have her bare cunt opened before a room full of people that she could not see. Someone slipped a finger into her pussy.

"Hmm," Robert said, "it's all wet and sticky. She's pretty randy for a corpse."

"Let me taste," said Marie. "I've never eaten a dead body before."

Lydia felt the lips against her lower lips, the tongue sliding into the moist sanctuary, lapping up the juices and then slipping up to rim the clitoris. She would have thrust her hips forward but her pelvis was still taped down.

"Nice," Marie said. "Tastes just like she did when she was alive."

"Her tits," Arthur said, "I want to see her tits."

The scissors went to work again and the top of her sheath dress was sliced open, baring her breasts to the room.

"Beautiful," said several people at once, and she felt hands skating up and down her rib cage and mouths descending on her nipples. From the impression, it seemed that five or six people were sucking on her tits at once. Squirmy sensations coursed through her immobile body.

It was then that she got the point. She was not to respond. She was to sense herself as a corpse. This was the fantasy exercise the others were imposing on her; it was not just for them to work something out, but for her to learn something. They were telling her that she did not have to carry the burden of responsibility all the time, that although they loved her and needed her, they existed independently of her, and even though they tended to flock about her and look to her for clues, they were quite capable of carrying on on their own.

Lydia let herself imagine her own death, that she had indeed passed from the realm of activity, and was now slowly decomposing and becoming one with the elements without her ego trying to convince her otherwise. And with that, a great peace descended. She saw that everything would continue. The universe would go on working out its mysterious and awesome patterns; the planet would continue to revolve around the sun; life would not cease from producing new forms; human beings would proceed to act out their scenarios.

Perhaps most importantly, people would go on fucking and loving and striving for freedom. And she did not have to do anything special, save to be herself. There was no success or failure, only process. It was possible for her to die, and for that to be all right. This was something she had known conceptually ever since the age of reason, but this was the first time it emerged as an emotional reality.

"Fuck me," she thought, "fuck my corpse. Pump living fluid into the dead so the dead may know that they are still alive."

From then on it was a feast for Lydia. The ritual lasted for several hours, during which there was not a second in which she was not being licked or prodded or spanked or kissed or fucked or fondled. After a while she could not easily distinguish her body from those of the others. It was all heat, all contact, all secretion, all sensation. Even the notion of orgasm lost its meaning. The entire thing was one long sustained climax. All the particular acts, the being fucked in the ass, the sperm on the tongue, the piss in the mouth, the fingers in the cunt, the cocks on the belly, the cunts on her lips, the bites on the nipples, lost all individual significance. Nothing existed but heat and movement and surging waves of yearning.

Through all of it she did not move. Her legs were lifted and parted and brought back together and manipulated in a hundred ways, but she exerted no effort. She allowed herself to be dead, the greatest luxury available to a human being.

The scene reached its own high point and then began to slacken, to falter. The men were the first to drop off, each having attained from two to five orgasms in her or on her. And then the women, one by one, stopped licking and finger fucking and smothering her face with their buttocks. And finally, they were all lying on the floor, some asleep, most in a tingling trance, and Lydia lay stunned and glimmering on the table. She was beyond all ability to give any name to her state of being at that moment.

At dawn, there was a stirring. The family began to move itself out of its collective stupor, a deep unconsciousness in which the most central aspects of the self were regenerated. And, something they were not to understand in all its implications until later, an unbreakable bond of understanding was formed. The way in which they had joined the relationship between fantasy and reality made it impossible that they could become anything but a permanent family.

It was John Abbot who cut Lydia loose. It took a half hour for her to get her full circulation back. And when she sat up, the entire universe tilted. She grabbed on to the edge of the table for she had started to float off its surface.

She shot John a glance to see whether he had noticed.

"Well, all the old books and the heavy yogis tell us that when you really understand reality, you become less and less subject to its laws. Levitation isn't that big a deal, unless you make a sideshow out of it."

"No," Lydia said, and then cleared her throat which was clogged with dried sperm. "I just don't want to start floating when I'm walking down Forty-second street, that's all."

"Well, the only solution to that is to get away from Forty-second street."

"You mean leave the city?"

"Sure," John said, "We all know that we have to go find our own land sooner or later."

"It's too much for me to think about right now."

"How do you feel?" he asked, "I mean aside from ravished and spaced."

"I'm hungry," she told him. "And I want a bath."

John turned around.

"Nora," he whispered. "Why don't you rustle these bums off the floor and see if we can get a breakfast together."

Then he turned back, slipped his arms under Lydia's knees and behind her shoulders, and lifted her from the table.

"I'm going to take you in and give you a bath," he said. "And then we'll all eat together, and figure out what happens next."

9

Lydia could not remember the last time she'd been in a basement. Of course, at the Warren Handman Institute for Psychoanalytic Systems (WHIPS), the place was not referred to as the basement. The members of that august body had shown a rare flash of humor by nicknaming it "the id" since it lay below the rest of the building's functions.

She sat on one side of a long redwood table while the five man panel examining her ranged across the opposite edge. The entire scene had been mounted with the precision of a Polanski period piece film. Six onyx ashtrays, six pads, six perfectly sharpened pencils, six glasses, and a pitcher of ice water provided the essential props. The massive tables and carved chairs with their velour cushions yielded the major furniture. On one wall an enlarged photograph of Freud peered down with a sour expression. Facing him, Warren Handman, the founder of the clinic, took the second place to the master he had assumed even in life, now represented by a slightly smaller photo in a less ornate frame. There was one window, but ventilation was provided by a discreet air conditioner which hummed to itself in one corner where it took the stale air out of a back alley and sent it, chastened, into the tribunal room.

Tom Norwood had followed through on his threat, writing a letter to the New York State Licensing Bureau outlining Lydia's activities and demanding her designation as a therapist be rescinded. The Board maintained a list of titles which citizens could not assume without official approval, such as Medical Doctor, Psychiatrist, Attorney at Law, and Psychologist. However, the term "therapist" was not on their list, and so anyone from a highly experienced physician to a raging lunatic could advertise himself or herself as a therapist. Tom Norwood hadn't known that and his letter was at first dismissed, but the clerk who read it, titillated by the juicy details of the way he had been taken through his fantasy and ended by fucking Lydia in the mouth, passed it around her office where it finally made its way into the hands of a woman who took her job as guardian of the public nomenclature quite seriously. She looked up Lydia's name, saw that she had passed the Licensing Exam for the title of psychologist, and forwarded the letter to the office which handled complaints against the abuse of that license.

Like all bureaucracies, the Board disliked involving itself in anything which wasn't routine and had perfected its own version of the process of passing the buck. Through a series of letters and phone calls, they arranged for the Handman Clinic to act as their investigative agent to decide whether Lydia had indeed overstepped her bounds in experimenting with radical forms of practice.

When Doctor Zugzwang was informed of what was going on, he literally did a little dance of delight, much like the skip executed by Hitler at the Austrian border. For months he had been receiving word-of-mouth reports on Lydia and growing more and more furious. His deepest rage involved what he considered to be the bastardization of analysis by generations of pipsqueaks who seized on one small corner of the vast Freudian tapestry and capitalized on selling strands of useless rationalizations. He would have dropped a small nuclear device on Esalen if he could have gotten away with it. He despised the touchie-feelie therapists, the sex therapists, the ones who experimented with drugs. He was capable, in his more expansive moments, of having a conversation with a very, very serious Jungian, but Reichians, Rogerians, Sullivanians, Behaviorists, and members of all other schools were anathema. His basic attitude was Inquisitorial. The world seethed with heretics, and it would be a better place once they were flushed out, forced to recant, or else be burned at the stake.

And now, one of the most dangerous and fiendish of them all had been delivered right into his hands! When he received the news he was beside himself with glee. If he could conduct a truly definitive investigation he might not merely wipe Lydia Stone off the therapeutic map, but institute guidelines that would be used to judge all future psychologists who wanted to tread the sacred ground of analysis. If he had his way, only medical doctors would even be considered, but he was realistic enough to know that the day of the lay analyst had definitely arrived. Ultimately, he would have it that no one could be an analyst without studying at the Handman clinic, under his supervision, which derived directly from Freud.

Zugzwang simmered even when he thought of his fellow Freudians who were filled with tales about how the old man had written to them, or held long conversations with them. The worst were those who had been analyzed by the Master. For Zugzwang knew, with the certainty of a suspicious husband who is convinced his wife is having an affair. He knew in his heart that the real transmission had been made to him. During a session of the International Psychoanalytic Association where Freud had addressed two thousand members, after the Founder had walked from the lectern and out of the hall, he passed Zugzwang on the steps, stopped, reached over and tugged his beard, and said in a loud voice, "Don't take yourself so seriously, Zugzwang." The then junior analyst understood the message at once. Freud was saying, "To all the others I give the outer shell, the mere form. But you and I understand the true, the central meaning. So much so that I can joke with you." It was the seal of esoteric knowledge, and Zugzwang had guarded it jealously for forty years.

To fill out the panel he had chosen Doctors Schaatz, Fick, Zwischen and von Gule. Not one of them was under sixty-five, and they all spoke with carefully nurtured accents which protected them from the rhythms of either their native or acquired tongues. Zugzwang had no need to tell the men what he expected, for they shared his cold anger at what they saw as the debasement of a noble ideal. Like clucking bishops, they were prepared to raise their miters in condemnation of the hussy who dared drag the legacy of Freud into the mud.

Lydia hadn't known quite how to meet them. The first

problem was dress. Should she wear something straightforward and treat the entire episode on the level of consensual reality, or ought she to approach the question of clothing with the attitude of emptiness and throw on whatever her hands reached for first in the morning? The family urged her not to go at all.

"What's the point?" Judy Bachrach said, "they're going to hang you anyway, unless you grovel and promise to mend your ways. So let them take your license away by mail. Why give them the satisfaction of doing it in person?"

"Unless you're thinking of giving in to them," John Abbot added.

"Of course not," Lydia replied. "But it's like the old witches' notion of looking up the devil's asshole. Zugzwang is the personification of everything that's horrible about the therapeutic world. Not for what he does, because classic analysis has its own validity in its own context. But because he can't allow anyone else to find their own way. He's the worst kind of fascist, ready to impose conformity on the entire species. And I suppose I want to confront him, to *taste* him. I think it will make me stronger."

By that time the group had decided that leaving for the country was only a question of money and momentum. It had become clear that all the arguments forced them in that direction. From Fred's accusation that their continuing to live in the city made them nothing more than a fancy brand of parasite to their own awareness that they would blossom best in a place where they weren't constantly being pressed in by a crush of people, the pressure was on them to leave. That being the case, Lydia's holding onto a New York State Psychologist's License was purely beside the point. If they didn't take it away from her she would let it lapse anyway. The question now was how to get the most mileage out of the situation.

They spent an hour tripping out on all the possibilities before they stripped Lydia naked, led her into the bedroom, and tried on every possible combination of clothing they could. The appointment was for two in the afternoon so they started dressing her at ten in the morning. Still, what with the giggling and fucking and horsing around, it was one-thirty before she was ready to leave, and she was sitting in the taxi before she realized that her outfit was outrageous beyond description for the meeting she was about to have.

Zugzwang had been dismayed when he first saw her, for she was wearing her mink and exuded an air of complete composure and self-confidence. He was prepared for a struggle with her, but was slightly fearful that she might have a few tricks prepared to catch him off balance. But when she removed the coat, his jaw fell open and he stared at her like an idiot gaping at the sun. Lydia was wearing a skin-tight blazing red knitted blouse two sizes too small which gripped every edge and curve of her torso with as much accuracy as a coat of paint. Her breasts were more naked than if she had worn nothing at all. Below the blouse was a pair of jet-black hotpants, cut well below her navel and molded in perfect contours around her pubic bone, revealing the cuntal bulge and split which did not carry the benefit of protection by panties. Her arms and legs were bare, and when she kicked off her mules she strode into the room barefoot. By the time she stood in front of the table she looked like nothing so much as an Eighth Avenue hooker on a summer night, except that she wore no jewelry and no makeup.

"Hello boys," she drawled, "how's tricks?"

Zugzwang almost bit his tongue. The woman had come into the very bowels of the Freudian body dressed and acting in such a way as to boast of her mockery of everything he stood for. At the same time, the sheer erotic power of her transfixed him and he felt something he had not known for more than twenty years, a distinct throb beginning in his right thigh and pulsing into his now finally dormant cock. The other men in the room shuffled about on their chairs, looking to Zugzwang for clues as to how to react. But he was struck dumb, leaning forward over the table, his eyes bulging.

Lydia laughed out loud, the chuckle of a whore watching a portly judge trip over his shoelaces in his haste to get to her.

"What's the matter, Zugzwang," she said in a nasal twang, "never see a libido walking before?" The clanging of that word in the context of having Lydia's raw cunty eroticism flung in his face, caused a jamming in the analyst's mind. The doctor possessed something like the Catholic's reflex of nodding the head upon hearing the name Jesus; only with him the action was not physically manifest and was connected to the long litany of terms which constitute the Freudian orthodoxy. But by that irony in which history delights, Zugzwang's reaction to Lydia was precisely the same as those doctors who first listened to Freud read his ideas on infantile sexuality. The brooding Viennese neurologist, fired up on cocaine, was greeted with hoots and catcalls and even had several chairs flung through the air at him. Now the nearly bald Zugzwang had to exert every bit of his will power to keep from picking up the heavy ashtray in front of him and crushing Lydia's skull with it.

"Please, Doctor, please sit down," said Zwischen. The clinic's leader looked as though he were on the brink of a heart seizure. No one could guess the depth of his murderous rage.

Zugzwang finally relaxed and eased himself into his chair. Lydia remained standing for a few seconds longer, gazing down on the assemblage of analytic inquisitors and, licking her lips and shaking her tits, she smiled to herself and sat down.

The six of them let the silence build around them for almost a full minute. Lydia and Zugzwang watched each other like gunfighters about to draw. She was the first to break the eyelock, and then raked the others with her amused glance.

"Well gents," she said, "the worst thing you can do is to recommend that I have my license revoked. And since it has less value to me than a sheet of high-grade toilet paper, your power covers a very limited area indeed. That is to say, the worst you can do is give me a pain in the ass for a brief time. So let's cut the pseudo-solemnities and talk straight."

The minute she spoke, a hundred cobwebs caught flame in her mind and burned away in an instant. Like a little child who has been naughty and who fears the wrath of her father, Lydia had retained a residual awe of the possible power of the men she was to meet. But once the words were out of her mouth, once she stood before them in her cataclysmic costume and hurled her challenge at them, she saw them as five pathetic creatures who lived in a dungeon of their own limitations. It wasn't until that instant that she saw that she had unconsciously been fearing this confrontation, that her dressing up was a bit of bravura intended to reassure herself more than to impress her accusers. It was the old father-figure problem that had hung her up on Doctor Monroe and the entire world of official attitudes. She almost laughed in relief at seeing, truly seeing, that these men had no power over her. They could strip her of her accreditation, smear her reputation in the therapeutic community, but all that had as much punch as an excommunication order issued by the Pope. She knew who these people were, for she had been one of them herself. They were the most clever of the intellectuals who grew fat on the offal of the civilization they fed off. They were incapable of independent thought, of free action. They accepted what they were told in school, and put curlicues on it, enough to make them seem mentally active, but their contribution to true knowledge was about as meaningful as the addition of fins on the bumpers of cars.

"All right," said Doctor Zugzwang, clearing his throat, composing himself. "Although, judging from your brazen attitude and absolutely infantile appearance, appearance . . . appear . . ." A tic had developed at the corner of his mouth and his head shook violently for a few seconds. Doctor von Gule leaned over and pounded his colleague on the back.

"Appearance," Zugzwang continued, "you are obviously already resigned to being dismissed from the community of your peers."

"Excuse me," Lydia said, "my former peers."

"As you like. At any rate, this hearing will probably not take very much time since you are not interested in making a defense."

"A defense?" Lydia asked. "I'm not aware of what charges have been brought against me."

Zugzwang looked down at the pad in front of him and smiled.

"Well, let's see," he said, "where shall we begin? The list is rather formidable. Using therapeutic procedures to seduce patients. Condoning illicit and immoral behavior. Holding orgies under the auspices of group therapy. Suspicious circumstances regarding the death of your control therapist, Doctor Monroe.' He turned to speak to his colleagues. "Minute traces of vaginal secretions were found at the base of Doctor Monroe's pe-pe-pe-penis." Then, turning back to Lydia. "Evidence of misconduct concerning the suicide of Marsha Seligson, a former patient of yours."

Doctor Zugzwang leaned back in his chair. "Quite a track record, *Doctor* Stone," he said, infusing the title with venomous sarcasm.

On an impulse, Lydia decided to cut through the rigmarole to see if she could address what little flexibility remained in the old man. This labored jousting wasn't even amusing, and she thought she might see if there was any value to be found in the meeting.

"All right, Zugzwang, let's drop the bullshit and talk about what's really important. And that is whether therapists have a responsibility to explore new ways of feeding life or whether we have to stay mired in the stale old rituals."

"What you call stale rituals," said Fick unexpectedly, breaking in on the line of tension between Lydia and the chief interrogator, "are modes of analysis which have proven themselves to be the most sound approach possible, despite the vogues which appear and disappear every few years. You know, since Freud developed his theory and technique, a hundred new ideas have been tried. Character analysis, drugs, massage, behavior modification, ego education, and so forth. And each has been like one of the blind men who held a piece of the elephant and thought he had the whole thing.

"Only Freud saw the whole, and only his approach gets to the heart of the matter. Now, I understand that you work with people lying on their backs. Well, you see, the circle comes back to the beginning. Freud discovered that. Of course, the posture is ancient, appearing in yoga and other disciplines. But he was the one to link it with free-association.

"Then the innovators came along and had the patient sit up. And after all the possible variations in that were tried, you come along and 'discover' what we have been doing all along. The difference is, we know that material cannot be pulled by force out of a patient, or seduced out of him. Freud used hypnosis and discarded it because of its artificiality. And as soon as you rediscover the analytic wheel, which Freud described more than seventy years ago, long before you were born, you get impatient, and want to rush in, inducing psychotic episodes, bringing about a melodramatic acting-out. And even this might not be bad.

"Not for theatre, perhaps, or for an evening's entertainment instead of playing charades. It is a game. And if you want to play, please go ahead. Some of my colleagues are outraged at your behavior, but I have seen much foolishness in my life and am no longer astonished at anything. But please, do us all a favor, including yourself, and turn in your license. And then you can let your conscience be your guide."

For a few moments Lydia was taken by the eminent level-headedness of the man who had just spoken to her. He seemed to let the air out of the balloon that Zugzwang seemed intent on blowing up so he could burst it.

In a way, Fick appeared to be sympathetic to her, but he couldn't let himself be open to recriminations by Zugzwang. So he added, "*If* you have a conscience left. Which I doubt. In any case, it has been interesting meeting you. I see your type on the street, of course, and, in modified form, on my couch, but this is the first time I have actually heard one of your kind in a context like this, one in which I am constrained to treat you as a balanced human being. I think you are sick, Doctor Stone. And I think you will cause great harm to a great many people. But please, do it without the benefit of your title."

"Yes, yes, well put," said Schaatz. "We imagined you would offer us some material to deal with, give some rational argument to defend what you are doing. If you could at least attempt to operate at a reasonable level, we might help you. But you are so perverse that you flaunt your condition."

As he spoke, his eyes were riveted on Lydia's nipples.

A long silence stretched over the room. The men, operating as a collective awareness, gradually recoiled from their own rambunctiousness. The shock of Lydia's vital and challenging presence, although it could be largely obviated by their ability to rationalize it, threw their attitude into a highlight of fanaticism. They could not admit this but were nonetheless affected by it. On her part, Lydia wondered why she had appeared in such a foolish costume. At her apartment, drenched in the giddy enthusiasm of the family, wearing the hotpants had sounded like a marvelous idea. But in the same way that marijuana notions dissipate in the arena of rigid social perception, this venture began to risk seeming silly.

Zugzwang was also having second thoughts. For months he had nurtured a slow dislike and hatred of Lydia, and he had spent agonizing hours analyzing his reactions. He was intelligent enough to realize that he was going overboard in this matter.

The thing he held in a back corner of his mind, however, was the certain knowledge that the totality of his life and work had amounted to nothing. Like most other people in the world, Zugzwang had made the error of equating his preoccupation with reality itself, and as the end of his life neared and his involvement with analysis proved to be no defense against death, the rubrics and relics of his crusade showed up as trivial toys.

The criticism most often brought against Freud in later years was that he was hopelessly provincial, not only culturally but cosmically. The power of his genius lay in its limitation. Who else could latch onto such stupendous banalities as the fact that children have erotic impulses and build an entire conceptual monument around it.

Zugzwang, like most of Freud's strict adherents, shared the tunnel vision of the Master, but lacked the burning intensity, or even the true spirit of innovation. Zugzwang would never consider snorting cocaine, or leaving cigarettes by the couch for one of his patients, things that Freud did as a matter of course. For Zugzwang, the central issue now was to avoid seeing his entire life as a grotesque parody, an inconsequential exercise in the obscure. The only thing that prevented this insight from crashing through was the constant reassurance by his peers. And the unrelenting attack he carried on against deviationists. He had planned on demolishing Lydia and thus provide himself with his most invincible bulwark to date against the encroachment of acid self-evaluation in terms outside the Freudian loop. But in her helter-skelter fashion, she had broken the spearhead of his attack.

Finally, von Gule, who was disposed to take the avuncular

attitude, cleared his throat. The sound exploded in the tense silence of the space.

"Well, she is just a child, isn't she?" he began. "She does not mean harm, she is not evil. Perhaps she truly thinks she has made a discovery. Perhaps she is filled with the zeal of the missionary. How much harm can she do? The people who follow her are all neurotic. So, she may make them a little more smug in their neurosis. She will either become a cult leader, or else come to her senses. What does it have to do with us? This is not a question for us to decide. I recommend that we turn it back to the License Board."

"I agree," said Zwischen. "They want our recommendation, I believe we can make a recommendation. Obviously, this woman is not qualified to hold the title of Psychologist."

The five men nodded at one another as though they were puppets connected by a single string. Zugzwang, who still hoped in part for a knock-down battle of ideas, was frightened enough to agree. He gave the final and definitive nod.

"Yes, Doctor Stone," he said to Lydia. "I can inform you that we shall simply send our recommendation that you have your license revoked to Albany. As you say, it means little enough to you, so I don't feel that we are harming you at all."

Lydia leaned back in her chair and took a deep breath.

"Actually, you are relieving me of a burden."

"Yes," added Fick, "if you had continued in this way, sooner or later someone would have brought a criminal suit against you."

"To be truthful," Zugzwang went on, "I am a bit disappointed in you. I had expected to find someone serious, someone who was trying to hurl a challenge against the tested Freudian understandings of the human psyche. And I would have welcomed discussing this with you, for I am positive that you would see the poverty of your ideas. You know, so many of the modern therapists denigrate analysis. I wonder what would happen if they, or you, would undergo a full seven year treatment. I think you might discover that all of your enthusiasms are merely one or another level of unfulfilled wish/projections that take shape because so many people out there are looking for the lost father or mother. Does this make sense to you?"

"Of course it does," Lydia answered. "I'm not an innocent or a fool. But everything you say is valid only within one context, on one level of consciousness. It is a definition of reality within which all the structures are self justifying and mutually supporting. What I have stumbled into is another truth altogether, and not a very novel one at that. It is the truth that Jesus and Buddha spoke of, that the mystics try to tell us about, and that most recently Don Juan has described. Essentially, I am learning about what I can only call *The Source*. I am learning about a space where everything is pure becoming, and the forms which result are incidental. You know, creation grows out of chaos, and chaos is then replenished by creation. But what you have done is to get stuck in the cauldron of creation, and you are afraid to let go, to let yourself come apart and realize that your form—that is, your body and thoughts and beliefs and artifacts—are just temporary, little better than an illusion. Thus, you are cut off from what really gives you energy, and so cannot feed anything back into the origin of all things. In a word, you have become stale. You have been afraid of love and death, and have sought refuge in conceptual perfection. You are your own museums."

She and Zugzwang stared at one another over the abyss of their mutually untranslatable languages, like two people from different countries who have tried, though hand signals and facial expressions to discuss something of ultimate meaning and subtlety and finally given up, retreating to their individual thought-forms.

Each was correct in his and her unique view of truth, and no consensus was possible. From the context of his world, he had done all he could do: he would see to it that Lydia lost her license. From the context of her world she had done all she could do: she had seen to it that Zugzwang would never venture outside the boundaries of his realm again.

"We are each living out our own fantasies," Lydia said to herself. "He has completely identified with his image of the world. He has his own private dream world, the same as anyone else, but he also possesses the arrogance to equate that with the actual flux of which we are momentary eruptions."

Then her vision became complete, the notion she'd been

struggling to find, to defend. Each human being is an entire universe of possibilities in terms of the way he or she sees the world. This private vision meets two antagonists. One is the world of brute physical reality, the enormous supra-galactic space in which the earth is an unmentionably tiny and irrelevant cinder. The second is the world of other human beings. And the whole question of survival in its widest sense involves those three points.

There has to be a way for each individual to bring his or her unique world view into harmony with those of every other human being, and then for all these to cooperate in dealing with the necessities of making it on the planet.

All the ills of the species involve disregarding one of the three points. Those who would discount the reality of the actual universe are escapists who fall into ersatz spirituality, cheap occultism, and other-worldly religions. Those who ignore the necessity for cooperation become the overlords, the competitors. And those who do away with the necessity to maintain the integrity of each individual's link to the source through fantasy are the fascists, the totalitarian tyrants.

Other variations are possible, such as the one represented by Fred, who maintained that these three aspects existed but should have nothing to do with one another. It was all right to dream but not to infuse one's dream world into the jungle of day-today survival.

Doctor Zugzwang's dilemma, which he did not recognize as such, was his inability to understand that each view of reality rarely included more than one person. And when there were more, these constituted a true family, a conceptual karaas. He had already put together his family, at the Institute, but he wasn't able to accept that, in the same way that Freud had to drive off each of his "sons". And, cut off from the succor of their actual families, such men drove themselves desperate trying to climb higher and higher cliffs of cerebral success, growing more bitter all the while.

It seemed to Lydia that the room grew dark. All that could be heard was the hum of the air conditioner, chanting monotonously to itself in the corner. The five men lost their features and became black shrouded statues at the edge of a low wall. The time might have been two thousand years earlier, or five centuries in the future. The place might have been anywhere, another planet, another solar system. They might have been any life form, not necessarily human beings. All that remained was consciousness, pure, empty, unattached. The shreds of the social context had burned away. Analytic institutes, licensing boards, orthodoxies, panels of judgment, dogmatic views of the mysterious existence . . . all these became two dimensional, one dimensional, and then disappeared, like Alice's pack of cards. Lydia could see auras, and fields of force, clusters of emotion, and vagrant thought forms whirring. She could see the whole chain of chaos and creation. All of human civilization, with its languages and arts and sciences and philosophies and religions was nothing more than the flimsiest ankle bracelet on the right leg of a minor god which itself held the most insignificant role in the overall scheme of what is.

In a sense, she did not know what she was doing, and yet she did. What the. five men saw, however, had the effect of a nitroglycerin charge set at the most critical stress point of a delicate bridge. They had a hundred different simultaneous impressions and attitudes. They gaped and looked away. They were aroused and repulsed. And, in short, they felt as though they had been kicked in the solar plexus and then pissed on by someone who did not even wish them harm or hold them in contempt.

Lydia snaked the hotpants down over her thighs. She ran her hands down her belly and pulled her cuntlips apart with her fingers, the violet painted nails glittering against the dark purple skin and the pale pink of the inner organ. The men gazed like children at a dazzling magician's trick, their eyes held by the magnetism of her crotch, the thatch of hair, the quivering lips, the moist center.

Slowly, deliberately, Lydia slid the middle finger of her right hand into the core and when she pulled it out it was wet and glistening with juice. The drowsy smell of parted cunt licked the air molecules in the room.

Carefully, she pulled her pants back up. She walked to the

door and threw her mink coat over her shoulders. Then she turned, and giving the doctors her most enigmatic smile, held the anointed finger straight up in the air.

They were still watching with febrile fascination as the door slammed in their faces.

10

"Well, what do you think?"

"I'm too overwhelmed to think right now. I haven't assimilated the change yet."

Fred sat on the edge of the high cliff and looked out three hundred miles into space. The pure air of the New Mexico heartland allowed unobstructed vision to the most extreme horizon and the eye unaccustomed to such a view was stunned that it could see so much. After the experience of sheer immensity, there was the detail. First, the color, the gash-pure vibrancy of hue from sun-shocked desert, wind-hewed outcroppings of ancient rock, and occasional rivers which gleamed like liquid diamonds.

Fred and Lydia sat on the lip of a mesa more than a thousand feet above the earth. She was like a child, her feet dangling into space, while Fred had folded his jacket under him and leaned back against a low tree. She was wearing a pair of overalls and nothing else. No shoes or shirt. Her breasts, brown and firm, showed clearly through the sides of the bib. Her hair had been drawn back into a ponytail, and her face carried no makeup except the effect of sun and wind. She exuded confidence and good health. Fred watched her with paternalistic amusement.

It had been a year since Lydia and twenty-three of her former patients had taken the final step, pulled up roots, and gone to find a place where they might start a new community. John Abbot revealed that he was the heir to a rather large fortune and while he had been using his money to play around in different city scenes, he now wanted to invest it in something he believed in. He made the five thousand acres he had inherited in the south of New Mexico available to Lydia and the group, and they all moved into the two sprawling ranch houses that had already been built on the land, there to begin a new way of being.

They had arrived with an almost even balance of advantages and disadvantages. On the plus side were an abundance of enthusiasm, no immediate financial worries, and a fairly high degree of personal knowledge about one another. Their most important sources of difficulty lay in culture shock, suffered when transporting oneself from one of the planet's most intense psychic centers to a space in which the nearest human neighbors were over three miles away; and in urban ignorance: not one of them knew anything about planting, growing, tending animals, or any of the hundred tasks necessary to keep a self-sufficient farm community going. For the first six months they had had to carry most of their food in from open air markets and only gradually made the transition to owning their own cows and sheep and chickens, and to raising their own soy beans and wheat and vegetables.

Learning the difference between actual survival effort and living an ecologically parasitic existence in the city was one of the most difficult tasks any of them had ever faced, especially since they were prone to all the excesses that utopian types fall into when they first find themselves in a secluded spot: nudity, orgies, reveling all night and sleeping through most of each day. Lydia's job involved getting everyone to do his or her necessary share of the labor while making sure that the group maintained its dedication to their real work.

They had decided, during one of their first meetings, to define themselves as a religious center. There were the usual legal advantages to such a move, but on another level they had all come to consider what they were doing as constituting a new religious sensibility.

As John Abbot put it, "There's only one true religion and all the religions of the world are more or less imperfect copies of that. So, why not make a new draft?"

Most of them were sophisticated enough to understand that the surest way to kill an impulse is to articulate it. Also, in the scramble to put down the structures, principles, and ground rules of a community, a power struggle is almost certain to ensue. Even though a number of people share the same vision, the formulation of that vision may differ radically from person to person.

They wrestled with the issue for more than a week and finally were able to agree upon three defining aspects of their religion. The first was that it have no name; the second was that its guiding spirit be universal compassion; the third was that the technique of fantasy trance states be its way of meditation and prayer.

Having attained to such a lofty evocation of ideals, they returned to the physical plane to deal with the same problems faced by every person on the planet: survival. Lydia was amazed at the stark simplicity of the questions they worked with, and what real complexity and strength was involved in answering them. They decided, for example, to divide the entire survival problem into seven essential categories: air, water, food, clothing, shelter, health, and social organization. This appeared straightforward enough on paper, but just a brief study of the food category yielded a world of considerations: buying stock and seed, housing and feeding the animals, all the steps necessary to plant, cultivate, harvest and store vegetables and beans, working out dietary requirements in terms of protein and vitamin intake. And this had to be coordinated with where and how houses were built, what medical facilities were available, and so on. In short, they had to reconstruct civilization.

Their essential life task then involved optimum survival for all in the context of their religious principles. And since they had just arrived from the most alienated, fragmented, and shallow civilization the world had ever seen, they were zealous about not allowing a split to take place between the two orders of business. For, to be "religious" with out concern for actual living conditions is the worst possible perversion of the mystical impulse; and to "survive" without any infusion of a truly religious sensibility is the road to the complete brutalization of humanity. The history of western culture has been the account of one society or another wandering or rushing down one of the two roads, or maintaining a hypocrisy in which the two were falsely commingled.

Cut off from the prying eyes of those whose interest could not be anything but hostile or benign curiosity, the members of the group began to flower into their most pointed individuality. In one sense they came to look more alike, with the men growing beards and the women letting their hair get long, and everyone wearing overalls most of the time. But the more they were able to rely upon the strength of the collective, the more each person could let his or her idiosyncrasies develop. Nora, for example, at one point went almost a month without saying a word. John Abbot had a bird tattooed on his forehead. And Eileen went through a six month spell of celibacy. As with any family, they learned to be tolerant of one another's foibles without letting anyone get away with too much egocentric foot-treading.

They met three times a week to get naked and enter a state of evocative fantasy together. There they expressed all those things that cannot be got to on the level of rational discourse. There they shook down the structure necessary to maintain their survival trip, making sure that they did not, either individually or as a group, get too compulsive or too loose. Physical labor kept them together, and psychic work kept them at the proper distances from one another. The sessions allowed them to see themselves and one another in ways that fell outside the essential roles they took in order to keep the community going.

As might have been expected, word of their existence leaked out, and before long they had their first visitors. In the first year some five hundred people came through; once the location and description of the community was fed into the counter-cultural information system, it became a stopping-off spot for those modern small caravans which crisscross the country in search of the ultimate utopia. Many went to satisfy a vague curiosity, some out of a kind of pathetic aggression; some because they were hungry and thought they might find one or another kind of food; and a few because they were looking for a home.

At the end of the year the community had more than fifty people.

And it was then that Fred visited. He arrived unannounced, and when Lydia first saw him it took her a full ten seconds to recognize the skinny, grey-faced man in the absurd clothing.

And when she saw who it was, she was caught between laughter and tears. He looked so ridiculous she wanted to laugh, and yet so miserable that she wanted to cry. He seemed like a little boy who'd lost his mother and was trying to pretend to be manly about it. To her amazement, Lydia realized that she felt like the mother he was looking for. She had not had a clear gauge of her development as measured by some criterion outside the community, but with Fred's visit, she could see that her advance had been breathtaking.

"Fred," she called out as he stood on the front porch twiddling his hat between his hands.

And when he glanced over at her, she knew that he was having as much trouble recognizing her as she'd had with him.

They moved toward one another tentatively and when they were standing several inches apart, they embraced, Lydia's strong arms, made firm by work in the fields, almost crushing Fred's rib cage. She'd taken him on a tour of the buildings, explaining the basic ground plan of the place, and then walked with him to the edge of the high plateau on which the entire community was housed, and they had stared into the vast distance for a long time before Lydia had asked what he thought of it all.

"I've missed you," Fred said, still staring down a fifth of a mile to the shrub covered ground below, his voice naked in the deep silence which drenched the land from horizon to horizon.

Lydia remained quiet. She was certain he wanted her to tell him that she had missed him also, but that hadn't been the case. Every once in a while she'd experienced a brief poignant memory of him, a searing flash that set her heart racing, her eyes stinging with tears, and a sense of eternal loss flooding her soul. But, in all honesty, she was generally too busy and involved to give Fred too much thought. She often considered that she would never see him again and that did not plunge her into any sort of ineradicable gloom.

"For a while," he went on, "after I'd heard that you left, I was very amused by the whole idea. I was certain you'd be back in a few months, your ego curled between your thighs, this entire utopian compulsion out of your system. But when it began to seem clear that you wouldn't be coming back to the city, I suddenly had to face the reality of what life would be like without you. And the more I looked at that, the more sad I became. I tried all the usual diversions: drink, drugs, orgies, cults, and even celibacy. Nothing distracted me long enough. I realized that for the first time in my adult life, I had allowed the reality of another human being to touch my heart, and now life without that touch would forever be empty, no matter how successful I became in other ways."

Lydia was astonished to hear him speak that way. She reached forward and touched her fingertips to his lips.

"Fred, that's so beautiful," she said.

"Like it?" he smiled. "It's a line from one of last week's soaps."

For an instant she tasted anger, but discarded it as unworthy of the moment. Fred's defenses against his feelings were still the dominant thing about him. And to her, living as she did in a state where the inner and outer lives continuously flowed into one another, each outburst as Fred was now indulging in, and then refusing to take responsibility for, was considered melodramatic.

It was the same reason why so much art was so phony; because it was only the rigidity and coldness of the culture which made certain expressions appear exalted, and these expressions were then surrounded by commercial-aesthetic frames of reference and exhibited as great works.

But when there is no split in a society between feeling and action, then everything anyone does is artistic, and art doesn't become a separate category somehow removed from the rest of life. One of the developments which had most revolted Lydia was the conceptual art movement, in which a comparative handful of snobs without great talent learned to surround unexceptional projects with the ideology of heightened banality in order to cash in on the trivial. The whole process was a bastardization of the ideas of Duchamps crossed with socialist realism.

"Fred," she said after she'd slalomed back into equilibrium, "you can have absolutely no idea of what an ass you sound like. I'm not saying that to sound superior, and you know it's not to hurt you, but we've been through too much together for me to deal with you on anything but a truthful basis. You have one of the most brilliant minds I have ever encountered. I mean, when you're on, it just glitters. The only trouble is that it isn't connected to anything. And so, ultimately, it will wear itself out, like scissor blades grinding on one another. You've taken a sparkling talent, a marvelous sense of humor, and a compelling insight into the nature of reality, and what have you done with it all? Written soap operas to put the anxiety ridden women of America to sleep. Don't you see what a dead end that is? And what's worse, you have begun to feel ashamed yourself and have become defensive, like you were a few moments ago."

"Yes, yes, I see that," Fred told her, "but now I don't know how to get out of it."

"I can't tell whether you are being real or acting out a melodrama," she said.

"You can't?" he replied, unable to keep a trace of sarcasm out of his voice. "I thought you had become an expert on distinguishing between fantasy and reality."

"Oh dear," she said, "you've come all this way just to make a point, to prove some tedious superiority, and all because you can't admit that you are lonely and tired and defeated and want to go home, but don't know how to get there." She looked at him a long time, the sun baking her skin.

"Come here," she urged.

"Here?" Fred repeated, as though he didn't understand the meaning of the word.

"With us," Lydia continued. "We've already sunk in our first roots. This is our new home, a real home. You can finally relax."

"Vegetate is the more accurate term."

He shook his head as though trying to discourage a fly.

"Come on, Lydia," he said, "a retreat into solipsistic fantasy may be pretty, and even viable for a while, but it's the worst kind of regression."

"Or the only kind of revolution."

Fred laughed, a harsh barking which made him sound like a coyote.

"I came here to try to educate you out of your obsession and because I truly missed you. But I imagine I missed the woman that I had fixed in my dreams, never dreaming that she might actually have become a parody of what she set out to be."

A second spark of anger flared in Lydia's eyes. Her ability to perceive people in terms of their total psychic structure had deepened in the past year, and Fred was more naked to her than he would have liked to believe possible. She saw his need, and his resistance, and the full complex of personality gimmicks which rose from his resistance. It was the latter facade, unfortunately, that he had come to identify as his self. Because she felt fondness for him still, and because, somewhere inside her a tiny but unmistakable biological itch yearned to be scratched she veered in from another angle.

It was a tactic she had used thousands of times, and there had been a time when she felt guilty for maneuvering in and out of people's heads and feelings in that way. It was based on a belief that there existed an authentic self beneath the manifestations of the social self. Lydia had now reached the state, however, where it was no longer a belief but a perception. She could literally *see* the child crying for its mother and the mother taking the guise of the person's adult personality telling it to be quiet, not to cry in public. In order for Lydia to reach the child she had to pass through the introjected parent, the society crystallized as muscular tension. And she knew that there was practically no way to manage that without creating a volatile situation, unless the person were willing to lie back, let go, and allow the suppressed energies to emerge as fantasy.

"Why put me down?" she asked. "I'm out here minding my own business and the business of those who want to be with me. I didn't send for you. You came because you had a need. And now you can't even admit that need, but just sit there and look foolish in your defenses. Imagine, having defenses on a day like this, in a place like this, and with me!"

"All right!" he shouted, "all right. I've admitted it. I missed you. I needed you. And I was willing to swallow my pride to be with you. But why do you want me to crawl? If you know what's inside me, why do you have to get me to jump through a hoop?"

"Then why did you come?" she replied, inconsistent and yet to the point.

"I was on my way to Los Angeles to close a deal," he told her. "And I thought it might be a lark to stop and see how you were doing. That's all."

"I don't know what to believe," she said.

"I told you, I was going crazy without you and I had to see you."

Fred was enjoying himself immensely. The air and sunlight had begun to render him euphoric and he was beginning to become infatuated with his little game.

Lydia jumped to her feet and walked over to the very edge. The two of them were poised against the sky, Lydia's feet just inches from the brink of the precipice, Fred sitting back from that existential line. There was no wind, no movement, only the sheer brilliant sunlight holding the planet in its sizzling palm. Not a person was visible, nor any animals. Just the patient plants in prickly meditation on the unalterable cycle of light and dark, cold and heat, that formed the substance of their lives.

"You make it ugly," she said at last, her back still toward him. "You take that inane bit of cleverness about the mythic structure of the age and play tawdry little games with it. How can you respect yourself at all?"

"Because I have only one criterion of my own worth, and that is to avoid vulgarity." Fred laughed to himself. "I know what you're thinking. How can a man who writes soap operas, of all things, consider himself to be above vulgarity? But it is precisely *because* I understand them in their vulgar aspect that that doesn't touch me. I *use* vulgarity; I *master* it. And it offends me deeply to see people who have succumbed to it. You've infused the gauzy beauty of the dream into the horrid reality of daily life in a way that can't compare to the work I do. With what you've done, the dream is bankrupt and the life is not any richer for it."

"Not any richer?" Lydia exclaimed. "Look at us. A year ago we were like you. Grey, nervous, complaining, proud, parasitic. And now we live in God's own sunshine, we breathe pure air and drink water so fresh and cold it brings tears to your eyes. And we grow our own food. The land we live on is ours. Don't you see? We are picking up where we forced the Indians to leave off. Living simply, honestly. Working hard. Paying attention to the optimum survival of all. And through all this, maintaining our sense of the sublime, keeping in touch with the great mystery of creation."

"But how absurd," Fred shot out. "You have become so enmeshed in your dreams that you have lost sight of THE DREAM. You have learned to pay so much attention to your survival realities that you no longer see THE REALITY. This"— he waved his hand to take in a 360 degree circle—"is fantastically pretty. And if the species had any sense, the whole earth would still be this unspoiled. But you know this is the last enclave. The machines are moving in. Strip mining contracts have already been signed for the land a hundred miles away. Soon this entire stretch will be dense with dust, and the air shattered with the noises of drilling and explosions. It's coming to an end, Lydia. The civilization is too foul, too stupid. It will kill everything. All beauty, all tenderness, all hope, all humanity. There are no human beings left, just locusts. A vicious hungry swarm sucking with monstrous greed at the juices of the planet, and growing thinner and thinner as it does, causing it to eat more and more. That's the real. The species is finished. We go the way of the dinosaurs. And if you want to ignore that and build a small zone where you can pretend that the sun isn't dying, that the galaxy isn't going to disappear in a black hole, that the entire universe isn't the most hideous illusion ever perpetrated, unless the universe next door isn't a more grisly joke, then go ahead and play your games. Roll around naked with your reformed neurotics. Live the good life. Pretty soon you'll be written up in the Spiritual Community Guide, and you will have joined the countercultural establishment. And you will have discovered that in your quest for freedom you have merely developed a more rounded form of fascism."

He took a deep breath, stood up, and stepped forward to look Lydia close in the eyes.

"Maybe I've failed. But I recognize my failure. I have liberty in a context of decadence and depravity, that is, within western culture. Now, you have evolved the beginning of a new culture, but you have sacrificed liberty. And by that I mean the only liberty that has meaning, the liberty to protest the fact of existence. Not to make nice with it by curling around your navels and swimming in smarmy fantasy group gropes."

To her surprise, Lydia found that her eyes were shedding tears.

"Why did you come?" she said. "Why did you come here with your despair and nihilism? Must you destroy what you can't have for yourself?"

"Well," he replied, a tinge of victory in his voice, "how can I affect you so strongly if you are really secure in what you're doing? I'll tell you why. It's because you're lonely, because you are suffering what every leader has to go through, the fact that there can only be one of you. You have to carry the burden, to keep the flock together. And it doesn't matter how much ideological hogwash you spout about your new-found religion, the scene is still an old-time happening. Get one thoroughly obsessed human being who wants to lead a tribe to a promised land and around him or her will gather all the standard types. Including the follower with money, and the follower with the organizing talent, and the follower with the child-parent fixation, and the follower who burns to be second-in-command, and the follower who will one day lead the first heretical revolt. It's nothing but the history of our history. You can read it in the books or see it actually happening in the communes around the nation.

"All you are doing is providing one more special case of the general rule. Don't you understand? You have missed the point about fantasy. You have not realized that the ruling fantasy is the unconscious mythos of the age. While you lie around and diddle one another's delicate parts, you are falling into a most humdrum pattern. And on one level it's fine. The goats and the soy beans and the fresh air are not the issue. The issue is that you are still operating at the level of second-class mind. You have not seen deeply enough into the essence."

As Fred unrolled his catalogue, Lydia felt herself shrinking into herself. Too much of what he said hit sore spots inside her. But, as always with him, it was more the manner of his speech which did her in. Now he was whirling verbally about like a brilliant and flashy swordsman, leaping on tables, swinging from chandeliers, parrying six thrusts at once, a sort of Douglas Fairbanks of the conceptual encounter.

"My, he sure can talk pretty when he wants to," she thought, admiring him despite her growing need to flee his presence. "If only I could grab hold of him at the center, shake him, make him see." And then, with the sadness of insight she was growing used to experiencing, she realized that he was probably thinking the same thing about her. No right, no wrong, simply the hopelessness of a man and a woman caught in the mutual vision of their separateness, with Lydia wanting to find union through merging at a deeper level, while Fred insisted that the deepest level was not available to experience. And each of them played leapfrog with the substance of the other's needs, Lydia calling Fred's "epochal myth" a form of alienation, and Fred referring to Lydia's "fantasy level" as a mediocre vulgarity.

Each human being has, or ought to have, a place or posture or mood which defines their ultimate sense of what's real, and at moments of high personal risk, there is a tendency for each of us to retreat to that circle of comfort. Fred had already found his in his attack; Lydia now drifted back from the hard edges of their confrontation into a world in which no other voice but her own carried meaning. From that viewpoint, Fred became a strange stick figure making unintelligible noises at the edge of a high cliff.

"Why won't you just accept that I can be happy living the way I am?" she asked as she swam under.

Fred did not notice that she was drifting, for from his space Lydia was an intelligent cunt with pretensions who underneath it all wanted to have a man tell her what was real and what wasn't.

"If you were happy, I'd let it go at that," he said "But you're not. I can tell. Don't forget, I know you in a way that these people can't. They're all so fogged up by confusing fantasy with myth that you could give them any reality and they would put it in their mouths like a pacifier. Honestly, you could talk this bunch into living in the Arctic and eating walrus turds and have them convinced that they were at the pinnacle of human accomplishment."

He reached forward suddenly, taking Lydia by the shoulders, his fingers digging hard into her flesh.

"Sweet Jesus, Lydia, can't you see? You've become just another dictator. You've betrayed the very freedom your entire life has been an effort to find."

They did not speak again. The feel of her skin in his hands electrified Fred's awareness. Then, all the paraphernalia of the novelistic necessities fell away. His concept, her fantasy; their names, all the circuitous plot turnings which brought them there. Now, it was simply man and woman alone at the beginning of the world.

Their movement was as simple and direct as that of two animals in the field, or that of two debauchees who know one another's tastes perfectly. There was not even communication, for that would imply time for the messages to be conveyed. And there was no time. Neither was it eternity. Nor could the instant be given any designation at all.

To Lydia, it happened as from a great distance. Fred was already a phantom, and the relationship between the ghost of her reverie and the actual figure who slipped the straps over her shoulders and tugged the overalls down to her ankles, was tenuous. For all practical purposes, Lydia was alone.

When Fred's sucking mouth pulled one of her breasts into its wet heat, she was alone.

When his fingers curled between her buttocks, slid up the quivering valley of clutching flesh, and danced into her pink, perspiring pussy, she was alone.

When he tore the clothing from his body and bared himself above her, his cock throwing a shadow across her belly, she was alone.

When he thrust his cock between her slack lips and her tongue lapped the bulky shaft and twirled around the purple head, she was alone.

He sank onto her body, grasping and stroking, licking and kissing, biting and sucking, spanking and holding. At the lip of the abyss he hunched his cock into her waiting cunt and fucked her.

They fucked in the position of simple coupling which lies at the core of all the translucent variations. Lydia lay on her back with her thighs spread, her legs lifting into the air, forming a double ski-slide invitation into the wet hairy hole at the center, now running with juice and the beckoning aroma of arousal. Fred lay between her knees, his erect cock throbbing, his pelvis pumping with slow fury.

They looked into one another's eyes. Fred saw the naked female, specific and anonymous. Lydia saw the naked male, abstract and personal. In giving birth to an idea, man discovers what is real. In giving birth to what is real, woman discovers the idea.

Fred leaned into her and was consumed by her embrace. Her cunt convulsed and sucked his cock as a mouth might, the mouth of some blind leech which feeds on hotblooded creatures which stray into the turgid waters of its jungle swamp.

For Fred, then, only pleasure existed. The cascading, surging sweetness of surrender and release, the extraordinary delight of getting laid. He felt like an orange being sucked dry through a hole made in its skin. But the juices which ran out of him were being pulled into another creature, were feeding someone else, were the seeds of creation.

"Yes," he sang, "yes, yes," as he spilled his guts.

And Lydia swooned with the intensity of her fantasy, a crowning projection in which she was being fucked at the edge of a lofty plateau under the scorching sun.

His orgasm blasted him out of consciousness. His toes curled and his spine melted. His eyes turned up in his head and saliva drooled from his mouth. It was not that he pumped his sperm into her, but that he was the handle being used by a force far greater than himself.

And when he was finished, when the last of his milk had been drawn into Lydia's gulping cunt, it was several seconds before he could distinguish his sensations of orgasmic flying from the fact that he was actually falling, that she had rolled him over onto his side and pushed him gently, that he had spun over the edge of the cliff and was now sailing through the air, gliding, plummeting, hurtling to his doom, to discover whether death was precisely what he thought it would be or whether existence had one last nasty surprise up its wrinkled sleeve.

11

"Fred. Fred!"

"Hunh?"

"Fred, wake up."

"What?"

"You were screaming in your sleep."

"Oh?" Lydia reached over and turned on the light next to the bed. Fred threw on arm over his eyes to protect them from the glare.

"Was it a nightmare?" she asked.

The words fought their way through the sleeping layers of his brain, tripping over snoring synapses, alarming napping axions, and stumbling through spun ganglia like a man catching cobwebs on his face as he crashes through the forest. After a long time as measured by the speed of impulses along a nerve, he made sense of what she was saying.

"Strange dream . . ." he muttered.

He lay still for a long while, breathing heavily. Then, slowly, he lowered his arm and pushed himself up to a sitting position.

"Want to tell me?" she asked.

"It's already starting to fade," he told her. "But the end!"

"What happened?"

"You were leading some kind of revivalist therapeutic commune in New Mexico. I went down to visit you and we argued, and then we fucked, and then you pushed me off a thousand foot cliff."

"That must have been some fuck," she said.

"A lot of that went on. Your patient . . . what's her name . . . Marsha, jumped off the World Trade Center building. And old Monroe had a heart attack while you were fucking him. And there was a weird orgy in Provincetown, with you dancing naked and getting gang-fucked by a bunch of freaks."

"Jesus, what did you have for dinner?"

"Lobster." He squinted and seemed to peer into a far distance. "That was another thing. A big scene between you and me at the Four Seasons. And you had your license revoked for holding orgies at your group sessions."

"My, more orgies," Lydia said.

They did not speak for a few minutes. It was three thirty in the morning. The light hum of the nighttime city kept watch outside the open window. A spring rain fell, washing the air.

Lydia's eyes grew heavy and she yawned. She put one hand on Fred's chest.

"Think you can sleep now?"

"I was doing fine until you woke me up."

"Well, so was I, until you screamed in my ear."

"Want to put out the light?"

"Mmmm."

They both slid down under the blankets and, as though on signal, rolled onto their left sides, her buttocks cradled into the hollow of his groin. He held her breasts gently.

"Heavy day tomorrow?" he asked.

"Not bad. Four patients and a group. You?"

"Script conference. We're thinking of adding a new character to the series."

They squirmed against one another for a while. Then, slowly, each mind began to melt and dissolve, like filters on a too-hot bulb, until they trickled into sleep, leaving behind all memory of the bodies lying on the bed. Drops of scorching wax dripped into the moon-struck sea and blossomed into rowboats. Two rowboats, separate and tied, rocked in undulating crescent rhythms by the same ceaseless waves.

As the city slumbered in its concrete husk, Fred and Lydia burrowed deeper into the rich texture of oblivion, and after a while, from the core of the long preconscious truth, a light began to flicker, like the beam from a projection booth in a darkened theatre, and bye and bye, they began, once again, to dream.

About the Author

MARCO VASSI was, without a doubt, the foremost erotic writer of our generation. Praised by Norman Malier, Kate Millett, Saul Bellow, and Gore Vidal, he was not only the ultimate sexual explorer, but a literary craftsman whose own life experiences became the stuff of his fiction—expanded, of course, by a grand imagination and a full sense of the absurd.

Tragically, Vassi died from pneumonia after he had contracted AIDS.

OPEN **(f)** ROAD

INTEGRATED MEDIA

Open Road Integrated Media is a digital publisher and multimedia content company. Open Road creates connections between authors and their audiences by marketing its ebooks through a new proprietary online platform, which uses premium video content and social media.

www.ingramcontent.com/pod-product-compliance
Lightning Source LLC
Chambersburg PA
CBHW020339260626
47156CB00004B/1602